ULTRAMAN

UltraSeven

THE OFFICIAL NOVEL OF THE SERIES

ULTRAMAN TITLES AVAILABLE FROM TITAN BOOKS

Ultraman: The Official Novel of the Series

ULTRAMAN

THE OFFICIAL NOVEL OF THE SERIES

PAT CADIGAN

TITAN BOOKS

Ultraseven: The Official Novel of the Series
Print edition ISBN: 9781803362441
E-book edition ISBN: 9781803363028

Published by Titan Books
A division of Titan Publishing Group Ltd
144 Southwark Street, London SE1 0UP
www.titanbooks.com

First edition: July 2025
10 9 8 7 6 5 4 3 2 1

A CIP catalogue record for this title is available from the British Library.

EU RP (for authorities only)
eucomply OÜ, Pärnu mnt. 139b-14, 11317 Tallinn, Estonia
hello@eucompliancepartner.com, +3375690241

Printed and bound by CPI Group (UK) Ltd, Croydon, CR0 4YY.

This one is for the Nova Expressions:

Lawrence Person, Dwight Brown, Glen and Jill Engel-Cox, Michael Sumbera, and Rich Simental.

Next time, the barbecue's on me.

And, like everything I do,

For Chris Fowler,
Always the most interesting person in the room

PROLOGUE

The Being of Light known as Agent 340 was in the midst of his latest assignment when a small, unassuming, but high-energy world called Earth caught his eye.

Not that he'd been looking for distractions. He'd drawn a real plum of a job—viz, mapping the Milky Way. Because of the dynamic nature of the galaxy, mapping and remapping had to be done periodically, and the Ultra Beings of the M78 Nebula chose the best and brightest among them for the task. There was no shortage of brilliance to choose from but Agent 340's active curiosity and relentless desire to learn made him perfect for the job. All the Ultras were eager to see what he would make of the information he gathered.

As with most galaxies, the Milky Way's greatest changes began at the outskirts and moved inward at varying rates toward the crowded center. It had always been thus, and Agent 340 found it curious. What this meant for him personally, his elders explained, was that he had to remain inconspicuous, if not virtually invisible, especially on the galactic fringe.

Unlike the teeming center, few of the populated planets were accustomed to alien visitors. In fact, most of those worlds had no direct knowledge or experience of any intelligent lifeforms other than their own, and it was policy not to engage if it could possibly be avoided.

Sometimes, of course, it was unavoidable, in which case, encryption had to be employed—not always easy, even for the wisest and most experienced of Ultras. Life on the galactic fringe was more unpredictable than it was anywhere else.

The standard procedure for mapping assignments was to start in the crowded middle and spiral outward, moving counter to galactic spin. As Agent 340 discovered, the areas where stars were most densely packed together practically mapped themselves. These were also the places with the least amount of change from the previous mapping.

Not that there weren't a few surprises—the odd, unexpected novae here and there. Agent 340 also found that, thanks to increased turbulence in the Orion Nebula, the Ultras had underestimated the number of new stars that had emerged.

As he moved outward and the main galactic arms became more defined and discrete, Agent 340 decided to map each of them in turn rather than continue moving in a widening spiral. There were few stars in the arms but more planetary systems, and therefore a greater percentage of inhabited planets. A good many of these had developed carbon-based lifeforms not terribly unlike the original form of his own people before the Plasma Spark had transformed and elevated their existence.

Some of these fringe worlds were pastoral, with no tool-using species that walked upright. Others had advanced just far enough to have the potential to destroy themselves; some already had, leaving only rubble for him to catalog. But most hadn't, and Agent 340 catalogued, annotated, speculated (personal observations were encouraged), recorded, and interpreted.

All the while, he dutifully kept his distance, until he didn't.

CHAPTER
ONE

Peple were disappearing.

In a crowded world where people passed in and out of each other's lives as a matter of course, it wasn't always taken as anything more than normal, or at least expected, human movement. But in the area to the south of Tokyo, along the coast and several kilometers inward, the increasing number of disappearances acquired a new twist. Reports came in from witnesses claiming to have seen someone vanish right in front of them, like a magic trick or a special effect in a movie.

At first, the police dismissed the first few calls. But calls kept coming in, the authorities finally realized that *something* was going on and it was definitely out of the ordinary. The police set up checkpoints in areas where disappearances seemed to be more frequent. There were a few complaints from drivers who didn't like having their commute or roadtrip interrupted, but most people took it in stride. Hey, that was life—if it wasn't one thing, it was another, and next week it would probably be something else, so what the hell.

Then everything changed.

＊ ＊ ＊

Officer Hiroshi Saijo had been a traffic cop for five years and he was bored; he'd been bored for some time now. Before his shift, he had another talk with his supervisor about making a change. His supervisor had said it looked like there'd be an opportunity for a transfer very soon, which was encouraging enough to make tonight's checkpoint duty seem less tedious.

Working a checkpoint wasn't difficult. Officers took it in teams so they could back each other up if drivers and/or passengers were difficult, belligerent, or under the influence. And if nothing happened at all, which was usually the case, they could take turns checking their email or playing the latest hot game, or just hang out and talk. Of course, some cops were better company than others.

The guys Officer Saijo was working with tonight were all dependable, stand-up guys, but their conversation did leave something to be desired. Not one of them had any good gossip or rumors. But then, Saijo thought as he watched another pair of headlights approach, he hadn't heard any good ones lately, either. Except for the unexplained disappearances, it seemed like nothing much was happening in Greater Tokyo, or possibly anywhere on Honshu Island.

Two officers waved the car into the breakdown lane where Saijo and his partner for the evening, a slightly older guy named Ken Hachisuka, were waiting. Saijo aimed his flashlight carefully so he could see the driver's face without blinding him.

The driver was obviously familiar with the routine—she already had her license out for inspection. Saijo looked it over, intending to hand it back to the woman and send her on her way, when some impulse made him ask for the car registration. The driver didn't get huffy or complain; she simply leaned over to get it out of the glovebox while Hachisuka watched for any concealed weapons or suspicious-looking packages.

The driver held out the registration politely, but when Saijo touched it, he saw the woman suddenly stiffen. Before Saijo could ask if she was all right, the car was suffused with a blinding white light. Then it was gone, and so was the driver.

Saijo let out a shocked cry that brought the other two officers rushing to his side. 'The driver—she just disappeared! Like, flash of light and bang! Car's empty!' He backed away, letting the other three search it for a trap door or a hidden panel. Despite his training and his record as a conscientious officer, Saijo couldn't bring himself to get within a meter of the vehicle.

It wasn't simply the woman disappearing—it was the way it had felt when the registration had vanished while he'd been touching it. The certificate hadn't been yanked or snatched away, he had felt it dematerialize. As Saijo told everyone later, he had never felt anything more disturbing, more... *unnatural.*

Several kilometers away and a few hundred meters underground in the Terrestrial Defense Force, Captain Kaoru Kiriyama of the Ultra Guard took one more look at the latest incident reports before heading over to Overwatch, where the TDF Joint Commanders were waiting for him. Six of them were on the premises today, including Commander Edwin Bogarde from North America, which was highly unusual.

The main headquarters of the TDF was in Paris; besides Tokyo, there were branches in Washington, DC, London, Berlin, Moscow, Rome, Cairo, Johannesburg, and the Arctic, as well as a host of other major cities. In Kiriyama's sixteen years of service, he had seen the original organization expand not only globally but beyond, to Lagrange point space stations and the moon.

Kiriyama was a bit on edge as he walked through the base, nodding at various TDF personnel. He still knew a lot of them by name, although new faces popped up all the time. The TDF numbered some three hundred souls, many more than when Kiriyama had been a shiny new recruit. Back then, he hadn't decided how long he was going to stay in. He'd never imagined he'd end up in command of an elite squad within the TDF, but here he was.

Minister Yamaoka had chosen him for his extensive experience with alien encounters. The four people under his command weren't as experienced but Yamaoka had chosen them as having exceptional potential. At first, Kiriyama had been dubious—he'd have preferred to choose his own personnel. But he had to admit that Yamaoka had a good eye and a talent for finding the right combination of people.

Two of them Kiriyama had already been acquainted with; the other two were new. One of the former had seven years of service, the others only two or three. According to Commander Manabe, this meant they had fewer bad habits to unlearn. They had gelled quickly as a team, to Kiriyama's great relief, and now he couldn't imagine swapping any of them out for someone else. Although he did wonder if Yamaoka planned to add to their number; five seemed to be a small group for something called the Ultra Guard, no matter how elite they were. But when Kiriyama had broached the subject with him, Yamaoka had dismissed it and Kiriyama decided not to push it. He'd made Yamaoka aware of his feelings. Now he simply had to wait and see if anything came of it.

The TDF guard outside Overwatch announced him via the intercom before opening the door. As Kiriyama went in, he saw the commanders gathered at a wall monitor displaying a topographical map of an area not far from the base.

'Glad you're here, Captain,' Yamaoka said. He turned to Kiriyama with a tense, uncertain expression. 'You're aware we've had another disappearance?'

'I am.' Kiriyama nodded to the other Joint Chiefs, some of whom he'd only seen onscreen until now.

'We have a difficult job for the Ultra Guard,' Yamaoka went on. 'Commander Takenaka can fill you in.'

Takenaka stepped forward holding a file folder. He was one of the old-school types who had to have hardcopy printouts.

'In the past week, we've had people vanish from parks, hotels, shops, restaurants, sports arenas, universities—anywhere and everywhere. And as far as we can tell, there's no pattern. Students, office workers, manual laborers, engineers—anyone can disappear from any place at any time and we still don't know why it's happening, let alone how.'

'And there's nothing left behind?' Kiriyama asked, although he knew the answer. 'No dust or residue?'

'Witnesses have reported a blinding white light, followed by nothing. Whoever's doing this has technology far beyond our own.' He looked around at the other commanders. 'After careful analysis and much discussion, we feel the phenomenon is… not of this Earth.'

Kiriyama nodded; he'd had come to the same conclusion, albeit very reluctantly. But if any country or organized group on Earth had developed the ability to pop people out of existence, it seemed highly improbable they'd have kept it so completely secret. Humans loved to show off, take credit, or worst of all, threaten.

'Witnesses have all described people just—' Yamaoka snapped his fingers. 'And you know what Sir Arthur C. Clarke said: any sufficiently advanced technology is indistinguishable from magic.'

But only if the observers believe in magic, Kiriyama added silently.

'We'd like the Ultra Guard to take point and investigate this more…' he hesitated, '…aggressively. You yourself have more experience with aliens than most of the people in the TDF— certainly more than any of us.'

'I'll assemble my team.' Kiriyama activated his wristcomm as he left.

Soga was at the target range, showing off his sharpshooting skills by way of demonstrating the latest model of the Ultra Gun for a new class of TDF recruits. The training officer was sorry to see him go—she'd already won a bundle from newbies who didn't know better than to bet Soga wouldn't miss even one target, and she'd been hoping to clean up with the next group of trainees.

Soga met up with Shigeru Furuhashi, fresh from a flexibility workout on the trampoline. At twenty-nine, Furuhashi was the most senior member on the team after Kiriyama, with seven years in. As the strongest member of the team, he had to make an effort to keep himself limber.

The third member of the team was poring over data in Planning and Scheduling when Kiriyama's summons reached him. Amagi was in his early twenties: tall, skinny, and gawky, which made him seem even younger. Nonetheless, Kiriyama had never met anyone with a better head for strategy.

Anne Yuri had joined the TDF at around the same time as Amagi, coming in with twin degrees in medicine and communications. Kiriyama's call found her in the clinic, wrapping a singed forearm and telling her patient to give the medication in the wrap enough time to regenerate new skin. She pretended not to notice the guy's disappointment at her having to leave as she gave him some mild analgesics. Under other circumstances, she might have been a bit disappointed herself—Mr. Second-Degree Burns was pretty cute. But the world was full of good-looking guys—there was only one Ultra Guard, and getting to work with Kiriyama was a dream come true.

She reminded her patient not to over-medicate, then ran to change out of her scrubs and into her Ultra Guard uniform.

* * *

All four arrived within seconds of each other in Overwatch. The room was full of TDF officers keeping a close eye on the surveillance feeds.

'Whatever entity or force that's been spiriting people away has upped their game,' Kiriyama said by way of hello. 'We've just received a report that two TDF officers on patrol have vanished on the same road where a woman disappeared at a checkpoint last night. Unlike the incident with the woman, however, their car disappeared with them. I don't have to tell you that's a brand-new wrinkle. We're still questioning witnesses, but so far, the car hasn't turned up and I don't think it's going to.'

'Where exactly was this?' Furuhashi asked.

'About fifty kilometers from Point V,' replied Kiriyama. 'Out in the hills. We're lucky to have any witnesses at all, as it's rather remote. I've sent all of you a map with the coordinates clearly marked.'

Soga's eyebrows went up as he checked the map on his wristcomm. 'That's closer to the base than any of the other incidents.'

Kiriyama nodded. 'I want you and Furuhashi to go to the scene. Amagi and Anne, you're with me—we'll keep an eye out for any more activity from here.'

Amagi was already bent over a monitor. Anne joined him; Kiriyama could tell by her expression that she was disappointed she hadn't been sent into the field.

One of the great things about being in the Ultra Guard, in Furuhashi's opinion, was driving the Pointer. Its official designation was TDF/Ultra Guard Pointer-1, and it had been designed for the kind of extraordinary situations the Ultra Guard had been established to handle. Among its many features, it had an energy barrier to repel weapons fire, puncture-proof tires, and a top speed of 365 kph. As much as Furuhashi enjoyed that last feature, this particular section of road through the countryside was twisty and narrow. The local police had closed the route to regular traffic, but Furuhashi kept the P-1 to a relatively sedate 100 kph.

When he saw the police car parked on the dirt shoulder, he slowed down, and as he did he heard Soga chuckle. 'Thank you, Lead Foot. I really like it when we don't crash and burn first thing in the morning.'

'I live to serve. And we weren't going *that* fast,' Furuhashi added under his breath.

They saw only one officer sitting in the driver's seat as they passed.

Furuhashi frowned. 'Don't the locals always work in pairs? Where do you suppose his partner is?'

'Napping in the back seat?' Soga guessed. 'Although satnav says this is only one and a half kilometers from the spot where the TDF guys disappeared.'

Furuhashi eased off the accelerator a little more as the fields and brush gave way to hills and rock walls, and the road became curvier. They were rounding a bend along a broken rockface when Soga suddenly yelled, '*Stop!*'

'I see him,' Furuhashi said, bringing the vehicle to a stop.

The guy standing in the middle of the road certainly was easy to see in a bright yellow jacket over t-shirt and jeans. If he was a hitchhiker, his last ride had dropped him off in the middle of nowhere. Furuhashi wondered if that had been at his request or the driver's insistence. He waited for the guy to move or ask for directions, or even a lift, but he only stood there.

Annoyed, Furuhashi leaned out the driver's-side window. 'Hey, you mind moving out of the way? You shouldn't be here anyway.'

The guy didn't answer, didn't even change expression. He was young—Furuhashi thought he was about Soga's age but something

PAT CADIGAN

about his posture suggested he might be a bit older. The Pointer had automatically taken his photo several times and Furuhashi decided to take a closer look later.

Soga stuck his head out of the passenger-side window. 'If you keep going that way—' he pointed back the way they had come, '—you'll find a police officer parked on the shoulder. He can probably help you get wherever you want to go. But you can't be here right now.'

The guy still said nothing, although Furuhashi thought he detected a hint of a smile on his face, which took his irritation up a couple of notches. Apparently, the guy was one of those people who felt compelled to defy authority. Furuhashi knew the type: some people believed that in a free society, they had a duty to give anyone in uniform a hard time.

Sighing, he turned to Soga. 'Looks like we'll have to smoke him out. Hit it.'

Soga opened a panel on the console between them and flipped a switch. Clouds of white smoke poured out of the Pointer's grille, enveloping the man in the road until he had disappeared completely.

Most people gave ground immediately, thinking the smoke was tear gas or worse. In fact, it was only harmless vapor, and Soga had triggered a very short blast. When the cloud dissipated, however, the man was gone.

Furuhashi had a flash of anxiety that the fog might have covered another disappearance, then decided that would have been far too neat a coincidence. Besides, whoever (or whatever) was behind the vanishing acts didn't do it under cover of anything but right out in the open, possibly for maximum shock effect.

He shifted gears and pressed on the accelerator. The engine revved and he heard the tires spinning, but the P-1 didn't move.

'Oh, for crying—what *now*?' Furuhashi fumed.

Soga opened his door and looked at the rear wheel. 'I don't see anything over here. Try it again, and really step on it.'

'I *am* stepping on it, I *always* step on it,' Furuhashi snapped as the engine continued to rev and the tires spun to no avail. He put on the parking brake and got out of the Pointer, then heard someone laughing. Anger surged in him; whoever was messing with them was going to be *very* sorry.

Then he looked up to find the guy in the yellow jacket was now sitting cross-legged on the roof of the Pointer and laughing like he'd never seen anything so funny.

'You get down from there!' Soga ordered, reaching for him. 'You should know better than to interfere with us when we're on duty!'

The guy was still laughing as he evaded both Soga and Furuhashi, sliding down the windshield to the hood, then jumping to the ground.

'You've got it backward, Officer Soga,' the guy said, laughing even harder at Soga's surprise. '*I'm* not in *your* way.'

'How do you know my name?' Soga demanded.

The guy shrugged one shoulder. 'I also know you're Officer Furuhashi,' he added, turning to him and grinning at his reaction. 'You're the strongest person in the Ultra Guard, if not the entire TDF.'

Furuhashi put a hand on the sidearm attached to his belt, even as his instincts were telling him he wasn't in danger. 'Who are you and what do you want?'

The stranger never stopped grinning. 'Well, I've been waiting around here for hours, hoping to save your lives.'

Furuhashi and Soga looked at each other, then burst into laughter. The Ultra Guard was always getting messages through the TDF website from cranks and fantasists claiming they had special secret knowledge, or super-powers, or some kind of device that would protect everyone from harm or bring about world peace or reveal the secret of life. Saving the lives of two members of the Ultra Guard was pretty tame by comparison, but the guy made it sound earth-shaking.

'Well, that's great, it really is,' said Soga. 'If you walk back to the police officer parked on the road, he can get all the details from you—'

'I'm not joking and I'm not crazy.' The guy spoke quite calmly but something about his face gave Furuhashi pause; he kept his hand on his weapon.

'That's considerate of you, but we protect other people, not just ourselves,' Soga was saying.

'If you keep going along this road, you won't be able to protect anyone,' the guy said.

'Listen carefully, fella,' Furuhashi said. 'Right now, we've got something we need to take care of. If you're here when we come back, we'll take you in.'

He and Soga were about to get back into the Pointer when they heard a vehicle approaching from behind. It was the police car they'd passed a few minutes earlier, now with two officers in the front seat. The driver pulled around them and stopped.

'Everything okay here?' the cop asked Furuhashi.

The stranger suddenly materialized at Furuhashi's elbow. 'Don't go any farther, there's danger ahead.'

The driver looked him up and down, as if he were something both unusual and ridiculous before turning back to Furuhashi. 'We've been patrolling the area since before dawn, including the forest. So far, there's nothing to report. Except maybe...' He jerked his head at the stranger.

Furuhashi stepped back from the car, pulling the guy with him by his sleeve. 'Okay. Stay safe, keep in touch.'

'Will do.' The driver released the brake and drove on.

To Furuhashi's surprise, the guy ran after the car, calling for them to stop, they were in danger. The driver responded by speeding up, leaving him in a small cloud of dust.

'And that's all the time we have for cranks, wackos, and weirdos today,' Furuhashi said, motioning for Soga to get back into the

Pointer. As he opened his own door, he heard a sound very similar to a plasma rifle, only much fuller and louder, more like a plasma cannon, from somewhere overhead. He looked up and saw a bright ball of energy zoom downward to make a direct hit on the police car.

Before he could yell to Soga, a second blast hit, making the car glow brightly for a second before it melted out of existence.

'I tried to warn them.' The stranger shook his head, looking deeply unhappy.

Furuhashi pounced on him. 'Who are you? What do you know about this? Who's behind it?'

'You're facing a deadly alien menace,' the guy said. 'I'm here to help.'

He was serious, Furuhashi thought, and in a better, more benign world, it might even have been true.

'They've been collecting human specimens for years,' the man went on. 'They're preparing for an invasion and I guess they're stepping things up. Why do you suppose that is?'

Furuhashi blinked at him, looked at Soga, then back at the guy. 'You got a theory?'

'It's because the Ultra Guard are responding now, investigating the disappearances. They've moved on to the next phase and things are gonna get a lot worse.'

'And just who in the world are you that you have this special knowledge?' Furuhashi asked.

'In *this* world?' The guy actually seemed to be thinking that one over. 'I'm only a traveler. Just passing through.'

'You got a *name*?' Soga said.

The guy hesitated; his expression gave Furuhashi the impression he was glad Soga had asked. 'You can call me Dan. I'm Dan Moroboshi.'

Soga opened his mouth to respond when Furuhashi heard the plasma-weapon sound again, still overhead but now much closer.

He looked around wildly, but Dan Moroboshi was shoving him and Soga roughly away from the Pointer and across the road toward a pile of broken rock just as something punched a crater in the center of the road, spraying them with stones, dirt, and chunks of asphalt.

Furuhashi looked up and saw another ball of plasma materialize out of thin air some fifteen meters above them. It hurtled down and hit only centimeters from his foot. The ground exploded and something sliced into Furuhashi's knee. He clapped both hands over it, feeling blood pouring out between his fingers.

'Something up there's firing on us!' Soga yelled. 'We gotta get outta—'

The rocks in front of them blew apart, leaving them completely exposed.

'Come on!' The guy dragged both of them back across the road, shoving them into the back seat of the Pointer so quickly that it didn't occur to Furuhashi until later how strong the guy was—easily as strong as himself. In the moment, all he could think of was how bolts of plasma were congealing out of nothing.

'Hit the barrier button!' Furuhashi shouted as the guy slid across the front seat to get behind the wheel. 'Gray one, left of the steering column!'

There was a deep hum as the Light Wave Barrier activated a fraction of a second before the next bolt would have hit the Pointer's roof. The whole car shook but remained undamaged.

'Step on it!' Furuhashi yelled.

Dan Moroboshi put the Pointer in gear as if he'd been driving it for years. But before he could accelerate, more plasma bolts hit a rockface not ten meters ahead of them. The impact sent boulders flying down onto the road, blocking their way.

Furuhashi opened his mouth to tell the guy to shut off the barrier and hit the blaster, to turn the boulders into crumbs. But the guy had already done it; Furuhashi fell back against the seat as the Pointer zoomed forward.

Soga was cradling one arm but had managed to activate his wristcomm.

'This is Anne Yuri at HQ,' said a cheerful female voice. 'Anything to report?'

'We've been attacked by a—' Soga floundered for a second. 'By an invisible flying plasma cannon!' he said finally. 'I know how that sounds but both Furuhashi and I are injured!'

Immediately, Kiriyama was on the line. 'Status?'

'Nothing critical,' Soga assured him. 'We'll be back at HQ shortly and, uh, we're bringing someone with us. A friendly.'

Anne's face on the small, flip-up screen was a mix of concern and confusion. 'If both of you are injured, who's driving?'

'I'd show you on the wristcomm,' Soga replied, 'but I think my arm is broken.'

Twenty minutes later, Anne had finished suturing Furuhashi's lacerated knee (while the Ultra Guard's strongest member kept his gaze averted from the needle). The on-call medic assisting her had determined Soga had a dislocated elbow rather than a fracture and had immobilized it with a splint.

'And that's the extent of the good news,' Kiriyama informed everyone in Overwatch. 'We have an enemy that's armed, dangerous, and worst of all, invisible, and they've added two police officers to their collection, plus their car. For anyone keeping count, that's two cars and possibly as many as two dozen people.'

Chief Yamagawa's lined face was grave. 'With those capabilities, they could have massacred us by the tens of thousands—except they haven't. So what are they up to?'

Kiriyama took a breath. 'The civilian who came in with

Furuhashi and Soga claims they've been collecting human specimens for research.'

Yamagawa nodded. 'Makes sense. Knowing your enemy would seem to be a ubiquitous practice.' He turned to Kiriyama. 'I'm sure they've traced the Pointer back here to us.' He raised his voice to address the entire room. 'Continue monitoring both ground and airspace in a one-hundred-kilometer radius. If we can't *see* them, maybe we can see the signs of their movements and locate them by changes in air currents, even atmospheric disturbances.'

Kiriyama was about to respond when Amagi suddenly appeared at his side. 'Captain, commanders—I think there's a transmission trying to come through.'

They followed him to the communications board, where several TDF officers were gathered in front of two wall monitors with flickering screens.

'What kind of transmission?' Kiriyama asked tensely, then saw what appeared to be the outlines of an image. It started to become more definite, then faded back into the static before the screen suddenly cleared up altogether.

Kiriyama blinked. The creature staring out from the monitor had an oversized bulge of a head that looked very much like an exposed brain, two wide-spaced, lidless eyes, and below them, six jointed limbs ending in claws and a vestigial body shaped like a cylinder.

'Attention, all Terrestrial Defense Force members,' said a high-pitched, nasal voice issuing from a flap just below the staring eyes. 'We are the Alien Cool. You will immediately disarm and surrender your planet unconditionally to us.'

The Joint Chiefs exchanged incredulous looks.

'We protect this world,' said Yamaoka. 'None of us would surrender it to you or anyone else.'

'Humans are nothing more to us than insects,' the alien said in its nasal whine. 'Watch. You'll see.'

The second monitor lit up and there were horrified gasps from everyone in the room at the sight of people floating in some dimly lit space. Some were upside down, others sideways, all with their arms and legs flailing as they struggled to right themselves while they called for help.

'What are you doing to them?' Yamaoka demanded angrily.

'Anything we want.' Now there was a gloating undertone in the thin, reedy voice. 'Their lives depend on your response. Answer *now*—will you surrender and give your planet over to us?'

Yamaoka drew himself up to his full height. '*No*. Of course not.'

Kiriyama braced himself for a high-pitched whining tirade of threats. Instead, both screens went dark, leaving the room in stunned silence.

'I think it hung up on us,' Furuhashi said finally.

The sound of his voice broke everyone out of their daze. But as the TDF members went back to work, the monitors lit up again to show two different views of the newly completed Keihin utility complex forty kilometers away. Visibility was good at the moment; across Keihin Lake, the Tokyo skyline was clearly visible, no haze at all.

Something bright streaked down from the sky into one of the power substations, which disappeared in a fiery explosion. There was a second strike, followed by a third, obliterating two immense cooling vats. Then it was raining fire and the entire complex became an inferno.

One of the screens flipped to show the alien again.

'This is how powerful we are,' it said in its grating voice. 'You have sixty of your minutes to decide, or Tokyo is next.'

Then it was gone and they were watching the complex burn.

Yamaoka turned to Kiriyama. 'We have to do something, Captain.'

'In an hour? How?' asked Commander Bogarde. 'We can't even *see* them.'

PAT CADIGAN

'We can't just let Tokyo burn!' Yamaoka said.

Beside him, Commander Manabe spoke up. 'Our ultra-sensitive detection system should be able to find anything in our atmosphere. If we can figure out where this thing is most likely to be, we could fire missiles—'

Takenaka was shaking his head. 'They've taken human hostages. We have to rescue them before we attack.'

'We can't rescue them if we can't find them,' Yamaoka said hotly.

'Captain.' Amagi was beside Kiriyama again. 'The Keihin complex is completely destroyed. Half of Tokyo is without power.'

'So what's the plan, Captain?' Yamaoka was glaring at Kiriyama as if he were personally responsible.

Kiriyama didn't blame him, but he had to take charge before blind panic descended on them and overrode training and discipline.

'All right, everyone, listen up!' Kiriyama raised his voice and the background murmur in the room cut off. 'We have to have a plan before we can act.' He looked around and his gaze fell on Anne, standing with the stranger, Dan Moroboshi.

For a split second, she looked startled, then composed herself. 'Dan, you seem to know more about these aliens than anyone else,' she said. 'Do you have any ideas?' Her gaze went from him to Kiriyama and back again.

Moroboshi frowned thoughtfully. 'When high tech fails, the solution calls for a simpler approach. If we can't *detect* the alien spaceship, why not try making it visible?'

Kiriyama gave a single, humorless laugh. 'That would be a neat trick.'

'As neat as spraying it with paint,' Moroboshi replied.

Kiriyama blinked, then shook his head slightly, as if to clear it. 'Of course,' he said after a few seconds. 'The hardware lab can throw some equipment together in no time at all. Amagi—'

26

'Already on my way,' Amagi called over his shoulder as he hurried out of the room.

Yamaoka looked at the other commanders, who nodded at him. 'All right, Kiriyama, this is your operation.'

Kiriyama barely heard him. His attention was on the stranger with the bright ideas, currently in conversation with the Ultra Guard's physician. He went over to join them. If Moroboshi had any other inspirations or special knowledge, he wanted to hear them first.

The stranger who had introduced himself as Dan Moroboshi listened intently to Anne Yuri as she gave him a quick rundown of the Ultra Guard and the TDF. He was aware of Captain Kiriyama making his way over to them. In fact, he had already gleaned quite a lot of what she was telling him, but despite the coincidence of the special squad's name, humans weren't Ultras; not even close. It was best to let humans share information in their usual way. On this world, very little ever went without saying or, at the very least, an opinion.

Captain Kiriyama had a lot of questions for him; he could sense them running through the man's mind. *Who are you? Where did you come from and where are you going? What are your intentions toward us, toward the world, toward anything?*

The only way he could help these people would be to gain Kiriyama's confidence, make him an ally, and that required meaningful communication. *I'm merely a traveler, just passing through* wouldn't cut it.

At the same time, however, he had to avoid interfering with their natural development by telling them too much. He'd already made a significant change in the scheme of things when he had saved the falling climber on the mountain.

He hadn't intended to take such crucial action, but when the climber had cut his own rope to prevent his companion from falling to his death with him, he had reacted automatically. But in truth, even if he'd had time to think about it, he'd have done the same thing. There was no good reason not to.

Humans, he had learned, didn't live very long—barely long enough to know they were alive. To let such a short life be cut even shorter was an inexcusable waste, especially since the man had put his climbing partner's life ahead of his own. Self-sacrifice was a virtue normally found only in the most advanced beings, and yet a lifeform that lived barely longer than an eye-blink had not hesitated. Such a species deserved a little extra help on their journey toward enlightenment.

The man had been unconscious when he'd caught him and flown him down to the floor of the valley. Placing him on a soft patch of grass in an open area, he had hidden and kept watch, curious. What would he do when he woke up, what would he think? After a bit, he realized that for the man to regain consciousness, he had to leave. He had given the man a second chance; now he had to go away and let the man's life continue, for good or ill.

Then Kiriyama and the one called Yamaoka joined him and Anne, who excused herself politely, giving him one last look of concern mixed with curiosity as she withdrew to the communications console.

'We have a great deal to talk about, don't we,' he said to Kiriyama.

Kiriyama took Dan Moroboshi to his office rather than an interrogation room. Yamaoka raised his eyebrows but said nothing, even when Kiriyama steered them away from his desk to the round conference table where, on his busier days, he ate lunch, reviewed incident reports, and organized the Ultra Guard schedule, sometimes simultaneously.

'I know you're wondering how I know so much about these aliens,' Moroboshi said. 'They call themselves the Alien Cool, yes?' His smile was fleeting.

'Something like that.' Yamaoka's neutral tone had a hint of expectation. 'Although the most important thing we need to know right now is what we can do about them. If you have any background information, you can tell us later.'

Moroboshi nodded. 'So you accept that these *are* aliens.'

'Well, of course.' Yamaoka frowned at him. 'The TDF was founded to deal with alien incursions. We've had quite a few, as Captain Kiriyama can tell you.'

'Some alien visitors have been friendly,' Kiriyama said, sitting forward, one hand piled atop the other. 'Or at least harmless. Some have done varying degrees of damage without meaning to, sometimes without even knowing it, because they didn't understand the local customs or laws. Others, like our current trespassers, have been hell-bent on conquering the planet and too bad for us insects.' He looked into Moroboshi's face and Moroboshi met his gaze evenly, openly, without a hint of defensiveness or dark intent; Kiriyama had seen enough faces to know.

'I've been... traveling for quite some time,' Moroboshi said after a bit. 'And to many far-flung places. We live in a world—universe—teeming with the miraculous, the wondrous, and the terrifying, and you'd be surprised at how many of them find their way to the outskirts of the Milky Way.'

Kiriyama and Yamaoka exchanged looks.

'I would think that we're well off the main travel routes.' Yamaoka spoke slowly, like a man who was choosing his words carefully. 'You might say, on the road not taken. By most travelers, anyway.'

'It is,' Moroboshi said with a small chuckle. 'Which paradoxically makes this world, and others like it, an ideal destination for those whose actions are deemed unacceptable in places with more inhabitants and more regulations. Or so it seems to me.'

'I can see that,' Yamaoka conceded. 'Aliens can do anything they want on a planet where the majority of indigenous lifeforms may not even believe they exist.'

'There are still people in the world today who will argue the Earth is flat,' Kiriyama noted. 'Although some of them do it simply to be contrary.'

'I've come to believe that a good part of humanity's charm is its capacity to inhabit an imagined reality that contradicts the one they live in,' Moroboshi said.

'I don't know about charm,' Yamaoka said, chuckling without humor. 'Most people find out that living in denial doesn't end well.'

'Denial is a universal phenomenon,' Moroboshi said. 'Although those societies that choose it instead of reality tend not to last very long.'

Kiriyama and Yamaoka traded looks again, and Kiriyama wondered just how well-traveled Dan Moroboshi was.

True to Kiriyama's prediction, the hardware lab had created a device for painting large structures and had it ready to install within half an hour. What Kiriyama hadn't expected was Yamaoka's decision to have Dan Moroboshi accompany the Ultra Guard on the operation as a provisional crew member.

On the one hand, it seemed like a good idea to have someone among them with a feel for what the aliens were up to. On the other, however, Moroboshi was a total stranger who had picked a very odd time to pop up out of nowhere. To all appearances, he was a good guy with a genuine desire to help—he had, after all, come to Furuhashi's and Soga's aid when they were under fire.

But truth to tell, they didn't actually know much more about him than the Alien Cool. Yamaoka was putting an awful lot of trust in a man who had literally wandered in off the road. If it turned out that Moroboshi was working with the aliens, or if he was actually a homicidal psycho planning to crash the Ultra Hawk 1…

Except he wasn't. Kiriyama felt as certain of that as he'd ever been about anything, and he was damned if he knew why. Something about him made Kiriyama want to trust him without question, and he wasn't the only one. Yamaoka was already there, and the other Joint Chiefs were close behind him. While the rest of the Ultra Guard treated the guy like he'd already made the team.

Kiriyama had never imagined that the Joint Chiefs or the Ultra Guard would ever trust someone they'd known only a few hours to help them release weather balloons, let alone participate in a mission to defend the entire planet. But here they were.

Furuhashi and Soga were mostly recovered from their injuries when the aerosol device was loaded onto the Hawk-1. In that time, TDF's communications specialists had, with Anne's and Amagi's help, picked up traces of the alien vessel. With a few suggestions from Moroboshi, they were able to configure the sensors at HQ and on the Ultra Hawk so they wouldn't lose it.

Everything was coming together, Kiriyama thought as he buckled himself in behind Furuhashi in the pilot's seat. Soga had the copilot's spot with the controls for the spray device. Anne took the seat behind Soga with Amagi on her left and Dan Moroboshi behind her at the very back. Kiriyama kept a discreet eye on him via a small wide-view mirror mounted on the ceiling, angled so he could see everybody in the cockpit. He wondered what Moroboshi would make of the Ultra Hawk. The first time he'd been aboard during midflight separation, he'd been astounded even though he'd known what was coming.

At the moment, Moroboshi was listening intently to Anne, who was twisted around in her seat explaining the Hawk-1's unique capabilities. Moroboshi seemed completely at ease, as if this were his millionth flight with the Ultra Guard rather than his first.

Whatever happened once they were airborne would tell them everything they needed to know about the guy, Kiriyama thought, and if it wasn't good...

But it would be. Kiriyama's instincts were sure of it.

'Initiating pre-flight,' Furuhashi announced. 'All passengers must now be in an upright position with safety harnesses securely fastened and *no talking*.' He looked over his shoulder at Anne, who was the picture of innocence.

'I didn't say anything,' she said.

'Commencing hangar opening,' said a filtered voice from a speaker in the ceiling.

A deep rumble passed through the aircraft as, far above them, a section of hillside slid sideways under the adjacent wooded area. The Ultra Hawk had VTOL capabilities but Furuhashi opted for a standard aircraft take-off and landing whenever possible, claiming it was easier on the eardrums. Acceleration pushed Kiriyama back into the seat padding and he glanced up at the wide-view mirror. Moroboshi still displayed the seasoned calm of a frequent flyer.

'Does HQ have sensor readings?' Kiriyama asked Amagi.

'Sending them to you now, captain,' Amagi replied. The screen in the seat-back directly in front of Kiriyama lit up with the figures.

'Levelling off,' Furuhashi informed everyone.

'Then let's not waste any time,' Kiriyama replied. 'Target registers at three o'clock. It's pacing us. Prepare to fire.' He felt more than heard the panel in the Ultra Hawk's belly opening to lower the adapted device in its launch cradle.

Soga thumbed a yellow button on the dashboard. Kiriyama watched from the side window as the device streaked away from the Ultra Hawk on a curved trajectory, then started to disgorge thick clouds of vivid red into the air.

For several excruciating moments the clouds were all Kiriyama could see, and he wondered if the hardware lab had screwed up the targeting. But as the scarlet began to dissipate, he saw a shape form, something round and a bit flat, with wings on either side.

'That's definitely not a charter flight to Kowloon,' Furuhashi said cheerfully.

'Sure isn't,' Kiriyama agreed. 'Initiate separation and begin attack maneuvers.'

'Separating,' Soga announced, one hand dancing across the control panel.

There was a *chunk!* as multiple mechanisms released the center section of the fuselage. Kiriyama's seat-back screen showed feeds from the external cameras; the section rose up and away, leaving a long, much skinnier body.

'Stage one complete,' Soga said. 'Your turn, Anne.'

'Beginning stage two,' Anne said, tapping the graphics display on the monitor in front of her. 'Disengaging tail subsection and activating autopilot.'

The vibrations from this process were much fainter but Kiriyama always felt them. Tail cameras showed the subsection withdrawing smoothly as the Ultra Hawk became three aircraft.

'Attack formation,' Kiriyama said briskly. 'Purpose is to harry and force it to land, *not* to shoot down, *not* to destroy. There are human hostages aboard and we want to keep them alive.'

'Damn, that thing looks like a toy,' Furuhashi said, circling the alien spacecraft.

'A really weird toy,' Soga added. 'Like a police-car-light with wings.'

'That's just the color,' said Anne.

'It's no toy.' Amagi sounded tense as the alien vessel began firing harsh bright bolts of energy at them.

Furuhashi evaded the shots easily and fired neutralizing charges at the bolts; they fizzled loudly in the air. With the other parts of the Hawk flanking them, Furuhashi herded the alien vessel toward the nearby canyon.

The bright red alien spacecraft dropped suddenly. Furuhashi went after it but was forced to pull up when the thing slipped between two tall rock formations and disappeared from view.

'Dammit!' Furuhashi fumed. 'Whoever's on the stick flies like they know the terrain.'

'If they've been collecting human specimens for as long as Dan says, they probably do,' Amagi said. 'Can you get a fix on it?'

'The mineral deposits here are messing with the Hawk's sensors,' Furuhashi said. 'I thought the TDF techs had upgraded the software to fix that.'

'And they probably thought *we'd* done that,' Soga said wryly.

'I *hate* when that happens,' Anne sighed.

'Never mind,' Kiriyama said in a sharp, no-nonsense tone. 'We've got it boxed in down there. Let's put the Hawk back together and find the damn thing before it breaks something we can't fix.'

Reassembling in flight was actually the more dangerous maneuver. Furuhashi took them up three hundred meters so the sections could reunite without any interference. Kiriyama had always found the procedure nerve-wracking, but Furuhashi breezed through it as if it were the easiest thing in the world.

'You know, Captain—' Anne began when the Hawk was back in one piece. But that was as far as she got before something big hit the tail-section. Furuhashi fought to keep them steady, but they were losing altitude quickly.

'Brace yourselves!' he shouted. 'We're coming in for an unscheduled—'

The impact drowned out the rest.

* * *

The Ultra Hawk 1 hit the canyon floor like a stone skipping across a lake before sliding to a stop. As crash landings went, it was one of the better ones, in that the newly reassembled body of the aircraft remained together.

The echoes of the crash died away, leaving the kind of heavy silence that always seemed to follow a disaster. No one in the Hawk was conscious so there was no one to note how long it lasted, but in fact it was quite brief. They were all still unconscious when, a short distance away in a hidden gully, the dome of the alien vessel split open with a loud, electronic whine and released eight smaller flyers into the air.

The flyers were also bright red and looked even more toylike than the mothership. They flew together in a formation that made the wind whistle oddly around them. It was the sound of their approach that roused Dan Moroboshi.

He was checking Anne's pulse when he heard an energy blast, followed by the sound of falling rocks hitting the Ultra Hawk. His new friends had no critical injuries. If he wanted to keep them that way, he had to draw the alien's flyers away from them.

Quickly, he found the emergency exit, climbed out, and ran from the downed aircraft, taking a narrow path between two towering rock formations. The machine-hum of the flyers rose in pitch to a whine, and he knew they'd picked up on him as another alien, albeit one different from the Alien Cool. Which meant they wouldn't be looking to make friends—to them, he was a competitor to be eliminated.

The crash had been more of a physical trauma for him than he'd expected. This body he'd made for himself was sturdy for a human but much weaker than his own, even with reinforcement from his

Ultra nature. Fortunately, his protector panels absorbed ambient light continuously, so he was ready to take on the Alien Cool.

He also had something to keep the alien flyers busy and away from the Ultra Hawk. The capsules were in his trouser pocket. He took them out, looked them over to make sure they weren't damaged, and selected one.

'We need you now, my friend—help us,' he whispered, then hurled the capsule away from himself as hard as he could.

The capsule landed in a fiery blast that shook the ground. There was a swirl of flames and thick white smoke that blew back to reveal the fifty-foot metallic being he had named Windom.

It had been a long time since he'd last released the creature from the safety and confinement of the capsule. Windom straightened up to his full height, stretching his bulky metal arms wide with a growl, and turned to see three of the red flyers coming toward him.

The growl became an angry roar as Windom swatted one away, straight into a wall of stone where it blew apart. The little flyers really were only drones; they had no live passengers, and unlike Windom, they weren't metal lifeforms.

Humans wouldn't have known the difference—they were unacquainted with any form of life not carbon-based. They'd have mistaken Windom for a robot rather than an autonomous being. Better that they didn't know about Windom yet, he thought. If Windom wiped out enough of the flyers, the Alien Cool would call the rest of them back. He could track them to the mothership, and with any luck, by the time the Ultra Guard came to, he'd have neutralized the alien threat.

It was a good idea but this world, this Earth, was one of those weird little places where you couldn't count on anything working out the way you wanted. Windom batted two more flyers out of the air and fired on a third with the Laser Shot from the lamp atop his head.

Instead of fleeing to the alien vessel, however, the remaining drones grouped themselves together in a way that reminded Dan of the Ultra Hawk reassembling. Together, they sent a concentrated beam of energy straight into Windom's lamp.

The metal giant fell to his knees with a sound that was more of a wail than a roar. Even from a distance, he could perceive Windom's suffering as the charge blasted into his head and ran through his body, overriding all his sensory input with pure agony. Dan had to call the creature back before the flyers damaged his electronic brain.

He raised his arm and called out, 'Windom, return!'

The faltering metal creature turned toward him and suddenly changed into a ball of white light. It zoomed through the canyon to his palm, resuming the form of an innocuous-looking capsule.

'It's all right, Windom,' he whispered, tucking it back into his pocket. 'As the humans say, I'll take it from here.'

The Ultra Eye in his jacket seemed to stir and awaken as he pulled it out and pressed it to his face.

The shift back to his Ultra state was a full-on shock, a blast of power that spread through him as it overwhelmed his smaller, more fragile human aspect. He took to the air, rising high above the canyon. The little flyers had separated, he saw, and were fleeing back to the alien ship nestled against a jagged rockface.

Touching down beside the spacecraft, he concentrated and assumed human proportions so he could enter the ship without tearing it apart and endangering the humans trapped within. Except, he saw now, the spacecraft had no visible points of entry.

That was no problem. He reached up and removed the Eye Slugger, sitting atop his head like a crest, and slung it at the ship. The Eye Slugger followed his unspoken command, cutting a wide rectangle in the spacecraft's bulkhead before it returned to him.

The neatly cut rectangle fell outward with a surprisingly quiet thump! and he stepped inside.

He paused for a second, expecting an alarm or possibly an attack from some kind of defense system, but there was nothing. It seemed the Alien Cool weren't used to active opposition, or at least nothing that a few flying drones couldn't take down. Extending his Ultra senses, he found the group of humans imprisoned in the center of the spaceship, but only one alien.

An alien on a solo mission to take over an entire planet? Granted, the planet was less advanced technologically, but still—what kind of invasion was this?

One that had been devised by a society that reveled in pride, vanity, and cruelty, he realized. These were preening creatures who enjoyed terrorizing other lifeforms, thinking a species not yet capable of interstellar travel would be an easy conquest.

He moved through a long, dimly lit passageway, following life-signs he could sense from both humans and the alien, until he came to an open space with two large consoles. These were the spacecraft's controls, he realized. Raising his hands to his lamp, he used the Emerium Beam to turn the consoles into scorched piles of junk.

With the controls gone, he found he could sense the Alien Cool much more strongly. It was hovering behind him in the passageway, he realized, and turned around.

No wonder the humans had been terrified, he thought. The alien was more like a grotesque insect or a sea creature that had escaped from a nightmare. And the Alien Cool knew it, reveled in it, even fed on it.

Anger surged in him at the alien's contempt for the way it saw humans—fleshy beasts whose only purpose was to cower before superior beings like itself. He reached up to the crest-shaped Eye Slugger again and hurled it at the alien.

The alien didn't try to dodge. It knew about Ultras, but apparently it wasn't familiar enough with them to know what the Eye Slugger could do. Or perhaps it was so arrogant, it really believed it was invincible.

The Eye Slugger sliced easily through the alien's body just above its staring eyes and then flew back to him. He watched the upper part of the thing's body—all of its brain—topple away, leaving only those eyes, its tube-shaped body, and the six clawed limbs to sink lifelessly to the floor.

In the absence of the alien's domineering disdain, the humans' terror and desperation came through to him much more strongly. He ran along the passageway, following their cries for help until he reached a gigantic chamber with transparent walls.

All the humans who had disappeared were there, trapped in a zero-gravity environment. Some had been there for months; all of them were disoriented and confused to some degree and a few had lost all sense of time or place, unsure if they were even still alive. Anger surged in him again.

Two hands suddenly slapped up against the glass directly in front of him. 'Is someone there?' asked a young woman plaintively. Her face was only inches away from his, but she couldn't see him, he realized; she couldn't see anything. He put his own hands on the wall as if he were touching hers.

She looked startled, then pressed one ear to the wall. 'I can almost hear you! Please, help us! Get us out of here!'

He tried to send her a reassuring thought, but she recoiled from the mental contact with a frightened cry. Withdrawing quickly, he searched the outside of the wall until he found a panel of unmarked controls in a vertical arrangement. There was no time for careful exploration; he pressed the top button.

Everyone in the room dropped to the floor as gravity was restored. The next button down turned up the lights and he found himself practically nose to nose with a familiar face—one of the police officers who had vanished only that morning.

'Open the door! Let us out!' he shouted. His thoughts shouted even louder.

The third button made the transparent wall disappear. The captives immediately rushed forward in a blind, panicky stampede and he drew back as they raced down the passageway, going back the way he had come, until they found the opening he had cut for himself. They didn't stop to wonder where it had come from or why. In the distance, he sensed the approach of the Ultra Guard and the TDF.

Once he sensed they were all outside and a safe distance away, he allowed himself to return to Ultra proportions, punching out the top of the spacecraft. The screams outside became louder and he looked around, wondering if he had missed some other danger, perhaps another of the Alien Cool.

No, he realized, they were screaming at the sight of him. After their ordeal with the floating alien brain, they saw him as a new threat. But that was all right—the Ultra Guard had just arrived with the TDF to take charge of the terrified humans. He gave them a friendly wave, saw Furuhashi, Soga, Amagi, Anne, and Kiriyama staring up at him in astonishment. But not fear. Gazing down at them, he drew on the sense of alliance and kinship all Ultras felt for each other and let a little of it flow from himself to his new friends. Only a little, so they wouldn't be overwhelmed.

Anne was the first to change expression, from incredulity to surprised joy. Everything is going to be all right—he felt the words in her mind so vividly that he heard them, distinctly, as if she were sitting on his shoulder. She was exuding calm and comfort to the terrified humans and to her teammates as he turned to the alien spacecraft.

* * *

Kiriyama and the rest of the Ultra Guard stopped short at the sight of people rushing up out of a wide gully and coming straight at them. For a moment, Kiriyama was sure the people were going to stampede over them in a blind panic. But the crowd swerved around them without slowing, some of them screaming at them to run. Before Kiriyama could contact the TDF members waiting behind them with medics and transport vehicles, a police officer grabbed him by the front of his uniform jacket and bellowed, 'What the hell is *that*?'

Kiriyama looked up and his jaw dropped. The red and silver figure towering over the gully was at least forty meters tall, humanoid but not human. *Another* alien?

He heard Furuhashi give a nervous laugh. 'Is it Take-Your-Giant-Alien-to-Work Day already?'

'It's okay,' Anne said. 'He won't hurt us. He's on our side.'

How the hell *would you know that?* The question was on the tip of Kiriyama's tongue. But when he opened his mouth, he heard himself say, 'Anne's right. We have nothing to fear from him.'

The police officer was still clutching Kiriyama's sleeve, demanding to know *what* that monster *was*, dammit! Then Amagi pulled the cop away, telling him they needed to gather everyone together before someone fell off a cliff. Amagi, the strategist. Kiriyama felt his own heartbeat start to slow, then speed up again as the red and silver colossus bent to take hold of the spacecraft in his arms.

'The giant just picked that spaceship up like it was a toy,' Amagi said later when they were all debriefed. 'He—I'm just guessing but I'm pretty sure that was a he—anyway, he just picked it up like he knew it wasn't supposed to be there and then he just—*flew away.*

'But the *strange* thing—I mean the really, *really* strange thing about the whole situation was, I wasn't afraid. Not for my team or the TDF or the hostages, who were all screaming and yelling with terror. I knew it was okay and he was there to help. But don't ask me how I knew. I just did.'

To Kiriyama's relief, the rest of the day was far less eventful.

All the captives had been accounted for and were undergoing treatment for trauma. On returning to HQ, the Ultra Guard found a party atmosphere in force; even the Joint Chiefs seemed to be in a celebratory state of mind.

Eventually, Kiriyama knew, things would calm down. When the TDF members who'd been captured were discharged from the clinic, they'd have a much longer debrief ahead of them— more than one, probably. But for now, they were all entitled to a break.

'I'd say we were lucky that stranger showed up when he did,' Anne said as they gathered in the Strategy Room for a review of the incident with the Joint Chiefs.

'You mean the red and silver guy, the giant?' Furuhashi asked.

Anne laughed a little. 'Yes, we're lucky he was there—whoever he is. But I was actually thinking of Dan Moroboshi. Who knows how many more people would have been taken if he hadn't warned us about what was going on.' She looked around at the others. 'Only now *he's* disappeared. Anyone know where he went?'

'For a fitting,' Kiriyama said.

As if on cue, the door opened and Yamaoka came in, looking more pleased than Kiriyama had ever seen.

'Attention, everyone,' Yamaoka said. 'I'd like to introduce the newest member of the Ultra Guard—Dan Moroboshi.'

Moroboshi stepped out from behind him and Kiriyama heard Anne gasp. He smiled to himself; apparently, she thought Moroboshi looked pretty good in full uniform. Judging from the smiles on many of the TDF's female members, she wasn't the only one. There was some scattered applause and people started lining up to shake Moroboshi's hand.

All except for one, that was. Kiriyama's gaze fell on a man standing off to one side; his old friend Kurata, looking slightly subdued. He'd applied for a spot on the Ultra Guard. His record was exemplary and his test scores near perfect across the board. On the face of it, he was one of the top members of the TDF, but when he had come up for consideration, Kiriyama had decided against him. There was something in his manner that suggested to Kiriyama that being part of a team wasn't Kurata's strong suit.

The guy was ambitious and he worked hard because he wanted to be the best—i.e., *the* best, a star. But Kiriyama didn't need a star, he needed a team player. Manabe had put Kurata on the CO track, and if he could learn to rein in his compulsion to prove how exceptional he was, he would probably end up running one of the Lagrange point space stations.

As if he'd picked up on the flavor of Kiriyama's thoughts, Kurata turned to meet his gaze. The man's face became a neutral mask as he nodded to Kiriyama, then checked his watch, seemed to remember something, and left the room.

'I'm surprised,' Anne said. 'But at the same time, I'm not.'

Kiriyama turned to her, baffled. 'Excuse me?'

'About Dan Moroboshi being asked to join the Ultra Guard,' she said cheerfully. 'I'm surprised, but at the same time, not surprised.'

'The Joint Chiefs thought it would be a good idea to keep him around,' Kiriyama said. 'I agreed with them.'

Anne nodded. 'There's something about him, isn't there?' She began making her way over to him.

'Yes,' Kiriyama said under his breath, watching her as she stood next to Moroboshi. 'There certainly is.'

CHAPTER
TWO

The party atmosphere persisted through the next shift change. For the newly official Dan Moroboshi, it was practically intoxicating. The good spirits of his new companions buoyed him up to the point where he had to make sure he wasn't literally floating. If he was going to remain among these people as one of them, Dan Moroboshi had to keep his feet on the ground both figuratively and literally—especially literally—even though he knew deep in his core that he should have left already.

After carrying the Alien Cool's spacecraft out of Earth's atmosphere and destroying it, he should have kept going, away from the beautiful little world, away from its solar system and its pretty if unremarkable yellow star. His work was done, it was time to resume his mapping assignment. That was his real work, significant on a galactic scale. The Alien Cool weren't the only sentient beings that preyed on weaker, less knowledgeable lifeforms, any more than humans were the only ones who could be victimized by an enemy they didn't even know existed. He had a duty as an Ultra to those who needed protection; mapping the galaxy would tell his fellow Ultras where they were.

Nonetheless, when he reached the point at which he would have departed and returned to interstellar space, he turned around and went back to Earth.

Something about these people resonated deeply with his spirit. They reminded him so much of his own people prior to their enlightenment. He could feel it in all of them, some a lot, some only a little, but it was there—the drive to connect, to create, to make a difference. To *be* the difference.

All of Earth's inhabitants were seeking enlightenment, whether they knew it or not. It wasn't something that came easily. Lifeforms could achieve it only by their own efforts, and not all species succeeded. There was no guarantee that humans would find the right course.

Oddly, humans seemed to understand there were no guarantees, no sure things. At first, he was baffled; how could they grasp this concept when they knew so little of the universe?

It was their abbreviated lifespans, he realized finally as he lay on the bed in his new living quarters, some hours after the celebrating had died down. There was still a jubilant feeling in the air, he could sense it all around him even though most of the other occupants of the rooms around his were asleep, insulated by the slowed rhythms of their hearts, becalmed in dreams they wouldn't remember. Their response to the brevity of their existence was to squeeze as much experience as possible into what little time they were allotted.

And that was *so* little—they had no idea how little it was. Even among short-lived species, they stood out.

As an Ultra who had already lived tens of thousands of years, he'd thought it would be difficult to adjust his sense of time. But as Dan Moroboshi, he'd adapted with very little effort.

In every way, it seemed, life was scalable.

* * *

Dan Moroboshi slipped into place in the Ultra Guard as if he'd been destined for it—or perhaps as if this had been his true assignment. Soga and Anne gave him a potted history of how the Ultra Guard had come to be, how it had started some years ago when a friendly alien called Ultraman had come to Earth and protected everyone from kaiju, until another Alien Being had arrived to take him home.

'They came from a nebula—Nebula M78, if I remember right,' Anne said as she, Soga, and Dan took an easy jog on the running track. 'But from what I can tell, they both looked an awful lot like the giant that flew away with the Alien Cool's spacecraft.'

'Humanoid for sure,' Soga said, panting a little. 'But not identical to the new one. The new one doesn't have a colored light in the middle of his chest, and his eyes are a different shape and color. They're about the same size, though—forty, fifty meters. Which comes out to a little over a hundred and thirty feet. That's *tall*.'

'The new one can change size,' Anne reminded him. 'When he let the captives out of that zero-gee chamber, they all said he was person sized. But after they got outside, he turned gigantic.'

'I can't figure out how he does it,' Soga said. 'I mean, what happened to the square-cube law? And we know he's not a holographic projection because holograms can't pick up alien spaceships and fly away with them.'

'I'm just glad he was there.' Anne pressed two fingers to her neck to check her pulse. 'Back in the day, Ultraman would show up just in time to help us when we were attacked by kaiju. I doubt we'd have survived without him—and by 'we', I don't just mean Tokyo or Japan. Life on Earth might be a lot different today without Ultraman.'

'And now there's another one,' said Soga as all three of them slowed to a walk. 'You think we're in for another series of attacks by bizarre monsters?'

'I don't know,' Anne said. 'I'm just glad he was there when we needed him, and I hope he sticks around.'

'Maybe Manabe would have put him on the Ultra Guard, too,' Soga said. 'But they don't make Ultra Guard uniforms in "humongous XXXL." Besides, what would we call him?'

'Well, I'm Ultra Six, right?' Dan said, smiling thoughtfully.

'So that would make him Ultraseven,' said Anne.

'Ultraseven,' Soga said. 'Lucky number seven. I like it.'

Kiriyama was waiting for Furuhashi and Dan Moroboshi when they returned from the first patrol of the day. He beckoned for them to join him at the enormous tabletop screen in the middle of Central Operations. Usually the room was bustling with activity, but there were only a few TDF members at the consoles tracking air and ground traffic, leaving Kiriyama alone at the big screen, presiding over a topographical display.

'A large object is reported to have fallen near the edge of Kiso Valley.' Kiriyama used a silver stylus to draw a circle on the screen.

'Guess we're going back out,' Furuhashi said as he put on his helmet again.

'Hey, I think it's someone else's turn,' Soga said, stepping up on Kiriyama's right. 'We can handle this.'

'"We" includes me,' Anne put in. She already had her helmet on. 'Right, Amagi?'

Amagi looked up from the tablet he was holding. 'Absolutely,' he said, then frowned. 'Wait, what?'

'Hold it, everybody.' Kiriyama put up both hands. 'I'm glad we're all good to go and ready for anything, but slow your rolls and let me finish. We've had a flurry of reports come in and most have been from children.'

'I thought comms had an algo to screen out the pranks,' said

Furuhashi, looking dubious.

'None of the kids were giggling,' Kiriyama said. 'And I don't like handing judgment calls over to algorithms anyway. We've always checked out every report, even those from kids. Furuhashi, you and Dan take the Ultra Hawk 3 and have a look. I've sent the coordinates to the cockpit.'

Kiriyama saw Anne's shoulders slump a couple of inches with disappointment. He knew she'd been hoping that the addition of a new member would mean she'd get more fieldwork.

Well, the day was still young.

The Ultra Hawk 3 was smaller than the Hawk-1, designed to transport heavy cargo in and out of remote areas under adverse conditions, although it was as fast and as maneuverable as any other aircraft.

'The Hawk-3 is simpler than the Hawk-1,' Furuhashi told Dan as they strapped themselves into the cockpit. 'If *this* one comes apart, you know you're in real trouble.'

Dan laughed, watching the hangar doors open, then turned to Furuhashi, startled at the wall of water between the Hawk-3 and the outside.

'Are we having a surprise monsoon?' He asked.

Furuhashi chuckled. 'Check this out, you're gonna love it.' He pulled back slowly on the controls and Dan felt the aircraft rise a couple of meters and move forward. It nosed through the waterfall, then ascended sharply into the bright open sky. 'Pretty cool, right?' He grinned. 'No one would ever guess what's behind the waterfall. It, uh, was actually my idea. Mostly.'

'Really? Why?' Dan asked, honestly curious.

'Well, it's great camouflage,' replied Furuhashi. 'And taking off through a waterfall is just pretty cool. I mean, there's no reason why something can't be useful *and* pretty cool, right?'

'I can't think of one, myself,' Dan said.

Furuhashi chuckled, radiating happiness. 'We're gonna get along great. I can tell.'

Kiso Valley's terrain made landing anything other than a VTOL difficult to impossible. Furuhashi set them down near a small wooded area close to the lake.

'This isn't exactly where we want to be,' he told Dan as they prepared to disembark. 'But we don't want to be too exposed. So we'll walk from here and see if we meet anyone. On any given day, you can find someone fishing.'

'Do they catch anything?' Dan asked.

'Beats me,' Furuhashi said, 'But maybe they saw something. Like, say, some kind of Big Dumb Object.'

As Furuhashi had predicted, they found a man dangling a line in the water from his perch atop a couple of stone slabs. Hearing their approach, he turned to see who they were, nodded hello, then went back to watching for some sign of movement under the water's still surface.

'Hey there,' Furuhashi said cheerfully. 'Are they biting today?'

The man turned to look at them again. He was an older man and Dan could see he'd settled in—besides the tackle box sitting next to him, he had a large thermos, what looked like two packed lunches, and a basket for his catch, if any. Dan picked up enough from him to know he was human, but screened out any further details. Mental communication didn't occur here, not between members of the same species or even the same family; if he was going to remain among them, it was crucial that he abide by that.

Furuhashi produced a map he'd printed out, and unfolded it on the rock beside the man. 'Can you tell me if we're anywhere near this spot?' He pointed to the circle Kiriyama had drawn.

'Oh, sure,' the man said, pointing off to their right. 'It's just over that hill. Don't think you'll find anything interesting, though. I've been here since sun-up and I haven't seen anything or anyone.'

'No kids?' Furuhashi asked. 'Maybe voices in the distance?'

'Nah.' The fisherman was about to say something else when a hard yank on his line bent his rod sharply. 'First bite I've had today!' He pulled back on the rod and wound the reel. 'You guys must be good luck!'

Several meters out, the water was stirring and splashing as the fish on his line fought to get away. Dan frowned; whatever it was seemed awfully strong for something in a relatively small, freshwater lake.

The fisherman leaned forward as his rod bent again and hauled back with a grunt of effort, struggling to wind the reel. 'I think it's trying to tire *me* out,' the man said between gritted teeth. 'Well, it'll take more than one little fish to beat this old—'

A girl suddenly popped up out of the water beside the flailing fish, which Dan now saw was actually more of an eel. She couldn't have been more than twelve or thirteen. Still beaming, she unhooked the eel with a quick, deft movement, gave them a friendly wave, then swam away, disappearing behind a rock outcropping.

'What the—hey, you!' The fisherman reeled in the slack line. 'You come back with my catch, you little thief!' He dropped the rod beside his tackle box and jumped down from the stone to stumble along the shore, parallel to the way she had swum.

'Who is she?' Dan asked as he and Furuhashi went after him.

'No idea!' the fisherman huffed angrily. 'Never seen her before! But I'm gonna have a serious talk with her parents!'

The large formations and scattered rocks gave way to a grassy, lightly wooded area. The fisherman spotted something at the water's edge and ran to pick it up. It was the float from his fishing line.

'Look at this!' He held it up so Dan and Furuhashi could see it. 'She cut my line! That little thief has a knife!'

* * *

The little thief watched the men from behind a clump of bushes, still smiling. If the big, clumsy men kept chasing her, they were going to find the ship—but they were supposed to. Their capturing Eleking, however, *wasn't* part of the plan. She released the little creature back into the lake with a whispered reminder to be more careful.

Although it really wasn't Eleking's fault. Who would have imagined that on this absurd planet, the dominant species sat by bodies of water dangling morsels of food on barbed metal hooks, tempting any unwary creatures in the vicinity? If she hadn't come along, that wrinkly old human would have *eaten* Eleking! Unthinkable!

The girl looked down at herself and remembered she had to change from this silly little 'bathing suit' into the silly little dress she had stashed in a stand of trees. But she had to wait for the men to go away or they might hear her moving around. One of them was like her—not what he appeared to be. He was the one she had to deal with. Getting him out of the way was vital to the mission—and yet, to her astonishment, the other two men seemed to have no idea he wasn't one of them. How could they not sense the truth? It was so obvious! Humans were so limited, their heads might as well have been solid rock.

Maybe their lack of awareness was due to the way their brains were sealed up in total confinement. They had to rely on the most basic sensory input just to find their way from one place to another. And yet one of them had managed to put a barbed hook in Eleking!

How glad she would be when the mission was accomplished. With all the humans gone, there would be no more dangling hooks, no more stupid little outfits to wear, and best of all, no more Ultra to fight their battles for them.

She just had to make sure the Ultra found the spacecraft,

which wouldn't be hard at all. Once he was inside, there she'd be to greet him. And if he brought any humans with him, well, so what? It wasn't like they'd be able to help him.

Dan finally convinced the fisherman to go back to his rod and tackle box before someone else came along and decided to help themselves to some free fishing gear. The prospect of losing more than just his catch sent him galumphing away on the rocky shore, holding onto his hat with one hand and the float with the other.

'We should check on him later,' Dan said as he and Furuhashi started up the wooded hill.

'If we have time,' Furuhashi said. 'That's really more a job for the local cops.' He paused for a few seconds, leaning on the slender trunk of a juniper tree to catch his breath. 'Damn, the hill didn't look this steep on the map. I knew I should've done more cardio.' He blew out a breath. 'What do you think is going on?'

'Your guess is as good as mine,' Dan said, echoing something he'd heard Soga say; it sounded better than *I don't know and neither do you.*

Furuhashi gave a short laugh. 'Well, there haven't been any reports of missing aircraft or satellites falling out of orbit.' He frowned up at the sky. 'Unless nobody knows yet.'

They resumed climbing, and were nearly at the top when Dan stopped short and put up a hand. 'Quiet—*listen.*'

Furuhashi tilted his head to one side. 'I don't hear anything,' he said in a half-whisper.

'It's something in the air,' Dan half-whispered back.

'Like what?' Furuhashi wanted to know.

Putting a finger to his lips, Dan shook his head, then motioned for them to move on. They moved as quietly as they could, and had to pause again at the summit to wipe mud off their boots.

'I didn't think it rained *that* much,' Furuhashi grumbled, scraping his soles on a half-buried rock.

Dan barely heard him. He could sense the spacecraft quite strongly now, giving off an energy that didn't belong to these surroundings or, indeed, any other place on Earth. It was so strong, it actually seemed to have a slight effect on Furuhashi—not enough that the man would understand what it was, just enough to make him uneasy.

He cleaned the worst of the mud off his own boots, then started down the other side of the hill, with Furuhashi behind him. Halfway down, Furuhashi grabbed his arm and pointed.

Something black and metallic was framed in the branches of the junipers. He could sense that Furuhashi was even more perturbed. Understandably: the black, metallic thing was a six-sided structure about half as large again as the Hawk-3, wide in the center, tapering at the top and bottom.

She was there, inside the spacecraft.

There was no flickering now, just the alien presence—or presences. More than one? To his dismay, he wasn't sure, which made him almost as apprehensive as Furuhashi.

He pushed the feeling away and steadied himself. As they continued down the hill, Dan angled their descent away from the thing so they could see the whole thing from what he hoped was a safe distance. The alien pilot had set it down right at the edge of the lake, so the water was lapping at the base.

'I'm gonna go out on a limb here,' Furuhashi whispered, 'and say this is the "large object" we haven't heard so much about.'

Dan nodded. 'Those are scorch marks around the bottom, from its trip through the atmosphere.' He drew his sidearm and Furuhashi did the same as they began to approach it.

'I don't see any numbers or other kinds of markings that would be like an ID,' Furuhashi said. 'So this definitely doesn't belong to any of the usual suspects, or even the usual unusual ones. Should we split up, circle around it?'

'*No*,' Dan said, so emphatically that Furuhashi's eyebrows went up. 'With only the two of us and no backup, we stick together. At least until we find out who's inside and what they want.'

'Copy that.' The undertone of relief in Furuhashi's voice made him smile inwardly.

They moved around the front of the thing through ankle-deep water until they came to a panel with a metal bracket or handle set close to the bottom. Dan looked at Furuhashi, who dipped his head to one side noncommittally.

Holstering his weapon, Dan took hold of the bracket and pulled. The panel gave immediately, opening out and up; a set of three steps slid out from the bottom, making both of them jump back.

Dan drew his weapon again and peered through the opening, saw only darkness.

'I guess that's the front door,' Furuhashi said. 'And I guess that means "Come in"?'

'I guess,' Dan said, frowning. The energy of the alien was no longer as distinct from the spacecraft as it had been. He was on the verge of pulling back and telling Furuhashi they should wait for backup when the other man climbed the steps.

As soon as he stepped through the doorway, lights went on. Furuhashi looked right and left, then moved to let Dan stand beside him.

'Well, after all the build-up, I gotta say this is pretty uninspiring,' Furuhashi said, gesturing at the plain, colorless walls. 'You see anything like a map or a floorplan anywhere?'

Dan moved into the hallway ahead of Furuhashi. 'I can't even see where the light's coming from.'

Furuhashi looked around. 'Oh, man, you're right. That's amazing.'

They'd gone about twenty feet along the passageway when

Furuhashi suddenly tapped him on the shoulder. 'Hey, look at that.' He moved around Dan to where a circular section of the wall was recessed two or three inches. It was at least five feet in diameter and decorated with straight dark lines going this way and that.

'What do you think this is for?' Furuhashi asked him.

'It looks like a giant porthole,' Dan said. 'Only I don't think this is an out-facing wall.' He could sense something on the other side, a lot of somethings, or possibly one big something, but he couldn't get a fix on it.

'Maybe it's a door,' Furuhashi said. 'For very short aliens.'

Dan lifted one foot and mimed a kick. 'Together, on three. You count.'

Furuhashi nodded and mouthed the numbers silently. *One... two...*

The panel flew open on the first try and they bent to look inside.

'*Wow!*' Furuhashi breathed, and ducked to go in first. 'Is this a control room or a video game arcade?'

Dan put a hand on his arm to stop him as he started toward the nearest console, which really did resemble one of the more popular video games in the rec room back at HQ, except there were three screens, too many buttons and switches, and no slot for tokens.

Wait, he mouthed.

Furuhashi nodded and Dan could sense his teammate's embarrassment for not exercising more caution, and his wondering what was wrong with him that he'd been about to make such a rookie mistake. Dan wished he could have told him it wasn't actually his fault, that the energy in the room was set to make anyone who entered drop their guard. But he wouldn't have been able to explain how he knew such a thing, and he had much bigger problems than that; the energy kept shifting and he couldn't tell if it were coming from a machine, something organic, or a combination of the two. Whatever it was, it was confounding the hell out of his Ultra senses, and the frustration emanating from Furuhashi wasn't helping.

Furuhashi pulled him back to the round doorway with him, then made a series of gestures indicating he wanted each of them to move from there along opposite sides of the room, looking for anything that might tell them why the aliens were here.

Dan made a dubious face. Furuhashi shrugged and looked expectant; if Dan had a better idea, he was ready to hear it. In fact, Dan didn't want to split up even if they were staying in the same room. But he nodded reluctantly—they had to do something other than just stand around waiting for something bad to happen. They started on either side of the round doorway, both staying close to the wall as they went.

Dan felt another odd shift in the energy around him. Keeping his sidearm raised, he paused to look at the instrument panel on a nearby console. He'd seen something like this before but the memory was vague, far removed in time and space from Earth. Like this spaceship should have been.

He went back to hugging the wall, inching along for another five or six feet until he came to an odd, asymmetrical cabinet. This housed part of the navigational system, he realized, and moved to get a closer look. As he did, he caught a sudden movement in his peripheral vision: a shadow slid behind another freestanding instrument console at the far end of the room.

Snapping his fingers to get Furuhashi's attention, he pointed at the console, mouthing, *Somebody.*

Furuhashi nodded and headed right to it, reaching it before Dan. Dan heard him gasp in surprise a second before he got to it himself and saw the girl crouching behind it.

Her presence didn't flicker or fluctuate as she stood up with the same bright smile as when she'd popped up in the lake to steal the fisherman's catch.

'You!' Furuhashi's jaw dropped.

'Me,' she agreed cheerfully. 'And you're those men I saw when I went swimming.'

'What are you doing here?' Furuhashi demanded.

'Hiding from you. I didn't think you'd chase me this long.' She laughed as if she was playing the most fun game in the world. 'Pretty neat hideout, isn't it?'

Furuhashi drew back from her as she came out from behind the console. 'Is this what you do when you're supposed to be in school—swim around and steal from fisherman?'

The girl laughed again. It was a lovely, musical sound, very distracting, at least for humans like Furuhashi, whose expression had already softened quite a bit. 'I just felt sorry for that little fish, about to get caught and eaten by that wrinkly old human.'

Dan looked down at his still muddy boots. They made a stark contrast to her clean and shiny black patent leather shoes. No human girl could have made it up or down the hill so quickly without getting her feet all muddy, or, for that matter, without breaking a sweat.

'Something's definitely wrong here,' Dan said.

Furuhashi seemed not to hear him. 'This is no place for you,' he was saying to the girl. 'This isn't "a pretty neat hideout," it's an alien spacecraft.'

'Oh, what are you talking about?' The girl laughed some more.

'You won't understand this—' But whatever Furuhashi had intended to say was lost in a sudden fit of coughing.

Dan looked up to see white clouds erupting from vents in the ceiling. He turned toward the round doorway but the clouds were rapidly thickening into a heavy fog that obscured everything. Turning back to the girl, he saw she was already lying on the floor, unconscious. If she was an alien, why would she knock *herself* out?

PAT CADIGAN

Good question. Dan fell to his knees, hoping he remembered it after he came to. Behind him, he heard a thump as Furuhashi collapsed just before he toppled over onto his back. He fought to stay conscious but his human eyelids were too heavy.

Some unmeasured time later, his Ultra senses registered a new presence looming over him, a dark silhouette, featureless except for two glowing eyes that were more than eyes, perceiving in greater breadth and depth than human organs of vision.

The figure knelt beside him, passed one dark hand over his face then down to his chest. As the hand slid into the left side pocket of his uniform jacket, Dan faded out.

Consciousness returned with a jolt.

Dan sat up and looked around. The air was clear now, no more fog or gas, although Furuhashi and the girl were still unconscious on the floor.

He pushed himself to his feet, checked his watch; he'd been out for barely three minutes. What was the point? Then he remembered the hand sliding into his jacket.

His Ultra Eye was gone.

The sight of his empty pocket was like a punch to the stomach, a reminder of how closely human emotions were tied to physical sensation. This was true of many species, but none more so than the humans of Earth. He went to Furuhashi, knelt down, gave him a small shake.

Furuhashi woke immediately but it took him a few seconds to focus. 'What… what happened?' he asked Dan, baffled.

'They hit us with knockout gas.' Dan hauled him to his feet.

'Who hit us?' Furuhashi looked around, wide-eyed with alarm.

'Whoever.' Dan turned him toward the girl, still motionless on the floor. 'Her friends, maybe.'

Furuhashi shook his head a little to clear it. 'Where are they?'

'Beats the hell out of me,' Dan said. 'Here, you get her back to HQ. I need to find something.'

'Okay.' Furuhashi crouched beside the girl to feel for a pulse, looked up and saw he was alone with her. 'Hey, what happened to not splitting up?' No answer; he sighed. 'What always happens, I guess.'

'How can Dan be missing?' Kiriyama asked Furuhashi testily as he stood over the tabletop screen in General Ops. 'You were just with him.'

'I don't know, Captain.' Furuhashi looked down at the topographical map. 'I flew over Kiso Valley a dozen times. Then I flew *through* it another half dozen and I couldn't pick up even a faint signal from his comm unit. I'd've kept looking but I had that girl strapped to a cot and I couldn't delay bringing her in any longer. Dan's a big boy who can take care of himself. *She's* just a kid.'

'You did the right thing,' Kiriyama said and turned to Soga. 'Has he tried to call in at all, even just from a telephone?'

'Negative, Captain.' Soga's expression was a mix of frustration and guilt, as if this was somehow his fault. Kiriyama made a mental note to give him a few more responsibilities; it would leave him less time to blame himself for mistakes he hadn't made.

'Maybe the alien found him first,' Amagi said.

'Then I feel sorry for the alien,' Furuhashi said stoutly.

'We should be out looking for him, for some sign of him,' Soga said. 'But I think he's back at the spacecraft. With your permission, captain, I'd like to—'

Kiriyama put up both hands. 'Hold it, everybody,' he said in a sharp, this-is-an-order tone, and everyone fell silent. They were all intelligent and well trained, but they were also very young—they wanted to be doing something, *anything*, just so they didn't feel like they were doing nothing. Not that Kiriyama could blame them; he felt the same way, but he knew action had to be directed, focused.

His thoughts were interrupted by a call from the sick bay. Anne appeared on the monitor, her young face full of worry.

'Captain, this girl is giving me a hard time about *everything*,' she said. 'She won't let me take her temperature or even just put my hand on her forehead, let alone examine her.'

Everything had complications today, Kiriyama thought. 'What can you tell just by looking at her? What's her general condition?'

Anne's worried expression deepened. 'I'm honestly not sure how well she is. Sometimes I think she's in pain, but I don't know what kind and not knowing anything about her, I don't dare give her anything, not even an aspirin.'

'Let me try talking to her,' Furuhashi said.

Kiriyama wasn't the only one who turned to look at him in surprise. Furuhashi had a lot of expertise in a wide range of things but not children.

'She met me and Dan first, so I'm a familiar face. I got knocked out with her in the spacecraft and I'm the one who brought her here. Maybe if I just talk with her for a while, she'll open up.'

'It's not a bad idea,' Anne said.

'No, it's not,' Kiriyama said. 'It's the best good idea I've heard today. Go ahead, Furuhashi, but remember to tread lightly.'

Furuhashi walked in as Anne was trying to listen to the girl's heartbeat.

'Stop it!' The girl rolled over on the bed, putting her back to Anne. 'Don't touch me!'

'Aw, come on now, don't be like that,' Furuhashi said, trying to sound casual and friendly. In fact, his only experience with thirteen-year-old girls had been as a thirteen-year-old boy; they'd confused the hell out of him back then, too. 'Anne here is a wonderful doctor—she keeps all three hundred of us at HQ running in peak condition. I don't know what we'd do without her—we'd be three hundred very unhappy people who got colds all the time because we kept forgetting to wash our hands.'

Anne smiled at him. 'It's nice to know I'm appreciated. Thank you.' She nodded at a hand sanitizer on the wall and Furuhashi automatically reached for it.

The girl still lay on her side, eyes shut, clutching the sheet to herself. 'Leave me *alone*!'

'Come on, kid, you've gotta let Anne make sure you're okay,' he said, and tapped her on the shoulder.

Her eyes flew open and she sat up, recoiling from him. 'There's *nothing* wrong with *me*, you can see that!' she snapped. 'I'm fine and I don't want any of you touching me!'

'Oh, for crying out loud,' Furuhashi groaned. 'Nobody's tried to hurt you. We've been very nice to you, but—'

'Furuhashi—back off.' Anne gave him a pointed look. 'It's okay,' she added to the girl in a soothing tone. 'I won't do anything. No one will touch you without your permission. You're safe here, I promise.'

The girl's shoulders rose and fell with a heavy sigh. 'I'm sorry. It's just—I'm so *tired*. Really, *really* tired.' Yawning, she lay down again and pulled the sheet up to her chin.

'Then have a nap,' Anne told her, straightening the sheet out so it covered her more evenly. 'I'm going to step out of the room for a minute, but I promise I'm not going far and I'll be right back.' She motioned for Furuhashi to follow her into the hall.

He waited for the door to close, then said, 'That's one stubborn little girl.'

'It might be more than adolescent bad temper.' Anne's face was solemn. 'Kids who don't want anyone to touch them often have a good reason, and it's not pretty.'

Furuhashi winced. 'Right—I wasn't thinking,' he admitted. 'I'm really worried about Dan. I didn't want to tell the captain he just flew the coop, but—' he shrugged one shoulder, '—that's what he did. The thing is, he seemed to know what he was doing—I'm sure of it, in fact. But he didn't let me in on it, so I don't know how to cover for him.'

'Then don't.' Anne put a gentle hand on his arm. 'If Dan knows what he's doing, he doesn't need anyone to cover for him. He's okay.'

'What if he's not?' Furuhashi asked.

'Then he needs you to find him, not cover for him,' Anne replied. 'But you can't just rush off without some kind of plan.'

'Yeah. And it'll take a minute or two to come up with something,' Furuhashi said, nodding. 'You really *are* a good doctor.'

'And I'm good with children—of all ages.' Her eyes twinkled.

Furuhashi was familiar with that twinkle. It was why half the people at HQ were infatuated with her at any given time.

'You go back to General Ops,' she was saying. 'I'll keep an eye on her while I wait for some test results.'

'I thought she wouldn't let you touch her,' Furuhashi said, frowning.

'Some things you can get *without* touching,' Anne said. 'Discarded tissues, stray hairs—hair especially. Hair can tell you what a person's been eating and drinking—medication as well as food—which can tell you where they've been or at least what they've been exposed to. Plus, anything *she* touches can tell us things about her she won't tell us herself, depending.'

She put her hand on his arm again, gave him a little squeeze. 'I'll let you know if I find out anything earth-shaking. See you later.'

A careful look around the spacecraft told Dan there were two aliens.

At first, he hadn't been sure—there might have been three or even four. But when he considered its size and how far it had traveled, he concluded there had been only two. Three passengers would have put more of a strain on the ship—they'd have had to stop more often to replenish food, fuel, and other supplies. The spaceship would have shown more wear and tear, inside and out.

And of course, two had been more than enough to relieve him of his Ultra Eye. One had remained in human form to play the innocent victim of knockout gas while the other one—well, who knew? He'd searched the ship over and over, and had nothing to show for it except a collection of interference patterns from the various materials in its structure. Nothing steady or consistent—everything fluctuated, confusing his wristcomm. As long as he was in sight of the ship, he couldn't send or receive messages.

Nor could he sense the alien. Those glowing eyes—perception of such a high degree would require a lot of energy but perhaps taking human form dampened the energy down, so the spacecraft's energy concealed it; Amagi would have said encrypted.

Now one of them was at HQ, leaving the other to keep an eye—correction: organ of perception—on the spaceship. From a distance? Or was the alien presence so encrypted that even his Ultra senses couldn't find it? Somehow, he didn't think so. After all, the front door was still open, with those three little steps like an invitation. He only had to be patient.

Dan made himself comfortable behind a small heap of boulders a few meters away, and waited, sidearm in hand with the safety off.

Some twenty minutes later, he heard rustling as something made its way quickly down the wooded incline. Dan opened his awareness very slightly, just enough to sense whether this was indigenous wildlife going about its business. What came to him wasn't the simple need of something hungry or curious or fleeing from something bigger, but a smudge in his awareness. Which had to mean it was the alien, blocking itself from detection.

The rustling ceased. Dan tensed, focusing on the area around the open door. Minutes passed.

Abruptly, he felt the alien presence very strongly some ten meters away, behind one of the large, irregular stone formations on the lake shore. Then, just as abruptly, the alien presence decreased sharply and a familiar figure stepped out from behind the rock.

The same long dark hair framing the same innocent face, the same pretty little dark blue dress with a white lace collar, the same tidy black patent leather shoes. If he hadn't seen Furuhashi taking the girl away, he'd have thought it was her.

The second girl spotted him right away. Her innocent face was terrified as she turned and ran back up the hill. Following, he saw she had chosen a very well-trodden path. Fine with him—she was going faster but he was gaining on her. She knew it, too, he could tell by the way her movements were becoming more frantic. Apparently the aliens didn't understand that an adult human could outrun an adolescent, even uphill.

The incline became steeper, slowing her down until he was almost within arm's reach. He was about to grab her by her lacy white collar when she suddenly plunged into a cluster of bushy undergrowth. Now he had her, he thought, and dived in after her.

He came up with two fistfuls of scrubby green branches and nothing else.

Dan held very still, listening, but he heard no sounds that could have been a kid running away from him. Suddenly it was very quiet, almost no sound at all, of any kind. He concentrated, opening his awareness again and extending it outward at a level too low to be noticed by another equally sensitive being.

Nothing and more nothing. The girl—alien—might have ceased to exist in any form. Or transported itself to another location… like HQ. He checked his wristcomm and discovered it was free of interference now. He told it to connect to the base; a second later, Anne's face appeared on the tiny screen.

'Dan!' Her face lit up. 'What's going on out there? We've been trying to raise you! Kiriyama's been tearing his hair out and I think he's ready to start on yours.'

'I'll explain later,' he promised. 'How's the girl Furuhashi brought in?'

Anne's smile faded significantly. 'Right now, she's taking a nap in sick bay.'

'Good. Has anyone showed up looking for her? Like maybe another girl about the same age?'

Anne blinked at him, mystified. 'No. Why? Did you find another one?'

'Just keep her there and don't let her leave,' Dan said. 'Put guards on her.'

'Already done,' Anne told him. 'HQ is secure. But Kiriyama's gonna want to know—'

'Tell him I'm still investigating,' he said. 'Something about the spacecraft interferes with our comms. Just make sure you have eyes on that girl at all times.'

'Understood.' She was about to ask something else when he broke the connection.

'Anne out,' she said to the blank wristcomm screen and flipped it shut.

When Furuhashi and Soga had first met Dan, they'd described him as an okay guy but kind of excitable. The man she had met was level-headed and even-tempered under pressure but always ready to act. Just now, however, he was more agitated than she'd ever seen him. Almost flustered.

What had he found out about the girl, and how she was connected to the alien spacecraft, she wondered. Feeling a bit uneasy, she peeked around the privacy curtain. Her patient was still napping. When she woke up, maybe she'd be in a better mood and she'd let Anne take her temperature. And after that, who knew? She might even get to listen to the kid's heart.

She called Kiriyama and told him about Dan's call. Interference or no interference, the captain was annoyed he'd been out of contact, and the admonition to keep the girl confined and under observation didn't help. It was on the tip of her tongue to tell him that the newest member of the Ultra Guard probably wasn't used to being part of a team rather than a lone wolf, then she thought better of it. Telling him something he already knew wasn't going to improve his disposition.

With that big stupid male blundering around among the flora and scaring the local wildlife while he looked for a pretty little girl, the alien was free to return to the spacecraft to enact the next phase undisturbed. She'd really been looking forward to this part. It was going to be so exciting, a spectacle like these silly humans couldn't imagine.

The best part was, they had nothing like it here, so they'd never be able to defend themselves. Nor could anyone come to their rescue as long as the special Ultra Eye was in her possession.

When they had arrived to find there was an Ultra on the planet, they had very nearly turned tail and run. But then they'd realized the limitations the world had put on the Ultra, and understood that this was a unique opportunity—they could take the planet and put an Ultra out of commission. No one had ever done anything like that before. And his fellow Ultras would never know until it was far too late.

Maintaining her guise as a human girl, she ran to one of the consoles and activated the circular screen. The image of the lake came up, looking lovely and tranquil. Her hands moved quickly over the controls.

'Eleking!' she said. 'Wake up, Eleking, it's time!'

If that awful old fisherman was still around, she thought, he was about to get the shock of his life.

The awful fisherman in question had decamped to a greener area of the lakeshore. The surroundings were prettier and the grass made a far nicer seat than a pile of rocks, so even if he didn't have better luck, at least he'd be more comfortable while he didn't catch anything.

That was how it went—some days, the fish were practically fighting each other for the bait on your hook, and other days, it was like they'd all moved and left no forwarding address. Today it was the latter. That awful child had ruined his chances at having a freshly caught dinner cooked on the hibachi on his apartment balcony. He could only hope the fishmonger had something appetizing.

Something flashed in his peripheral vision and he turned to look, thinking yet another hobbyist with a camera was out trying to be the next Hiroshi Hamaya. Occasionally one would ask to take his picture and he always said yes. Why not? These days, everybody ended up on camera one way or another, anyway.

Now he caught another flash, not from an amateur photographer but from the lake—from the water. No, from *under* the water. The fisherman struggled to his feet as more flashes came more quickly. Time to go, he thought, reeling his line in as quickly as he could.

Water suddenly geysered up in the center of the lake, startling him so much he dropped his rod. He'd heard about things like this—one moment, everything was okay, nice and calm, and the next, lights were flashing and the water was churning, shooting up like a fountain, and then—

No, this was *Kiso Valley*—this was *Lake Azusa*, for crying out loud. Nothing ever happened here, absolutely nothing, especially not today, when the fish were too bored to bite—

And then the creature emerged.

The fisherman couldn't move, couldn't speak, barely dared to breathe. All he could do was gape at the thing, fifty meters tall—at least fifty—its pale cream-colored bulk covered with thin black markings. It waded up out of the lake on powerful, thick hind legs, lashing a very long, very agile tail around behind it.

But that wasn't what sent the fisherman running for his life in a blind panic, nor was it the creature's oddly humanoid arms that ended in paddle-like hands, or even that its long-muzzled head had rows of flashing lights where its mouth was supposed to be.

What sent him tearing through the long grass screaming for help were the two antler-type protrusions it had in place of eyes, and the antlers were *rotating*. Like *antennae*.

As the fisherman told anyone who would listen later on, he was going to see that in his nightmares for the rest of his life. And he was right.

Dan had intended to search the alien spacecraft again, in case the disappearing girl had somehow slipped around behind him and gotten back inside. But when he heard the fisherman's screams, he headed back toward the other part of the lake. He heard something else as well, a grating, high-pitched noise as harsh as metal grinding metal. It sounded like something was tearing the air itself.

As he came out of the woods, the terrified fisherman ran right into him. '*Kaiju! Kaiju!*' the man babbled at him, showing no sign of recognition. 'It was in the lake! Save me!' But instead of waiting for Dan to save him, the man plunged past him into the woods.

Dan stared after him. If the guy kept running that way, he'd come to the Park Ranger Station. They'd take care of him, get him somewhere safe. And when they saw the creature that had come up out of the lake, they'd go with him in a hurry.

'Moroboshi calling HQ—please respond, anybody!' Dan shouted at his wristcomm. But the static on the screen told him he wasn't going to get through. There was enough interference to play hell with all transmissions going into or out of Kiso Valley.

Dan drew his sidearm, flipped off the safety. It was good tech for what it was, but compared to the creature, it seemed flimsy. Still, sometimes a well-placed shot from a small weapon could be quite effective; you just had to pick your target. He took aim at the creature's neck and fired, and was surprised when the target spot burst into flames.

The monster let out a long, grating screech, writhing in pain, the paddle-paws beating at the fire and its long, snaky tail whipping through the water. But when the flames died away, there was only a small scorch mark on its pale flesh.

The monster's antennae were twirling even faster as it turned its head toward him. The lights that were its mouth flared brightly and sent a stream of crescent-shaped yellow blades of energy at him. Dan dodged to one side and the large rock he'd just been standing in front of exploded into fragments.

The monster reared back, and Dan scrambled away a moment before a second blast hit the large stones behind him, spraying him with sharp bites of rock. He barely managed to dodge the third blast. It passed close enough that he heard the air crackle as a stone formation blew into powder.

He needed a hell of a lot more than his sidearm, Dan thought, but until he recovered the Ultra Eye, he had only one thing that might keep Lake Azuma's least desirable new resident busy, and maybe even tire it out a little.

Digging into his trouser pocket, he came up with a few capsules, selected one.

'Miclas, you're up,' he whispered to it. 'Kick that monster's ass a little for me, okay?' He stood up and flung the capsule at the lake.

'A giant *what* came out of Lake Azuma?' Soga held the phone away from his ear. Everyone in General Ops could hear the hysterical man on the other end of the line, along with random bursts of static. 'I'm sorry, sir,' Soga said finally, talking over him, 'but this is a *terrible* line, you have to slow down…'

Kiriyama watched Soga take the report, using a stylus to make notes on a tablet. Soga never had trouble writing legibly on a tablet. Kiriyama envied his dexterity; anything he wrote on a screen was illegible.

'All righty, got it,' Soga said after a bit. 'Now—yes, I know there's a monster, you just told me—sir, please let the Park Rangers take you—' He broke off and put the receiver down. 'The guy hung up on me,' he said to Kiriyama. 'Says there's a giant monster in Lake Azusa and he thinks it's—and I quote—"the one that got away with the girl." If that makes any sense to anyone?'

'Moroboshi's still out there,' Kiriyama said. 'Someone get him on the line for me.'

Furuhashi tried, first by wristcomm, and then using the console. 'Sorry, Captain,' he said finally. 'Nothing but snow and white noise.'

'But he just called Anne,' Kiriyama said, annoyed.

'I don't think he's talking to anyone right now,' Furuhashi said.

'You think something happened to him?' Amagi asked, his long face filled with worry.

'I think we'd better get out there,' Kiriyama said. He raised his voice to address everyone in the room. 'I want the Hawk-1 ready to go right now.'

'Standing by, sir,' said one of the TDF members, already at the instrument panel for the hillside hangar.

'Ultra Guard, you're with me,' Kiriyama announced, and headed for the door with his helmet under his arm.

'What about Anne?' said Soga, picking up his own helmet. 'She's still in sick bay with that girl.'

'Then she's right where we need her to be,' Kiriyama said. 'Now let's go!'

If the fisherman had been terrified of the creature with the antennae, Dan thought, he probably would have fainted at the sight of Miclas. Humans here put a lot of stock in appearances, and Miclas appeared to be just as monstrous as the thing Dan was sending him to fight.

Any Earth person who looked closely at Miclas might have thought him similar to what humans called a buffalo, except he walked upright, on two legs. Miclas also had two pairs of horns, one very long and the other quite a bit smaller. All the horns had red and green bands. Fur had been replaced by hide with the texture of bark, albeit far more durable, and his strength matched his stamina. If anyone other than an Ultra could take down the monster from the lake, it would be Miclas, or so Dan hoped as he watched the two creatures square off, sizing each other up like a couple of human fighters.

There was a sudden smell of ozone and Dan felt the small hairs on the back of his neck and his arms stand up. The monsters rushed at each other, collided, and were thrown backward, as if repelled by some force. Both seemed startled, but they got up and waded in for another try.

This time they connected and Miclas forced the monster down into the water, where they grappled like wrestlers. The black and white beast kept trying to wrap its freakishly long tail around Miclas, who broke its hold and managed to take the fight out of the lake and up onto dry land.

It was a good move, forcing something that lived in water to fight outside of its natural habitat, or it would have been. Unfortunately, the pale monster didn't seem to have any trouble on land. The thing parried Miclas's blows clumsily but with great force while slapping at him with its tail. Finally, it found an opening to wind the tail around Miclas's thick upper body.

Miclas grabbed the tail in his powerful paws and used it to swing the creature around in a circle, then let go. It flew thirty meters before crash-landing heavily on a couple of young trees, making the ground shake.

The monster rolled with the motion and regained its feet. Its mouth-lights brightened suddenly as it sent a series of yellow energy blasts at Miclas, one after another, setting the ground and everything on it on fire, trapping Miclas in the flames.

Lying on the silly little bed in what humans referred to as 'sick bay', the girl feigned sleep until she sensed the ones that called themselves the Ultra Guard (silly name!) had left in their silly flying machine.

Well, except for the one who had stayed behind. That was the one they called Anne, the doctor—whatever that was. Anne was the silliest one of all, pretty but too old to be cute like her and her mission-partner.

But at least she could handle this one. She slipped off the bed without making a sound, though the Anne-thing probably wouldn't have heard anything, being so engrossed in whatever she was looking at in that silly thing she called a 'microscope.' By the time she got her hands around the Anne-thing's neck, the girl thought, it would be too late.

* * *

Miclas stamped down on the fire surrounding him and advanced on the piebald monster, which simply turned and ran, leading Miclas away from the lake.

Dan moved in parallel through the trees. He'd expected the monster to go on bombarding Miclas with blasts of energy, but it looked like there was a limit on the amount of energy it could expend in that way.

When he resumed mapping as Agent 340, Dan thought, he was going to investigate this creature and the alien aggressors that had brought it here—most likely the Alien Pitt, they loved to breed monsters. But there was no telling when that would be. *Or if,* he thought as the pale beast wrapped its snakelike tail around Miclas's body.

Miclas fought to break out, but this time the monster had him. Dan saw its mouth-light brighten and he heard a terrible sizzling noise as raw energy surged through its tail into Miclas, making him shudder violently for several seconds. Then the creature unwound its tail to let Miclas fall forward.

He couldn't let this continue, Dan thought. Miclas had done what he could, and he didn't deserve any more punishment. Holding the capsule up, he called out, 'Miclas, come back!'

Miclas's bulky form disappeared as the capsule reappeared in Dan's palm. He tucked it away and started to reach for his sidearm when he heard—no, *felt*—a sharp, high-pitched keening.

The creature was standing very still while those antennae twirled and twirled and twirled. It was receiving orders from the Alien Pitt, Dan realized. He turned and sprinted along the shoreline toward the spacecraft.

* * *

'What the *hell* is *that*?' In the pilot's seat of the Ultra Hawk 1, Furuhashi changed course sharply, giving the monster a wide berth while letting the team get a good look at it.

'Fire!' Kiriyama shouted, although Furuhashi already had. A monster over a hundred feet tall with light-up jaws and two spinning antler-like things for eyes was the kind of creature Furuhashi shot at automatically, especially if it was standing in an area popular with campers, nature-lovers, and families.

'Those antennae-things work just as well as eyes!' Amagi said, watching its every move. 'It's tracking us!'

Furuhashi changed course again, dodging a sudden bright yellow blast from the creature's mouth. 'If that's how it talks, I don't want to chat!'

'How the hell does it *eat*?' Amagi asked incredulously.

'Don't know, don't care,' Furuhashi growled and fired on it again, hitting it dead center.

The monster responded with another yellow blast of energy. Furuhashi dodged it easily and came around to take another shot, this time hitting it low on its right flank.

'It felt that one, I can tell,' Furuhashi said with grim satisfaction. He executed another hard turn, fired again, and hit its neck. Smoke and flames obscured its head for a couple of seconds.

Furuhashi started to ask Kiriyama when he should initiate separation for a three-pronged attack when something hit the Hawk's tail-section. It was more of a glancing blow than a direct hit, but that was enough.

'Aw, *dam*mit! We just got that fixed!' Furuhashi fought to regain altitude and couldn't. 'Brace yourselves, guys, the VTOL's out, too. We'll be sliding into home on our belly!'

Furuhashi managed to keep the nose up until they were nearly on the ground, then retracted the wings in the hope that they wouldn't be torn off the fuselage. They hit the ground hard enough to bounce once, then plowed forward, scraping dirt, rock, and trees.

It seemed to go on forever, until they finally scrape-slid to a stop. Furuhashi waited in the ensuing silence, hoping the fire suppression system was online. Seconds ticked by. When he was sure they weren't about to go out in a blaze of glory—or gory, Furuhashi thought—he undid his safety harness and gave his passengers the all-clear. They all looked pale and ashy, but from what he could tell, no one seemed to be seriously injured.

'Sorry about the toboggan ride,' Furuhashi said, and flinched inwardly at how awkwardly loud his voice seemed to be. 'But when you got no brakes, you go with friction and hope for the best.'

'All take-offs are optional, all landings are mandatory,' Kiriyama said, his voice surprisingly steady as he undid his safety harness. 'And any landing you can walk away from is a good one. So let's walk away. *Fast.*'

Still in the guise of a sweet little girl, the Alien Pitt stood over silly Anne Yuri, lying motionless on the floor.

Taking the form of this species' immature female was great for deceiving them but there were a few disadvantages as well. One of the more serious drawbacks was size: the Alien Pitt's strength was undiminished, but its human hands were too small to finish this human off, so it had to settle for simply immobilizing her. It could have used any number of available tools to kill her but there wasn't time to do it right and get away. Killing one silly human wasn't the priority anyway—they *all* had to go, and it couldn't do that if it was trapped in this 'sick bay.'

Better to leave her on the floor like trash, to be crushed when Eleking rampaged through the place. The woman was only human—it wasn't like she deserved anything better.

Still careful not to make a sound, the alien tried the door and was relieved when it opened for her. She stepped into the hall and found another door, which also opened for her. But behind this one was one of those silly human males in a silly uniform.

'Where do you think *you're* going?' he blustered at her.

Simpering prettily, she grasped the pendant she was wearing. Green rays of light streamed out to envelop the human, who drew back, raising one hand defensively. The light whirled around him, sparking and trembling until the man stood frozen, his face set in an expression of shocked confusion, his weapon useless in his hands. Eleking could stamp him flat, too, she thought as she slipped past him into another room.

There was a lot of equipment here and it seemed to be some kind of monitoring or security system; one instrument panel ran the entire width of the room. The silly humans probably thought it was the most sophisticated technology ever. It was fun showing them how crude it really was, she thought, her hands dancing over the buttons and switches and dials. Crude and flimsy!

She pried a couple of knobs off the console, but as she was about to set the power to overload, she heard voices right outside in the hall. Time to go; she broke off one last knob, then ran to hide behind some other pitiful piece of hardware just before the door opened and several uniformed people ran in, all of them carrying weapons. Maybe she could trick them into using them on each other, she thought, listening to them cry out as sparks erupted from the console. That should keep them busy, she thought, getting ready to run as they gathered around it, chattering in their silly language.

As soon as she bolted from her hiding place, one of them yelled, 'There she is! Don't let her get away!'

As if they had a choice! Smiling at them, she clutched her pendant again and told it where to take her, hoping there was enough energy left in it.

There was, but only just. This planet's thick atmosphere meant even the simplest operations required a lot of energy. She had to get back to the ship to recharge the pendant, and herself. Fortunately, the vehicle she was standing in front of would take her anywhere she needed to go in minutes.

She had to climb a long, narrow ladder to the small hatch in the nose cone, but that was easy. Settling into the padded seat, she found the right controls, listening happily as far above her, a section of the hill slid to one side. This set off a lot of harsh klaxons to alert the base that an unauthorized launch was imminent.

The silly humans would be scrambling, but they'd get here just in time to see their silly rocket with the silly name—Ultra Hawk 2 receding into the blue before the hillside closed again. It was ridiculous, using a rocket for such a short hop, but it meant they'd have no way to pursue her and her mission-partner. And Eleking could stomp them all to nothing.

If he hadn't realized this girl was an alien before, Dan thought as he entered the spacecraft, her failure to shut the front door was a dead giveaway. He crept up behind her with no problem—all her attention was on the monster on the screen. She was so focused, he was able to slip his hands under her arms and clasp his hands behind her neck almost before she knew what was happening.

'Let me *go!*' she demanded, squirming in his grasp with a surprising amount of strength for someone so much smaller than he was. Dan hung on; according to Furuhashi, this was a wrestling hold called 'a full Nelson', and it was extremely useful since most people couldn't break out of it. He was glad to know Furuhashi was right, although the girl was thrashing and kicking so violently that he was staggering to keep his grip on her.

'I said *let me go!*' the girl shrieked, her arms flailing. She didn't seem to know this was an unbreakable grip, he thought as she whipped her head back and forth. In the midst of the struggle he heard something clatter on the floor, and shifted her to one side so he could see what it was.

The Ultra Eye.

Immediately, Dan pushed her away hard and moved to scoop it up, only to have a small foot in a shiny black patent leather shoe kick it across the floor.

Both of them dived for it. The girl was closer and very nearly grabbed it, but he blocked her arm, shoved her back, and swept up the Ultra Eye practically in one smooth motion.

The girl cried out as he stood up. She was glaring at him with such intense hostility and desperation, Dan thought she was going to attack him. He took a step toward her and she jumped back, startled, only to trip over her own feet and lose her balance. Her head struck the console with an alarmingly loud *crack!* and Dan saw her go limp as she dropped. Under other circumstances, he would have checked on her condition. But he could see she was breathing and that was good enough, he thought, as he ran for the door.

Outside again, he clapped the Ultra Eye over his human eyes, feeling as if the sunlight was embracing him. The transformation felt extraordinary—power flowed over him and into his head, his arms, his chest, like his Ultra nature was welcoming him back to himself after an exile.

Raising his arms, he took to the sky.

Kiriyama hadn't realized how far the toboggan ride in the dirt had taken them from where they wanted to be until they disembarked. They had come to rest on the banks of Lake Azuma's main feeder river, and after last night's rain, the water level was high and turbulent, running more like rapids.

'So do we swim for it?' Soba looked down at the white caps apprehensively.

'Nope.' Furuhashi appeared beside him with a large flat yellow something under one arm. Smiling, he tossed it on the ground, produced a key-fob, and pressed a button.

There was a startling *whoomf!* as the thing unfolded itself and started swelling up to become a raft.

'*Ta-da!*' Furuhashi made a flourish like a magician and bowed. 'Behold, I give you the Ultra Guard Raft-O-Matic!'

'That's not what it's called,' Amagi murmured under his breath. But he was smiling as he detached one of the rods stuck to the stern. A hard shake made it telescope to three times its original length, one end fanning out to make an oar. 'It pays to be prepared for a landing on water, or even just near it.'

Amagi handed him the oar. 'You can say that again.'

'But not now,' Kiriyama said before Furuhashi could oblige. 'We're a little pressed for time.'

Two kilometers downstream, the river widened and became less turbulent. Kiriyama had stationed himself in the bow, using his paddle to push them out of the shallows or away from rocks, while Amagi did the same in the stern and Soga and Furuhashi rowed on either side.

By Kiriyama's estimate, Lake Azusa was still a couple of kilometers ahead, but as long as the river didn't have any surprises for them—

'Hey, Captain!' Furuhashi called out. 'You think there are any more monsters on the loose?'

'No idea!' Kiriyama called back. 'Why?'

Whatever Furuhashi's answer might have been was lost as the cluster of rocks Kiriyama had just poled them away from exploded, pelting them with shards of broken stone. Kiriyama looked up to see the pale kaiju moving along a ridge high above the river, pacing them.

'Fire!' he yelled.

Their first shots hit the thing's long neck, sending it into a rage. The monster gave several high-pitched screeches and pounded the boulders lining the ridge, causing an impromptu landslide aimed directly at the raft.

The water here was barely knee deep, Kiriyama saw. He jumped out of the raft and the other men followed suit; together, they dragged the raft to shore while boulders and broken chunks of stone tumbled down around them.

Kiriyama spotted a rock formation, and they all took shelter behind it. He drew his weapon again and Furuhashi suddenly grabbed his arm.

'Captain, look! It's him! It's Ultraseven!'

'Ultra *what*?' Kiriyama said, then saw the giant red and silver figure land squarely on the kaiju's head and knock it down. 'Ultra*seven*?'

'He didn't leave a name.' Furuhashi shrugged. 'But if Dan's Ultra Six, he must be Ultraseven.'

'Ultraseven,' Kiriyama said again. He liked the sound of that, a hell of a lot more than he liked the harsh, high-pitch shrieks coming from the kaiju.

The screeches grew louder and even more unpleasant. Underneath them was a new sound, distant but unmistakably a rocket coming in for a landing. Kiriyama had a mental picture of another spacecraft arriving, opening up to let out an endless stream of pretty little thirteen-year-olds in pretty little dresses with white lace collars and patent leather shoes.

But as the noise grew louder, he recognized it as the Ultra Hawk 2. Either HQ had decided it *wasn't* a colossal waste to send a spacecraft to Lake Azuma, or a certain alien had taken it for a joyride.

* * *

As the alien monster struggled in his grip, he could feel how hard and dense its muscles were under its tough rubbery hide. Finally, he managed to get an awkward grip on the thing's upper body, lifted it off the ground, then slammed it down as hard he could.

The beast's screeches took on a slight keening quality. He definitely had its attention now. *Get used to it*, he told the creature silently, grabbing it at the base of its long, flexible tail. Holding on tightly, he whirled around in a half circle, and let go. The thing crashed down hard enough to make the ground tremble. More boulders tumbled down from the ridge into the river below and he hoped his teammates were quick enough to dodge them.

Instead of getting up, the creature whipped its tail at him. He jumped over it as it whistled through the air, then ducked as it came back the other way. The beast turned its strange head toward him, its antennae twirling, and he understood that he'd surprised it. With that came a second realization: that the Alien Pitt had implanted it with a basic artificial intelligence. This was what he'd been sensing, with plenty of interference from the aliens' tech.

Anger surged in him. If the Alien Pitt hadn't bred this creature as a living weapon, it would have been peaceful and placid, roughly equivalent to the animal humans called a cow.

The monster was up on its feet again. Dan took several steps back, drawing it away from the river. Eleking, he remembered, as the beast stomped toward him, its tail lashing the air.

She had sensed something was very wrong even before she'd landed the toy that humans dared to call a spacecraft. There was just enough power left in her pendant to send her to her own spacecraft, where she was greeted by the sight of her mission partner face down on the floor, still in human guise. If that red and silver alien had killed her to get his Ultra Eye back—

'Wake up! Wake *up*!' She lifted her partner's upper body off the cold metal floor and gave her a hard shake. When she didn't respond, she shook her again, harder, until she finally let out a moan and opened her eyes.

She let go of her still-groggy partner and ran to the nearest console, where the screen showed Eleking facing off with the Ultra. So he had recovered his precious Ultra Eye. Well, it wouldn't matter, she promised silently.

'Eleking! Kill that alien—kill him!' A name popped into her mind from nowhere. 'Kill Ultraseven! Kill him before he kills us!'

He saw the monster raise its head, as if it was listening to something only it could hear. Its antennae were rotating faster and faster; it was receiving instructions, of course, and it wasn't hard to guess what they were.

The beast whirled, putting its back to him, and he knew what was coming. This time, he didn't dodge the tail, he let it wrap around him as he braced himself. But the energy coursing through the monster's body wasn't as strong as before. It had expended too much on Miclas and what was left was barely enough to tickle him.

It took only one try to break out of the coils. The creature turned to him, its antennae spinning. He stepped back as it advanced on him, positioning his arms to awaken the lamp in his forehead. In the next moment, the Emerium Beam destroyed one antenna, then the other.

The kaiju stood motionless before him, blind, deaf, helpless. He felt a surge of intense pity as he removed the Eye Slugger from his head and let fly. It sliced through the creature's tail, went on to its center mass, and up to its neck before returning to him.

For some unmeasured time, nothing happened. Then the creature came apart, sections of its body sliding away from each other in gushes of pale red blood. Sparks erupted from the stubs where its antennae had been, and Dan felt the interference that had been plaguing communications drop to nothing. He could sense the Alien Pitt more clearly than ever as their spaceship took off.

Agent 340 went after them with the intention of sending them as far from Earth as possible. Drawing nearer, he felt them become clearer and more vivid than ever in his awareness, filling his head with their existence, their thoughts and emotions, their determination.

The one that had stolen his Ultra Eye was bristling with frustration and anger. *Our plan failed*, she complained to the other. *We lost the Ultra Eye.* Her memory of taking it was so vivid. *We underestimated these humans.*

How were we to know an Ultra was watching over them? her partner replied.

We don't have to give up, said the first one. *We can raise a monster even stronger than Eleking to wipe them out. How lovely it will be when there are no more ugly humans and this beautiful planet is all ours!*

And it will be so much easier next time, the other said, exuding a powerful wave of joy that enveloped both of them. *Now that we know the mature form of this species has such a weakness for cute young girls!*

He sensed them shedding their human guises and returning to their own form. As they did, the last bit of interference died away and he could perceive the truth of their nature, and the darkness that they had embraced so completely.

In doing so, however, he allowed them to sense him as well. They fired on him, and he let the energy stream past him and fall away while he considered what to do next.

He could fling the ship out of this arm of the galaxy to a place so distant they wouldn't bother coming back. But then they would simply turn their attention to exterminating the population of some other beautiful world. The Alien Pitt claimed to live for beauty; in fact, they cared only for conquest. There was no success for them unless they had an enemy to wipe out, even if the so-called enemy posed no threat. Their idea of existence didn't involve coexistence.

Sending them elsewhere would only make them someone else's problem: the next species they targeted might be far more primitive than the people here, without an Ultra to keep an eye on them. When the Alien Pitt wiped them out, he would be complicit.

He positioned his arms and let the Emerium Beam shine bright.

The explosion left only clouds of smoke that dissipated quickly in the upper atmosphere.

Even so, he felt a deep, terrible ache in his core that even Earth's brilliant sunlight couldn't dispel. He was a young Ultra. If he'd been older and wiser, would he have found a different solution, a better one that was merciful on all sides?

Or was this just how life was on Earth—that some choices, even the most well-intentioned, would be painful?

He changed course, flying back toward the Ultra Guard at Lake Azuma.

CHAPTER

THREE

S tanding on the terrace outside the cafeteria after breakfast, Dan Moroboshi inhaled deeply, enjoying the first-thing-in-the-morning-after-a-rainstorm fragrance. Anne had told him this aroma was called *petrichor* and she thought it was the best thing about the rainy season (humidity, she said, was the worst). He was reserving judgment himself, but he had to admit that Earth was a feast for the senses.

As if his thoughts had summoned her, Anne materialized beside him, sipping a cup of tea. 'Rained really hard last night,' she said cheerfully. 'Did you hear it?'

''Fraid not,' he told her. 'I was pretty tired.'

She gave him a sympathetic smile. 'The last few callouts have been pretty, ah, strenuous. I'm a sound sleeper most of the time, but last night there was a crash of thunder so loud I almost fell out of bed.'

'I never heard it,' Dan said.

'I looked out the window and the rain was coming down in sheets.' Anne sipped her tea. 'I couldn't see a thing except when lightning flashed.'

'Did you see anything interesting?'

Anne shrugged one shoulder. 'In the middle of the night, when you're trying to sleep, your eyes can play tricks on you. I could have sworn I saw a long, snaky, metallic something flying around in the storm, maybe something blown off a tower or a satellite dish. But I didn't see anything in any of the overnight incident reports. Just...' She sipped her tea again.

'"Just"?' Dan prompted when she didn't go on.

She blew out a short breath. 'A few deaths.' Pause. 'Sort of.'

Dan suppressed the urge to put a comforting arm around her shoulders; she might think him presumptuous, if not actually aggressive. Had she been Soga or Furuhashi or even Kiriyama, he'd have sensed her feelings more clearly. But Anne was the most guarded member of the team. A brief peek at her mind would have clarified what she meant but he couldn't bring himself to violate her privacy just for his own edification.

'"Sort of" deaths?' Dan asked, after a few seconds. 'Do you mean the weather conditions, or—'

But Anne was shaking her head. 'These sort-of deaths have nothing to do with the weather. Half a dozen people just... stopped living. For no reason that anyone can see. All within about a thirty-mile radius or so.'

Furuhashi, Amagi, and Soga came out to join them. Seeing Anne's expression, Soga put an arm around her and gave her a quick squeeze. 'Our good doctor is creeped out by the recent fatality rate,' he said to Dan.

'They're not fatalities,' Anne said. 'They're not dead. They're just not alive. And we can't find a cause. That creeps me out a lot more than normal death.'

'Can't blame you,' Dan said. 'I'm a little creeped out myself.' It wasn't a total lie, he thought; if he'd been human, he would have been just as unsettled.

ULTRASEVEN | THE OFFICIAL NOVEL OF THE SERIES

'I've got a cousin in the US,' Furuhashi said. 'He says, "When it rains, it pours." And he's right—sometimes literally.'

Dan nodded. 'There are times when bad things seem to happen in clusters.'

'Or good things,' Amagi added. 'Sometimes.'

Soga made a face. 'Yeah, but I've got a bad feeling. And you know what Friday is?' He looked around at them. 'It's the thirteenth.'

'I forgot how superstitious you are, Soga,' Anne said with a tiny smile. 'You know, a feeling of impending doom is usually due to low potassium. Your doctor prescribes a banana—maybe even two. Eating a banana will cure it.'

'Unless it actually is imminent doom,' said Soga, a bit defensive. 'All the bananas in the world won't cure that.'

Furuhashi gave him a hearty pat on the back that knocked him off balance. 'Let's just see how the week goes before we declare the end is nigh. Or near. Or here.'

'Very good idea,' Anne said, and Furuhashi beamed as if she'd pinned a medal on his chest. 'Whatever it is, you guys are going to have to handle it—I'm going to be out recruiting all this week.' She patted Soga's shoulder. 'While I'm away, try to remember that just because something bad happens, it doesn't mean something good won't.'

'Yeah, of course,' Soga said, although it was easy to see he wasn't convinced.

Four days later, Kiriyama called them into his office to tell them the number of sudden, unexplained deaths had risen to twenty-six, all of them occurring in the area of Mt. Iwami, which people called Devil Mountain.

'We've actually got the latest casualties on video,' Kiriyama told them gravely. 'Purely accidental.' He picked up a remote and pointed it at a monitor on the wall nearest the small conference table.

The screen lit up to show them four people, two men and two women, all very young, out in the country posing in front of what looked like a mutant cactus.

'C'mon, Ken!' called one of the guys, laughing. 'We're taking a photo, not remaking *Rashomon*!'

'Oh, so *now* you're fussy,' said one of the women, making the other one giggle. Ken finally appeared, running into the frame and trying to squeeze between them. They made him kneel and leaned heavily on him, laughing.

'Okay, everybody!' Ken said. 'Don't move!'

They all obediently held still, maintaining big smiles, and nothing happened.

'You set this for *today*, right?' one of the women giggled.

'Just hold still!' Ken said through a toothy grin.

The group waited a little longer, still smiling. A second later, they all collapsed face down on the muddy ground.

Kiriyama paused the video. 'And that's all there is, until the battery runs flat. The camera was new, and somehow the owner, Ken, set it on video rather than delayed photo.'

Amagi got up from the table and went over to the screen for a closer look. 'And they're all dead?'

'They'd still be out there in the drying mud,' Kiriyama was saying, 'except the camera automatically uploads everything to Ken's storage in the cloud, which he shares with his brother Riku. Riku couldn't get him on the phone, so he checked for any new photos and saw this.' Pause. 'Riku is eleven.'

Everyone groaned.

'And they have no idea what killed them?' Furuhashi said.

Kiriyama shook his head. 'I'll tell you what we *do* know: all the deaths occurred in a certain area of Mt. Iwami and all the victims were young, with promising futures ahead of them. Those five—' he nodded at the screen, '—they were finishing up in the accelerated degree program at Tokyo University. One of them was about to start a doctorate at the Massachusetts Institute of Technology, one had a place at Oxford, and the other three put in applications for the TDF.'

'Those are some big losses,' Soga said, looking perturbed.

'Big losses times twenty-six,' said Kiriyama.

'So, someone's targeting the best and the brightest,' Amagi said thoughtfully. 'Or rather, the best and the brightest who happen to set foot on Mt. Iwami near the old Devil Mountain volcano.'

'So what do we do?' Furuhashi said. 'Issue a public warning—stay away from Devil Mountain unless you're kinda stupid?'

'I'm sure all the local businesses would be thrilled,' Amagi said drily.

'Especially the Cool Dude Ranch,' added Kiriyama with a humorless chuckle.

'The what?' Dan looked at him, baffled.

'It opened fairly recently,' Kiriyama told him. 'The owner went on holiday to a dude ranch in the US and loved it so much, he decided to open one here.' He aimed the remote at the monitor and the screen changed to display a large wooden cabin with a sign in front: *Welcome to the Cool Dude Ranch.* Below that, in smaller letters, was the legend: *Find your inner cowboy.* 'It's an actual ranch—they've even got a few head of cattle.'

'Is that where those five were?' asked Soga.

Kiriyama shook his head. 'They were on the ranch's land but they weren't guests. When emergency workers arrived, they found a jeep parked nearby but off camera. Which brings me to something else: this incident is a first. Up till now, it was always just one person at a time. Then suddenly, this morning, it was five people at once.'

'That's a bad sign,' Amagi said. 'Whoever's behind this is escalating. Have the autopsies told us anything useful?'

Kiriyama's uneasy expression deepened. 'And that brings me to something else we know for sure but have held back from news media and anyone not directly involved: there haven't been any autopsies.'

'Why not?' Amagi asked sharply.

'None of the bodies have begun to decompose.'

The Ultra Guard members all exchanged incredulous looks. 'Does that mean they aren't really dead?' Soga asked.

'We don't know what it means,' Kiriyama said. 'Local authorities consulted with us and we've decided to hold off, except for X-rays, CT scans, sonograms, or any other non-invasive procedure.' He took a breath, let it out. 'There was a theory that it might be something in the soil or the water on Mt. Iwami, or even the air. But even after the bodies were removed, they didn't deteriorate.'

'It's theoretically possible that there may be something acting as a permanent preservative,' Amagi said. 'I wish Anne was here. She knows so much more about this.'

'Maybe it's something about those people in particular,' Furuhashi suggested. 'Maybe they were all exposed to some substance not normally found on Earth.'

'More aliens?' Soga said.

'Or a meteor,' suggested Furuhashi. 'People don't just stop living for no reason.'

'And yet we have twenty-six people who seemed to have done exactly that,' Kiriyama said, and turned to Dan. 'I've sent a map of the area where the latest deaths occurred to you and Soga. I'd like you both to go out there, take samples of everything where those five dropped—soil, water, vegetation. Analyze that cactus all the way down to the roots, get samples from other plants for comparison. If you find trash, bag and bring it in. Check radiation levels, look for anything anomalous. Take the Hawk-3.'

'Will do, Captain,' Dan said.

* * *

'We've been in the air for twenty minutes and I don't think you've said two words.' Dan looked over at Soga in the copilot's seat. 'Anything on your mind?'

Soga took a breath. 'Remember how I said I had a bad feeling? Well, today's the big day—Friday the thirteenth. Something bad's gonna happen, I can feel it in my bones.'

'Like what?' Dan asked, curious.

Soga sighed heavily. 'That's the thing—I just don't know. But it's gonna happen and we're not gonna like it.'

Dan let it go. Humans had no psychic abilities—their brains were locked up tight in their skulls. Despite this, some were highly adept at intuiting something about to happen or someone else's feelings, but only under the right conditions. Most of the time, however, they couldn't divine the future or the exact content of another person's thoughts.

He didn't have to invade Soga's mental privacy to know how he was feeling right now—it radiated from him like heat, or a bright light. Or his aftershave, which as far as Dan knew was something unique to Earth, or at least this part of the galaxy. Normally just the thought of Soga's aftershave made him smile, but at the moment, Soga's apprehension seemed to overpower everything else.

Well, even the most cheerful and upbeat humans had an off-key day. Soga wasn't normally given to jumping at shadows or reading omens, good or bad, into happenstance. But Dan wished his teammate could have tamped his feelings back even just a little. They were getting to be a real nuisance, like a sliver in his finger or a stone in his shoe, phenomena that also seemed to be unique to this planet.

* * *

PAT CADIGAN

The TDF had blocked access to the area from the main road and set up a no-go perimeter to keep the ranch guests and employees from contaminating the site, and vice versa. Dan and Soga started by measuring radiation. As they'd both expected, there was no change from previous readings.

'I'm glad that's out of the way,' Soga said, setting aside the Geiger Counter and opening the sample case. 'My Materials Analysis professor used to say that if an investigation wasn't tedious, you weren't being thorough enough.'

Dan burst out laughing. 'Insightful teacher,' he said as Soga passed him several small plastic bags with blank labels.

'If you see me nodding out over a bag of dirt—' Soga held one up, '—just wake me. Remind me it's not my breakfast so I won't eat it.'

Dan laughed again as they went to work collecting stones, fallen cactus needles, and a few careful scrapings from the cactus itself, which the ranch owner had pleaded with them to treat with extreme care. It was actually a mutation bred to survive outside of a desert climate.

'It's pretty amazing that they actually got it to thrive,' Soga said. 'The owner said there are half a dozen of them over the whole place. I think it's kinda—I don't know—over the top myself. I mean, develop a whole new plant to make a dude ranch look more authentic?'

Dan dipped his head noncommittally as he sealed a bag with a square he had shaved from the underside of the cactus's single arm. 'A lot of discoveries are made for reasons that were frivolous at the time.'

'I guess,' Soga said but he didn't sound convinced. 'I guess I'm really thorough today.'

'How so?' Dan asked.

'I know we said we'd stick together, but this'll go a lot faster if we each take half of the area the captain marked.' He picked up the tablet leaning on the sample case and tapped it to bring up the map.

Looking at it with him, Dan was sympathetic. His Ultra senses would tell him most of what they'd learn from analysis of the samples they were gathering. But living among humans meant doing things their way; speeding things up even just a little would be criminal interference with human development.

'You're right,' he said to Soga. 'We just need to stay within sight of each other. Which won't be hard, considering how flat the terrain is.' He looked around. 'And to be honest, I'd rather not spend more time here than we have to.'

'Okay, now you're on my wavelength!' Soga said feelingly. 'This place feels wrong to you too, doesn't it? I mean, there's something about it that's just... *wrong*.'

Dan floundered for a moment, searching for the right response. 'Well, five people dropped dead here,' he said finally. 'That's wrong enough for me.'

'You're right,' Soga replied, giving his arm a soft buddy-punch. 'Look, I'll take this section here—' he turned in a slow circle until the onscreen compass pointed north '—on the northwest side of the cactus. You keep working on the other side.'

Dan gave him a thumbs-up, a gesture he'd learned from Anne that he liked a lot, and began combing through the damp, lumpy ground around the base of the cactus. In his peripheral vision, he saw Soga approaching a small grassy mound with a cluster of wet, bedraggled wildflowers. Now that he was all wrapped up in what he was doing, Friday the thirteenth was no longer front and center in his awareness. Perhaps by the time they finished taking samples and measuring the air quality and all those other tediously thorough yet absolutely crucial (for humans) tasks, his superstitious dread might have slipped his mind completely—

Snik.

A tiny, contained noise, barely audible, but Dan was downwind of it so he wouldn't have missed it even with human hearing. He knew immediately it was *wrong*—for these surroundings and these conditions, for this time of day, and this planet. *All wrong.*

He looked around. Soga was kneeling with his back to him, still examining the wildflowers. There was nothing wrong with them.

Dan knelt with the cactus at his back and drew his weapon. After a few seconds, he inched forward about a foot, and then another.

The hum was so deep, he felt it pass through him before he heard it, and then it was gone. Dan held still, opening his awareness, sensed Soga was still indulging his secret fondness for wildflowers; still safe.

Snik.

Metal, Dan thought; a cutter with sharp edges.

The hum returned, passed through him again and became more of a buzz. Whatever it was, Dan realized it was for him—aimed at him. But from where? The land was so flat—

Except for that hillock some twenty feet to his right. He gazed at it and finally discerned a long metal tube nestled in the scrubby vegetation, pointed directly at him. Not a weapon, but not harmless.

Snik.

Something like scissors, cutting him off from the land, the overcast gray sky, Soga, the samples, the planet Earth, and all the rest of the universe.

Soga looked up to see someone on horseback galloping away from him. Horse and rider were too distant for him to make out anything more than the horse's brown and white markings. Generic horse, ridden by a generic guy wearing a generic cowboy hat.

He walked a few yards in the same direction, stopped when he spotted something shiny on the ground: a spur, with a little bit of leather still attached. Soga picked it up, looking it over. Quite a novelty—he'd never actually seen spurs except in movies or TV shows. One of the Cool Dudes must have lost it, maybe the one he'd just seen on horseback. It looked new and rather fancy, but now that he saw the sharp edges up close, he thought using it on a horse was kind of mean.

Soga looked for the rider again but he was gone. How had he gotten through the TDF perimeter? Someone on guard duty needed a talking-to. As he tucked the spur into a sample bag, he turned to see what Dan was up to and spotted him lying face down on the ground.

'Dan!' Horrified, he ran to him and rolled him carefully onto his side. 'Dan, can you hear me?' Soga felt for a pulse, first at his wrist, then his throat, and finally at his temple. 'Dan, *please*—wake *up*!' he begged, ignoring how cold Dan was already, so much colder than he should have been.

Standing in the quarantine area of sick bay, Kiriyama gazed down at the inert body of Ultra Guard Six and hoped he was doing the right thing by not announcing to the entire base that Dan Moroboshi was the latest unexplained death.

With Anne away, he'd called in three TDF physicians who doubled as medical examiners. All three had agreed Dan was the latest victim of the force that left people in a state of—well, not suspended animation. More like suspended death. Even the doctors weren't sure what to call it. Kiriyama wanted to believe that the absence of decomposition meant the victims weren't permanently dead, that there was some way to call them back to life. It was a preposterous notion, to be sure—his sensible side told him this was pure wish-fulfilment fantasy. But his experienced side reminded him that there were far stranger things abroad in the universe and some of them had already visited Earth.

'I should have done something,' Soga said. His voice was bleak as he stood looking down at Dan on the gurney.

'If there'd been anything you could have done, you would have,' Kiriyama told him a bit briskly. 'We have to think about what to do next.'

'Any ideas?' Furuhashi asked glumly.

'The only people who know about Dan are the four of us and the doctors who examined him, and I want to keep it that way for now.'

The other three men exchanged anxious looks. 'What about Anne?' asked Amagi.

'Anne is still interviewing TDF applicants at the Okinawa Technological Institute,' Kiriyama said. 'If we tell her what happened, she'll drop everything and rush back here to do exactly what we're doing now. It won't help Dan or her or anyone else.'

'I don't like keeping secrets from a teammate,' Furuhashi said, and the reproach in his voice couldn't have been clearer.

'I don't either,' Kiriyama said evenly. 'I'm not saying we *never* tell her, just not right now.'

Furuhashi opened his mouth to argue, then didn't. But it was plain that he didn't agree.

'Be clear on this, all of you,' Kiriyama said. 'This is not the time to mourn—this is where we do something. There's an enemy out there and we can be pretty sure it's not of this Earth, running loose and taking lives, and Dan isn't the only victim. We don't know how this is happening or why, but we do know one more thing than we did before.'

He turned to Soga, who held up an evidence bag.

'We know it wears spurs,' Soga said. 'Because it's missing one.'

While Kiriyama had never had the urge to visit a ranch, he had to admit the sight of five people on horseback was quite stirring.

Four of them were wearing what he supposed were typical cowboy clothes—flannel shirts, jeans, boots, and cowboy hats. The fifth had opted for a colorful serape and a sombrero.

The idea was so incongruous, he thought—Japanese cowboys, not to mention that one of them happened to be a cow*girl*—but in reality, right here and now on the ranch, it didn't seem that way. Perhaps the ranch owner was onto something, and everyone, regardless of origin or geography, really did have an inner cowboy. Or cowgirl.

The owner, an ebullient man named Minamimura, stood beside him, leaning casually on the Pointer-1, smiling broadly. As enthusiastic as the man was about the cowboy lifestyle, his inner cowboy hadn't come out today. He was dressed in a black turtleneck and black trousers, with a suit coat, a knit cap, and dark green wellies.

The five riders came to a stop in front of them and the man in the lead touched the brim of his cowboy hat in greeting. 'Important business today, boss?' he said to Minamimura.

'Today and every day.' Minamimura took the spur in the evidence bag from Kiriyama and handed it to the lead rider. 'Does this look familiar to anybody?'

The riders passed it around, all of them shaking their heads. The lead rider was about to hand it back to the owner, then stopped to take a closer look.

'Hey, doesn't this belong to Yukimura?' He held the bag up.

'I think you're right,' said the cowgirl.

Kiriyama looked a question at the owner.

'Yukimura's our most recent hire.' Minamimura chuckled. 'Not a contender for Cowboy of the Month. Seems to have an allergy to hard work. Last time I saw him was…' He paused, then frowned. 'You know, I'm not sure. When was the last time any of you saw him?'

'He's been gone about three days,' the lead rider said as he leaned forward to hand the bag to Kiriyama.

'Couldn't find his inner cowboy?' asked Furuhashi, slightly amused in spite of everything.

'Found his inner slacker,' said the rider in the serape, making the other riders laugh.

'Look, until we know more, it's best for your staff and guests to stay close to the main house rather than riding the wide open spaces,' said Kiriyama. 'I know, that's not what people come here for, but we have to think of everyone's safety, and you're all safer with more people around.'

'Safety in numbers? We're covered,' the lead rider said. 'There are five of us.'

'What a coincidence,' Soga said. 'The killer took five people all at once this morning. Before he took, uh, one more from pretty much the same place.'

The riders' smiles faded.

'I know what you're thinking,' the owner said to Kiriyama. 'We're kinda loose and disorganized for someone to go missing without our noticing.'

'I don't know anything about running a dude ranch,' Kiriyama replied, his tone neutral.

'What it is, is, I don't chase anybody who doesn't want to work here,' Minamimura went on. 'I can always find a replacement. Frankly, I don't think Yukimura knew how hard the work was when he signed up. So when he didn't show, I didn't bother looking for him, I just hired someone else.'

The rider in the serape raised his hand. 'And I'm glad you did.'

Kiriyama was about to ask something else when his wristcomm chimed with an incoming call from Amagi. 'Captain, we've just had a call from the Gunma Prefecture Police,' he said. 'They want to rendezvous at a cave just southeast of Mt. Iwami Ranger Station number three. I've sent the coordinates to the Pointer's nav system.'

'Copy that.' Kiriyama looked up at Minamimura and his ranch

hands. 'Keep those happy trails close to home, okay?' he said, then turned to Furuhashi and Soga. 'Let's go.'

Two police officers were waiting in a car parked some twenty or so feet from the mouth of a cave. Soga pulled up beside them and they all got out of their respective vehicles, Kiriyama making sure they stayed back while they talked. There was a strange noise coming from the cave, airy but low-pitched, like growling wind.

'What *is* that?' Furuhashi asked.

'At first, I thought it was just air passing through a natural vent somewhere in the rock,' said one of the police officers; he was name-tagged Sato. 'But I looked it up and supposedly you only find those near fumaroles.'

'*Funerals?*' Soga blinked at him, incredulous. 'What would a *funeral* have to do with this?'

'Not funerals, *fumaroles.*' The other officer, named Kinoshita, spelled it for him. 'Those are holes near a volcano that let vapors escape—except there's no volcanic activity here and hasn't been for a few hundred thousand years. Still, the locals call this area Devil Mountain, maybe because of noises like that.'

'Okay,' Furuhashi said, unsnapping the holster on his right hip. 'We'll go in and have a look around. You two should wait out here.'

Kinoshita made a face. 'Would you?'

'Furuhashi and I will go in first,' Kiriyama said in his no-nonsense command voice. 'You two behind us, and Soga, you've got our six.'

He could tell by Furuhashi's uncomfortable expression that he felt he should take point by himself, but he knew better than to argue in front of the police. In fact, Kiriyama had been tempted to let him go first; he wasn't fond of caves, whether they made strange noises or not.

Once they were inside, Kiriyama was dismayed to find their torches didn't throw much light. Ten feet in, he called a halt while they took stock of their surroundings.

'Low ceiling,' Furuhashi said, pressing his free hand against it with a small humorless laugh.

'Don't anybody get rambunctious,' Kiriyama said. 'Or noisy.' He turned to look at the police behind him. Only Sato was there; he pointed to his left with his flashlight and Kiriyama saw Kinoshita examining some marks on the wall. Instead of scolding him for getting out of formation, Kiriyama said, 'Did you find something, Officer?'

'Not really, but—' Kinoshita froze, looking terrified. His whole body turned a harsh, glowing sepia for a second or two, before he keeled over sideways.

'Kinoshita!' Sato ran to him, asking if he was okay in a high, panicky voice. Kiriyama suddenly became aware of a very low, deep hum, but only because it had stopped. While Soga and Furuhashi tried to keep Sato calm, Kiriyama looked around, shining his torch over the walls, the low ceiling, and the cave floor, but there was nothing to see except dust and shadows. Another unexplained death, this one his responsibility; he should have made the cops stay outside.

The hum returned then, loud enough that they all heard it.

'Everybody down!' Kiriyama ordered.

Furuhashi and Soga dropped immediately but Officer Sato just stood, staring at him blankly, as if he'd spoken in a foreign language. In the next moment, he turned the same glowing sepia as his partner before he toppled over.

Kiriyama was about to call retreat when he heard a new sound, something very much like a rifle cocking. 'Fifty percent power, twelve o'clock—fire!'

The three of them opened up on the shadows directly ahead of them for five seconds, until Kiriyama ordered them to cease firing. They stood up, and for some unmeasured time they kept completely still, listening to the silence. Then a yellow light came up beside a chunk of broken stone ten feet from where Kiriyama was standing, and for a moment he had a wild hope that it might be the cavalry coming to save them.

Something flew out from behind the rock to land at Kiriyama's feet with a small *clink!* He waited to see if anything else was going to fly at him. When nothing did, he stooped to pick it up. It was a spur, the mate to the one he'd shown the dude-ranchers.

'I wonder where Yukimura went, that he left his spurs in two different places,' he said in a low voice just above a whisper.

'Uh, Captain?' Furuhashi motioned to his right and Kiriyama saw two jeans-clad legs poking out from behind another rock formation. No boots, only socks; one had a hole with his big toe poking through.

'You want to go out on a limb here and say that's the missing ranch hand?' Soga asked.

Furuhashi shook his head. 'Nah. You can do it.'

Kiriyama shushed them just as a new figure popped up from behind the rock where the spur had come from. It was mostly humanoid but covered with blue fur; on its head were two antennae topped by tiny glowing red balls.

'Down!' Kiriyama ordered and they all hugged the ground again. When he looked up, it was gone.

Kiriyama scuttled forward a few inches, stopped, moved a little farther and stopped again for a couple of seconds, before going all the way to the rock. Keeping his weapon up and ready, he peered around it to see what was lying in wait for them.

All he found was a silvery metal device lying on the ground. It looked something like an advanced version of a plasma rifle, except the edges at the end of the barrel curved back in, as if the device was meant to take something in rather than eject a projectile or a bolt of energy.

He crawled back to Furuhashi and Soga and showed it to them.

Furuhashi shook his head. 'I can't tell if that's a gun or something that fell off a sports car.' He passed it to Soga.

Soga ran his hands over the thing's length, keeping the barrel pointed away from them while he felt the small protrusions along its length.

'It *looks* like a weapon,' Soga said finally, 'but I don't think it is. Not in the classic sense, I mean. Look here.' He turned it upside down and ran his hand along the length of what could have been a rifle barrel. 'It's way too long and too narrow. There's no way I can see to load ammunition. And if you sent a plasma charge through this thing, it wouldn't fire—the whole thing would melt. Amagi needs to see this.'

Kiriyama took the device from him and got to his feet. No humming, no sepia glow; as they turned to leave, his gaze fell on the two police officers. He and Soga carried Sato out while Furuhashi slung Kinoshita over his shoulder in a fireman's carry. After placing him in the front seat of the police car, he went back in for Yukimura.

'Captain, you and Furuhashi can take the cops and the ranch hand to HQ,' Soga said. 'I'll stay here and keep an eye on things.'

Kiriyama considered it, then nodded. 'But I'm calling out half a dozen TDF stealth drones to back you up,' he told Soga.

'That many?' Soga said uncertainly.

'If the alien shoots them down, the R&D lab can send me the bill,' Kiriyama said.

'Okay,' Soga said. 'But call me as soon as Amagi figures out what that instrument is, because I'm dying to know.'

Kiriyama looked aghast. 'I really hope not.'

'It's a camera,' said Amagi.

Kiriyama wasn't sure he'd heard him right, and by the way

Furuhashi was looking at him, he wasn't alone.

It had only been two hours since Kiriyama had put the alien device in Amagi's hands, sure that it was some kind of weapon. Now they were gathered around a workbench in Tech Lab 3, along with Amagi's assistant du jour, Hayashi, who had brought in a guinea pig in a cage and was now standing by, presumably awaiting instructions.

The guinea pig had made Kiriyama wonder, somewhat nervously. It wasn't like Amagi to demonstrate weapons on living creatures. But apparently the alien hardware wasn't a weapon after all.

Still… a camera?

Furuhashi cleared his throat. 'Film? Or digital?'

'Neither.' Amagi chuckled. 'Okay, it's a *sort* of a camera. I have to say, I had a hell of a time trying to figure this thing out.' He nodded at the device where it was lying on the worksurface beside the guinea pig's cage. 'But as soon as I found the right comparison, it all became clear. A metaphor is a powerful thing. Handy, too.'

'Okay, so how does this "camera" work?' Furuhashi asked. 'What kind of pictures does it take?'

Amagi turned to his assistant. 'Hayashi?'

The assistant raised one side of the cage. The little animal looked up with bright, curious eyes, twitching its whiskers.

'Sorry about this, little buddy.'

Amagi picked up the device and aimed the barrel at it. Kiriyama heard a familiar hum; the guinea pig glowed sepia for a second, then fell over on its side.

'I know what you're thinking,' Amagi said as everyone turned to look at him reproachfully. 'But our little friend isn't *quite* gone. His body is inert but his life-force is in here.' He patted the device directly behind the trigger. Or shutter-release, Kiriyama thought. 'It's been captured on film. Or maybe that should be "in film."'

'So it's film, not digital,' Furuhashi said.

'Most serious photographers I know still use film,' Amagi said. 'These aliens are old-school.'

'It looks more like an old-school death ray to me,' Kiriyama said.

'I thought so, too,' Amagi said. 'But then I figured out how to pair a monitor to it.' He put one hand on the underside of the section that resembled a rifle butt. Kiriyama heard the hum again, though it was much fainter and had a metallic quality. Amagi picked up a remote and aimed it at the monitor on the wall behind them. For a second there was only static. Then they gasped.

The people on the screen floated in some kind of weightless space, some upright, some prone, others at what seemed to be random angles. It was hard to see what any of them looked like as the image was a sepia-colored negative. Kiriyama went over to take a closer look.

'Are they talking to each other?' he asked.

'I don't think so,' Amagi said. 'I don't think they're aware of each other.'

As Kiriyama watched, the guinea pig appeared, drifted across the top of the screen and out of the frame.

'How on Earth did you figure it out?' Kiriyama asked Amagi.

'By accident,' Amagi replied, looking a bit sheepish. 'My tablet paired itself to the device. At first, I thought someone was watching old music videos.' He looked at his assistant, who shrugged. 'But then I spotted this guy.' He tapped the image of a man; the uniform he was wearing was instantly recognizable, even in sepia negative.

'That's Dan!' Furuhashi said excitedly. 'Isn't it?'

Amagi nodded.

'We gotta show him the recording,' Furuhashi said, laughing a little. 'He'll never believe it.'

'You know, there are cultures that believe a camera can steal souls,' Amagi said. 'If they saw this, they'd be saying, "Told you so."'

'Do you think they're conscious in there?' Kiriyama asked, still watching the monitor.

'To be honest, I don't know,' Amagi replied. '"Conscious" and "unconscious" are physical states and none of them exists in a physical state right now. Each life-force is discrete, unto itself, but they're contained in a two-dimensional medium.' His expression took on a deeper solemnity. 'I don't know how long three-dimensional life-forces can remain viable in a two-dimensional medium. But if we leave them in there too long, there's a chance they'll come back... *different*.' Pause. 'If they come back at all.'

'Any guesses as to how long is too long?' Kiriyama asked.

Amagi shook his head. 'I won't know until I get someone out, and I don't know how to do that yet. I don't even know if I can— for all I know, this is a one-way trip, like the final one we're more familiar with.'

Kiriyama studied him for a moment. 'But you don't think so.'

'No, I don't,' Amagi replied. 'None of the bodies have started to decompose. To me, that says the connection between body and soul is still unbroken.'

In spite of everything, Kiriyama smiled inwardly. There was something reassuring about hearing Amagi refer to body and soul. Aloud, he said, 'Let's make sure we have all the people affected here at the base so we can keep them under observation. If any of them start decomposing, we'll know immediately. Furuhashi and I will track down the, uh, photographer. Maybe we can talk them into loaning us the instructions.'

'And I'll do my best to figure out how to get everyone's life-force back where it belongs,' Amagi said. 'I'm also going to try to make contact with Dan, while he's still...' He motioned at the alien device.

'From what you've said, that might be impossible,' said Furuhashi.

'Maybe,' Amagi said. 'But "impossible" seems to be today's speciality.'

* * *

Soga hadn't really intended to disobey Kiriyama's orders to stay out of the cave, but deep in his heart of hearts, he knew he hadn't really planned to obey, either. If he saw anything unusual, untoward, or just downright freaky, he was prepared to investigate and take any necessary actions. That was what the Ultra Guard did, after all: they took action, they didn't just watch from a safe distance.

For the first hour, however, that seemed to be exactly what he was doing, except there was nothing to watch. He was considering calling Kiriyama to say he was going to let the drones handle surveillance while he came back to HQ.

Then he saw a bright, white flash of light inside the cave.

Another weird device or weapon? Probably—no one ever brought just one. But who or what were they using it on? Had one of the cowboys slipped past the perimeter and found another way in? Tell people they couldn't go someplace and they immediately had to go there.

Or it could be kids, Soga thought uneasily. Kids were so good at finding their way into dangerous places like caves, often by some access point too small for adults.

He looked at his wristcomm. If he called HQ, Kiriyama would tell him to sit tight and send in a couple of the drones while he waited for TDF backup. But that could take at least fifteen minutes, and a lot could happen in fifteen minutes.

Two more flashes from within the cave decided him. Soga recorded a logbook entry on his wristcomm for immediate upload to the cloud. Then he climbed down from the tree branch where he'd been perched for the last twenty minutes and headed toward the cave.

As he did, there were more flashes of light before he reached the mouth, where he stopped and waited. Minutes passed but the flashes seemed to have stopped. Maybe the alien was getting ready to leave?

No, Soga thought, it wouldn't leave without its device, whether it was a weapon or not.

Kiriyama wouldn't be thrilled if he disobeyed orders, but the Ultra Guard wasn't like the military, or even the TDF. Members of the Ultra Guard were allowed to exercise discretion in certain situations. If he felt it was absolutely necessary to enter the cave again, he wouldn't automatically be subject to a tribunal for insubordination, even if everything went wrong. And maybe it wouldn't go wrong. Maybe he'd capture the alien and disarm it. Or several of them.

Soga moved up to the cave entrance, drew his sidearm, and poked his head in. 'Marco?' he said, then felt ridiculous; no one was going to say 'Polo.' 'Anybody home?'

Light flashed again and the furry blue alien was standing directly in front of him. Soga jumped, raised his weapon.

'Don't shoot!' the alien begged, holding up its furry hands. '*Please* don't shoot! We are the Alien Wild.'

'You are?' For a long moment, Soga was at a total loss. Then he pulled himself together and straightened up to his full height. 'We are the Human, uh, Humans. Why are you here?'

'We haven't come to invade or conquer you,' the alien said in the same pleading tone.

'Okay,' Soga said slowly, unsure what to say. How did diplomats handle this kind of thing, he wondered. 'We're very glad to hear that,' he said finally.

'We just need a few young human lives,' the alien added.

'Say again?' Soga asked, glad he hadn't holstered his weapon.

'We—which is to say, our race—have grown so old, we've begun to die out,' the alien went on. 'We're desperate for young lives to keep us extant!'

'So... what, then? You're taking *our* lives?' Soga drew back from it. 'You can just forget that, we won't let you.'

He raised the barrel of his sidearm so it was pointed directly at the alien's face. Alien anatomy could be tricky; you couldn't always tell just by looking where a species was vulnerable. But in general, most intelligent lifeforms had a strong aversion to head shots.

'We thought you'd feel that way,' the alien said, its hands still raised. 'Which was why we didn't ask. You humans have a saying here: it's easier to get forgiveness than permission.'

'Not for taking our lives, it isn't,' Soga said darkly.

'But you don't understand what's at stake for us,' the alien protested.

'Then let me tell you what I *do* understand.' Soga discreetly flipped the safety off his weapon with his thumb. 'You think you can just come here and help yourselves to our lives, deprive us of our existence. You're not entitled to those lives—they belong to the people born into them, who are living them right now.'

'Can't you try to see it from our point of view? To understand what we're facing?' the alien implored. 'Without an infusion of fresh, young, vigorous life-forces, we face extinction. We will be deleted—erased—*obliterated*. We'll be *gone*.'

'Okay, I get it, you're a—an endangered species,' Soga said. 'That doesn't give you the right to take other people's lives. And in case you haven't noticed, we're not even the *same* species.'

'We're not asking for the Earth's *entire* population.' Now there was a wheedling undertone in the alien's voice. 'We just need a few fresh lives—life-forces. When we have those, we can make more, we know how. All you have to do is give back what you took from us. Our _____.' The last word was half-growl, half-chirp,

'Your *what*?' Soga blinked at it. 'You mean that weapon?'

'It's *not* a weapon!' The alien clenched its raised fists and shook them; not what Soga would have called a pleading gesture. 'What few of our species that still survive are waiting on our home world. Without the lives our _____ contains, we are doomed!'

'If this is how you treat other lifeforms, I'm not surprised,' Soga replied. 'There is nothing for you here. *Nothing*.'

'Even after what I've told you?' the alien whined.

'Did I stutter?' Soga snapped. 'You heard me. You get *nothing* from us, now or ever. Now get the hell off our planet!'

The light that flashed this time was bright red. Soga remained conscious long enough to see what looked like two jagged bolts of red lightning coming at him from the alien's antennae.

So that's what those are for, he thought. Then everything went away.

'Uh-oh,' Hayashi said.

Amagi, Kiriyama, and Furuhashi turned to look at him in trepidation.

'What is it?' Amagi asked him, his voice calm but tense.

'I accidentally used this thing on the guinea pig again,' Hayashi replied. He looked at the cage; Kiriyama and the others followed his gaze. The guinea pig had vanished.

Amagi was silent for a couple of seconds. Then: 'I really wish you hadn't done that.' Pause. 'What did you think was going to happen?'

'Well… not that,' Hayashi said.

'Where do you think it went?' Kiriyama asked Amagi. 'Or is it… disintegrated?' Abruptly, his wristcomm chimed with an incoming call from Soga. *Timing,* Kiriyama thought, and flipped the screen up.

Soga's face was devoid of all expression; that was never good, Kiriyama thought. He started to speak but Soga talked over him.

'Captain, you must bring the alien instrument back to the cave.' He stared straight ahead, his eyes empty. 'It's urgent, captain. The return of this item is *imperative*.' The connection cut off before Kiriyama could respond.

'I don't think he's okay,' Furuhashi said after a moment.

'I *know* he's not,' Kiriyama said. To his knowledge, Soga had never used the word *imperative* in his life. He turned to Amagi, motioned at the device in his hands. 'How long would it take to put together a mockup of this thing?'

'Well...' Amagi frowned. 'No more than ten minutes, as long as you don't need it to do anything except look real. But even if the alien's fooled, it won't be for long. The alien might have some kind of biological or mental connection to it. No, maybe not,' he added suddenly. 'Since anyone can make it work. But—'

'Just do it,' Kiriyama said. 'Build me a prop. Even if it only fools the alien for a couple of seconds, that might be all the time we need.' He turned to Furuhashi. 'And since this is so *imperative,* let's leave the Pointer in the garage. Get the Hawk-1 prepped.'

Kiriyama and Furuhashi were back at the cave with the fake alien instrument in under thirty minutes.

'Hey, Soga!' Furuhashi called as he entered the cave ahead of Kiriyama, who was carrying the fake device. 'We're here with that alien thing. You know, because it's *imperative—*' He was inching forward when there was a buzz-hum and then the furry blue alien appeared.

'Stop where you are!' The alien's voice vibrated strongly and Kiriyama's apprehension increased. Excessive and intense vibrations could destabilize solid matter and bring most of Devil Mountain down on them.

'Where is our friend?' Kiriyama demanded.

'Here, with me.' The alien stepped to one side. Soga was frozen in a defensive posture, one arm raised, his weapon in his other hand. 'If you value this human's life, you will hand over my _____.'

'If we give this to you, you'll let us take our man?' Kiriyama asked. Without waiting for an answer, he gestured for Furuhashi to go to Soga. The moment he lifted Soga's feet off the ground to carry him fireman-style, Soga's body went limp. Kiriyama moved to put himself between the alien and Furuhashi and Soga, and stooped to set the fake device on the ground.

'Let's go,' he said to Furuhashi sharply. Then, in a much lower voice, he added, '*Run.*'

They had reached the mouth of the cave when they heard the alien cry out in anger.

'Hundred-yard dash!' Kiriyama ordered as he drew his weapon.

They had dashed all one hundred yards when Kiriyama realized the alien wasn't chasing them, and slowed to a stop. Soga, however, was waking up, trying to squirm away from Furuhashi, who set him down.

'What the hell was that about?' Soga asked him, then turned to Kiriyama. 'I thought you left! And where's that furry blue creep?'

Before Kiriyama could tell him, they felt the ground shudder under them. The shuddering became more intense as the sound of thunder rolled through the air.

'Never mind—what the hell is *that*?' Soga pointed at Devil Mountain. Kiriyama saw smoke had started pouring out of the top. In the next second, it blew off altogether in a deafening explosion.

Furuhashi was gaping at the cave mouth, which was now completely blocked by boulders, broken chunks of rock, and soil. 'If we'd still been in there…' he said.

'So much for no volcanic activity,' Soga said. 'I think Devil Mountain's awake after all.'

'That's not volcanic,' Kiriyama said grimly. Within the dense clouds of smoke, he could make out a form rising into the air, something long and slender, writhing furiously. 'The alien didn't come here without backup.'

'Damn,' Furuhashi said as Kiriyama began pushing him and Soga toward the place where they'd hidden the Hawk-1. 'It never ends, does it?'

'Wait a minute.' Soga dug his heels in, forcing the three of them to a halt. 'Is that—is that a *dragon*?'

Kiriyama stared at the long, jointed creature undulating in the sky. 'Incident reports from earlier in the week included calls from people claiming they'd seen a demon riding a lightning bolt down to Devil Mountain,' he said. 'Local authorities dismissed them as figments of frightened imaginations.'

'That figment just blew the top off Demon Mountain,' Soga said. 'What do you think it'll do for an encore?'

'Probably not air ballet,' Kiriyama said as he got them moving toward the Hawk-1 again.

'That was ingenious, sir,' Hayashi said to Amagi with admiration. He picked up the newly restored guinea pig from the adapted output plate of the 3D printer. The little animal cuddled up to him as he cradled it gently in his arms. 'And our friend here seems none the worse for wear.'

'Time will tell if that's true,' Amagi said. 'Did I mention I'd rather Anne didn't know about this?'

'A while back,' Hayashi said. 'When we first—well, you know.'

'I'm not kidding.' Amagi's serious tone made Hayashi look at him in mild surprise. 'I know, it looks like a happy outcome for our little friend, but to Anne, that's not the point.'

'Okay,' Hayashi said as he placed the guinea pig back in his cage. Amagi was pretty sure his assistant didn't really understand, but that was okay. Hayashi didn't have to understand, he just had to keep quiet. 'Should we elevate the printer?'

'No,' Amagi said, 'we just have to position it so there's plenty of room for the output.'

'Should we have a gurney? Or even a chair? For when they come out—'

Amagi shook his head. 'We should make sure the area is clear of any foreign objects larger than the average thumbnail. I'd rather not restore Dan and then have to surgically remove a chair from his body.'

The two of them wheeled the 3D printer into a spot normally occupied by the digital radiography system, now closed up and out of the way.

'If we weren't so pressed for time,' Amagi said as he powered up the printer, 'I'd have done a lot more trial runs. Although I'm not sure how much more we'd have learned.'

'And our little buddy would have had to wait an extra day to be restored,' Hayashi said. 'And when did you say Anne comes back?'

'Exactly,' Amagi said, turning to look at the little creature. 'Run him over to Life Sciences for me, will you? Tell them I want a full checkup every thirty minutes and a full-body sonogram ever two hours, results to me immediately. Unless he starts deteriorating—then they should call me right away.'

'And if he develops super-powers?' Hayashi said, not quite deadpan.

Amagi made shooing motions at him; Hayashi picked up the cage and left. As soon as the door closed behind him, Amagi dropped into the nearest chair and took several slow, deep breaths before calling up Dan's profile on the workstation.

He read it over several times, hoping he might have missed something, but he hadn't. Dan's profile was strangely sparse. Apparently, he hadn't had a complete medical workup since his arrival and there were no records from any other source, no indication that he'd even had the standard inoculations.

That couldn't be right, Amagi decided; obviously there had been a major software glitch somewhere. Well, there was no time to run down clerical errors right now, but when this was over, someone was going to have to straighten out the virtual paperwork.

Fortunately, that wasn't his responsibility. Then Hayashi came back and he put it out of his mind completely.

'Life Sciences wanted me to explain what happened to the guinea pig,' he told Amagi. 'I said they'd have to ask you later, when we put everybody back the way they're supposed to be.' Pause. 'Maybe you'll explain it to me, too.'

'I'll give you the simplified version right now,' Amagi said as he wired one end of an old-fashioned coaxial cable to the part of the alien device he'd been referring to as the film container. He'd removed the connector and stripped two inches of plastic coating off the wires by hand, being careful not to scrape the wires themselves before cementing the exposed wires to the film container. Then he plugged the other end into a slot on the printer marked *Input*.

'When this alien "camera" absorbs a physical body, that body and its life-force are on the same, oh—call it wavelength or frequency,' Amagi continued. 'But the two can't combine in a two-dimensional medium. When the printer is set to print out, they can reunite and return to their original state.'

'That doesn't sound very simplified to me,' Hayashi said. 'How can you store something three-dimensional in two dimensions?'

'The short answer is fractals,' Amagi said. He put on the printer's status monitor. 'I'll tell you the rest later, but it involves a whole lot of math.'

'Doesn't everything?' Hayashi said in a long-suffering tone of voice.

'Uh-huh.' Amagi went to the gurney where Dan Moroboshi's body lay.

'Wait!' Hayashi grabbed Dan's helmet from a shelf and went over to put it on him. 'It might not matter,' he said to Amagi. 'But I think he should be wearing everything he had on when the alien took his, uh, picture.'

'Good thinking,' Amagi said, genuinely pleased, and made a mental note to put an attaboy in Hayashi's file.

Hayashi finished working the helmet onto Dan's head, then stood back. Amagi steadied himself, took aim, and pressed the device's activation button. Dan's body disappeared in a sweep that started at his feet and rolled up to his head. It gave Amagi pause; he'd expected Dan to disappear all at once, or maybe to fade out.

'Man, that's spooky even when you know it's coming,' Hayashi said.

'Copy that,' replied Amagi with a small nervous laugh. He looked down at the alien device in his hands.

'What happens now?' his assistant asked.

'Well, we've reduced Dan's body to data,' Amagi said, putting the device aside on a nearby desk. 'His life-force will recognize it, and as they come together, they'll move from the device to the nearest space with greater capacity, which is the printer. We set it to print out completely and there he'll be. Just like our little furry friend.' *I hope*, he added silently as he flipped on the printer's small status screen.

The screen was only six inches square, but it lit up right away with two schematics of a human being. Amagi's heart gave a hard thump; Dan's head, his upper chest, and most of his central nervous system was indistinct.

'I hope it's supposed to look like that,' Hayashi said. 'The guinea pig was a lot more defined.'

'The guinea pig was a lot smaller,' Amagi said.

Hayashi looked doubtful. 'It's still a pretty complex organism.' He pointed at the blurry cloud in Dan's skull. 'How is he supposed to function with just a vague idea of a brain?'

'Think of electrons,' Amagi said.

Now Hayashi looked baffled.

'You only know where electrons are likely to be,' Amagi went on, 'but that's close enough to make chairs, buildings, mountains, spacecraft, aliens, and humans—you, me, and Dan Moroboshi, among others.'

The printer beeped to tell them it was about to print out. Amagi held his breath as he watched Dan melt back into existence. His body reappeared first as a transparent figure, and gradually became more substantial.

'How do we know when he's, uh, done?' Hayashi whispered to Amagi.

Amagi gave a small chuckle. 'Oh, I think he'll tell us.'

Furuhashi flew the Hawk-1 in a wide curve around the golden serpent-dragon slithering through the air with a flexible grace that sent a chill through Kiriyama. Soga had been scanning it in an effort to determine whether it was alive or not. It seemed to be a blend of organic and inorganic matter but the proportions of each kept shifting.

'It's hard to believe that thing comes from the same planet as the furry blue guy,' Soga said.

'Maybe it doesn't,' Kiriyama said, thinking out loud. 'Maybe the blue guy took its picture, and then retouched it.'

'Or vice versa,' suggested Furuhashi.

'Nah,' said Soga. 'No hands.'

'Unless the blue alien is its hands,' Furuhashi said, firing on the gold monster. 'So to speak.'

Soga made a face. 'I wouldn't think they could live in the same atmosphere.'

'Just going by appearances, the same could be said about humans and spiders,' said Kiriyama. 'And yet all of us can breathe on Earth.'

'Anybody see the blue furry guy anywhere?' Soga asked.

'The serpent or dragon or whatever-it-is is tracking us,

captain,' Furuhashi said tensely. He was still flying rings around the creature. It opened its jaws and screeched at the Hawk-1, showing enormous gold fangs.

'Jeez, that's a hideous sound,' Soga said, wincing. 'Like stainless steel spikes on an old-fashioned chalkboard.'

'Nine inches long,' said Furuhashi. 'The spikes, not the chalkboard.'

The reference zipped past Soga but Kiriyama chuckled. 'Let's get rid of this thing,' he said to Furuhashi. 'Then we can all go home and listen to oldies.'

'Golden oldies,' Furuhashi said and fired on the creature. Sparks burst from the center of its length and it screeched even more loudly, still tracking them but not attacking.

Not a fire-breathing dragon, then, Kiriyama thought, but it gave him no comfort. If it didn't breathe fire, what *did* it do?

There was another torturous shriek that seemed to go through the entire aircraft, shaking every inch. Kiriyama wondered if that was its weapon—sound waves that incapacitated and/or damaged? He took a quick look at the control panel and was relieved to see the Hawk-1's structural integrity was uncompromised, at least for the moment.

Furuhashi fired again and hit the creature near its tail. It shrieked as sparks erupted from its body. 'It's losing altitude, captain!'

'Then let's land and finish this monster off on the ground,' Kiriyama said.

'Are you sure, captain?' Furuhashi asked.

'I'd rather we don't get shot down,' Kiriyama said drily. 'If the crash didn't kill us, the paperwork would.'

'Point taken,' Furuhashi said, one hand moving rapidly over the control panel. 'Taking us to a safe distance and switching to VTOL.'

* * *

Dan became aware of movement, then light. The next thing he knew, he was standing between two people holding him upright. For a few seconds, he was at a complete loss. Then he found himself practically nose-to-nose with Amagi.

'Easy there, big guy.' Amagi sounded upbeat but his eyes were serious. 'Do you know where you are?'

Dan never hesitated. 'Earth.'

'Can you narrow that down?' asked a second voice. Dan turned toward it; this nose was unfamiliar but he recognized the uniform.

'I'm at TDF HQ,' Dan said. 'Is there anything else or can I go help my team?'

'I'd rather give you a quick checkup—' Amagi started.

'Later,' Dan said, pulling away from him. 'My team needs me.'

'Do you even know where they are?' Amagi asked.

'Yes, and I've got to get to them *now*.' Dan headed for the door.

'How're you gonna get there?' Amagi's voice was rather plaintive.

'I'll get a ride,' Dan said over his shoulder. 'On horseback, if I have to!'

'I guess we didn't hurt it as much as we thought,' Furuhashi said unhappily. He stood behind a cluster of trees with Soga and Kiriyama, watching as the dragon wound its long, slender body into coils on the ground.

Not just coiling but interlocking, Kiriyama realized. It was making itself into a structure—a stronghold for the furry blue alien?

'It looks like a flying saucer,' Soga said. 'A flying saucer with a dragon's head on top.' He paused to look at Furuhashi and Kiriyama nervously. 'That's what I see. You guys see it, too, right?'

'Yeah,' Furuhashi said, drawing his sidearm and flipping the safety off. 'And vice versa.'

Soga looked from him to the dragon head atop the gold coils. Its big angry eyes seemed to be fixed on them. 'You really think *it* can see *us*? From there?'

'It's a spacecraft,' Furuhashi said in a sour tone. 'It can probably see us from Jupiter.'

Abruptly, they heard someone yelling desperately in a strange language. Kiriyama spotted the blue alien from the cave running across the open area toward the dragon saucer, waving its arms wildly. In the daylight, its blue fur was far less vivid, closer to gunmetal gray.

'What do you think he's saying?' Soga said, peering through a tangle of leaves on his left.

'"Hey, wait, don't leave me here!" More or less,' Furuhashi said. 'Minus the profanity.'

'Alien profanity,' Soga mused. He braced his forearm against one lopsided tree and steadied his weapon, taking aim at the blue alien. 'Hey, buddy, didn't anybody ever tell you it's not polite to take people's lives and then leave without saying goodbye?' He fired.

The energy bolt hit the alien low on one leg. Instead of falling over and howling in pain, however, the alien burst into flames. Kiriyama felt his jaw drop.

'I swear I didn't know that would happen,' Soga said in a small voice.

'Nobody did,' Furuhashi assured him. They watched as the alien went on burning for over a minute, until the flames started to die down, leaving nothing except a charred husk already disintegrating in the wind.

Soga turned away from the sight. 'I swear, I didn't mean to—I didn't know—'

'Shake it off!' Kiriyama snapped at him. He pinched Soga's bicep for good measure and felt a small, secret joy when he flinched. 'Cry about it later!'

'I'm *not* crying,' Soga said, coming back into focus. Kiriyama could practically see his training assert itself, overriding the horror of what had just happened.

'Captain—look!' Furuhashi yelled.

Kiriyama turned to see that the dragon's coils were spinning now as it rose into the air, the angry dragon eyes seeming to glare directly at them. When it was thirty or so feet above the ground, a bolt of energy shot out from its underside; the stand of trees they'd been hiding behind exploded into fragments.

They turned and ran, and the dragon-saucer kept firing, nipping at their heels. Hot pellets of rock peppered the backs of their legs. Kiriyama heard Soga cry out in pain and saw that something was eating holes in the sleeves of his uniform; as he helped Soga tear the material away from his body, he could see ragged-looking welts in his flesh.

Twenty feet from the Hawk-1, the saucer caught up to them. Kiriyama started to motion for them to disperse in different directions when he heard a hard-edged electronic squeal that went through his head like a white-hot steel rod. He tried to keep running, but his legs buckled and he went down.

Kiriyama let himself roll with the momentum and came up on his knees, still holding his weapon. Taking a two-handed grip on it, he aimed at the bottom of the saucer, now directly overhead, when he caught a flash in his peripheral vision of something red and silver.

'He found us!' Furuhashi yelled joyfully. 'Here to save our butts *again*!'

Kiriyama keeled over but somehow managed to keep his weapon pointed at the saucer. 'Took him long enough,' he muttered. 'What kept you?' He started to laugh, then clamped down on it. If he started laughing now, he might never stop.

* * *

His first thought on returning to his normal state had been, *I'm Dan Moroboshi again!*

The comfort those four little words gave him was ineffable, which should have been surprising, and yet it wasn't in the least. The life he'd been inhabiting on this world had felt exactly right from the start. Now it felt even more so, and he was overjoyed to return to it.

He knew he'd been trapped in the two-dimensional space for only a few hours—not very long even by human measure—but it had seemed much longer. Being reduced to 2D had robbed him of his ability to simultaneously think and perceive. If Amagi hadn't figured out how to retrieve him, he wasn't sure how long it would have been before he was 2D permanently, which would have allowed a whole lot of furry blue aliens to appropriate all the humans lives they wanted.

Of course, they'd have gotten a nasty surprise when they found out how short those lives were. But then, the planet had over seven billion humans; the furry blue aliens could have eaten them like peanuts while they scouted out a more lasting supply.

His Ultra teachers had warned him when they'd assigned him the mapping task that he would learn things about various lifeforms in the galaxy that he'd never wanted to know, things he'd wish he could un-know.

What do I do about that? he'd asked.

You do what good there is to do, they'd told him.

His Ultra teachers, he concluded, had never been trapped in two dimensions. Intelligence, consciousness, and any hope for enlightenment were possible only in a minimum of three dimensions.

In the distance, he heard Furuhashi cheering at the top of his lungs, looked down and spotted him, Soga, and Kiriyama waving at him, and he was glad that none of them had had to suffer the ordeal of 2D. As he flew over them, he spared them a good thought, then focused on the gold dragon-headed saucer zooming up and away. Without the blue alien, there was only an artificial intelligence left and he had no qualms about probing its mentation.

The spacecraft was no longer accelerating upward. The AI had sensed his pursuit and it had decided to take him on, logging everything for the Alien Wild's benefit so they would know how to defeat any inconvenient Ultra that came to Earth's defense.

'*Jeez!*' Soga blurted, wincing as he pressed both hands to either side of his helmet. 'You guys don't hear that?'

'Hear what?' Furuhashi said, honestly puzzled.

'That horribly shrill machine noise,' Soga said, raising his voice as if he was trying to make himself heard over something louder. 'It's coming from that dragon and it's getting worse!'

Furuhashi shook his head. 'You must have ears like a bat. I don't hear anything.'

Kiriyama gave a sudden surprised laugh. 'It's because we're too old!'

'For what?' Furuhashi asked.

'To hear sounds above a certain frequency,' Kiriyama said. 'Happens right around age thirty.'

'But I'm only twenty-nine,' Furuhashi protested.

'It's not exact,' Kiriyama said.

'Like electrons,' Furuhashi said, which jerked another surprised laugh out of Kiriyama.

'Uh-oh,' Soga said, looking around with wide, frightened eyes.

'What now?' Furuhashi asked. 'More noises only you can hear?'

'No, it's gone,' Soga told him. 'It was rising in pitch and then, nothing. And I'm not twenty-nine.'

'Never mind.' Kiriyama was looking past them at Ultraseven. 'Someone else heard.'

* * *

The sound was like having a long, thick needle of fiery cold driven into the Color Gem in his forehead, then downward to the base of his skull. Pain radiated outward from it until it seemed like there was nothing in his head but agony.

All the while, the dragon-saucer flew crazy circles around him until he wasn't sure how many saucers there were—dozens? Hundreds? Thousands?

The noise receded a bit and he saw the dragon was unwinding itself in front of him, but when he tried to focus on it, the pain in his head surged. He was trying to will the pain into nonexistence when the dragon head suddenly lunged at him with open jaws.

Before it could sink its fangs into him, he batted it away, but it was coiling its body around him now and things were jabbing at him from every direction. The connectors, he realized, that had let it keep its saucer shape; they did double duty as weapons. Were the Alien Wild that clever? Or had they gotten the idea from another civilization they'd used up?

There was another burst of the awful machine scream-whine, very brief, barely a second, but when the pain loosened its grip and he could see again, he discovered the gold dragon was tightly coiled around him and had begun to squeeze. The pain in his head returned in a tidal wave; he felt himself go down on one knee, tried to push himself back up to his feet, and almost made it before he fell over on his side.

The dragon's intentions came to him with the relentless clarity of machine-thought; the spacecraft was programmed to send a raw log of everything that had occurred as soon as it had left Earth's atmosphere. Once the Alien Wild knew what had happened, they could decide on their next move, and they would have no inclination to be restrained or merciful to the people of Earth. They would descend on the planet and pick it clean at their leisure, till they ran out of humans. Then they would simply find another world to victimize.

It was as if a bright light in some secret place within himself suddenly went on, illuminating everything he was and wanted to be. The Color Lamp gave him the power to pull himself up off the ground. The dragon was trying to squeeze him harder when he simply burst out of the metal bonds, sending pieces of the dragon's body in all directions.

The AI tried to ask one last question—*Why?*—and then disintegrated. There would be no message to the Alien Wild.

In the distance, he could see Soga and Furuhashi jumping up and down and hugging each other while Kiriyama maintained a dignified but happy composure as he raised his wristcomm. That would be Amagi calling, to tell him that Dan Moroboshi was back among the living and on his way to them, possibly on horseback.

That was his cue to exit, skyward.

Kiriyama finished talking to Amagi and stood watching with Soga and Furuhashi as the unofficial seventh member of the Ultra Guard disappeared into the blue sky.

'Damnedest thing, though,' Soga said suddenly. The other two men turned to look at him. 'Once again, he showed up when we needed him most.'

'And you think that's strange?' Furuhashi asked.

'Hell, no. It's just—' Soga made a pained face, '—we're all safe now but Dan isn't.'

'Isn't he?' Kiriyama chuckled, pointing at a horse and rider in the distance, galloping toward them.

'Hey.' Furuhashi shaded his eyes with one hand. 'Is that—?'

Soga's face lit up. 'It is! Dan Moroboshi, you're such a *jerk*, I could *kill* you!' They ran forward to meet him.

Dan brought the horse to a stop with an easy expertise that raised Kiriyama's eyebrows. Apparently, he was an equestrian, too; Kiriyama made a mental note to ask him later if he had any more hidden talents or abilities. Right now, Soga was bawling him out for making them all worry.

'Does this mean I'm getting written up?' Dan asked when Soga finally paused for breath.

'Not by me,' Furuhashi said. 'Unless you drop dead again today. Then I'd have to report you.'

Kiriyama chuckled. 'I'm just glad you're all right.' His wristcomm chimed; it was Amagi again.

'Just wanted to let you and everyone else know, Captain, we've started restoring all the victims without any problems. Although I'm insisting they stay in the clinic for the next few days, just for observation.' Amagi's smile faded a bit. 'I'd've kept Dan here but he was gone before I could stop him. Said he was going to meet up with you, on horseback if necessary. Any sign of him?'

'See for yourself.' Kiriyama angled his arm toward Dan. 'He's a man of his word, right down to the horse.'

'I'm a *live* man, thanks to you, Amagi.' Dan leaned forward to talk into Kiriyama's wristcomm. 'It's no exaggeration to say I owe you my life. Thank you.'

Kiriyama turned the screen back to himself; Amagi looked as if he'd just been given a medal. 'I'll send him straight to sick bay when we get back,' he told Amagi. 'We can chain him and the horse to the wall if we have to.'

'Don't worry, captain, I'll behave.' Dan was smiling but his eyes were deeply serious. 'Going through that really made me appreciate being alive.'

Kiriyama blinked, momentarily lost for words. But that was Dan—he never seemed to have any hangups about expressing himself.

'Glad to hear it,' he said after a moment. 'After all, you only get one life—you can't just let some alien take it.'

Furuhashi and Soga burst into hearty laughter. Dan's smile widened, although his eyes were more serious than ever.

CHAPTER

FOUR

The twenty-four hours that followed saw everyone in high spirits. Kiriyama noted in his private command notes that it was as close to a full-on party atmosphere as he'd ever seen on base. But, he supposed, the presence of over two dozen civilians who were thrilled to be alive and grateful to the TDF and the Ultra Guard, and in particular to the man who had figured out how to save them, would have an effect on the general ambience.

'You'll probably never have to buy yourself a drink for as long as you live—at least in this part of the country,' Furuhashi said to Amagi after watching him run a gauntlet of people dying to show their appreciation. It was a more frequent occurrence since Kiriyama had given the civilians slightly wider access to areas of the base on Anne's recommendation.

'If you insist on confining them to sick bay, they'll spend all their time trying to get out,' Anne had told him. 'Let them use the gym and the jogging track—the runners will love the selectable environments. And give them access to Lounge Delta-4—it has the best vending machines as well as the largest number of game terminals. Those'll keep them so busy they might actually forget they can't leave for another couple of days. It'll be more like an impromptu summer camp for adults who don't know they're still kids.'

And as usual, Anne had been right. She hadn't been even slightly fazed at finding twenty-four-plus people under observation. She had reviewed all the medical records herself and personally examined half of them. Although the person who got most of her attention was Dan Moroboshi, which didn't surprise Kiriyama in the least.

'How do I feel?' Dan considered the question, then smiled. 'You may have noticed what a good mood everyone's in, even with a mob of civilians cluttering up the place. That tends to be contagious.'

Anne laughed a little. 'Yeah, the civilians were hard to miss. And you're right, good spirits are contagious.'

They were sitting in her tiny office off the main ward in sick bay. Even with the door closed, they could hear people laughing about something with a TDF officer.

'It was a good idea you had, about reserving that lounge for them while they're here,' Dan told her.

'All those people confined solely to sick bay for three days?' Anne shook her head. 'There'd have been no survivors. Which kinda defeats the whole purpose of saving their lives, don't you think?'

'True,' Dan said. 'And if there's one thing I always try to avoid, it's defeating the whole purpose of anything.'

Anne burst into hearty giggles, then put a hand over her mouth, blushing a little.

'If you're laughing at my jokes, I must be back to normal,' he said.

'Yes, but *you're* confined to the base, too,' she informed him, sitting up straighter in her chair. 'Which means you obey your doctor's orders and don't try to sneak out till I clear you.'

'I will, and I won't,' he promised.

'You better, and you better not,' she said, wagging her finger at him.

They laughed together, although she was serious; it was all there on the surface of her mind. Anne, he had discovered, was most open and unguarded in her role as a doctor—but only for him. To her patients, she was friendly and easy to talk to, always composed and reassuring, but ultimately circumspect, especially where her own feelings were concerned.

The fact that he could read her most easily when she was at her least forthcoming with other humans was fascinating to him. He'd have liked to examine that puzzle much more closely, but the course he had chosen to follow here didn't leave time for that kind of contemplation. No doubt that was down to the brevity of the human lifespan—when you had to squeeze as much living as possible into such a limited period, things got hectic.

Now he caught a tiny spark of anger from her; she was still upset at having been away during this particular crisis, although she was trying very hard not to be. Part of it was because of him, but mostly it stemmed from a secret fear that Kiriyama might decide they could get along without having a medical doctor in the Ultra Guard.

'That's scary,' he said, without thinking.

Anne's smile vanished. 'What is?'

'Dying,' he replied; it was the first thing he could think of. 'Even when you're, uh—' he caught a memory from her, so fleeting she hadn't noticed it. 'Even when you're not even merely dead, let alone most sincerely dead.'

Anne burst into laughter. 'I *loved* that movie when I was a kid. All my friends were afraid of the green-faced witch but the thing that scared me was the tornado.' She shuddered; the picture in her mind's eye was so intense, Dan almost shuddered with her. 'You know,

I looked it up, thinking it was just the States. But I found out that Japan actually averages twenty tornadoes a year. Plus, we have one extra thing they don't get in Kansas.' She leaned forward and lowered her voice. '*Waterspouts*. Tornadoes *on the ocean*.' She shuddered again.

'Did you ever see one?' he asked.

Anne shook her head. 'But for a while, you couldn't get me out on a boat even at gunpoint. My worst nightmare was being caught on the beach between a tornado and a waterspout.' She laughed at herself. 'Luckily, I got over it.'

'Good,' Dan said. 'Because I hate to think of you being afraid.' The words sounded more serious than he'd meant them to, but he was mildly surprised to find that wasn't why Anne shifted uncomfortably in her chair.

'I never told anyone else on the team that,' she said, her voice tentative.

'Your secret's safe with me,' he assured her.

'Thanks.' Her relieved smile faded quickly. 'You know, Dan, if there's anything you ever want to talk about, it would be safe with me, too.' Pause. 'Even if it's just how you feel since you were revived.'

'I guess I feel pretty much like everyone else who had their picture taken by an alien,' he said. There was another burst of laughter from the hallway. 'Jolly.'

It wasn't until all the civilians were discharged and the noise level was appreciably lower that the fatigue finally hit Dan.

The human body he had fashioned for himself wasn't nearly as strong as his own, but it was a good deal sturdier than the one he had modeled it on. Not that any of the improvements he'd made were obvious—his physical vessel had to pass for the standard adult male human. Some minor fiddling with his personal files had allowed him to avoid the more intrusive kinds of examinations—things like an MRI or a CT scan, which would have exposed certain physical anomalies of his human-like body.

But it had been his teeth, of all things, that had drawn attention to him: he had no fillings.

'I've never seen anybody who didn't have at least one or two fillings,' Anne had said. 'You must use floss by the kilometer. I keep a supply in my desk—if you ever run out after a big dinner, just help yourself. Maybe I should use you as an example for my next dental health lecture.'

'I don't think I'd enjoy being an example,' he told her.

Anne was nothing if not considerate. She agreed to use photos and keep his teeth anonymous.

Life at the base finally returned to normal, much to Kiriyama's relief. Good morale was one thing, but the TDF wasn't a theme park. High spirits over an extended period could interfere with discipline. It was also more energetic than was really necessary, which he thought was probably why Dan was so tired. Well, that and being brought back from two dimensions. He asked Anne to keep an eye on Dan for a bit longer.

A few days later, after a complicated emergency involving aliens disguised as humans and a rather formidable robot monster, Anne told Kiriyama that Dan Moroboshi was the same great guy he'd always been and she didn't think his fatigue was cause for concern.

'My honest opinion, Captain, is that he goes all-out every time,' she said over an informal, late-night pot of tea. 'And this time, he had to put up with Kurata before the guy finally went to Space Station 3.' She hesitated. 'You know, the way Kurata is still resentful that Dan got a spot in the Ultra Guard instead of him doesn't speak well of him.'

'Kurata's performance record is still close to perfect,' Kiriyama pointed out.

'I know. But if, in six months' time or a year, he comes back to HQ and he's still taking little passive-aggressive shots at Dan, I'm going to put a note in his file.'

'Really?' Kiriyama sat up straighter.

'I don't *want* to,' Anne said. 'But I don't think it's a good sign that he hasn't let this go.'

Kiriyama tilted his head to one side and shrugged. 'The people chosen for the TDF—and the Ultra Guard—are dedicated to excellence. They don't let things go easily.' He smiled. 'I know *you* don't.'

Anne gave a small, embarrassed laugh. 'Okay, yes, guilty as charged. I get protective about our people. It comes with the territory of being the doc.'

'I know,' Kiriyama said, his voice kind. 'And I don't expect you to change who you are because it might rub someone else the wrong way. Especially if you outrank them.'

She grinned broadly. 'All right, I get it,' she said, then sobered. 'I'd only put a note like that in someone's file under extreme circumstances. I'm not the regulator of human behavior.'

'I wasn't worried,' Kiriyama said, chuckling a little.

'Good,' Anne said brightly. 'And you don't have to worry about Dan. He's mostly over his fatigue and generally fit for duty.'

Kiriyama's wristcomm chimed then with a call from Amagi with the news that the *Sakura 9* spacecraft, which had vanished on its way to explore one of Saturn's moons two years ago, had just reappeared and was on its way back to Earth.

'Obviously, it's Six-Impossible-Things-Before-Breakfast Day,' Anne said after Kiriyama broke the connection. 'We can pick this up later, if you like.'

'Sure,' Kiriyama said, wondering if this was the real thing at last or just another false alarm. There had been two previous sightings of the *Sakura 9* that had turned out to be strangely shaped asteroids. Now he headed to Strategy, unaware that all hell was about to break loose.

'I'm not asking about traffic patterns,' the TDF communications officer was saying patiently. 'I'm asking if the Space Center has sent anyone out to the area where *Sakura 9* is expected to land.' The officer's name was Daguchi and he was the official liaison between the TDF and other government agencies, a job he'd gotten by virtue of his ability to talk to any other government employee without becoming rude, testy, or hysterical. At the moment, however, there was an edge in his voice.

Daguchi listened to the reply in his earpiece. 'All right, that was all I needed to know,' he said. 'No, don't send *anyone* out. *We'll* investigate and let you know what we find. As soon as *we* know, *you'll* know.' He broke the connection and swiveled around in his chair to Manabe, who stood behind him with Kiriyama.

'Are they still fussing about whether this is *Sakura 9* or not?' Manabe asked him.

'Fortunately, no,' Daguchi said. 'I convinced them the transmissions we received were encrypted in the form designed specifically for *Sakura 9* as a unique identifier.'

'I didn't realize they were giving you a hard time,' Kiriyama said, slightly perturbed.

'Oh, they weren't really,' Daguchi said with a brief smile. 'They've just got a lot of new hires over there right now and it took a while to get someone with a little experience on the line. The first guy I talked to wanted to send out a crew with a flatbed to pick it up and take it to their garage.'

'Seriously?' Kiriyama blinked at him, amazed. '*Why?*'

'No idea,' Daguchi said with a short laugh. 'Maybe to let their mechanic take a look at it first?'

'The Space Center was the public face of the Sakura Project for a long time before it got off the ground,' Manabe said. 'They called it Project Titan over there since that was Sakura's destination. Although for the last two years, everyone called it "lost."'

In Kiriyama's opinion, the Space Center needed a major organizational revamp, but it wasn't up to him. 'Send its trajectory and projected landing zone to Furuhashi and Soga on the Ultra Hawk 1. They might have the data already but send it anyway.'

'On it.' Daguchi's fingers danced rapidly over a keyboard on the console.

'I'd really like to know why *Sakura 9* suddenly showed up now,' Manabe said thoughtfully. 'And who or what brought it back.'

Kiriyama remembered belatedly that Manabe had been one of the prime movers behind the Sakura Project long before the spacecraft had been launched, when some committee members had been arguing to send the unmanned probe to Ganymede instead of Titan. The pro-Titan contingent had won because calculations showed Titan would be in a better position by the time the probe reached Saturn's orbit. And then the probe had disappeared just as it reached the asteroid belt.

Which was too bad for everyone. Even the pro-Ganymede faction hadn't been able to blame that one on choice of target.

'I can hardly believe it's back,' said Soga. 'It looks exactly the same as it did the day it was launched.'

'Yeah,' said Furuhashi, making sure *Sakura 9*'s descent was being recorded in infrared and UV as well as standard light. 'You'd think after being lost for two years, there'd be a few more marks or dents. But there isn't even a bumper sticker.'

Soga chuckled. 'You mean fin sticker.'

'"I was lost in outer space for two years and all I got was this lousy fin sticker.'" Furuhashi made a face. 'Doesn't exactly roll off the tongue.'

'No, but if you're ever lost in outer space, I know exactly what I'm getting you as a welcome-home present,' Soga told him.

'Wow, thanks. I think.' Furuhashi hit the comm button. 'Ultra Hawk 1 to Captain Kiriyama.'

'This is Kiriyama,' came the reply in the cockpit speaker. 'Go ahead, Furuhashi.'

'It's definitely *Sakura 9*,' Furuhashi told him. 'Currently making a controlled descent. Projected LZ will be in Jigokuyama.'

'I've had local authorities close off all roads into and out of the area,' Kiriyama said. 'You haven't spotted anyone on the ground, have you?'

'So far, no innocent bystanders. Or by-hikers,' said Furuhashi. 'But to be honest, captain, we haven't really been looking for anyone. We've been completely focused on *Sakura 9*.'

'Good.' Manabe's voice was somewhat farther from the microphone but perfectly clear. 'We don't know where that thing's really been or what it may have brought back.'

'Copy that, sir,' Furuhashi said. 'But just looking at it, I can't see anything different about it.'

'Ah, but the day is young,' Kiriyama said. 'Continue observing from a safe distance, let us know if anything changes.'

Kiriyama ended the call just as Dan Moroboshi arrived. 'First patrol of the day completed, Captain.' Dan nodded a greeting to Manabe, smiled at Anne and Amagi.

'Great,' Kiriyama said, 'you're just in time. I want you, Anne, and Amagi to go out and get a look at *Sakura 9* on the ground. Scan for the presence of anything unusual, untoward, or just odd.'

'You think we'll find anything?' Amagi asked him.

Kiriyama gave a single laugh. 'Frankly, I'll be surprised if you don't.'

'Hawk-1 to Pointer! Hawk-1 to Pointer!'

Dan flicked the switch on the dashboard for the in-car comm. 'Pointer-1 receiving, you've got Dan, Anne, and Amagi. Go ahead, Furuhashi.'

'Sakura's coordinates have shifted again. I'm sending you a new set for the LZ.'

'Copy that,' Dan said. 'Coordinates received. Anything else?'

'Nothing so far,' said Furuhashi. 'Still reading no extra presence, inside or out.'

'Thanks, Furuhashi,' Dan said. 'Be careful up there.'

'Will do, and you watch your six down there. Furuhashi out.'

'Is it a big change?' Dan asked Anne as she copied the new coordinates to their wristcomms.

'No, it's in the same vicinity.' She was studying a topographical map on her tablet. 'But the terrain makes it harder to get to. And of course, there's no decent parking. We'll have to hike a hundred or so yards.'

Amagi sat forward in the back seat. 'On the other hand, would we really want to park right next to it?'

'You're so literal, Amagi,' Anne laughed.

'I know,' he fake-sighed. 'It's a gift *and* a curse.'

'You know, that's going around,' Dan said.

'What's going around?' Amagi asked, puzzled now.

'Things that are both a gift and a curse,' Dan replied. 'In fact, that seems to be the human condition.'

'Sounds like someone majored in philosophy,' Amagi said knowingly.

'*So* literal,' Anne said, and they all laughed again.

* * *

Low-lying mist blew through the area as Dan, Amagi, and Anne strode briskly along a wide stone ridge toward the *Sakura 9* where it sat half-hidden amid some tall, jagged standing stones.

'That had to be a tricky landing,' Amagi said as they paused thirty yards from the spacecraft.

Dan nodded. 'Way too risky for an unmanned vehicle.'

'You think there's someone inside?' Amagi asked. 'Or maybe controlling it remotely?'

'No idea,' Dan said. 'But right now, I don't think we should get any closer. If there *is* some… entity, individual in there, I'm sure they know we're here. And if something's controlling it remotely, they won't be all that remote—they'll be nearby and we don't know where.'

Dan backed them up a few steps, although what he really wanted to do was get them as far from the spaceship as possible. What he could sense from *Sakura 9* was a garbled mix of organic and inorganic elements, along with something else that he couldn't make sense of because it seemed to be shielded or covered in a way that confounded his perceptions.

He was about to suggest they withdraw to the Pointer when twinkling lights suddenly appeared all over *Sakura 9*.

'Everybody get back!' Amagi yelled, pulling Dan and Anne behind an untidy heap of broken stones. Dan pushed them all down, automatically throwing himself over Anne and Amagi just as the spaceship blew apart in a deafening explosion that seemed to shake the air as well as the ground below them. Dirt and stone fragments rained down on them.

Dan gave it a slow count of five, then raised his head. There was nothing left of *Sakura 9* except a scatter of flaming wreckage.

'How did you know what was going to happen?' Dan asked Amagi as they stood up slowly.

Amagi stared at him blankly; Dan raised his voice and repeated the question.

'I didn't,' Amagi said in the too-loud voice of someone unable to hear. 'I just got a bad feeling. I thought it was going to fire on us.'

Anne patted his arm. 'Good instincts!' she said in the same too-loud voice.

'Any bad feelings now?' Dan asked, not quite shouting.

Amagi shook his head. 'But remind me never to complain about wearing a helmet. My ears are ringing as it is. If we hadn't had helmets on, we'd probably have ruptured eardrums.'

Dan smiled inwardly. Furuhashi had once said Amagi would probably be able to find the upside of a punch in the face; he hadn't really understood at the time, but now he did. He was trying to decide how long he should pretend to be deafened when his wristcomm buzzed and he realized he wasn't pretending as much as he'd thought.

'Kiriyama to Moroboshi.' The captain didn't bother trying to cover his apprehension. 'What's going on out there? We're getting readings of an explosion.'

'That would be *Sakura 9*, Captain.' Dan showed him the burning wreckage on his wristcomm screen.

'Do we need to send in a TDF disaster team?' Kiriyama asked when he turned the wristcomm back to himself.

'I wouldn't, Captain,' Dan said. 'It's all rock where it landed. The flames'll die down without spreading.'

'I'm putting a team on standby anyway,' Kiriyama said. 'Hit the alarm if the wind picks up.'

'Copy that, Captain. Moroboshi out.'

'I don't get it,' Anne said, her voice not quite as loud as before. 'I'd've thought if it was going to blow up, it would be on landing.'

'Maybe it self-destructed before we could board it?' Amagi blared.

'Would that indicate a passenger?' Anne asked. 'One that got off before it exploded, of course. Unless they accidentally blew themselves up before they could say hello or make threats, whatever.'

Dan frowned. 'Does anyone else hear that?'

Amagi winced. 'If it sounds like ringing, it's probably my ears.'

'It's the fire,' Anne said, catching hold of Dan's arm as he took a step toward the wreckage. 'A fire that big is *loud*.'

'No,' Dan said, shaking his head. 'It's more like metal screeching.'

Amagi tilted his head to one side. 'Nope. Just ringing.'

'I only hear fire,' Anne said.

'Wait here, you two,' Dan said. 'I want to check something out.'

He pulled away from Anne, drew his sidearm, and ran toward the now-dying fire, stopping at the edge of the blast radius to look around. Something was present, he could only just sense it. There seemed to be some screen or barrier between it and himself—and he was suddenly certain something was watching him.

Dan moved toward the nearby rock wall. Nothing there but inanimate stone, of course. Had he really seen anything—maybe an eye staring out of the solid rock? Frowning, he turned to look at the fire dying in the stone alcove.

After an explosion that powerful, there should have been fragments of spaceship all over the place and a crater where the rocks had been. So what the hell—

'Found anything?' Amagi asked, materializing on his left with Anne.

You were supposed to wait, Dan managed not to say. It would only cause Anne to point out, quite rightly, that he wasn't in command, and the discussion that followed wouldn't be as useful as what she was doing right now, viz, taking photos with her wristcomm.

'I don't see anything unusual,' she said, getting a few shots of the stone wall. Dan had to force himself not to pull her away; something about it gave him what Soga called 'the creeps.' 'Amagi, you're right about our helmets,' she went on, almost chattily. 'I can tell my hearing—'

'It's back!' Dan said excitedly. 'That screeching—I hear it again. But I can't tell where it's coming from. It's like it's all around, from all directions.'

Amagi was about to answer when a sudden fit of coughing bent him double.

Dan moved to his side. 'What's wrong?' he asked but Amagi couldn't stop coughing to answer.

'Toxic fumes and gases,' Anne said helpfully. 'I should've realized. Amagi's always been more sensitive to air quality than the rest of us, but now I can feel my chest starting to get tight. I recommend we find better air to breathe *stat*. Damn, it's been a long day already and it's only going to get longer.'

They turned away from the detritus that had been *Sakura 9* and headed back to the Pointer.

Some distance away, on the other side of the wreckage, an eight-year-old boy named Hiroshi would have agreed with Anne's assessment. He had also had a long day already and experience told him it would probably last forever.

The day had started out okay. He'd been in the playground area for his section of the apartment complex with some other kids—nice kids, not the jerks. They'd all been having fun, and they might have continued having fun all day long, but then Ken and his pals had shown up. It was like they had an alarm or something that alerted them whenever kids were having a good time so they could run in and spoil everything.

They were all bigger kids who liked to push littler kids around, but lately, to Hiroshi's dismay, Ken had focused on him and he didn't know why. Not that bullies needed a reason—all they needed was a likely victim, and he was Ken's, at least until Ken got bored and found someone weaker, geekier, and easier to scare. Although Ken had been pushing him around so much, Hiroshi thought he had the dubious privilege of being the weakest, geekiest, and fraidiest of all the fraidy-cats in the complex. It would be just his luck.

As usual, Ken and his gang had wasted no time breaking things up. Hiroshi had run for the hills—more specifically, Jigokuyama. He wasn't supposed to go there alone because of the danger of falling rocks. And nobody, kids or grownups, was supposed to go there today—Hiroshi had met two cops blocking the main road into the area with a police car. They'd told him to go home because there was some kind of crash or chemical spill or something.

On any other day, Hiroshi would have turned around, taken the long way home to avoid Ken, and spent the rest of the day playing in his room till dinnertime. Today, however, he'd had enough of people telling him what he couldn't do and where he couldn't go to not do it. The road wasn't the only way to Jigokuyama.

The wooded hillside on the other side of the apartment complex's access road went right into it. It was awfully steep, and if he'd met more cops while he'd been climbing, he might have given up. But there hadn't been any, and he'd made it all the way up the hill just in time to see the spaceship land.

More than anything, he wanted to get a closer look, but something told him to keep his distance. Not in so many words—the thought had just popped into his head. This happened sometimes, albeit not very often. But when it did, Hiroshi paid attention because he knew if he didn't, Something Bad would happen.

At the top of the hill, he paused to look around and discovered he was well west of where he'd meant to be. But he could see the spaceship just fine. He was seeing it and Ken wasn't. Now he could tell all his friends—the kids who were nice when Ken wasn't around—how it looked sitting in the place with those tall stones. That was *great*. And if something came out of it, that would be the *greatest*.

As he sat down to rest, he heard a tiny, distant voice yell, '*Get back!*' The next thing he knew, an invisible giant hand gave him a hard shove and sent him tumbling head over heels back down the hill until he fetched up against the base of a tree.

For a few seconds, he lay there panting while he tried to figure out what had just happened. He hadn't fallen very far; only a few yards, really. But who—or what—had pushed him? Even if there were invisible people, he doubted any of them were bullies. Ken would have happily shoved and kicked him all the way down the hill, but not without an audience to show off for.

Hiroshi climbed back up to where he'd been sitting. He felt strange, but everything felt strange, even the dirt and grass. The first thing he saw when he got to the top was the burning wreckage but there was something strange about that, too. The whole world had gone strange—

Finally, he realized what it was: he could hardly hear anything. It was like wads and wads of cotton had been stuffed into his ears.

'I can't go home like this,' he said aloud, just to find out if he could even hear himself. He could but his voice seemed to be coming through layers of thick woolen blankets. If that far-away voice yelled another warning, he'd never hear it.

Not that the voice had been yelling at him. Or had it? Suddenly he wasn't sure of anything except that *Sakura 9* had blown up.

If it even *had* been *Sakura 9*.

Hiroshi remembered his teacher telling the class that in real life, explosions weren't anything like that you saw in movies or on TV. People who were too close to an explosion could be hurt even if they weren't hit by fragments of burning metal or stuff. They also couldn't hear after a big explosion, which reminded him that he couldn't go home like this. He'd never be able to explain it to his mother. Even if he told her the truth, she probably wouldn't believe him.

Well, not at first, maybe, but the explosion would make the news. Then he'd *really* be in for it—would he ever! His mother would be so angry that he'd disobeyed her and gone to Jigokuyama, especially because he'd been so close to an explosion that he wouldn't be able to hear her yelling at him.

He tried to think, remembered his teacher had also said hearing loss was usually temporary. Okay, that was good... only, what if he were *un*usual and he'd lost his hearing for good?

No one would feel bad for him because he'd brought it on himself by disobeying his mother. People would whisper, *Serves him right*, behind his back, even though he couldn't have heard them anyway. Except for Ken—he'd yell it at the top of his lungs and laugh in Hiroshi's face.

His life was getting worse by the second, Hiroshi thought as his throat tightened. Any second now, his eyes would start filling up—

No, he ordered himself. *You will* not *cry. You're* not *a crybaby.*

Hiroshi took a deep breath that trembled on the way in but wasn't as shaky coming out. No tears spilled out of his eyes, either. He inhaled again, slowly and deeply; this time his breath wasn't as shaky going in and was perfectly steady coming out. The next breath was steady both ways and so was the one after that. Tears weren't threatening anymore, which was like some kind of miracle.

His Uncle Junpei had taught him the breathing trick, saying it had always worked for him. Hiroshi was glad to know it was a real thing and not just another lie grownups told kids, like, *If someone's teasing you, ignore them—they'll give up and go away.* Talk about a big lie—that had to be the biggest one ever. The only problem with the breathing trick was, bullies never gave you a chance to breathe, they just kept at you till you broke.

Then you were really in for it. Any kid who cried outside of their own room was doomed to a beatdown. And bullies were like sharks—they could smell tears a mile away. Good thing Ken was nowhere near him, but Ken wasn't the only bully in the world. The last thing Hiroshi needed was another bully in his life.

Well, no problem there—since he couldn't go home, he'd have *no* bullies in his life. But there wouldn't be any of the good things, either, and he was really going to miss those.

Hiroshi was about to sit down on the same spot when a sudden superstitious impulse made him shift a few feet to his left. How simple his life had been once, he thought sadly. Back when he'd gotten up this morning—a lifetime ago—he'd gone out to play, and that had been fun until Ken had come along and run him off the play area. Maybe coming to Jigokuyama hadn't been his best idea ever but Ken had wanted to make him run home crying. So in that way, coming to Jigokuyama had been kind of like fighting back, striking a blow against Ken. Well, in secret, but still. Except now that he couldn't go home, he supposed it didn't matter anymore.

Hiroshi sat glumly poking at a round pebble with a twig. After some unmeasured time, he realized he'd been listening to the distant crackle of flames, which faded in and out depending on the wind direction. He could also hear the whispery rustle of leaves in the trees. His hearing was coming back after all.

Limp with relief, Hiroshi let himself fall back on the grass and lay spread-eagle, smiling up at the sky. Now nobody would ever have to know what had happened—not his mother, or the cops, and certainly not Ken.

'I got away with it,' he said aloud, then laughed because his voice sounded almost normal again. He sat up, thinking that he might as well get away with a souvenir. It would remind him of how he'd thought he'd have to live wild on Jigokuyama for the rest of his life, with berries for food and leaves instead of toilet paper.

And seeing as how nobody was ever going to know, he might as well look for something really special—like, say, for instance, a piece of *Sakura 9*. Maybe he could find a piece small enough to fit in his pocket. Nobody would ever suspect, but then nobody would even believe he'd been there to see *Sakura 9* blow.

Besides, he needed a little more time for his hearing to come back all the way.

As soon as Hiroshi pushed himself to his feet, he spotted it. It was half-hidden in a patch of grass twenty or so feet away. At first, he wasn't sure it could have been from *Sakura 9*, since that was awfully far away from the explosion. But then he noticed brown scorch marks on the grass.

Hiroshi went over to it and crouched, holding one hand over it to see if it was still hot. It was kind of warm but cooling off fast. By the time he'd worked up enough nerve to actually touch it, it was only a little bit warm, no warmer than his own skin.

He smiled.

Ken was bossing everyone around in the play area when Hiroshi finally came down the hill with the treasure he'd found. It definitely wasn't pocket-sized, but when he'd found it lying on the ground, something had told him he had to have it, even though it wasn't part of the spaceship.

Or was it? In truth, he didn't know. The thing he'd picked up was about the size of his mother's mantel clock but it wasn't as heavy as most rocks that big. The color was strange, too—most of the rocks around Jigokuyama were dark, but this was a sort of sandy-pinkish color with shiny flecks. But Hiroshi thought the weirdest thing about it was the shape.

To him, it looked like something that might have been alive once. It had lines and contours that made him think of pictures of fossils he'd seen in the natural history museum. But why would a fossil be on *Sakura 9*?

Hiroshi stopped for a moment to examine his find again. Maybe a creature had gotten aboard the spaceship and this was all that was left of it after it had blown up? No, that couldn't be right, either. If a creature had blown up on *Sakura 9*, it sure wouldn't look like a fossil.

After spending most of the day at Jigokuyama, he was too tired to take the long way around to the back entrance of his apartment building, which was the only way to avoid the playground. If he kept to the very edge, he thought, maybe he could just slip by without anyone knowing—

'Hey, everybody!' hollered a familiar spiteful voice. 'It's Hiroshi!'

So much for that plan, he thought unhappily. Maybe if he kept walking very fast and made like he hadn't heard Ken…

Then he was surrounded by kids and Ken was looming over him.

'Ooh, that's a really pretty rock!' said Mari, who lived in the apartment one floor up from Hiroshi.

'*Pretty?!*' Ken hooted in that nasty-happy way he did before punching someone in the head. 'Is *that* why you're carrying it around—because it's *so pretty*?'

'Where'd you get it?' asked Chiba, one of Ken's assistant bullies, but in a very un-bully-like way.

'Found it hanging out at Jigokuyama,' Hiroshi said, doing his best to sound super-casual, like it was no big deal.

'That's way cool,' Ken said, talking over everyone else. 'But you're way too geeky to have cool stuff. You better give it to me.' He took hold of it with one chubby hand.

'*No!*' Hiroshi pulled away from him. 'You want a cool rock, go find your own.'

Later, Hiroshi remembered the hush that fell over the group as being almost as loud as *Sakura 9* exploding. Ken was gaping at him open-mouthed, obviously astounded that one of his regular victims would dare to defy him. All the other kids were gawking, too, unable to believe that Hiroshi had, in effect, just asked Ken to kill him.

But oh, wow, it had felt *so good* to stand up for himself. Hiroshi hoped he could remember how good it felt after Ken killed him.

Ken finally remembered where he was and pulled himself together. 'Do you *really* want to cry, Hiroshi?' he said. 'Because you're gonna cry your eyes out and give me that rock *right now!*' He took hold of the rock again. 'C'mon, just gimme it, and after I punch you out, we'll all play with you for the rest of the day.'

Not much of an offer—the afternoon was slipping away quickly and it wouldn't be long before everyone's parents started calling them in. Ken was really hoping he'd just let go and run.

'*No*,' Hiroshi said again. 'I *won't*.' He tried to shove through the kids around him.

Ken got a better grip on his rock and tried to work it out of Hiroshi's arms. Hiroshi tightened his own hold on it.

'You give me that! *Gimme!*' Ken demanded, and he wasn't just bully-angry now, he was angry for real. That was bad, but Hiroshi decided he had come too far to give up now.

'I said no!' he shouted into Ken's face.

'*Gimme!*' Ken bellowed and wedged his hand between the rock and Hiroshi's chest. In another few seconds, Ken would have it, Hiroshi thought, close to panic. Then he'd show Hiroshi what happened when he didn't do as Ken told him. Ken would take the rock home, and then tomorrow, or the next day, he'd use his father's hammer on it and Hiroshi would find pieces of it scattered all over the complex.

The next thing he knew, Ken and all the other kids were rolling around on the grass, holding their heads and crying out in pain.

Hiroshi looked around at them, blinking in confusion. What had done this? Nothing had ever come to his rescue before. Was this some mysterious justice? He wanted so much for that to be true, but even as he thought that, he knew better. Things just didn't work that way, and besides, anything that hurt kids, even bullies, was a Bad Thing for real. He should run and get an adult, because adults would know what to do.

Except then they'd want to know why *he* wasn't hurt, too, and he couldn't explain that. And when the hurting stopped, Ken would say *he'd* done it because he didn't want to show anyone his pretty rock from Jigokuyama. The grownups would believe Ken because that's how it always went in these situations and OMG, what if he ended up *getting arrested*?

What if they sent him to *juvie*? Juvie was full of kids like Ken, only bigger and meaner, with baseball bats and knives—

Hiroshi ran.

Dan pulled up as close as he could to the kids rolling around on the grass and crying out in pain. He'd intended to go straight back to HQ, but as soon as they'd neared the apartment complex, he'd heard the screeching again and changed course.

And then, of course, the moment he parked the Pointer, the screeching stopped. It just figured, Dan thought as he and his teammates got out of the Pointer. There was no possible way any debris from *Sakura 9* could have been blown this far. Nonetheless, he'd heard that screeching and it had led him to a bunch of kids in obvious physical distress, so clearly he was right where he was supposed to be.

None of them could see any injuries on the kids, but even without his Ultra senses, he'd have known their pain was real. Amagi called emergency services, and while they waited for the ambulances, they tried to talk to the kids. Dan was kneeling beside the biggest kid, a huge lump of a boy named Ken, yelling for someone named Hiroshi to make it stop when the screeching came back.

Now Dan got to his feet and looked around in the twilight, at the swings, the slide, the sandbox, the slender trees.

'Something?' Anne asked him.

'I hear the screeching again. It—' He cut off. Something was watching him. He put one hand on his weapon and turned in a slow circle until he saw the eye on the tree.

An *eye*? On a *tree*?

Dan felt a dropping sensation in his middle. It looked like a human eye but it was impossibly big, gigantic, the size of his head, and he could feel it *observing* him, waiting to see what he'd do next. The sight seemed to burn itself into his mind, like it was marking him.

A second later, the eye closed.

He drew his weapon and took aim at the place on the tree where it had been.

'Dan!' Anne shouted, her voice high and urgent.

He turned to look at her, realizing belatedly that the screeching had stopped again. She glared at his weapon, then looked significantly at the children still crying on the ground.

He holstered his sidearm and went to the tree, running his hands over the bark. Nothing there but plain old bark—no secret panels that might be hiding an eye, no eye-shaped gnarls, just nothing, nothing, and nothing.

Anne got up and went to him. 'What did you see?' she whispered.

'No idea,' he said. 'But I heard the screeching while it was here. Now it's gone and so is the screeching.'

There were sirens in the distance as he called Kiriyama to give him an update.

Twilight had morphed into night by the time Anne came out of the hospital's emergency entrance and got into the Pointer, where Dan and Amagi were waiting for her.

'*Really* glad I rode with the girls,' she told them. 'I learned so much about life in the Comfort Palais apartment complex. More than I actually wanted to know, but I'll give you the highlights.'

She twisted around to address Dan as well as Amagi in the back seat. 'The biggest kid's name is Ken and I guess he's the apex predator for that part of the complex. All the kids are afraid of him and his bully boys. Who *are* all boys, by the way, because Ken says, "girls are yucky." Unquote.'

'Are they all okay?' Amagi asked.

Anne nodded. 'The kids all say the pain was lessening just before the ambulances arrived. They said it started when a boy named Hiroshi came along and showed them a "really cool rock." Also unquote.'

'What'd he do, hit them with it?' Amagi said.

'No, not at all,' Anne replied. 'Hiroshi claimed he found it on Jigokuyama earlier today. I don't know if I believe that since the local police had every route into or out of Jigokuyama blocked off.

'Anyway, all the kids told me pretty much the same story. Ken wanted to get a closer look at the rock and Hiroshi wouldn't let him. When Ken tried to take it, they all suddenly got a terrible sharp pain in their heads—all of them except Hiroshi. He ran home with his treasure and hasn't been seen since.'

'Did they happen to mention his apartment number?' Dan asked, starting the Pointer.

'They did,' Anne said. 'And better yet, there's decent parking.'

The soft polishing cloth his mother had given him didn't seem to make the rock any shinier, but it didn't hurt anything and it felt really nice. Besides, it was late now. Maybe he'd see the difference tomorrow in the daylight. Then he could decide where he wanted to keep it—on his desk or the bureau? Or maybe his mother would think it was pretty enough to go on a shelf in the living room.

Hiroshi thought that one over for a minute. No, he decided, he was going to keep it in his room because, after all, it was *his*. Even the biggest bully in Comfort Palais hadn't been able to take it from him.

His desk lamp went out suddenly and he jumped, startled.

'I'm *not* afraid of the dark,' he whispered. 'I'm too big to be afraid of the dark. Only babies are afraid of the dark and I'm *not* a baby.'

Hiroshi shifted in his chair. His mother had said courage would replace fear, only she hadn't told him how long that would take. So far, he didn't feel any different. But then, just because he was too big to be afraid of the dark didn't mean he had to *like* it. That was how he felt, he decided—he *disliked* the dark. Lots of people who weren't babies probably felt the same way.

He tried turning the lamp off, then on again, twice. When that didn't work, he decided it was time to call in an expert, and went to get his mother.

Or he tried to, except his door wouldn't open. He pulled at the knob, yanked and twisted it, but it was like the door was glued shut. 'Mama?' he called. 'My door's stuck and my light went out.'

No answer. Maybe she had her earbuds in?

'Give it up, kid,' said a deep male voice. 'There's nothing you can do.'

Hiroshi backed up against the door, looking around, his heart pounding. 'Who said that?' he demanded. 'Who's there? What do you want?'

'My body, of course,' the Voice replied. 'I'm here to take my body back.'

'I don't know what you're talking about,' Hiroshi said, trying to sound tough rather than terrified.

The darkness in his room seemed to deepen and something... *happened*; Hiroshi felt it as distinctly as a change in temperature or humidity, although it wasn't either of those things.

I'm not alone, he thought, and he had never been more certain of anything. He looked over at his bed in the far corner of the room; the ceiling above it was slanted, so it was kind of like a little shelter. But it was also the darkest part of the room, the one place that got no direct light from outside, not even in the daytime. Staring into the shadows, he reminded himself that his mother had said there was nothing in the dark that wasn't there when the lights were on.

And then an enormous Eye opened. And *looked* at him.

Hiroshi's inner temperature plummeted to absolute zero.

His mother hadn't lied on purpose, she just hadn't known. It wasn't the first time she'd been wrong, but it was definitely the worst. Next to that, Ken the bully was like a mosquito.

After a bit, Hiroshi felt his heartbeat start to slow from jackhammer to more like human. He tried the breathing trick again but he felt a little silly. No matter how he breathed, there would still be a giant Eye twice the size of his mother's new flatscreen TV in the shadows over his bed.

'My body is right there, on your desk,' the Voice said, as if he'd asked. 'You've been polishing it.'

Hiroshi was so flabbergasted, he forgot he was afraid. 'No it isn't. That's just a rock I found lying around on the ground. A *rock*.'

'No, that's my body,' the Voice said in a reasonable tone. 'I temporarily lost track of it when the spaceship blew up.'

Hiroshi sidled over to his desk and put a possessive hand on his treasure. 'How can a *rock* be your body? Bodies have—' He frowned, trying to find the right words. 'Bodies have body stuff that makes them alive. A rock doesn't. A rock never *was* alive and never will be.'

The Eye went on looking at him, never blinking, not even once. Hiroshi thought that was as weird as it claiming a rock was its body.

'Suppose we make a deal,' said the Voice, sounding more kindly now.

Alarm bells went off in Hiroshi's mind. Whenever a grownup said this, it meant you had something they were desperate to get their hands on. They'd make it sound like if you gave it to them, you'd get something really great in return, something you'd always wanted. But the way it usually worked out was, they got what they wanted and you got to watch them walk away with it.

Which meant this big old Eye, as scary as it looked, was really just another grownup that wanted something. Understanding this made Hiroshi feel much less afraid.

'All the kids here pick on you, don't they?' the Voice said. 'I saw it earlier, when they tried to take my body away from you. But I could make you stronger than all of them—so strong that no one would ever dare pick on you again.' Pause; Hiroshi waited. 'I just need you to do one little favor for me.'

There it was, Hiroshi thought. 'What's the favor?'

'Go back to that place—what's it called, Jigokuyama? Yes, go there, right now, without telling anyone or letting anyone see you, and drop the stone into the smoke.'

Hiroshi replayed the words in his head and was still confused. 'The "smoke?" *What* smoke?'

'You'll see it when you get there,' the Voice assured him. 'Go, and you'll see the place I mean.'

'I'm not going to some place full of smoke,' Hiroshi said stoutly. 'People can *die* from breathing smoke, they taught us that at school.'

'It's not that kind of smoke,' the Voice replied. 'You'll see. Do this favor for me and no one will ever bully you or pick on you again. Can you leave this place without anyone knowing?'

'I s'pose...' Hiroshi thought it over. 'But is it true? You can really fix things so Ken never picks on me ever again?'

'Yes, I can,' the Voice said, and Hiroshi could hear a very slight edge of impatience in its tone now. 'So, what do you say— do we have a deal?'

Hiroshi hesitated. His instincts were screaming at him to say no; at the same time, he knew deep in his bones that if he did, he'd miss his one and only chance to become the strongest boy in the whole complex.

'Yes, we have a deal,' he said finally. He'd have felt a little better if they could have shaken hands on it, except judging by the size of the Eye, its hand would have been bigger than the whole apartment. 'Can you fix the door so I can get out?'

'It is done,' the Voice told him. 'Now, if you *really* want to be the strongest boy, you will hurry!'

Dan knew Hiroshi's mother Shiori was a single working parent the moment he saw her. In the relatively short time he'd been on Earth, he had come to recognize certain characteristics. Single working parents all presented as self-possessed, competent, and tired, although that last was usually well-hidden, perceptible only to his Ultra senses.

As soon as he knocked on Hiroshi's apartment door, he picked up on the fading traces of a strange energy. Shiori was clearly oblivious to it as she welcomed him in, though he could see she was taken aback to hear the Ultra Guard asking about her son. She listened calmly to his account of finding the children in the play area, how they'd been taken to the hospital, and what Anne had learned.

'I saw the rock,' she told Dan. 'Quite unusual looking. Hiroshi said he wanted to clean it, so I gave him an old chamois. He's still in his room, trying to polish it.'

'Was there anything about it in particular that stood out to you?' Dan asked.

'Well…' She grimaced. 'He didn't say where he'd picked it up, so I figured he must have been somewhere he wasn't supposed to be. You say he told the other kids he went to Jigokuyama?'

Dan nodded, following her down a hallway to a closed door with a sign that said, *Hiroshi! Private!* Whatever the strange energy was, it had been there, but his Ultra senses detected only residue now.

'I told him to stay away from that place,' Hiroshi's mother said. Anxiety was starting to break through her poise. 'It's too far away from Comfort Palais and it's not safe.' She knocked on the door. When there was no answer, she tried the knob; it wasn't locked.

'Hiroshi?' she asked, poking her head in. 'Good heavens, why are you sitting in the dark?' She felt along the wall, found the light switch.

The overhead light went on to show them an empty room except for the residue Dan had sensed, which most definitely wasn't that of an eight-year-old boy. Hiroshi had left alive and well, not forced, but without full understanding.

'Was there anything odd about Hiroshi's behavior?' Dan asked as the woman stood in the center of the room looking around helplessly. 'Did he do or say anything that was—well, not *bad*, but not like him?'

'The rock.' Her gaze fell on the desk where it had been. 'He's never showed any interest in rocks. Superheroes, outer space, aliens, kaiju—he can't get enough of them. The rock surprised me. I planned to get him to talk to me about it over dinner. I don't know much about rocks or geology, but I looked a few things up.' She gave a short, humorless laugh. 'If it matters, I can tell you that rock wasn't igneous. I think it was sedimentary. Rather pretty but you'll have to take my word for it, since he took the thing with him.'

'It is possible Hiroshi ran away?' Dan asked, as gently as he could.

She shook her head. 'He knows he's not supposed to be out by himself after dark. That's a strict rule and he'd never break it unless he really believed he had to. But don't ask me why he'd think such a thing,' she added with a shrug. 'Considering he took the rock with him, I'm pretty sure he's heading back to Jigokuyama.'

'You're probably right,' Dan said, knowing she was. 'We'll look for him there first. I know you want to come with us, but we'd like you to remain here—'

'In case he calls or comes back on his own,' the woman finished for him, her voice weary and sad. 'I want to run through the streets calling his name till he answers but I know you're right. Just please—find my son quickly, because I'm not sure how long I can make myself wait here.'

'I'm going to call a couple of police officers to stay with you,' Dan told her. 'They'll keep you updated so you won't be sitting alone wondering what's going on.' He used her phone to do just that and waited with her until two women officers arrived.

'There are a couple of things you should know about Hiroshi,' Shiori said as she saw Dan to the door. 'One is, I've been trying to help him overcome his fear of the dark.' She smiled fleetingly. 'I was afraid of the dark, too, at his age, and I know what it's like. He's been doing pretty well, but as soon as I opened his door and saw the light was off, I knew something was wrong. He's not as afraid of the dark as he used to be, but he'd never just sit in a room with the lights off.'

Dan nodded. 'Anything else?'

'The children who were hurt,' she began, then hesitated. 'Did they say Hiroshi did something to them?'

'No,' Dan replied and perceived her secret relief. 'Just that an awful noise made their heads hurt.'

'Was there a big boy named Ken with them?' she asked and nodded knowingly when Dan told her there was. 'That's the other thing we're working on—the bully problem. Ken's the local tough guy. He picks on all the kids, and I guess he's been rough on Hiroshi lately. But if Ken was hurt, too, it wouldn't be anything Hiroshi did. I know Hiroshi would never do anything to hurt any of the kids here, not even Ken. Bullied kids can turn around and become bullies themselves, but Hiroshi wouldn't. It's not in his nature, or his character.'

'I believe you,' Dan said truthfully. 'We don't know what hurt the kids, only that Hiroshi was with them at the time. We just want to find him and make sure nothing bad happens to him.'

Hiroshi's mother didn't have tears in her eyes but Dan could sense how close she was to breaking down. 'Just bring him home,' she said, by way of farewell.

Even with the police officers supporting her, Dan knew it was going to be a long night. This parenting thing, he thought as he went back to the Pointer; it sure wasn't for the faint of heart.

He wasn't ever going to like the dark, Hiroshi thought as he rode his bike along the road to Jigokuyama with the rock in the basket, but he was feeling a lot less uncomfortable about the nighttime. In fact, he'd always been secretly fascinated by the night—things happened then that never could in the daytime. Fireworks, for one thing; you couldn't see those in the daylight. And the way the city looked all lit up—like it was a magic land filled with unimaginable wonders.

Best of all, though, was right now. Here he was, riding his bike, and nobody was bothering him. Ken wasn't chasing him or sending an assistant bully after him. He hadn't seen anyone at all, not even a single car, even though it wasn't really that late. The cops must still have the road closed, although he didn't see any of them, either. Well, except for the one at the traffic checkpoint.

At least there had only been one, sitting at the desk in the little checkpoint house or whatever it was, scrolling through something on his tablet and looking bored out of his mind. Hiroshi had considered walking his bike around behind the checkpoint, except it had looked awfully dark and he didn't know what was back there. Probably just tall grass and bushes, but if he got stuck in a thorn bush, the cop would hear him struggling and grab him. Then he'd never get to Jigokuyama, the Eye would never get its body back, and bullies like Ken would pick on him for the rest of his very unhappy life.

Hiroshi decided to zip past without looking left or right, but when he got closer, he saw the police had put up a barrier. It was just a bunch of cones and barrels, but he'd have to walk his bike past them after all. He'd just have to walk fast.

Except he knocked over one of the stupid cones. *Should've known*, he thought as the cop looked up from the tablet and saw him.

Hiroshi jumped on his bike and rode away as quickly as his little legs could pump the pedals, pretending he couldn't hear the cop calling after him to stop.

'It was the weirdest thing,' Officer Goto said to Dan a few minutes after the boy rode through on his bike. 'I looked up and there he was, under the streetlight, with his bike and some kind of big rock in the basket. When I called out to him, he took off up the road.'

Dan grimaced. 'How quickly can you put together a search party?' he asked the cop.

'On it,' the officer said, already dialing the phone.

'He came this way on his bike,' Dan told Anne and Amagi as he slipped back into the driver's seat in the Pointer. 'And he's definitely on his way to Jigokuyama. If we hurry, we might catch up with him.'

'Unless he doesn't stay on the road,' said Amagi, looking troubled.

'Why wouldn't he?' Anne asked him.

'He doesn't have to,' Amagi replied. 'He's not riding a ten-speed racer, he can go off-road.'

'With a big rock in his basket?' Anne said with a half-smile. 'Which means it's not a dirt bike, those don't have baskets. Even if it were a BMX, he's *eight*—he doesn't have the muscles to ride dirt all the way to Jigokuyama. I doubt it would even occur to him. Eight-year-olds aren't strong on strategy. Present company excepted,' she added, patting Amagi's arm. 'I'm sure you were a prodigy.'

She turned to Dan. 'And just for the record, I guarantee you he's going to Jigokuyama—the one place he was told to stay away from.'

'Astute as always,' Dan said. 'But I don't think that's the only reason. I think he was there when *Sakura 9* blew up. And I think this rock of his has some kind of direct connection to it.'

'How so?' Anne asked, her expression turning serious.

'I think that so-called rock of Hiroshi's is actually part of whatever *Sakura 9* brought back with it. Whatever it is could be drawing him back.

'Why?' Amagi said, frowning. 'To do what?'

'No idea,' Dan said, keeping his eyes on the dark road ahead. 'But I think we'd better get there before the kid returns the rock to whomever or whatever's calling to him.'

By now, his mother would have reported him missing, which meant he had to get off the road before he was spotted. Too bad, but the land here was just too tough for his bike; he'd have to walk to Little Gap Bridge. He found a good hiding place amid some thick brush in a gully only a few yards off the road. From there, he had to climb Bridge Hill, which wasn't as steep as the wooded incline he'd climbed earlier. Like the kids said on some US TV show Ken thought was so great, *Easy-peasy, lemon-squeezy!*

Then he could go home, and with any luck his mother would never know where he'd been. He could tell her he'd run to a shop to get some more new pencils for school—

Or not. He stopped short at the sight of handheld torch-beams sweeping through the darkness like searchlights. Because that's what they were—searchlights, carried by people searching for him. Only they couldn't be, could they? Already?

'Hiroshi! Where are you?' called a voice in the distance.

'Your mother's worried sick, Hiroshi-kun!'

Hiroshi closed his eyes, let out a long breath, opened them again. Nope, not a bad dream, there really was a search party looking for him. How had his mother gotten them together so quickly?

'Why did you stop?' the Voice wanted to know. It seemed so loud, he thought for sure the search party must have heard it, but they just kept waving their flashlights around and calling for him.

'How am I supposed to get past *them*?' Hiroshi said, feeling his leg muscles starting to knot up along with his shoulders. 'They're all looking for me and when they see me—'

'Don't worry about them,' the Voice told him. 'I won't let them stop you. Now, go—and hurry! I need the smoke to restore my body.'

'Okay,' Hiroshi said uncertainly. Maybe he could find a way around them. There seemed to be nobody to the left of where he was, and they were all making so much noise, they'd never hear him sneak past.

To his dismay, however, he found it wasn't very easy to sneak through grass taller than he was. He struggled through the rough stalks, clutching the rock to his chest and trying to will himself to be invisible.

Suddenly there was a blinking light in his eyes and someone was yelling, *'I've got him!'*

Hiroshi found himself face-to-face with what seemed to be most of the people in his apartment building. His mother must have gone door-to-door, he thought, as a man he recognized as living across the hall took a step toward him. 'Hand over the rock, kid, and let us take you home.'

He hugged the rock tighter to himself. 'No.'

'Don't you know your mother's going crazy with worry?' asked an older woman who lived on the next floor down.

Hiroshi was about to answer when the Eye opened just above them in the dark. It looked down at them and all the people fell to the ground, holding their heads and crying out in pain, just like Ken and all the kids on the playground.

'They can't get you now,' said the Eye-Voice, more impatient than ever. 'Move along!'

Hiroshi moved along, picking his way through the people on the ground, many of whom had passed out—*not* like Ken and the other kids, which was a lot scarier. He rushed past them and ran the rest of the way to Bridge Hill, where he half-climbed, half-crawled to the top.

And there was Little Gap Bridge, just waiting for him. The way things had been going, he'd almost expected to find the bridge closed as unsafe, if it hadn't actually fallen down altogether. But no, it was the same old steel framework, looking a little drab under the yellowish streetlight but sturdy as ever.

After he got across, he'd be very close to where *Sakura 9* had blown up. But he didn't see any sign of the smoke he was supposed to throw the rock into. It had better still be there, he thought; then nobody would ever mess with him again. Or else this whole thing would've been for nothing.

True to its name, Little Gap Bridge wasn't very long but the chasm below had always seemed really deep to him. Normally when he walked across, he stopped in the middle to look down. Sometimes he couldn't see anything but shadows; other times, it was like a bowl of mist. He loved the idea that the mist might be a portal to another world full of amazing creatures like dragons or gryphons or—

'Why did you stop?' asked the Eye-Voice irritably. 'You need to keep moving before someone else catches up with you. If they do, they'll take my body away and I'll never get it back.'

Hiroshi looked up and saw the Eye was open again above him. 'Why would anyone do that?'

'Because they're afraid,' the Eye-Voice said. 'Afraid of what I'll do when I'm whole again.'

'Oh.' Hiroshi looked back but there was no sign that any of the search party was coming after him. 'So, um, what *are* you gonna do?'

'I'm going to make sure no one disturbs the peace of our world again.'

Hiroshi thought this over. He still didn't know what the Eye-Voice was planning but he had a bad feeling.

'Come now—you *want* to fight those who pick on you, don't you?' the Eye-Voice prodded. 'You want to defeat them so they can never hurt you again. That's true, isn't it?'

Now the Eye-Voice had a wheedling tone, like Ken sounded when he was trying to get another kid to do something they knew was wrong. Usually the other kid got caught while Ken got away.

'Well, isn't it?' demanded the Eye-Voice.

Hiroshi remembered the kids in the playground rolling on the floor, holding their heads and crying. Like the grownups in the search party, who'd been lying motionless on the ground.

'No!' he shouted at the Eye. 'I *don't* want to do that! I don't want to hurt *anyone*, not even Ken! I'm going home!' He put the rock down on the bridge and turned to go.

'But you *promised*!' the Eye-Voice boomed at him. 'You don't break promises, do you?'

Hiroshi's heart sank. He *had* promised—more than that, he'd *sworn*. Everybody knew you couldn't go back on anything you'd sworn to do. Sighing, he picked up the rock again.

'Good, good,' said the Eye-Voice. 'You *have* to do this or you'll never be strong enough to defeat your enemies.'

'My enemies?' said Hiroshi. 'I have *enemies*?'

'Everyone has enemies,' the Eye-Voice assured him. 'And

enemies must be defeated, there's no other way. Now keep going!'

Hiroshi meant to take a step forward but doubt held him in place. Somehow, he'd never thought of any of the kids he knew as enemies, not even Ken. Sometimes they were nice—even Ken could be nice—and sometimes they were mean, himself included. He'd been playing with all of them for as long as he and his mother had lived at Comfort Palais, which was as long as he could remember, and he'd never once thought of any of them as enemies, just other kids.

He wished with all his heart his mother had made him promise not to go to Jigokuyama. Then he could have told the Eye-Voice he'd made the promise to his mother first and it would have to find someone else. But his mother always said she didn't want promises, she just wanted him to do what he knew was right. Now he couldn't even lie to the Eye-Voice about a promise to his mother, although he had a feeling the Eye-Voice would have known it wasn't true.

All at once, he realized the bridge was vibrating under his feet. Only a little at first, but then it got stronger and stronger until the whole thing was shaking. Terrified, Hiroshi ran to the other side and looked back to see one of the Ultra Guard standing where he'd just been.

The man started to say something when Little Gap Bridge just… came apart all around him. Hiroshi watched open-mouthed as the metal support beams, the struts, and the cables parted ways and fell into the darkness below, taking the Ultra Guard with it.

'Well? What are you waiting for?' the Eye-Voice demanded. 'Go! *Now!*'

Hiroshi went.

Should've seen that *coming*, Dan thought ruefully as he sat up, moving with care in case some part of his human body was bruised, twisted, or broken. Humans weren't made to fall great distances. Luckily, this hadn't been a very long one, but even so, if anyone had been with him—Amagi, or worse, Anne—or worst of all, the boy…

But Hiroshi had gotten safely across and was on his way to the site of the *Sakura 9* explosion. The alien presence had become strong enough now that Dan was able to track it. When he'd reached the bridge, he'd picked up on the alien's intentions, albeit in fairly broad strokes. Not that he needed more detail to know he had to stop it. He used his wristcomm to call Anne.

'Where *are* you?' she asked, her voice full of concern. 'We heard a godawful noise and someone said Little Gap Bridge collapsed!'

'It did, indeed,' Dan confirmed. 'Don't worry about me, only my pride is sprained. But the boy, Hiroshi—he's on his way to where *Sakura 9* exploded. We've got to stop him. That rock—' He broke off, momentarily lost for a way to explain. 'It's all about the rock,' he said finally. 'Whatever came back with *Sakura 9* is using the rock to control him.'

'Uh, okay,' Anne said. 'We'll try to intercept him.'

'If you do, hold him for me,' Dan said, pushing himself to his feet. 'Moroboshi out.'

Anne called HQ to give them a quick update, then turned to Amagi. 'The captain says we should protect the kid and hold onto the rock till he gets here with Soga and Furuhashi.'

Amagi gave a short laugh. 'Furuhashi just *loves* flying the Hawk-1 at night.'

'The Hawk-1 has the largest containment chamber for hazardous materials,' Anne replied. 'You know, for things like alien rocks that might be more than just rocks.'

One of the police officers that had organized the search party came over to her and Amagi to show them a map on his tablet of the area that the police and volunteers would be covering. After assuring the officer they would be on comms, she and Amagi drove back to where they'd been when *Sakura 9* had landed.

'I keep having to remind myself it was just this morning we were here,' Anne said as they walked across the same stone ridge. 'Only a few hours ago. Not days.'

'This is right about where we were standing when *Sakura 9* blew,' Amagi said as he and Anne lowered their visors and activated the night-vision utility. 'See anything new or different?'

Anne pulled her binoculars out of the case on her belt and took a look around.

'There he is!' she said suddenly. 'The kid, I mean—approach at ten o'clock. Well, more like nine fifty-three.'

'Nine fifty-three it is,' Amagi said, using his own binoculars. 'We'd better stick to night vision—the terrain between us and him is pretty tricky.'

'Copy that,' Anne said as they began making their way toward the little boy cradling the rock in his arms.

Hiroshi concentrated on putting one foot in front of the other, trying to crowd out any other thoughts, especially the way the Ultra Guard guy had dropped into the darkness with Little Gap Bridge. In truth, he couldn't stop seeing it; it played over and over in his head on a loop. Sometimes when the bridge collapsed, he thought he caught sight of the man's confused face a fraction of a second before he went down. Other times, all he could see was how the pieces of the bridge just fell apart under the guy so that he fell with them. When he'd looked at the gap without the bridge, it hadn't seemed all that little to him.

Still, he kept his eyes on his feet as he clambered up an incline, then picked his way along an old footpath through overgrowth that seemed as thick as a jungle. From now on, he told himself, he was going to be a lot more careful about what he said, especially when it came to making promises. *Especially* to aliens.

Hiroshi had pushed through the thickest tangle of overgrowth to a much clearer stretch of footpath that would take him to where *Sakura 9* had landed. Once he got there, he had to find the smoke. The Eye-Voice claimed he'd see it, but so far—

'Hiroshi!'

Startled, he looked up and saw two more Ultra Guards in front of him, one of them a very pretty lady. Where had *they* come from? Didn't matter, he had to run away before the Eye opened and hurt them.

Too late.

The man and woman grabbed their heads as they fell to the ground, crying out in pain just like the search party and the other kids. Hiroshi watched, unable to move or speak as their cries died away and they lay still. He looked up at the Eye.

'You can go now,' said the Eye-Voice, still with that impatient edge. 'They can't stop us. No one can.'

Hiroshi rushed past them, afraid to look at them but more afraid not to. *Please let them be okay,* he prayed silently. *And please let this be over before anyone else gets hurt.*

As Hiroshi approached the spot where the spaceship had blown up, he noticed a change in the air. He smelled something burning, but it wasn't like leaves or a wood stove or even a bonfire. It smelled like someone had set his chemistry set on fire, the whole thing with all the chemicals, and every breath he took seemed to scrape the back of his throat. This definitely wasn't going to be his favorite day ever, Hiroshi thought, going up a small incline to a long flat area, like a platform or a stage made out of stone.

This had to be the place, he thought, looking around at the scorch marks from *Sakura 9*. If there were any pieces of the spaceship left, he couldn't see them. But now he saw the smoke, drifting up over the edge of flat stone he was standing on. It wasn't gray like mist or fog but a weird green color, like poison, and he didn't want to be anywhere near it.

I promise never to make another promise to an alien, he vowed, taking one shuffling step forward. He meant to peer over the edge, but a poison-green cloud puffed up into his face, making his eyes sting and water, and his mouth taste like *yuck*.

Hiroshi turned away to wipe his eyes, but they wouldn't stop stinging and he couldn't spit the *yuck* taste out of his mouth. He moved back from the edge, keeping his face turned away, took two deep breaths, and held the third. Then he shuffled all the way to the edge, raising the stone high over his head. Maybe if he threw it down hard enough, it would break and the Eye-Voice would be gone forever.

Two strong arms caught him up and pulled him back.

'Let go! I have to do this!' Hiroshi shouted, squeezing his streaming eyes shut.

'Hiroshi, listen to me!'

Not the Eye-Voice, but one he knew. Only it couldn't be, he thought, as he twisted around to see who was holding him. It *couldn't* be the Ultra Guard who had fallen into the dark, deep chasm under Little Gap Bridge, it *just couldn't be*. But there he was.

'How'd *you* get here?' Hiroshi asked, flabbergasted.

'Never mind, I *am* here,' the man insisted, 'and you mustn't do this. You'll put everyone in terrible danger!'

'*Leave—me—alone!*' Hiroshi yelled, squirming desperately in the man's arms. Why was this so hard? All he had to do was throw a rock into some smoke, just this one simple thing, and the Eye-Voice would make him the strongest, toughest kid in Comfort Palais. He'd never have to run from Ken or anyone else. But this

PAT CADIGAN

Ultra Guard was acting like it was some kind of terrible crime when it wasn't. It wasn't!

'Hiroshi, please listen to me,' said the man's voice, close to his ear. 'Give me the rock and let me take you home.'

The man was gazing into his face now in such a kindly way that suddenly Hiroshi wanted more than anything else in the world to do what *he* wanted. But then the image of Ken bloomed in his mind—Ken laughing at him, Ken chasing him, knocking him down, throwing rocks at him. Was the Ultra Guard going to come to his rescue the next time Ken made him hand over his after-school snack money?

Desperate now, Hiroshi broke away and ran to the edge, but the man grabbed him again and begged him—actually *begged* him—not to throw the rock into the green mist. Hiroshi felt his resolve start to weaken again but he kept struggling anyway, and the Ultra Guard kept begging him not to throw the rock into the smoke, and in the end, he didn't.

The stupid thing slipped out of his hands and fell.

'I didn't mean to do that!' Hiroshi wailed, not caring about the tears running down his face. He really was sorry he'd dropped it, but the moment the stone had fallen from his hands, it had been like an enormous weight had been lifted off him. The Ultra Guard was still holding him tightly, only now it felt protective.

'It's all right, Hiroshi,' the man said. 'I'm going to take you home—'

Above them in the darkness, the Eye opened again and it looked gigantic as it radiated poison-green light. Only, instead of telling Hiroshi what to do or hurting the man, it zoomed down into the green smoke. Hiroshi and the Ultra Guard inched closer to the edge and peered over it together.

The green smoke was gone, leaving a cavern too deep even

for shadows. Then two small lights appeared, glowing the same poison green.

'It told me it would make me the strongest and toughest kid in our apartment complex if I kept my promise to throw the rock into the smoke,' Hiroshi said mournfully, knuckling tears from his eyes. 'And I had to do it because I *promised*.'

'Uh-huh.' The man went down on one knee and sat Hiroshi on the other one. 'Did *it* promise?'

Hiroshi couldn't speak without bursting into loud sobs, so he just shook his head.

The man was about to say something else when they heard a deep sort of growling noise. It actually sounded a lot like boulders grinding against each other, but Hiroshi knew instinctively that it came from something alive, and that wasn't its let's-be-friends sound. He and the man took another peek into the darkness below.

The poison-green lights glowed in the darkness, closer now. Hiroshi saw they were set into a chunk of a head that moved from side to side. Now he could make out two bulky front legs that ended in long, sharp claws and a large, misshapen body, like a bunch of broken stones glued together to look like a stegosaurus. Except next to this creature, a real stegosaurus was like a butterfly.

Hiroshi turned back to the Ultra Guard. 'Oh, man, I *really* didn't mean to!'

'I know,' the man said in his kind voice. 'Can you find your way home from here?' Hiroshi nodded. 'Head for the road and you'll meet a bunch of people who are looking for you. They'll take care of you. Okay?'

Hiroshi nodded again, not caring there were still tears running down his face.

'Good,' the man said. 'Let's just back up a little more—'

In the next moment, both of them were falling backward into darkness.

* * *

Furuhashi had been gracious when he'd ceded the Hawk-1 piloting to his commanding officer. Kiriyama had expected nothing less, but he also knew it was a sacrifice for him. When this was over, he planned to reward Furuhashi and the rest of the Ultra Guard with an extra day of personal leave, just to show his appreciation.

Now he was following what Soga had described as 'a whopping great alien signal' that had shown up on the scanner right where *Sakura 9* had blown up. As they neared the area, Kiriyama flipped on the floodlights on the underside of the aircraft, aiming them at the enclave of standing stones just as what looked like a kaiju made of boulders was pulling itself up out of a gully.

'Captain, I'm picking up Dan's locator beacon!' Soga said excitedly.

'Where?'

'Not too far from that thing, whatever it is,' Furuhashi said as the boulder-creature turned its head and fixed its bright, nasty-green eyes on them.

Kiriyama kept them at a distance as the Hawk-1 descended, looking for some sign of Dan or anyone else. 'Are you sure he's here?'

'Lots of gullies and ditches down there,' Soga replied. 'Maybe he crawled into one to hide from Old Green Eyes.'

'Switching to infrared,' Furuhashi said, and immediately added, 'Got him! And someone else, much smaller!' Pause. 'They're not moving.'

The pit that had just opened in Kiriyama's stomach felt a thousand feet deep.

'Their heat signatures are constant, not decreasing,' Soga said. 'They're alive, Captain—location coordinates onscreen.'

Kiriyama made a wide turn and a small screen to the left of the yoke lit up in night-vision, showing him Dan lying on the ground with a small boy sprawled on top of him.

'That creature's practically invisible in infrared,' Furuhashi said. 'Maybe it really *is* made of rock.'

'Remember that for the incident report,' Kiriyama said, pulling the Hawk's nose up and putting Dan and the boy behind them. 'Furuhashi, fire at will!'

Furuhashi hit the creature's left flank. There was a showy burst of sparks and smoke and sparks, but when it cleared, the monster was still moving, apparently unharmed.

'Is it me,' said Soga, 'or does that beast look like a half-baked cross between a dinosaur and an anteater?'

'Put together by a kid whose parents never help him with his homework,' added Furuhashi. 'It's a mess, all right. I'm gonna try shooting where its joints should be. Maybe I can dismember it.'

'Good idea,' said Soga. 'And I'm going to—'

But they never found out what Soga had in mind. The monster looked up at the Hawk-1 and two beams of light shot out of its glowing green eyes. They struck a glancing blow across the Hawk-1's bow, barely a yard from the cockpit.

'Okay, brace yourselves,' Furuhashi said unhappily. 'It's gonna be one of *those* landings.'

'Again?' Soga laughed nervously.

'Don't rub it in,' Furuhashi growled.

'But the good news is, we've done this before,' Soga said with another nervous laugh. 'So we'll probably live through it. *Probably.*'

The bar for good news was set exceptionally low of late, Kiriyama thought as he fought to keep the Hawk's nose up long enough to lower the wheels.

It was raining dirt.

Why was he sleeping out in dirt-rain, Dan wondered, and why was there a bag of laundry on top of him?

He lowered his visor, started to push the laundry bag aside so he could sit up, and discovered it was actually a little boy. Dan switched his visor to night-vision just as more dirt rained down on him.

Memory returned in a burst. Dan sat up, careful to move Hiroshi gently, and stretched forth his awareness. The process went more slowly than usual, which was disturbing, though not as much as the fault in his memory, as brief as it was. But he'd have to agonize about it later—right now, his commanding officer and two teammates were facing a monster and he had to do something about the unconscious child lying on top of him before he could help them.

As if to underscore the thought, more dirt fell on him and the boy. Dan slipped the Ultra Eye out of his jacket pocket, then caught himself. It was night; the Protector on his chest would still have plenty of charge but he couldn't let this become a lengthy fight.

Above him, he heard the sound of the Hawk's weapons firing. Kiriyama, Soga, and Furuhashi were up there, ready to take on any threat, anytime, and none of them had Protectors. Besides, this wouldn't be the first time he'd had to fight in the dark.

But first he had to get Hiroshi to a safe place. The Pointer, of course—it was out of the monster's reach but not so far away he'd use up too much energy getting there and back.

Dan pressed the Ultra Eye to his face, felt the Ultra energy surge within him. Good thing kids slept like mountains, he thought, as he flew Hiroshi to the Pointer and placed him carefully in the back seat. The boy never stirred.

For once, the Hawk-1's crash-landing was more landing than crash. Always good to get the wheels down instead of skidding to a stop, Kiriyama thought as he, Furuhashi, and Soga armed themselves and climbed out of the emergency exit in the roof. They had come to rest not quite a hundred yards from where the kaiju was screaming into the night. Kiriyama led them back toward the creature through a wooded area that came to an abrupt end at a gully carved into the ground during the last monsoon season. It was just deep enough to give them cover while they fired on the monster.

Furuhashi had the heavy gun, while Soga and Kiriyama used the plasma rifles. From the way the monster was screeching, Kiriyama thought it had felt every hit from their weapons. But when the fiery bursts and the smoke cleared, it was still whole and moving around with barely a mark on its hide, its eyes glowing like bizarre green coals. The thing had no trouble figuring out where the shots were coming from; it gave another of those raw-throated, high-pitched screech-bellows as it plodded toward them.

Kiriyama set his rifle on Incendiary—Lethal, motioned for Furuhashi and Soga to move farther away from him. If they fired on the creature simultaneously while he had its undivided attention—i.e., just as the beast tried to blast him with its eye-beams—they just might hit it at its most vulnerable. He took a deep breath and hoped the trench would afford him enough protection that it wouldn't be his last—

'*Enough!* Stop this! Do you hear me? *Stop!*'

The screechy rasp was actually quite clear and yet Kiriyama couldn't quite believe he'd heard it. He looked to Soga, then to Furuhashi. Both were as dumbfounded as he was. He raised up and peered over the top of the trench. The creature was only a few yards away, its shiny green eyes fixed on him.

Because it knows I'm in charge, Kiriyama thought, calmly and rationally, even though he still wasn't ready to believe the monster had just demanded a time-out. He pushed himself up out of the trench and stood before the kaiju. If it changed its mind and decided it wanted to fight after all, they'd be having his funeral *after* his cremation. Not that he'd have to worry about it.

Kiriyama straightened to his full height, pointing his pulse rifle away from the kaiju but keeping it up and ready. 'What do you want with us?' he said, loudly enough for Furuhashi and Soga to hear.

'I came here to destroy your world for attacking us,' the monster replied.

Kiriyama felt his jaw drop, not because it was the first time he'd ever heard an alien claim humans had struck first, but because he'd never even heard of a kaiju so articulate, much less met one.

'We never attacked you,' Kiriyama said. 'We don't even know who you are or where you come from!'

'Lies,' the kaiju said. 'Many years ago, we were forced to leave our planet and search for a new home. It was a long, difficult search, but we finally found it. The sixth planet in orbit around your star, the one with such prominent rings—'

'*Saturn?!*' Soga hopped up out of the trench to stand beside Kiriyama. 'How can you live on *Saturn*?'

'We live on that planet's largest satellite,' the alien said.

'We call that moon Titan,' Kiriyama said.

'*We* call it Annon,' the creature informed him, and it sounded almost huffy now. 'We had traveled so far and so long, we had used up nearly all of our fuel and provisions when the largest planet in this system exerted its gravitational force on our small fleet of ships and drew us inward. As we entered the system, we scanned every orbiting body—planets, moons, even asteroids— desperate to find somewhere to survive. Annon has ice, bodies of liquid, and a thick nitrogen atmosphere. We had just enough fuel left to change course and go into orbit around it and finally land.'

Kiriyama looked at Soga, and then at Furuhashi who had come up to stand on his other side. 'That doesn't explain why you think we attacked you.'

The creature's green eyes flared more brightly for a second. 'We knew this planet was inhabited,' the creature went on its rumble growl. 'But we also knew that Annon would be inimical to human lifeforms, so we assumed you would be no threat to us, and you weren't—until you fired that missile at us.'

'What missile?' Soga asked, bristling with exasperation.

'You mean *Sakura 9*,' Kiriyama said as he realized, meeting the creature's eyes steadily, although he felt as if its green stare were boring into his head. 'The spacecraft you used to bring you here. But it wasn't a missile or any other kind of weapon.'

The green eyes flared again. 'We calculated its trajectory,' the kaiju said, 'and determined Annon was its target. Scans showed no living passengers. A vessel aimed at a specific target with no life aboard—what else could it be but a missile, sent to wipe us out!'

'Well, maybe where *you* come from,' Furuhashi said defensively, then grimaced as Kiriyama stepped on his foot.

'Here on Earth, we send out unmanned probes for purposes of exploration,' Kiriyama said to the creature, careful to keep any hostility out of his voice. 'If our probe had discovered you had colonized Ti— *Annon*, we would have greeted you in peace with the respect we show to friends and allies.'

'I don't believe you,' the creature said, its growl becoming harsher. 'Scans of your planet show you Earthlings have weapons stored everywhere. There is no place on your world without weapons, no safe place for visitors to land where you couldn't annihilate them in seconds.'

Kiriyama considered telling the creature humans had been making the same complaint for over a hundred years, then decided it wasn't much of a defense.

'We are a people with a long, troubled history,' Kiriyama said after a moment. 'There are many sovereign nations on this planet and all of them have, at one time or another, had to defend themselves against threats to their existence. Trying to explain in any greater detail would take a very long time and I'm not sure we could make things any clearer. For now, however, can you take us at our word when we say no one intended to use any of Earth's weapons on you?'

'No,' the alien said flatly. 'Do you take me for a fool? No intelligent species would keep so many weapons of such destructive force if they really had no intention of using them. We will destroy you before you can destroy us.'

The creature lifted its unwieldy head and took a step toward him. Kiriyama heard a high-pitched noise, faint but building in intensity as it rose even higher. In a few moments it would be beyond human hearing, but, he knew, not beyond feeling; he could actually sense the coming pain, sharp and piercing and inescapable—

Abruptly he heard something else, a different, painless sound, one that he had come to like a great deal.

As dark as it was, he saw the red and silver figure flying toward them in the night sky. His eyes glowed, too, but they were a warm, comforting amber. Kiriyama leaped across the trench, motioning for Furuhashi and Soga to follow, so the unofficial seventh member of the Ultra Guard had a clear LZ.

Ultraseven touched down with the effortless grace Kiriyama still found breathtaking, placing himself between the men and the kaiju. For a single, pristine second, the two faced each other in silence.

The monster gave a throat-scraping shriek and lunged at Ultraseven with a speed that belied its lumbering bulk.

'Uh-oh,' blurted Soga. Kiriyama shushed him.

He met the creature with a hard kick to the head that drove it back, farther from the Ultra Guard. It could have been worse, he thought; they could have been fighting on Titan/Annon, where the alien would have been coated with ice and the sun would have been too distant to provide the energy he needed to defeat it, or even just survive its attack.

The alien gathered itself and came at him again. He pounced on it, wrapping both arms around its rugged head, then pivoted to execute a throw Furuhashi had shown him in the gym. The massive stone body slammed down with a noise like a mountain cracking open.

The creature rolled over to face him and he braced himself. But instead of rushing him, the creature lowered its head and he saw the curved spike high on its back light up as it sprayed a stream of fire at him.

He crossed his arms to activate the Ultra V Barrier, maintaining it until the creature realized its attack couldn't get through. Before it could do anything else, he positioned his left arm across his chest and kept the right one at his side, fist clenched. The Emerium Beam burst forth from the lamp in his forehead in a hard, invincible line of power.

The monster screeched in outrage and pain. He was about to fire again when it suddenly leaped high into the air. *Let that be the last surprise this beast has in store for me*, he thought as he stepped back. Instead of coming down squarely on top of him to dig in with all four sets of claws, the alien landed in front of him and he jumped on it, delivering a flurry of punches.

The alien heaved him off and twisted around to look at him; hard green beams of light shot out of its eyes. Dan countered with his own eye-beams. After a few seconds, the creature broke off the attack, turned, and began to lumber away.

Dan pressed his palms together, trapping the alien within the Spiral Beam, freezing it in place, then stole a glance at his teammates; they were shaken up and practically reeling but they were still on their feet. And so was he, although he could feel how much his strength had decreased. Either he talked this creature into a more peaceful resolution or he killed it, and he wasn't sure which one was within his power.

But then, the alien didn't know that.

Digging deep within himself, Dan found the strength he needed for one last show of power and willed the alien to rise up off the ground.

'The Earth human didn't lie to you,' he told the creature as he watched it turn slowly in midair. 'The people of this world had no intention of attacking you. They didn't even know you were there.'

'You seem very sure about that,' the alien replied. Dan sensed it had weakened as well, although he wasn't sure how much.

'I'm also an alien and I live here in peace, among the humans. *With* the humans,' Dan said. 'If they were as belligerent as you claim, I wouldn't be here.'

There was a long moment of silence as the alien thought this one over.

'All right,' it said after some unmeasured period of time. 'I believe you. But I won't allow my people to be the target of an invasion.'

'I believe we all understand that,' Dan said drily. 'You can return to Annon in peace—no one will try to stop you. You and your people are free to thrive and grow on your new home world. Earth will leave you alone if you agree to leave Earth alone.'

'Agreed,' said the alien.

Its eyes glowed bright and brighter, then suddenly zoomed up into the night sky, merging into one bright green light as its body fell to pieces, the life gone. Dan took to the air to follow it; he had just enough power remaining to make sure the creature left the atmosphere and was on course to Titan/Annon before he returned to human form.

Dan found Hiroshi waiting with Amagi and Anne in the Pointer, exhausted but otherwise all right.

'I think someone's going to sleep late tomorrow morning,'

Anne said as Dan slipped into the driver's seat.

'I think we all will,' Dan said, making her and Amagi laugh.

'Hey, what happened to that alien?' Hiroshi wanted to know.

'Oh, the seventh member of the Ultra Guard convinced it to go home instead of fighting,' Dan said.

'We call him Ultraseven,' Amagi put in.

'Yeah, I knew that,' Hiroshi told him in a lofty tone that had them all suppressing laughter.

'And now that the alien's gone home,' Dan said as he started the Pointer, 'it's time for all of us to do the same. You included, Hiroshi.'

The kid made a discouraged noise. 'Well, that's just great. I'm not the strongest, toughest kid in Comfort Palais, and tomorrow it's all going to be just like always, with everyone picking on me. Nothing's changed, *nothing*.'

'I wouldn't say that,' Dan chuckled.

'*I* would,' Hiroshi said glumly.

Anne tried to cheer him up, but despite her best efforts, Hiroshi rode in dejected silence until they reached the traffic checkpoint, where a small crowd of people, mostly search party volunteers, as well as a surprising number of children, were waiting with the police officer and Hiroshi's mother.

'Well, will you look at that,' Dan said as he pulled up and parked. 'Your search party is now a welcome home party—all for you, Hiroshi. That's a *big* change, don't you think?'

His mother was smiling like she really was happy to see him and wasn't even a little bit cross after he'd made her worry. If it had just been her and a few other grownups, Hiroshi would have jumped out of the car and run to her. But there were a lot of kids there, too, including Ken. Hugging your mother where Ken could see you was a good way to get mean-teased for *weeks*.

'Hiroshi-kun, look at all these friends of yours,' said the Ultra Guard named Dan. 'They came to meet you because they're glad you're okay!'

Ken was glad he was okay? Yeah, right, he thought; Ken was glad Hiroshi could still be his punching bag.

'I don't wanna go,' he mumbled as Anne helped him out of the back seat. She gave his arm a gentle tug but he stayed where he was, one hand on the seat and the other on the open door, digging in his heels. Maybe he could just live in the Pointer's back seat from now on. 'I *can't* go. I'm not strong.'

'Oh, Hiroshi.' Dan couched down and looked into his face in that kindly way. 'Only a truly strong boy could do what *you* did tonight—you led that alien *away* from the apartment complex, away from your friends, your family, and everyone else who lives here. You saved them from getting badly hurt.' Dan leaned closer and lowered his voice. 'Or worse.'

'I did?' Hiroshi said in a small voice, feeling his resolve melt away. 'Me?'

'*You*—only you, and none other,' Dan assured him. 'It also takes great strength to get along with other people, whether they're kids or members of the Ultra Guard, which I'm pretty sure makes you the strongest kid *I* ever met. And certainly the strongest kid in Comfort Palais.'

Dan smiled and Hiroshi felt as if the sun was shining inside of him.

'Go ahead,' Anne said, and her smile was like even more sunshine. So much light, Hiroshi thought; he was never going to be afraid of the dark again. 'Go to them—everyone's dying to know what happened.'

Hiroshi looked up at all the smiling faces waiting for him—his mother, the search party, all the kids, even Ken. He gathered his great strength, took a deep breath, and marched over to his mother.

Everyone crowded around him like he'd just scored the winning goal in the national football championship. Kids were patting him on the back, asking questions, and he wanted to answer them, except suddenly he was so tired that when he opened his mouth, all that came out was a yawn.

'Hey, Hiroshi—thanks for all your help!' Dan said, giving him a snappy salute as he started the Pointer. 'See you around!'

'Yeah, see you around,' Hiroshi sighed, staring after the car's taillights. It was all so amazing. This had turned out to be the best day of his life, and it wouldn't be the last good day, because Dan had thanked *him* for helping the Ultra Guard.

And then he'd said, *See you around!* In front of everyone! Like Dan really expected they'd see each other around, because they were friends. He just wished he wasn't so *tired*.

He wasn't the only one.

CHAPTER

FIVE

The human body Dan had fashioned for himself was comfortable for what it was, and it was aesthetically pleasant but not too attention-getting. Unfortunately, it also had less stamina than he'd have liked. After the situation with the Alien Wild and the Eye, he needed two days to recover, and he spent most of the second day fending off Anne and her stethoscope.

'I checked with clerical and we still haven't received any medical records for you,' she told him. 'If I don't get them soon, I'll have to schedule a complete checkup for you.'

'I'll call my previous doctor again,' Dan promised. 'I'm sure they've just forgotten.'

'Again? Or still?' Anne's eyes twinkled. 'Everybody in that office must have some sort of amnesia.' Her expression changed to what he'd come to think of as her medium-urgent look of concern; no more twinkling. 'We have to have a medical history for you, Dan. Kiriyama can't send you out on assignments unless he's sure you're physically fit for duty, or at least not likely to drop dead in the course of a normal emergency.'

'Is that really what you're afraid of?' Dan grinned with half his mouth. 'That I'll keel over in the middle of an alien invasion?'

Anne gave a perfunctory laugh. 'Obviously, you won't. But there are other things to think about. Are you allergic to anything? And I mean seriously allergic, like, say, to penicillin? Or tree nuts? Or wheat? What if you get stung by a bee and die of anaphylactic shock because I didn't know you needed to carry an EpiPen? We don't know—and I don't think *you* do, either.'

Somewhat alarmed now, he promised to look into the (nonexistent) status of his (nonexistent) records. The easiest thing to do would be to find the medical records of the man whose appearance he'd duplicated; he could make copies, put his own name on them, and then he and Anne would have other things to talk about.

Unless, of course, Jiro Satsuma put in an application to join the TDF—the records department would flag the duplication immediately. How would he explain that one?

But even as he considered it, he knew the chance of such a thing happening was so small as to be nonexistent. It wasn't a complete impossibility, but he'd had a glimpse of Jiro Satsuma's path and there was nothing that would lead him to become part of the TDF or the Ultra Guard.

He'd found Jiro during his first day on Earth, while he'd been flying around marveling at the lovely blue color Rayleigh scattering had given the sky. How long ago had that been? They marked time very differently here; it kept their abbreviated lives organized but it wasn't at all flexible. Nonetheless, his choosing to remain here meant agreeing to live by that system as both Dan Moroboshi and Ultraseven. This was their world, after all; he was the secret interloper.

On a personal level, producing the medical records Anne kept asking for would make her very happy. And making Anne happy, he discovered, had become very important to him.

Learning how interpersonal relationships played out among these short-lived beings who were so strictly regulated physically, mentally, and temporally was fascinating to him. The experience of coincidence, for example, was unique to each person. Sometimes it was delightful; other times, it was downright unsettling.

Then there was a mine cave-in and he learned about serendipity, Earth style.

When Kiriyama told them they'd been called to deal with the collapse of an old coalmine, Dan sensed immediately that there was more to the disaster than there appeared to be.

He drove out to the mine with Kiriyama, Soga, Anne, and Furuhashi while Amagi stayed at HQ in Overwatch. Anne was thrilled not to be left behind and her good spirits affected all of them.

Underneath the upbeat mood in the Pointer, however, Dan sensed Kiriyama's emotions were mixed. He was tempted to probe the captain more deeply but lately he was more hesitant to invade the privacy of the human mind, especially those minds closest to him. Probing a human mind to save a life was one thing; just being curious, however, was less a connection than it was a violation. Humans had no Ultra senses but they found ways to communicate profoundly enough to bond with each other, often for many years.

Dan thought the most amazing thing about that was how humans saw this as commonplace, ordinary, when it was really close to miraculous.

'Correct me if I'm wrong, Captain,' Dan said as he drove the Pointer out to the site, 'but we aren't usually on call when a mine caves in, are we?'

'The circumstances are unusual,' Kiriyama said, looking up from the tablet he was studying. 'Which is to say, the mine itself. Coalmining in Japan isn't a growing industry. The Earth Sciences department at the Tokyo Technological Institute has developed new ground-penetrating sensors that can detect the presence of all kinds of things—gold and silver deposits, for example.'

'So, what then—did they find gold in an old coalmine?' Soga asked.

Kiriyama didn't answer.

'Oh, my goodness!' Anne said excitedly. 'They really found gold in a coalmine!'

Dan glanced at her doubtfully; she winked at him.

'How nice that would be,' Kiriyama chuckled. 'In fact, the presence of gold was detected, albeit only in very small amounts, along with copper, titanium, platinum, lithium, and a number of other things that are never found in close proximity to each other.'

'Are they sure their detectors are working right?' Soga said. 'I've never heard of lithium deposits in Japan.'

'Neither have I,' said Kiriyama. 'But the thing about the Japanese archipelago is, it's a subduction zone with a lot of tectonic plate movement. Over millions of years, these have uplifted the islands and created three oceanic trenches—the Japan Trench, the Kuril-Kamchatka Trench, and the Izu-Ogasawara Trench.'

'I had no idea you were such an expert on trenches and subduction, Captain,' Anne said, and Dan knew her eyes were twinkling.

Kiriyama chuckled. 'Oh, I'm not. Or I wasn't, but then I got an earful from Akira Tokuda, the president of the mining company. More than I ever wanted to know, fascinating though it was.'

'Are they trying to mine the gold?' Anne asked.

'Tokuda told me they weren't,' Kiriyama replied. 'This was supposed to be an exploratory operation to try to determine the feasibility of digging up whatever's down there. These shafts have been undisturbed for decades, indicating the area should be stable. But I guess something woke up and slipped sideways or something. Tokuda said it happened fast—faster than it should have. The miners felt the tremor and the next thing they knew, a dozen of them were trapped. Rescuers managed to get eleven of them out.'

'And the twelfth?' Soga asked.

'A young guy named Jiro—' Kiriyama scrolled upward on the tablet. 'Jiro Satsuma.'

Dan's heart gave a thump so hard he was a bit surprised Kiriyama hadn't heard it. 'Who?' he asked.

Anne tapped him on the head. 'Hey, eyes on the road, driver.'

'Is that name familiar to you?' Kiriyama asked him. 'Someone you know? Old friend or coworker?'

'No, just an interesting name,' Dan said, doing his best to sound casual.

'Yeah, it kinda is,' Soga said. 'What happened that they couldn't get him out with the others?'

'That's quite a tale,' Kiriyama said, chuckling some more. 'As in, a mouse tail. Jiro Satsuma was the self-appointed keeper of the crew mascot—' he scrolled again, '—Chukichi. When the rest were running to get out, Satsuma ran back to get him. Now they're both trapped.'

'But why would they bring their mascot into the mine?' Soga said.

'Because the pet shop was all out of canaries.' Kiriyama looked around at the others. 'Do I have to explain canaries in coalmines?'

'Not a bit,' Dan chuckled. 'We're all familiar with canaries, coalmines, subduction zones, and, uh, what's the other one?'

'Tectonics,' Anne said. 'You're welcome.'

'The ground shook and there was a flash of light,' said a young miner named Mizuki. He was tall and lanky, with a pinched, worried expression and a fine layer of black dust covering him from head to foot, as if he'd actually been mining coal. According to the other miners, he was Jiro Satsuma's best friend, which had given Dan pause.

But Mizuki had shaken his hand without noticing that one of the Ultra Guard just happened to be a dead ringer for the man still trapped underground. Human perception varied from person to person, Dan reminded himself; since his helmet completely covered his hair, it made the resemblance less marked, at least for Mizuki, who was explaining why he called Jiro Satsuma the Miracle Man.

'It was just one of those things that happens sometimes,' he said over a cup of tea in the canteen. 'We'd climbed that rockface before, several times, and never had anything go wrong. But that day...' He shook his head. 'We had a piton come out. I couldn't believe it, I was so sure it was solidly in there, secure. But as soon as Jiro touched it, it was like the rock just spat it out. Suddenly, I had all of Jiro's weight hanging off me, and both of us were hanging from the piton just above me and I could feel that it wasn't going to hold.'

Mizuki took another sip of tea, as if fortifying himself against the memory. 'So there was Jiro, dangling below me. He tried to get a handhold or foothold but he couldn't reach the wall. He started swinging and I could practically *hear* the piton above me start working its way out of the stone. Then I look down and I see Jiro's sawing away at the rope between us so he wouldn't pull me down with him.'

'What happened?' Anne asked.

'He cut the rope.' Mizuki shook his head. 'Two hundred meters straight down and he cuts the rope. I couldn't believe it.'

'What did you do?' Dan asked.

The man gave a single laugh. 'I made the fastest non-falling descent of my life and went looking for his body. Found him lying in a patch of clover, unconscious but perfectly okay, not a scratch or a scrape on him, not even a bruise. I woke him and asked him how the hell he managed that one.'

'What did he say?' Furuhashi asked, fascinated.

'Said he didn't know. Still doesn't. We've all been calling him Miracle Man ever since.'

'Sure sounds miraculous to me,' said Soga, looking from him to Dan. 'Maybe he's got more than one miracle in him?'

'Or maybe someone's loaned him one they aren't using?' Anne said. Soga and Furuhashi laughed.

'Hey, stranger things have been known to happen,' Dan said, keeping his tone light. He looked around the canteen dining room for Kiriyama and saw him sitting a few tables away with President Tokuda. Dan excused himself and went over to join them just as Kiriyama's wristcomm chimed with an incoming call from Amagi.

'I contacted the Earthquake Research Center, captain.' Amagi's voice sounded filtered, as if he were on an old-fashioned radio, and Dan wondered what was causing such interference. 'There was no tectonic activity close enough to affect Japan. If the earth moved—and I guess it did—' he allowed himself a small laugh, '—it wasn't a quake.'

Tokuda's lined face seemed to sag a little more. 'To be honest, I never thought it was an earthquake.'

'Neither did I,' Kiriyama said. 'But now we can officially rule that out.'

Tokuda scowled. 'This is our third accident this year.'

Kiriyama sat up a bit straighter. 'In the same mine?'

'No, the other two were in two different locations. But they occurred at about the same depth.'

Dan wanted to ask for more details, but Anne caught his eye from the other table; she wanted him to come back. Sensing Tokuda would probably talk more freely to Kiriyama alone, Dan returned to his original seat.

'Tell Dan what you told us just now,' Anne said to Mizuki.

Mizuki looked down at the table in front of him. 'It sounds kinda silly.'

'Lots of things that sound silly aren't,' Soga assured him. 'Right, Dan?'

Dan nodded. 'Go ahead. You never know, it might be helpful.'

'Okay.' Mizuki took a breath and finished his tea. 'When I was running for my life, I looked back and I swear I saw these—' he made a pained face, '—I saw these round, bright lights. They were smaller than headlights but they were too big to be hard hats or flashlights. And they were close together, so that they looked like great big eyes.'

More eyes shining in the darkness? Dan wondered. 'They weren't green, were they?'

'No, they were just lights. White, no colors.' Mizuki seemed a bit puzzled by the question.

'Did anyone else see them?' Dan asked him.

'Everybody says no, so I guess I'm the only one.' Mizuki made a face. 'The more we talk about it, the sillier it sounds.'

'Not to me,' Dan said. 'You saw *something*, and they wouldn't have hired you if you were prone to hallucinations so it's definitely worth investigating. And you should lead the way, at least to begin with.' Pause. 'If you're up to it, of course.'

'This is as far as I can take you,' Mizuki said, bringing the small group to a stop about twenty-five feet in from the entrance, to the place where the miners had dug through the dirt and rocks to free eleven of the twelve trapped miners. All the lights here were still on, although the one closest to the collapse had begun to flicker slightly.

Soga moved ahead of the group with a portable remote sensor. He held it high, then low to the ground, first on one side, then the other. After a minute or two, he turned to Kiriyama.

'I'm getting no signs of life, Captain,' Soga said, his voice apologetic. 'But I think there's some kind of interference blocking or distorting the readings. Let me keep trying.'

In the relative quiet, Dan heard a faint *ping!* like two metal objects colliding. No, he realized, like someone banging on a metal pipe with a tool or a rock, trying to let people know he was still alive.

Dan beckoned to Soga and had him position the portable sensor on one of the pipes that ran along the righthand side wall of the tunnel, from the entrance to the place where it curved down and disappeared into the ground, right in front of the caved-in section.

Soga's face lit up. 'Okay, *now* I'm getting signs of life! Really faint but definitely there!' He looked at Dan, who simply shrugged and moved out of the way so Kiriyama could look at the readout, and went to the larger pipes on the opposite wall. He bent slightly to sight along it and stretched forth his Ultra awareness.

And there he was, Jiro Satsuma himself, very much alive and well enough to bang on a pipe with a wrench. Dan sensed him remembering the day when he had cut the rope tying him to Mizuki, with no hope of survival. No one could fall two hundred meters and live.

In truth, he'd fallen all of three meters before Dan had swooped in to catch him. Jiro had already passed out, overwhelmed by events, so it had been easy to give him a soft landing on a bed of clover, leaving him with more than a few unanswered questions and a preposterous story no one would have taken seriously if Mizuki hadn't been there to back him up.

This time, instead of cutting a rope to spare a friend's life, he had run back into the collapsing mine to save the crew's mascot. Dan didn't have to probe any of the miners to know they thought Jiro was crazy to try to rescue a mouse instead of just saving himself. But crazy or not, they didn't want to lose him.

Dan's Ultra awareness told him Jiro was hoping for an ingenious rescue or, failing that, one more miracle. At the same time, he could also sense the interference that wasn't really interference. There was no way to describe it except as strange, extrinsic. Alien.

He straightened up and went to Kiriyama. 'Captain, I'd like to try going in, to rescue this man but also to find the source of whatever that interference is. Something may be going on down there and it may explain why a mine that's been stable for years would suddenly cave in.'

Kiriyama nodded, and activated his wristcomm to call Amagi and request that he use the Hawk-3 to bring them a particular piece of equipment.

The Magma Riser was based on standard tunneling hardware, although the design had been given an extensive makeover by Amagi and the R&D department. The new machine had proved itself in the field several times over—or perhaps that should have been '*under* the field.' Amagi and the Research and Development team had managed to beef up its power while making it more streamlined, indestructible, and, best of all as far as Dan was concerned, fast.

'Jiro Satsuma is your priority,' Kiriyama told the five members of the Ultra Guard. 'And when you find him, *please don't forget the mouse*. Because if you do, this guy is gonna hop out and run back for him.'

The Ultra Guard laughed; Kiriyama didn't.

'And of course, keep your eyes open for anything that shouldn't be there,' he went on. 'Tokuda told me neither of the previous incidents was as bad as this one, but the miners involved also reported flashes of light and interference with electronics, communications, and equipment.'

'You think the earth tremors were caused deliberately?' asked Furuhashi.

'Nobody knows,' Kiriyama said. 'So we should find out.'

* * *

'Isn't anyone going to say it?' Furuhashi said as the Magma Riser arrived at its target depth and levelled off.

'Say what?' Anne asked, baffled.

Furuhashi gave an exaggerated, put-upon sigh and looked around at the others expectantly; no response. 'Okay, I'll say it. That was really *boring*.'

Everyone groaned.

'That was really *awful*,' Anne told him.

'I know.' Furuhashi shrugged. 'And I was the only one brave enough to say so.'

'Obstacle ahead,' Dan said, raising his voice to get their attention. He was in the copilot's chair next to Amagi. 'It's showing on instruments as a solid sheet of granite.'

'Does granite come in sheets?' Soga wanted to know as Amagi brought the Magma Riser to a stop.

'Apparently it does in these parts,' Amagi replied. He flipped up the plastic cover over the weapons controls on the dashboard. 'Demolishing obstacle ahead.'

Dan watched the granite in front of them tremble. A multitude of thin lines spread across the stone; in the next moment, it disintegrated into millions of tiny pieces.

All of them sat in silence, staring through the windshield. 'Well,' Amagi said after a bit, and turned to Dan. 'You see that too, right?'

'If you see an enormous underground cavern, then yes, I do,' Dan said.

'Wow, that's—that's breathtaking,' Soga declared, sitting forward. 'Guys, what we see before us is nothing less than a volcanic wind hole.' He glanced down at the tablet in his hand. 'And if I'm reading the coordinates correctly, Jiro Satsuma's right on the other side of that far wall directly opposite. I guess we took the shortcut and didn't even know it.' He called Kiriyama to update him as Amagi steered the Magma Riser into the cavern.

'Be careful,' Kiriyama told them. 'Tokuda says the original geological surveys showed no caverns or pockets at your current location.'

'I can't speak to that, Captain,' Amagi said as Soga held his wristcomm closer. 'But this isn't a new formation. How old are those surveys? Maybe that interference was masking it or distorting the readings somehow.'

'Just make sure you keep recording everything as you go. And don't dawdle. Kiriyama out.'

'Hey, Furuhashi, guess what?' Anne said brightly. 'It's not boring anymore.'

Everyone groaned again.

Not far from the Magma Riser, water had begun to drop into the tiny space where Jiro Satsuma watched the crew mascot alternately running around in his little cage and running on his exercise wheel. Jiro had no idea where the water was coming from but it was fresh and cold, and the mouse seemed to appreciate it as much as he did.

After some vague period of time, Jiro realized the dripping had increased almost to a stream. It was very gentle as yet, but now he had something new to worry about. The good news was, he and Chukichi were alive and well and, under the circumstances, still pretty comfortable. The bad news was, the small breeze he'd been feeling had died away.

Died was probably not the word he wanted to use.

He looked down at a small puddle by his feet. How long had that been there? As long as the breeze had been gone? *Think*, he ordered himself; *concentrate*. But it seemed his concentration was on a tea break.

The rattle of the wheel in the mouse cage made him smile in spite of everything. 'I'm glad you're feeling energetic, Chukichi,' he said. 'Enjoy yourself while you can. Drowning in a coalmine isn't a whole lot of laughs.'

Hearing his voice, the mouse stopped running on the wheel and poked its nose through the bars of the cage, wiggling its whiskers as it regarded him with bright black eyes.

Jiro couldn't help laughing. 'You're right, Chukichi—I *shouldn't* give up so easily. After all, I'm the Miracle Man, right?' He took a deep breath, let it out slowly. 'So, uh, if you can hear me, oh great forces of the universe or whoever's in charge, maybe you've got one more miracle you can spare me? And if you do, could you kinda sorta hurry it up, please? Give me just this one miracle and that's all I need. Just this one miracle and I'll never ask for another, I promise.'

And then, to his surprise, he was yawning, hugely, enormously, and for a moment he was strongly tempted to let himself doze off. Waiting for a miracle really took a lot out of a person; somehow he'd failed to notice how strenuous it was the first time around.

'Jiro Satsuma's air supply has been cut off,' said Kiriyama's voice in the ceiling speaker; he seemed to be speaking through steel wool. 'The engineers say something shifted and resettled, and now he's sealed in.'

'We didn't feel any movement where we are,' Amagi said. 'How much air does he have?'

'Between thirty and forty-five minutes,' Kiriyama said. 'And that's assuming he continues to breathe normally and doesn't have a panic attack. But the good news doesn't stop there. Air quality monitors show gases are starting to build up. Advise you get Satsuma and get the hell out within the next twenty-five minutes at most. Twenty would be better.'

'Copy that, Captain,' Amagi said. 'Flooring it now. Expect us back in time for the late-afternoon tea break, if good fortune's with us and the creek don't rise. Amagi out.'

The Magma Riser bumped along for another fifty feet or so before Amagi brought it to a halt at the opposite wall of the cavern.

'Soga, you said Jiro Satsuma's right on the other side here, right?' Amagi looked to Soga, who didn't look up from the tablet in his hands. 'How strong a blast will get us through without killing him?'

'Well…' Soga grimaced. 'I'm not getting the same readings as before. There's actually a barrier and a big gap between us and Satsuma.'

Amagi blew out a long breath. 'You mind explaining how you didn't see that before?'

'I don't know,' Soga said unhappily.

'Okay, let's take it one thing at a time,' Amagi said, and Dan could sense him forcing himself not to yell at the other man. 'What kind of barrier is it?'

Soga looked from Amagi to the cavern wall and back again. 'Mostly stone?'

Amagi lifted the plastic over on the dash, set the laser on low-medium strength, and fired. He produced a formidable cloud of dust but did no damage that anyone could see.

'Upping the strength,' Amagi said and fired again.

Shards of rock flew in every direction. The clouds of smoke and dust dissipated, revealing smooth, featureless metal underneath the stone.

'Upping the strength *again*,' Amagi announced defiantly and fired on the barrier for close to half a minute.

The metal wasn't even scorched.

'Damn,' Amagi declared, shifted into the reverse, and started to back up. A screen on Dan's side of the dashboard lit up with a video feed from an exterior camera at the rear, showing another metal barrier slamming down to cut them off.

Anne was on her wristcomm immediately. 'Anne calling Captain Kiriyama, please respond. Doc calling captain, respond.'

'Save your breath, Anne,' Soga said. 'Our comms are blocked, too.'

'I don't think we should hang around to see what's coming up next,' Dan said. 'Amagi, we're carrying bunker-busters, aren't we?'

'Yes, but…' Amagi's long face took on an apprehensive look. 'We could end up flattened under umpteen tons of rock. Or maybe the Magma Riser'll hold up, but that'll only mean we'll be mint condition when we run out of air.'

'Got it—we're sitting ducks,' Dan said unhappily. 'I really hate when that happens.' He unhooked his safety harness, got up, and went to a cabinet on the righthand side.

Now Amagi looked alarmed. 'Those are really just revamped concussion grenades. They're not incendiary but I'm not so sure we want to use them in a confined space where gas has been building up.'

Dan glanced over his shoulder at him as he tucked grenades into the front pocket of his uniform. 'You have a better idea?'

'I don't even have a worse one,' Amagi said with a humorless laugh. 'So whatever you've got in mind, go to it.'

'I'll come with you,' Soga offered, undoing his harness and going over to Dan.

'No, it's better if you stay here,' Dan told him. 'I can go faster if I only have myself to keep track of. I'll set the charges so the blast is directed outward, away from us. Just batten down the hatches and keep your helmets on. And maybe strap in, because there's gonna be a jolt.'

He started to leave and Anne caught his arm. 'Listen, just…' She floundered for a second. 'Don't die.'

Dan smiled at her. 'I won't if you won't.'

* * *

Anne's first thought as the blast shook the Magma Riser and the right side of the vehicle tilted down under a hail of dirt and rock was that it had come too quickly for Dan to have taken shelter. But she had to be wrong, she thought. Dan was too sharp to make himself a casualty. And if she kept telling herself that, maybe she would believe it.

She looked around at her teammates, who, like her, were listening to the sound of rocks and dirt falling on the Magma Riser's hull. Eventually it trailed off and stopped, although they all waited a bit longer, just in case.

A loud metallic click made her jump; it was only Furuhashi in the seat beside her, undoing his safety harness. He started to get up and she caught his arm.

'No sudden moves,' she told him. 'We don't know how stable we are.'

'We should be okay,' Amagi said, looking at the video feeds from the Magma Riser's exterior cameras. 'We're sort of wedged in. The right exit's blocked but we can get out on the left side. Assuming the door still works.'

Furuhashi had already made his way over to it. He tried the controls. The door slid open halfway, then stopped. 'I think everyone's skinny enough to squeeze through,' he said as he pried open a panel just above the doorway, revealing a compartment with a flexible ladder.

'Is that long enough so we don't have to jump?' Sofa asked, watching him unroll it so it hung out of the door.

Furuhashi leaned out to look. 'Not quite. But it's only about five feet from the end of the ladder to the ground. I'll go first and catch you guys as you come down.'

As if on cue, they heard the sound of more dirt and rocks coming down on the Magma Riser. *Maybe we should get out while we still can*, Anne thought, undoing her safety harness.

'Think there's more to come?' Sofa asked.

'Hard to say.' Furuhashi turned to Amagi. 'You're in command, what do you think?'

'I think we can't just sit here waiting for Dan to come back,' Amagi said, with an uncertain edge in his voice that made Anne even more uneasy.

'No, we sure can't,' Soga said, checking the dashboard. 'There's nothing showing but interference. I can't even find Dan's locator beacon.'

'You think they lost all our signals on the surface?' Furuhashi looked upward.

'They should still be picking up the Magma Riser's position if nothing else,' Amagi said, then turned to Anne. 'You're our comms expert. Is there any way to piggyback signals to communicate with everyone upstairs?'

Anne thought for a minute. 'Yes and no. As in yes, it's possible, but no, we don't have the right tools on board to do it.'

'I'll fix *that* when we get back to HQ,' Amagi said, and Anne could all but see him checking a box on a mental to-do list.

'Go to it with my blessing,' Furuhashi said. 'It's just the getting-back part that'll be tricky.'

'We should block the door so it stays open,' Soga said suddenly. 'If there's another tremor—or even if there isn't—it could snap shut on us.'

'Good thinking,' Amagi said, with a mix of admiration and surprise. He did something to the mechanism in the door itself using a tool from his belt.

'That really was a good idea,' Anne said to Soga. 'It never occurred to me.'

'Only because you haven't locked yourself out as many times as I have,' Soga said drily.

Amagi turned off climate control but left the fans on for ventilation, then paused to check the armory. 'We should take the rest of the grenades,' he said, pulling out a courier bag.

'You really think we'll need them?' Anne asked, her uneasiness going up another few notches.

'I have no idea,' Amagi said. 'But I'd rather have them and not need them—'

'—than need them and not have them,' she finished with him, nodding. 'Of all the things humans have invented, explosives are my least favorite, but you're right.'

Furuhashi took the courier bag of grenades, slung it across his back, and climbed down the ladder easily. 'So far, so good,' he called up to them. 'Let me take a quick look around before the rest of you come down.'

He picked his way through the broken chunks of rock around to the front of the Magma Riser, and then came stumbling back in a hurry. 'You guys have *gotta* see this!'

Anne knelt at the opening and leaned out to look around. 'Did you find Dan?'

Furuhashi shook his head. 'It's easier if you just come down.'

Amagi had Soga climb down next, followed by Anne, and finally himself.

'You feel that draft?' Furuhashi said when they were all together. 'I'll show you where it's coming from. Follow me.' He led them around the lopsided nose of the Magma Riser.

Anne gasped; the charges Dan had set had blown a ragged hole clear through the metal. For a moment, all she could see was soft light illuminating countless dust motes floating in the air. *Like a room that had remained closed and unoccupied for a very long time, months, maybe years*, she thought, *except this wasn't anywhere near that innocuous.*

'That's nothing,' Furuhashi assured her. He herded them all

right up to the hole and Anne's mind went blank. After some unmeasured time, she heard Soga say, 'Is that a city?'

'It's like a tech-head's idea of fairyland,' Furuhashi said.

Anne nodded, thinking that was exactly what it looked like—a fantasy world with tall cylindrical buildings in shimmering crystal, many of them topped with round platforms in soap-bubble colors. She couldn't tell where the soft, indirect light was coming from, if it was shining out of the crystal structures or shining on them from some place she couldn't see.

'It's like they designed a city where all the buildings are based on the Tokyo Skytree,' Soga said. 'You think those round things could be like umbrellas—shields against falling rocks?' He leaned a little farther into the hole. 'Hey, I think I see a way we can get—'

'Slow down, everybody,' Furuhashi said, his voice low and tense. 'That doesn't look like a city to me. It looks more like a power station.'

Anne felt her jaw drop. *Of course* it was a power station. Now that Furuhashi had said it, she couldn't see the arrangement of shining crystal shapes any other way. The cylinders were beautiful but not meant to shelter living things. Cities were meant to exist on the surface, under the sun; they weren't supposed to be hidden a thousand meters underground.

'Well, I suppose that would explain the complete absence of any inhabitants,' Soga said. 'But if it's a power station, what kind of power?'

'Geothermal,' Furuhashi said. 'Like, earthquakes.'

'That would be one way to get rid of indigenous lifeforms,' Amagi said thoughtfully. 'And leave the planet free for the taking. Ashes to ashes, dust to dust, and when the dust settles, they can just show up and make themselves at home.'

Everyone was silent for a long moment. Then Soga said, 'If the aliens aren't here yet, who built this?'

'Funny you should ask,' said Amagi, looking back toward the Magma Riser with his weapon up and ready. Anne turned to follow his gaze.

At first, she didn't know what she was seeing. The bulky metal figure was completely out of place—it seemed to have been cobbled together from spare or discarded parts. It had a box for a head but it looked like someone had glued half the contents of her mother's junk drawer to the front of it, dumped a lot of silver paint on it to make it shiny, then stuck on a couple of lights as an afterthought.

Its body was more symmetrical but no less messy. There was a frame on its chest containing what could have been spare clock parts, and a partial sketch of a boat or a large spacecraft made by a child who'd lost interest before finishing. The thick, unwieldy arms had two extra joints and ended in peculiar grappling tools that didn't resemble hands or even paws. She wouldn't have thought it could move without falling down if she hadn't been watching it lumber toward them on its chunky, angular feet.

Abruptly, the thing stopped as it drew even with a bit of stone jutting out from the cavern wall, raised one bulky arm, and slammed it down hard. The rock crumbled; it brought up its other hand and Anne saw the weapon.

Soga jumped in front of the group and fired, hitting the robot's center mass. To no effect—the robot shot Soga's sidearm out of his hand and continued stomping toward them. Amagi pushed Soga aside with a motion that seemed almost casual and fired his own weapon.

The robot stopped short as its square head was engulfed in a bright burst of loudly crackling energy. After a few seconds, the energy died away. Amagi prepared to fire again, but the robot didn't move except to lower its weapon before dropping to its knees and finally falling forward on its indecipherable face.

'I *really* didn't see that coming,' said Soga, rubbing his injured hand.

'They didn't see us coming, either,' Furuhashi said. 'I mean, they probably weren't expecting much resistance.' He picked up Soga's sidearm and gave it back to him.

After a quick examination of Soga's hand showed no serious injury, Anne turned back to gaze out at the crystal vista below them. 'Do you think Dan's down there?'

Amagi never hesitated. 'I'm sure of it. We can plant more charges while we search for him and then, after we find him—'

'We bring this whole place down,' Furuhashi said. 'Right?'

'But what if we can't find Dan?' Soga looked sick. 'I'm sorry, I didn't even want to *think* that. But… well, I did.'

Amagi shook his head. 'First we have to get down there and search.'

Furuhashi was leaning out of the hole to look at the stone wall. 'And I think I just found a way to do that.'

Getting down to the bottom of the alien installation turned out to be easier than anything else. A pathway had been carved into the stone itself; it was completely smooth, without steps, and meandered from side to side like a river.

'You think that's how the robot came to meet us?' Soga asked as they stood at the bottom catching their breath.

Amagi gave a single, humorless laugh. 'I'd look for a secret elevator first. These things don't seem like fast climbers.'

'Unless they fly,' Anne said before she could think better of it.

Now Amagi looked stricken. 'Oh my God, I hope not.' For a few moments, he gazed up at the towers with their strange circular tops aglow with soft, pulsing light. 'No, I'm pretty sure they don't,' he said after a bit. 'Otherwise, I think we'd have already seen them flying around.'

Furuhashi turned to him with a solemn expression. 'I'm

embarrassed to tell you how much I want you to be right about that. How many do you think there are?'

Amagi spread his hands. 'No idea. As many as they need to build and maintain a place like this. We're bound to meet some more now that we're down here. However, it looks like they operate individually, not in packs, so I don't think they'll swarm us or anything. Just remember—head shot, not center mass. It shorts them out.'

Anne could practically hear him add, *I hope*, silently.

Now that they were actually in the alien complex, it made Amagi think of an amusement park. He couldn't imagine why aliens would build an underground theme park on another planet, but who knew why aliens did anything?

As the group moved farther into the installation, however, he found himself thinking more of an escape room, albeit on a gargantuan scale. Perhaps the aliens were giants? No, he decided; giant aliens would have chosen a much larger planet. He filed the idea away for later examination.

He stopped in the middle of a narrow yellow lane to look at a wide, cylindrical structure. Next to it was a pile of crystal rods, piled up like lumber in a logging camp. Crystal lumber, with high-tech crystal lumberjack robots? It seemed like a silly idea.

Amagi moved closer to the pile of crystal rods. Each rod had tiny flakes of gold and silver in them. Alien gold-rush? Or alien amber? 'I can't tell what any of this stuff is for,' he said aloud.

'Because it's theirs,' Furuhashi said. 'The aliens', I mean. They know what to do with it, so they don't put any instructions on it.'

'And the robots would simply be programmed,' Amagi said, nodding.

'Hey, guys—I think I found the janitor's closet!' Soga called to them from farther along the yellow walkway. He was standing next to a low, asymmetrical structure with a chunky protrusion stuck onto it at shoulder height. He pressed his hand to it and a section of the wall swung inward.

Furuhashi was on him in a couple of strides, pulling him back from it as he drew his weapon. He peered inside, frowning. 'You want me to go in and check it out?' he asked Amagi.

Amagi shook his head. 'I said we don't split up and I mean it.' He looked around at the nearby structures. 'This is the first one of these we've found with a door. There must be more.'

'Do you want to look for them?' Anne asked, looking uneasy.

'If we had all the time in the world, sure,' Amagi said. 'But we don't and Dan's missing.' He turned to Soga. 'Sharpshooter goes first this time.'

'Headshot,' Soga said before he could go on. 'I remember.' He drew his sidearm and stepped inside. Amagi followed, with Anne behind him and Furuhashi bringing up the rear.

The group moved into a dimly lit passageway that became brighter as they went, although Amagi couldn't see where the light was coming from. Even with more light, however, there was something off about the passageway; something made it seem smaller than it was. Finally, as they moved around a corner, he realized it was because the space was wider at the bottom; the walls slanted inward. The passageway was shaped like a trapezoid. But the angle of the walls wasn't uniform—they widened and narrowed, seemingly at random.

He was about to say something about it as they rounded another corner but then Soga was shoving them all back, gesturing for them to be quiet. Then he went to peek around the corner. Amagi moved up beside him to see what was going on.

The robot in the hallway was plodding away from them. It wasn't any more graceful than the first one they'd seen, but somehow, it moved silently—no clanking, no clicking, no sound at all. Either the acoustics were crazy or the robots had noise dampeners that worked like magic.

Amagi drew back and tried to think, then took another look at the robot. It was much farther up the passageway than he'd expected, almost as if it had teleported. But who would teleport to go ten feet? With no one watching? The problem with aliens was they were aliens.

He turned back to say something to the others and saw what was coming up behind them silently, on its thick feet. Soga saw his face, whirled, and fired, hitting the robot's non-face on the first try. The robot toppled forward and hit the floor with a muted thump.

'Good shooting, Dead-Eye,' said Furuhashi.

'Where the hell did that come from?' Soga demanded. 'And how many more are there?'

'I don't know,' Amagi said, 'but I think this is a good time to start planting charges.' He nodded at Furuhashi, who shifted the courier bag around to his front and opened the flap.

'I brought a few incendiaries, too,' Furuhashi said, handing the charges out. 'We can plant them as we go. We can set them so they won't go off until they get a signal showing the Magma Riser is back on the surface. That should give us enough time to find Dan.'

Consciousness returned gradually, bringing with it the awareness that he was lying on his back on a hard, flat surface with something gripping his wrists and ankles too tightly. But it wasn't until Dan realized how warm he was that he opened his eyes.

He was clamped to a smooth round metal table in a room full of control panels and consoles. Somewhere out of his field of vision, he could hear the heavy clumping steps of a robot, doing whatever it was doing, leaving him to reflect on the inconvenient weaknesses of the human form he had adopted.

After setting the concussion charges, he'd taken cover behind the Magma Riser. The blast had been more forceful than he'd expected, but it hadn't brought everything down on him and his teammates still safely in the vehicle. When he had ventured out from behind the Magma Riser and seen the complex alien structures, he'd known immediately what he was looking at. He'd seen it before in the course of his mapping assignment. Earth scientists would have called it terraforming.

He wasn't sure what they'd have called the process of converting Earth's environment to support alien life. Exo-forming, maybe. Not that it mattered; he had to destroy this place before the aliens put the plan into motion. And he had to do it soon—the metal table was already too warm.

Dan flexed his arm and leg muscles one at a time, testing his restraints. The manacle on his right wrist was slightly looser than the others. Keeping his movements small, he twisted his arm back and forth, wincing when his fingers touched hot metal. If he didn't get out of this soon, he was going to fry like one of those cheeseburgers Furuhashi was so fond of.

The robot was still stumping around in the area near his head, apparently paying no attention to him. At any moment, he expected it to turn around and bring a thickset metal arm down on his face. But whatever it was doing kept it too busy to see him finally work his wrist free so he could reach into his jacket.

The Ultra Eye was gone.

Dan's heart skipped a beat and went into high gear. He looked around frantically. In his human body, he didn't stand a chance against even one of these robots. Were they programmed to recognize the Ultra Eye for what it was?

He stretched forth his awareness with extra care, sensed the utterly mechanical nature of the robot's guidance system, searched through its stored database of images and finally found a picture of his helmet on a small table. It took another few seconds to locate the table against the far wall, some fifteen feet away on his left. His gloves were there, too, dropped carelessly on top of what might have been a pair of sunglasses with red frames.

Keeping both his outer and inner gaze fixed on the Ultra Eye, he reached his freed hand toward it and stretched forth a different and deeper awareness, drawing on the sense-memory of the Ultra Eye in his hand. He held his concentration steady until he could feel its contours on his skin. Because it was there, right in the palm of his hand.

For a moment, he was so exhausted by the effort, he was tempted to let himself pass out. Then he slapped the Ultra Eye into place and the feeling was gone.

The transformation broke the rest of the manacles, allowing him to hop off the table just as the robot turned and fired on him. He ducked, moving quickly to position his arms—left arm horizontal to steady his other, upright arm. The Wide Shot flooded out of him in a blinding blast that enveloped the robot from head to toe; it dropped to the floor, motionless.

He waited a beat to see if anything else was going to come at him; there was nothing. He expanded his awareness and sensed the rest of the robots as vague presences here and there. His awareness deepened and he found his teammates, their lives shining brightly as they moved around searching for him. They were all right but they weren't the only ones he had to worry about.

It would have been so much easier if he'd been on the surface; then he'd have had daylight to boost his Ultra senses. He'd have been able to save his friends with one hand, grab up Jiro Satsuma (plus the mouse) with his other, and fly them all to safety.

Too bad; this was what he had and that would have to be enough.

After some unmeasured time, he sensed the tiniest human spark, faint but burning as bright as it could, along with another, much smaller one, about to flicker out.

He flew upward, across the shining crystal panorama, all the way back to the Magma Riser, to break through stone, earth, and water until he hit the now airless pocket where Jiro Satsuma lay unconscious, one hand resting protectively on a small metal cage with a mouse.

Dan gathered them up in his arms and flew them to the Magma Riser. As he lay Jiro Satsuma on a stretcher at the rear of the passenger compartment, he saw the mouse had awakened and was observing him with curious diamond-bright eyes.

'And you must be Chukichi,' he said as he took an oxygen cannula from a drawer marked *First Aid*. He plugged the other end of the tube into an outlet marked 02 and adjusted the flow. 'Pleased to make your acquaintance.' Once he was sure the man was breathing easily, he clasped his hands together and returned to his human appearance. The mouse watched this with calm interest.

'I'm Dan Moroboshi. You might notice there's a strong resemblance between me and your best friend.'

The mouse looked at Jiro Satsuma and twitched its whiskers as if it had understood every word. Dan laughed a little. 'Okay. You keep an eye on things here, I'll be back with the rest of the Ultra Guard and we'll get out of here. Sound good?'

The mouse's consciousness was a dimly lit tangle of instinct and memories. He was pretty sure it couldn't have known what he was saying but he thought it looked skeptical. Or maybe that was just the whiskers.

* * *

'What the hell is *that*?' said Furuhashi, staring at the round metal table in the middle of the room. It was smooth and unmarked except for four broken clamps.

Soga frowned, holding his hand a few inches above the surface. 'It's hot, like a grill. Or a giant frying pan.' He glanced at the strange consoles and control panels lining the walls around them. 'With a lot of temperature controls.'

'That all looks like communication hardware to me,' Anne said. 'What would robots do with a grill? And what kind of a grill has *manacles*?'

'The kind that serves man,' Amagi said grimly. 'Except these are broken. Dinner must have escaped. I'll give you three guesses as to what's not on the menu—excuse me, *who's* not on the menu.' He nudged the robot on the floor with his foot, then bent to turn it over.

'Don't!' Anne grabbed his arm and pulled him back. 'We already know they shoot first and don't ask questions later.'

'That one's not getting up.' Amagi rolled it onto its back and they all stared at the scorch marks running from the top of its boxy head to the center of its body. 'Definitely plant incendiaries here.'

'It'll probably bring the whole mine down,' Anne said.

'Good,' said Soga with a vehemence that surprised her. 'No more mine, no more cave, and no more free meals for aliens.'

'We don't know what this place is really for,' Amagi said. 'But we should destroy it anyway, before it caves in by itself and traps more people underground.'

They planted a few incendiaries and turned to leave just as another robot appeared in the open doorway. Before any of them could raise their weapons, the robot's entire body was enveloped in crackling energy. Unable to move, Anne could only gape as it shuddered, then fell forward, revealing a more pleasing sight behind it.

'Everybody all right?' Dan asked cheerfully, as if he'd just disposed of a minor but annoying problem.

'I guess we are,' Amagi said, grinning broadly

'Good,' Dan replied. 'Because I want us out of here five minutes ago.'

Since there was no way to explain how Jiro Satsuma and his mouse had come to be in the Magma Riser, Dan decided not to try.

'I came back looking for you guys and I found him here, just like this,' he told his flabbergasted teammates.

Anne immediately became Dr. Yuri, kneeling beside the stretcher to take the man's vitals. 'Good, strong heartbeat,' she told them, looking pleased. 'I think his little friend is doing well, too.' She poked a finger through the cage to pet the mouse.

'Could he have gotten here on his own? Escaped from wherever he was trapped and found the Magma Riser?' Soga asked. 'We *did* leave the door open.'

'It's possible,' Anne replied, making sure the stretcher was properly secured for the trip back to the surface. 'But I doubt he'd have known where to find the oxygen or how to adjust the flow.'

Dan chuckled. 'Maybe he's a lot smarter than we thought. Or maybe he had help from someone who didn't have time to stick around.'

'You really think Ultraseven blew through here without stopping to say hello?' Furuhashi asked.

'I think that's more likely than Jiro Satsuma finding the Magma Riser on his own,' Dan said as he took the copilot's seat next to Amagi. 'On the other hand, he *is* known as the Miracle Man, so who knows?'

'Let's wake him and ask him to miracle a way out of here for us,' Furuhashi suggested.

'No need,' Amagi said, looking at his control panel. 'Someone accessed navigation and laid in a course for us.'

'Ultraseven,' said Anne, Soga, and Furuhashi in perfect unison.

Amagi started the Magma Riser's engine with an amused smile. 'Just make sure you're all belted in securely because it's going to be a bumpy ride home. Ready? Heading is twelve o'clock straight up, in three… two…'

The journey straight up was shorter than the journey down had been, thanks to the new route. Once they reached the level-off point, the going became a bit rougher; after ten minutes of what Amagi called 'white-water driving', they burst out of a hillside half a kilometer from their original entry point.

'I'd have sworn we were farther from where we went in,' Soga said, looking out the window and blinking in the daylight.

'We've got a welcoming committee,' Amagi told them as they approached the cheering miners waiting for them in the middle of the camp. He brought the Magma Riser to a stop and the group spontaneously ran toward them.

As Soga and Furuhashi were about to carry Jiro Satsuma and his mouse out of the vehicle, Dan folded a soft towel and laid it over the man's eyes. 'Because he's been underground for so long,' he said in response to their curious looks. 'He'll need time for his eyes to adjust.'

Anne gave him an approving nod, then guided Furuhashi and Soga out of the Magma Riser. Dan hung back, watching as the miners crowded around the Miracle Man.

'So, what do *you* think that was down there?'

Dan turned to find Amagi beside him, watching the impromptu celebration. 'Pardon?'

'Do you think we found an underground city or a power station?' Amagi asked in a chatty tone, as if he really were just making conversation and there wasn't a deeper question in his mind.

'Could've been both,' Dan said. 'Or it could have been something else entirely.'

There was a vibration in the ground below his feet, faint at first, then growing more powerful, followed by a deep, barely audible sound like very distant thunder.

'Whatever it was,' Amagi said, 'it is no longer.' He looked down at the ground. 'You know, I didn't really like the idea of blowing it up. I wish we could have studied it.' He took a breath, let it out. 'At the same time, I've got a strong feeling we did the right thing. I'm going to tell Kiriyama we should contact other branches of the TDF. We don't know how many other installations may still exist. Or where.'

Dan found himself at a loss for words. He couldn't tell Amagi anything, couldn't even speculate. Introducing information that no one on Earth could possibly know would be existential tampering, which was an offence against all intelligent life, not just humans.

'I guess we'll never know,' Amagi added.

Dan looked at him blankly. 'What?'

'What the aliens were doing,' Amagi clarified. 'Whether they were going to kill us off with earthquakes or not.' He frowned. 'If they were, they'd take possession of rubble and wreckage and nothing else. What would be the point?'

'Amagi,' Dan said. 'They're *aliens*.'

The other man nodded as they wandered over to the group around the stretcher. Jiro Satsuma had regained consciousness and was sitting up, holding the mouse cage in one hand and keeping the towel over his eyes with the other as he and the rest of the miners talked excitedly. Anne kept trying to make him lie down again so they could carry him into the infirmary, and finally got her way by confiscating the mouse cage.

'You're right, Dan,' Amagi said. 'Who knows why aliens do anything? Alien reasoning is an enigma wrapped in a mystery wrapped in the square root of an imaginary number. Miracles, on the other hand—those are easy.'

'Of course they are,' Dan said, thinking of how absolutely no one had noticed any resemblance between himself and Jiro Satsuma. 'Miracles are just that—miraculous.'

Amagi sighed. 'Well, you're not wrong.'

'And some days,' Dan chuckled, 'not being wrong is just right enough.'

CHAPTER

SIX

Fatigue hit Dan the moment they returned to HQ.

He managed to stay all of fifteen minutes at the impromptu celebration for the six of them in Kiriyama's office. Fortunately, Amagi got a phone call about a project he was working on with the lab; it gave Dan an opening to make his excuses and head for his quarters. The disappointed expression on Anne's face made him want to stay but he felt too close to actual collapse.

Kiriyama made it easier by giving everyone the next few days off. Dan had it in mind to ask Anne if she'd care to spend at least some of that time with him. And because there was so much about life on Earth that was utterly predictable, he could imagine how the sequence would go: he would make the suggestion to her politely, she would agree. From there, things were less predictable, but the variations were limited to a narrow range of possibilities, which were themselves predictable and, as he was learning, predictable could be something to look forward to.

Of course, life on Earth wasn't *always* predictable.

'Anne? She's gone to the beach,' Soga told him when Dan asked if he'd seen her. 'She's got an old friend living in Iritahama, in Izu, and it's her birthday.'

Dan thanked him for the information. He had sensed her absence from the base but hadn't realized she'd planned to stay away for a few days. Well, why not? Humans got tired too, he knew that, although he wondered if any of them ever felt as weighed down as he did.

For once, Dan Moroboshi was the farthest thing from Anne's mind. All her attention was on her friend Ruriko, who was enduring what had to be the most off-key rendition of 'Happy Birthday' since last year's party. All the partygoers finished murdering the last line and Ruriko blushed as they broke into applause.

As Ruriko went about blowing out the candles on her fancy three-tiered cake, Anne noted there were some new faces among the people crowded into the townhouse. That was Ruriko—she made friends everywhere she went. People were drawn to her kind and friendly nature. Next year, they'd probably have to hire a banquet hall.

Finished with the candles, Ruriko blushed again as everyone applauded. But she left the cake-cutting and serving to someone else, instead grabbing Anne's hand and leading her to a quieter spot near the patio door.

'I feel like I haven't seen you in forever,' she said to Anne. 'The Ultra Guard keeps you busier than you were in med school. Please tell me you're happy.'

'Oh, I am,' Anne assured her. 'I get to practice medicine and have exciting adventures.' She gave her friend a quick summary of finding an alien installation underground and how Ultraseven had come to their rescue.

'Wow,' said Ruriko. 'I thought you'd be too busy for anything, what with having three hundred patients.'

Anne laughed. 'Well, I'm not the only doctor on the base—'

'Just the best one,' Ruriko said, glancing toward the patio. Somewhere nearby, a dog was barking furiously.

'I've got something for you,' Anne said, laughing some more. Her eyes twinkled as she handed the other woman a small bag containing a small puffy cloud of pink tissue paper.

'Oh! You didn't have to!' Ruriko said, holding up the bag to admire it. 'It's almost too pretty to unwrap!'

'It's too pretty not to,' Anne said, watching her as she found her way through the tissue paper to the red velvet box inside.

'Oh, Anne, you *didn't*—'

Anne beamed as Ruriko opened the box and saw the brooch inside.

'It's lovely!' Ruriko sat forward to hug her. 'Just like you!'

'Put it on,' Anne urged her. 'It'll look great with your dress.'

Ruriko took it out of the box and held it up to the light; the vintage rhinestones sparkled like stars. 'It looks like a comet. Or a falling star with streamers.' She pinned it to her left shoulder. 'Is it straight?'

Anne was about to say something to the effect of comets not needing to be straight when she realized the barking dog outside had become louder and more frantic.

'That dog is really upset he wasn't invited,' she said. 'Maybe we should bring him a piece of cake?'

'Oh, that's just my neighbor's dog, John,' Ruriko said, still admiring her comet. 'He's probably telling off a cat that dared to cut across his yard.'

Anne gave a short, incredulous laugh. 'You neighbor named his dog *John*?'

'I don't judge,' Ruriko said.

Anne was about to say something else when the dog's barking cut off sharply. She waited for it to resume but it didn't. 'Dogs don't usually do that, do they?' she asked after a few seconds.

'No, they don't,' Ruriko said, looking concerned now. 'I'm going to check on him.'

'I'll come with you,' Anne said.

They slipped out the patio door without anyone noticing.

Hunger. So much hunger, insistent, relentless. It would not stop.

The journey to this remote rock on the outskirts of the galaxy had depleted its supplies, leaving it with nothing. But the signal from the Initiator had promised that all Braco with the strength of will to make the trip would find a world of unending plenty.

It had expected that on its arrival, there would be a magnificent banquet that stretched as far as the eye could see in every direction. But as it had followed the signal into the largest body of water, it had seen the dominant indigenous lifeforms going about their pursuits as if they still mattered. As if they'd been created to do something other than provide sustenance to superior beings like the Braco.

The Initiator explained the situation in a dispatch: yes, there was a plethora of fresh consumables but they were as yet unprocessed. Mass processing could not begin until there was an adequate number of Braco on the planet to impose the necessary order and conditions.

This wasn't simply a matter of rounding up food providers so they could be cleaned and cultivated. They had to find the best breeding stock. Breeding itself was the easy part—the stock could breed themselves without even having to leave their pens. It listened, showing appropriate respect as the Initiator outlined what sounded like food paradise, although it had some misgivings.

An unending supply of food would be wonderful. But on the outskirts of the galaxy, so far from the Braco homeworlds? It seemed inefficient. The Braco diet was, after all, unique; no other lifeforms in the galaxy consumed food this way, so why cultivate it on such a remote planet?

'There was an incident,' the Initiator told it in private, one-to-one communication. 'A Braco spacecraft was seized and its food supply confiscated as misbegotten.'

'By whom?' it had asked, shocked.

'You know by whom,' the Initiator replied. 'By those known as the Beings of Light.'

'They police us now?' it said, dismayed. 'They can dictate what we consume and deny us food?'

The Initiator went into an explanation about how conscious intelligent lifeforms, no matter how primitive or backward, were now and forever off-limits for use as tools, beasts of burden, or nutrition, but it was too hungry to pay attention. It had crossed the galaxy on a mission for its homeworld but the mission had fallen apart, leaving it farther from home than it had ever been with its resources almost gone. This had been the only suitable world it could reach with its depleted fuel supply. It had followed the Initiator's beacon, expecting to share food and assuage its homesickness and loneliness before attempting the long trip home.

Instead, it had found two dozen spacecraft huddled together at the bottom of an ocean while the Braco whispered to each other about what they would do when there were enough of them. By the time the Initiator had concluded the conversation, it couldn't decide whether it was furious or traumatized. Then the relentless hunger, briefly forgotten in the face of the Initiator's preposterous plan, reasserted itself with new intensity and it had no choice but to act.

According to custom, the Initiator, as the first to arrive on a planet, would determine how food and other resources would be obtained and distributed. Challenging the Initiator's authority was taboo in the extreme. Its choices were limited: it could accede to the established order, or it could leave. Leaving was impossible; it could not bear one more moment of hunger.

It reviewed the Initiator's declaration and discovered the Initiator's rules had no order, explicit or implied, that forbade individual action.

None of the other Braco noticed when it detached its vessel from the group formation underwater and rose to ride the incoming tide to the local landmass. It was the time of darkness, the time the Initiator said the local lifeforms called *night*, which they designated as the time for rest. But the lifeforms didn't rest right away—they defied the onset of dark with artificial light, and there was still plenty of activity among both the growth medium and the breeding stock. This might have given the new arrival pause had it not been crazed with hunger.

When it reached the shallower water near the land, it left its vessel for the first time since its departure from home and made its way through the massively impure saline mix to the shore. There it found a collection of repositories voluntarily occupied by the dominant animalia. Each repository—receptacle? Reticule? Storage pen?—held various numbers of the creatures. Some had only one or two, while others contained four or even more.

Then, in a subsection of the organized storage, it found a receptacle containing over a dozen of the creatures. Half were suitable for cultivation; the others were strictly breeders. It was considering how to approach when it encountered something unexpected.

Noise! Noise, noise, *noise! NOISE!*

The sound wasn't completely unfamiliar, but it had never heard it produced by such a small organism. Also harmless, it discovered, since the creature was restrained. But it continued with its noise, apparently feeling obligated to be as loud as possible.

Because, it realized with dismay, the creature had detected its presence. This was its way of announcing that to all within range.

None of the lifeforms seemed disturbed, but then, they didn't speak the little creature's noise—they didn't know what it was telling them. Still, such discordance attacking the air was objectionable. Annoyed, it found the noisy creature and made it stop.

Moments later, two of the cultivatable stock left the crowded container, calling out for *djahn*, or maybe *zhon*. The noisy beast, it realized; they were searching for it. Why? Were they hungry, too? It didn't care, the cultivatables were within reach...

And then it discovered neither of the organisms could produce food as is. They were *almost* ready, but they had to be processed first.

The two pre-comestibles found the scrap it had excised from the noisy beast. Their vocalizations indicated disquietude. Then, to its surprise, the pair parted ways, going in opposite directions.

Whether they were observing a custom, a law, or an individual indulgence didn't matter. It followed one into an area of deeper darkness.

Ruriko bent to pick something up—a broken dog collar attached to a chain.

'This is John's.' Ruriko's eyes filled with tears. 'Something's happened to him.'

'Maybe he just broke out of it somehow,' Anne said, wincing; that sounded lame even to her. This was going to ruin Ruriko's birthday. 'Listen, you look around here in case John comes back—dogs always come back to their territory.'

'I thought I'd look over by the shed for him,' Ruriko said. She pointed at a small structure a few meters away.

'I'm going to look around front,' Anne said. 'Why don't you wait for me, and we'll look in the shed together?'

'Okay,' Ruriko said. 'I'll be right here.'

But she wasn't.

* * *

The Initiator was a fool, it decided as it approached the animal. There was no reason to delay processing these creatures. Had the Initiator forgotten what short lifespans they had?

As expected, the creature panicked at the sight of a being so much more advanced than itself. It had to render the creature unconscious before it could make any loud noises, then carried it back to its vessel, stripping off a couple of annoying attachments from the body—shiny stones. Of all things! Were these creatures descended from *birds*?

It wasn't like Ruriko to go off on her own in the dark, Anne thought, looking around. Maybe John the dog had come back and she was chasing him. No, she'd have heard Ruriko calling him.

For the thousandth time, or maybe the millionth, she wondered what kind of person would name a dog *John*.

An awful feeling of creepiness suddenly swept over her again, stronger than before, making her want to run as far away as she could, as fast as she could. After three years with the Ultra Guard, she was too well-trained and disciplined to give in to that urge. She just hoped the feeling didn't get any more intense or she might not be able to help herself.

The triumph of civilization is intellect tempered with emotion, not ruled by it. The memory of her old history professor's words made her feel steadier even if it didn't relieve her uneasiness.

'Ruriko? Ruriko?' Anne took a step toward the beach and felt something strange under one foot. She pulled her penlight from the inside of her boot. In the tight round beam of the torch, she saw a pair of high heels, black silk, with red roses embroidered on the toes.

Something cold and hard started to gather in the pit of Anne's stomach. She shined the penlight on the ground around herself, spotted what she thought might be a footprint. A closer look, however, told Anne the impression in the dirt hadn't been made by any foot, paw, claw, or hoof that she knew of.

She looked around for another and found it a meter away, along with a little something extra. It was a small thing, almost completely covered with dirt and sand but the tiny glint had caught her eye. Even before she picked it up, she knew it was the pin she had given Ruriko.

The disquiet she had felt before returned even more strongly. She looked up from the pin in time to see a large round *something* sinking below the waves in the moonlight.

'Dr. Anne Yuri calling Headquarters, please respond!'

The transmission wasn't all that loud but everyone in Communications went quiet as soon as they heard Anne's voice.

Kiriyama picked up immediately. 'What's wrong, Anne?'

'Everything,' Anne replied. 'My friend Ruriko is missing and there's something in the water here, near the beach. It's big, and *dangerous*. And *wrong*.'

'We're on our way,' Kiriyama promised.

By the time the other five members of the Ultra Guard arrived in the Pointer, Anne had briefed them on what had happened. She met them at the front door and led them around to the back. Through the patio door, Dan could see the party had become a rather somber gathering. Clearly none of them had had anything to do with Ruriko's disappearance (or the dog with the peculiar name) but they had to let the procedures unfold in the usual way.

Anne was giving Kiriyama an account of what the object in the water looked like and how far it had been from shore when Furuhashi grabbed Dan's arm and pulled him off to one side.

'I found the dog,' he said in a low voice. 'It was either dropped from a great height or something slammed it down on the ground with incredible force.' Pause. 'Don't tell Anne. Not yet, anyway.'

Dan frowned. 'That must have been, uh, messy. You didn't find any trace of another, bigger mess, did you? The size of a human?'

'No, there's no sign that Anne's friend got the same treatment,' Furuhashi said. 'But all that means is—'

'We didn't find her,' Dan finished for him. He turned his flashlight on Soga, who was kneeling beside one of the bizarre tracks Anne had showed them.

'These tracks go straight down the beach into the water,' Soga said, standing up. 'The tide's still coming in so we'll lose most of them, but I took plenty of pictures."

'Good thinking,' Dan said absently, looking over his shoulder at Anne, still talking to Kiriyama.

He couldn't help marveling at her; she was one of the most complex individuals he had ever encountered. All humans were complex—it was their lot as beings who were far removed both literally and figuratively from the endless glow of enlightenment but still felt its pull. Anne in particular was pulled in so many different ways—doctor, protector, friend, daughter, sister—but all ultimately toward illumination.

Kiriyama materialized beside Dan and Soga. 'I've asked Anne and Amagi to finish taking witness statements from the partygoers,' he said. 'I'd like to have a look at the area where Anne saw the saucer or whatever it was submerge.'

The four of them got into the Pointer with Furuhashi in the driver's seat. He started the Pointer and headed straight for the waves rolling in on the beach. 'I love this part,' he said, shifting with one hand while he pulled back slightly on the steering wheel.

Dan felt the Pointer's tires leave the ground as the vehicle rose a meter into the air over the still incoming tide, and couldn't help giving a surprised laugh.

'I knew the Pointer could do this,' he said as everyone else looked at him. 'I just didn't know how it felt.'

'Experience is always so much more,' Soga agreed.

Kiriyama slid open a panel on the dashboard to reveal a small screen. It lit up with a quick shot of dark water sliding past beneath them, then changed to a very blue picture of the shallow bottom.

'Hey, look—there's my watch!' Furuhashi said as a chunky round clockface went by. 'And it's still running!'

'It is?' Soga said, incredulous.

'You're *way* too easy,' Furuhashi told him.

'What are you looking for, Captain?' Dan asked, talking over them.

'I'll know it when I see it,' Kiriyama said shortly, and Dan could sense how his frustration was mixing with anxiety and worry for Anne, and not only because the missing woman was a friend of hers. The captain had Furuhashi fly back and forth over the area where Anne had seen something submerge, while he eyed the monitor and peered out the window. 'But I guess I won't be seeing it tonight,' he added with a sigh. 'Take us back to HQ. On the road.'

Dan looked back at the water glittering under the moon. Anne had indeed felt something wrong; he could feel it, too. Anything strong enough for humans to sense was very wrong indeed.

Happy Birthday, dear Ruriko, Happy Birthday to you!

Ruriko smiled to herself. Her friends were just the *best*. Every year they had a party for her birthday, and it was always so much fun. This year, she had decided to have them all come to her new place in Iritahama to thank them for being such good friends with a day at the beach. Then it turned out that the tide was out for most of the day, but nobody seemed to mind, which made her doubly glad that she'd baked her special mini-cheesecakes as a surprise. In fact, it was probably time to get them out of the refrigerator before people started leaving. They'd probably have to take them home because everyone would be full from all the birthday cake.

So why wasn't she moving? She had to get up and ask Anne to help her with the trays. Where *was* Anne?

Where was *she*?

She was sitting, she knew that much, but something was off. It felt like she was sitting on the floor, except it wasn't carpeted, so it couldn't be *her* floor. And now she realized she didn't hear any of her friends talking and laughing, even though she'd been listening to them all night. When had it gone so quiet?

Had everyone left already? Or had she left them?

But why would she leave? To go where, do what?

Get up and go back to your friends, she told herself; nothing happened. She tried to concentrate and for a little while—a minute? An hour?—she sort of drifted off. After a bit, she became aware of her arms, positioned so her hands rested side by side on her legs, which were demurely tucked beneath her; what her mother called the proper technique for sitting on the floor in a dress.

Something brushed against her arm.

Get it off, get it off! she screamed soundlessly, trying to recoil from the contact. But she still couldn't move, couldn't make a sound.

'These were found in a sheep pasture in the Swiss Alps,' said Professor Takenada as the largest screen in the briefing room lit up with an exact duplicate of the weird tracks the Ultra Guard had found on the beach.

The scene changed to show the same tracks on a more hard-packed surface. 'This is from a cattle ranch in Montana in the US, near the Canadian border,' Takenada told them. He was a plump, older man with an unruly head of silver hair, glasses that seemed impossibly thick, and a deep rumbling voice. A longtime friend and colleague of Professor Kitamura's, his specialty was unusual diseases in exotic animals, which was why the professor had consulted him.

The picture onscreen changed again to a silicone cast of the track. 'And this was made from a print found in Hwange National Park in Zimbabwe.'

'And we're only just now hearing about this?' Kiriyama asked tensely.

'Authorities at each location thought the prints might be fakes, made by pranksters or poachers involved in smuggling exotic animals.'

'Do they find a lot of exotic animals on American cattle ranches?' said Soga.

'In general, no,' Takenada said with a hint of amusement in his voice. 'But officials do find a lot of contraband in transit near international borders.'

'Ah.' Soga nodded. 'We don't share a lot of borders.'

'True,' Takenada said. 'And perhaps cattle is exotic to those unfamiliar with it. As with the other locations, one animal was stolen from the ranch where the print was found.'

'Only one of each?' said Furuhashi. 'That's one really lousy poacher. Everyone knows if you're going to breed your own, you have to start with at least two. Of the same species.'

'Not if they just plan to clone them,' Soga pointed out.

'These are just the ones we know about,' Takenada said. 'And only because the prints were found before they disappeared.'

'But they didn't take an animal this time,' Dan said. 'This time they took a person.' Dan's words seemed to hang in the air ominously. Then Kiriyama's wristcomm chimed with an incoming call, giving them all a start.

It was Amagi, calling to say that they had found Ruriko on the beach just above the high-water mark. She was alive but unconscious.

Dan arrived to find Anne, Amagi, and most of the party guests gathered around Ruriko's still form.

'She looks like she just decided to lie down and sleep here,' Anne said, kneeling beside her friend. She brushed a few loose hairs back from Ruriko's face, laid one hand over her forehead, checked her pulse. 'Except I haven't seen any signs of REM sleep and I haven't been able to wake her. She hasn't stirred even the slightest bit. But her heartbeat is strong and steady.'

'We'd better get her to HQ asap,' Amagi said. His expression was so serious, Dan had an urge to comfort him.

Instead, he knelt beside Anne. As his shadow fell across Ruriko's face in the pale light of the new day, her eyes opened.

'Ruriko! I'm so glad you're awake!' Anne grabbed her hand and held it in both of hers. 'Say something!'

Dan put a gentle hand on Anne's shoulder. Ruriko's eyes had opened slowly, without fluttering; she hadn't looked around or tried to get up. Anne turned to him with a fearful expression and he wished he could tell her everything—who he was, where he'd come from, why he was here. But right now, all she wanted to know was what was wrong with Ruriko and how to help her.

'Hello, Ruriko.' Dan put his hand on her forehead and immediately withdrew it. Instead of the usual jumble of thoughts, vague notions, pictures, and memories, he felt only an absence that was gradually becoming more pronounced. Ruriko hadn't disappeared completely, but she was fading and there was no time to waste.

'Dan.' Amagi pointed at something on the woman's arm.

The shapeless, dark green blotch wasn't very large; it could have been a piece of seaweed or other flotsam she'd picked up after a swim, except there was no brushing it off. Dan took a closer look in the beam of his flashlight. It was raised, with a rougher texture than the surrounding skin, and it was growing—too slowly for humans to perceive right now but it would pick up momentum the same way she was disappearing.

'She didn't have that yesterday,' said one of the party guests.

Dan looked to Anne, who nodded. 'I've never seen anything like that on her arms or legs. We need to get her back to HQ for tests,' she said briskly. Dr Yuri was in charge now, the calm professional who oversaw the health and wellbeing of three hundred souls when she wasn't out on a mission with the Ultra Guard. She leaned toward Dan and lowered her voice to a near-whisper. 'I've never seen anything like that on anyone. We need to bring everyone else in and put them in quarantine. That includes us.'

The TDF sent out a mobile medical unit for the party guests; Amagi waited with them while Dan headed back to HQ with Anne and Ruriko. Anne's composure belied how worried she really was—her anxiety seemed to fill every empty space in the Pointer, making Dan wish he could simply teleport them all to HQ. But teleportation was one more thing they didn't have on Earth.

Professor Kitamura, the exotic disease specialist, was prepared for their arrival. He insisted on doing the biopsy on Ruriko personally while Anne supervised. Half an hour later, he gave everyone else a clean bill of health and released them from quarantine. Ruriko remained in isolation.

'Just in case whatever's attached itself to the young lady still has some surprises for us,' he told the Ultra Guard at a meeting in his office. 'Although whatever she has doesn't seem to be communicable and she shows no sign of disease or physical impairment. If anything, her health has improved and continues to do so.'

Sitting in front of Kitamura's desk, Anne looked baffled. 'But she's catatonic. I don't understand.'

'I don't either, Dr. Yuri,' said the professor. 'Right now, your friend has the strongest immune system I've ever seen. If it gets any better, she'll be bulletproof.'

'Because of that thing on her arm?' asked Soga. 'How?'

Kitamura's expression turned mildly apologetic. 'I'm afraid I haven't figured that out yet. I'm certain there are nano-mechanisms involved but they're extremely elusive. If it's all right with you, Dr. Yuri, I want to have some equipment brought over from the lab at Public Health.'

'Of course,' Anne said. 'We don't have a lot of call for nanotech here—it's mostly sprains, fractures, and the occasional case of man-flu.'

'Oh, come *on*,' said Furuhashi. 'I really *was* sick—I had a temperature of *thirty-eight point nine*!'

'I didn't mean *you*.' Anne looked around, caught Dan's eye, and mouthed, *Man-flu.*

'Well, obviously this isn't, er, man-flu,' Kitamura said. 'Or any other kind. She's sedated—what we call a chemical cosh, and a very effective one. It's keeping her subdued by blocking or neutralizing her brain's response to stimuli.' Kitamura's troubled expression deepened. 'A CT scan showed no permanent changes in her brain as yet. But if she stays like this for too long—'

'Then she'll stay like this for good,' Anne finished for him. 'So how do we get rid of that thing on her arm?'

Kitamura shook his head. 'We can't. Whatever it is, it's connected to her autonomic nervous system in a way that I haven't figured out yet. But when I tried to take a sample of it to biopsy, her heart went into fibrillation. She's all right now,' he added quickly in response to Anne's alarmed expression. 'Her heart is very healthy and strong, just like the rest of her. At least for the time being.'

'For the time being,' Anne echoed. 'However long that is.'

Kiriyama sent Furuhashi, Soga, and Amagi out in the Ultra Hawk 1 to explore Iritahama while Dan stayed at HQ to scan for possible alien signals. Anne wondered how Dan felt about having to stay behind. She'd never liked it herself, but for once she felt torn between wanting to be out doing something and staying with her patient. As for Dan, she was sure he'd be fine. He was always fine; things always seemed to work out that way for him.

Meanwhile, the professor's equipment had arrived, which meant rearranging a lot of things to make room. It was just temporary and the nursing staff had been willing to do all the heavy lifting or tedious jobs, but she had banished them all on the grounds that she had to place everything herself or she'd never be able to find anything. In truth, being alone meant she could check on Ruriko whenever she liked. Or rather, needed to.

It wasn't lost on her that she was doing the opposite of what she would have advised for someone else in the same situation. But it wasn't like she was trying to do everything alone, she told herself. In the middle of HQ, help was only a call or a shout away. She was keeping things organized.

As she was trying to decide what to do with a stack of trays, she heard Ruriko moan. It was the first time Ruriko had made any sound at all, and Anne was glad she'd stayed close; otherwise, she might have missed it. She pulled the privacy curtain aside and found that her friend had somehow managed to pull the sheet up over her face. If she was also moving now, that had to be a good sign. *Please, let it be a good sign*, Anne prayed.

'Hey, girlfriend, are you all the way awake now?' she asked, forcing a light tone into her voice.

Ruriko moaned again, this time as if she was in pain. Alarmed, Anne pulled the sheet down and let out a shocked cry. Ruriko's skin had turned a bright, bilious green.

There was a noise behind her. Help really was just a shout or a shocked cry away and Dan was nearby, she thought as she turned around.

But it wasn't Dan coming to help her. Not even close.

Dan had just left Kiriyama in the strategy room when he heard Anne cry out. He sprinted down the hall to the sick bay, burst through the entrance to Isolation, and found Anne face down amid a scatter of towels, gauze pads, and bottles of hand sanitizer.

In the same moment, the feeling of the alien's presence buffeted his awareness like a sudden gust of wind. He whirled and saw it in the corner beside Ruriko's bed, glaring at him with green eyes that bulged out of its misshapen, lumpy body. The thing moved from side to side on thick hind legs, waving two appendages resembling sharp knives at him.

It was making a trilling noise but not as an attempt to communicate; the pitch and tempo told Dan it was a show of hostility. And not *just* for show—it suddenly unfurled two muscular upper limbs ending in three-fingered hands that made rather impressive fists.

The alien wasn't merely hostile, Dan realized—it was enraged. For a few moments, that was all his Ultra awareness could pick up, rage, and underneath that a terrible need—no, a hunger, so intense it had turned to pain. Because they'd brought Ruriko here; because they'd touched her; because they were acting like she was more than a growth medium for food: the alien took these as offensive actions.

Dan turned to see if Ruriko was all right and saw that her skin had turned the same awful green as the alien's eyes.

It waved its fists threateningly and Dan knew it had used them on Anne. He launched himself at the alien, discovering as he drove it back against the wall that the lumpy body was harder than it appeared. Not to mention stronger; he sensed the creature's expertise as it grappled with him, forcing him backward across the room. Trilling more loudly, it twisted one hand out of his grip and tried to grab his neck.

Dan grabbed the limb again but the alien shoved him down to his knees. He pushed upward with all his strength; the alien's hand slipped into place around his neck and began to squeeze.

Brown patches appeared in his vision. *Anne!* he thought, pulling at the alien's arm. But Anne couldn't hear him, he was too far away and getting more distant all the time. The sound of the standard-issue Ultra Guard sidearm was barely audible.

The echoes, however, were loud enough to clear the brown patches in his vision. Then Kiriyama was helping him up, asking if he was all right.

'I'm fine, Captain, just foolish not to call for backup. I heard Anne shout and—' Dan looked around.

'And you charged in like you were Ultraseven,' Kiriyama said.

Dan ignored him, spotted a nurse kneeling beside Anne, and automatically tried to go to her, but Kiriyama held him back.

'Wait,' said the captain. 'Look.'

Anne was turning the same poison green as Ruriko, but in stages, the color becoming progressively darker at different rates on different areas of her body. Dan looked around for the alien, saw it on the floor in an ungainly heap.

'I wasn't really trying to kill it,' Kiriyama said. 'But I wasn't trying not to, either.' The captain looked from it to Anne to Ruriko, and finally to Dan. 'Maybe now that we have the actual alien, Professor

Kitamura will be able to tell us something useful. Starting with whether it's really dead.'

'It *looks* dead,' said the nurse with Anne.

'It's an alien,' Kiriyama said. 'All bets are off.'

'You're not going to like this,' said the professor's voice on the speaker. There was rustling in the background as he removed his hazmat suit.

Out in the waiting room, Kiriyama gave a short laugh. 'At least we're consistent.' He glanced at Dan sitting beside him on the couch.

Now that Anne had been infected, Professor Kitamura had reinstituted quarantine protocols. The birthday party guests were confined to the base so they could be kept under observation and tested hourly, while Ruriko and Anne remained in isolation, with hazmat suits mandatory for all visitors. The dead alien was, for the time being, sealed up in an anti-contagion capsule in cold storage with round-the-clock monitoring.

Isolation's glass airlock-style exit whispered as Kitamura stepped into it, looking bleary-eyed and overworked in wrinkled, light blue scrubs. He stood for a couple of seconds with his arms over his head while he was scanned for contaminants, then joined Kiriyama and Dan, taking the chair facing the sofa.

'I'll give you the short version,' he told them, then let out a long breath as he sat back. 'Sorry, I'm more tired than I realized.'

'It's going around,' Dan said. 'We're ready when you are.'

'I don't know if I'm ready for any of this,' Kitamura said and took another breath. 'The alien is a mix of organic and inorganic matter.'

Kiriyama nodded. 'We've seen this sort of thing before.'

'Yes, well, in this particular lifeform, the two are so melded I can't tell you if it occurred naturally or if it was something they did to themselves.'

'With every other species we've seen, it's been the latter,' the captain said. 'I've yet to find a stone with a naturally occurring nervous system.'

'No, but I've seen a live person develop stones,' Kitamura said. 'Gallstones, kidney stones.' He gave a single short laugh. 'Both of which I'm acquainted with. But what I've discovered about its diet is much more disturbing.'

Kiriyama shifted on the couch cushion as the professor hesitated. Dan could sense him wanting to prod Kitamura. In truth, he was feeling slightly impatient himself. Sometimes he was amazed that such short-lived creatures could be so good at dragging things out, as if they had all the time in the universe.

'I double-checked the information we had on the animals in the Alps, the US, and in Zimbabwe,' Kitamura said after a bit. 'They were all female.'

'This species eats only females?' Kiriyama said, incredulous.

'Not exactly,' the professor said. 'The only food it eats is grown *on* females. To be precise, it's produced by making use of the double-X chromosomes.'

Kiriyama looked puzzled for a second, then revolted.

'New growths have appeared on the first young lady and Dr. Yuri both,' Kitamura went on. 'These growths are leeching vital nutrients from them while producing a biochemical cocktail meant to keep them docile and placid while they're being used up in slow-motion.'

'Can't we excise the growths or neutralize them?' Dan asked.

Kitamura shook his head. 'Cutting them off or amputating an affected limb won't do any good. Once a growth appears, the entire body has been compromised. New growths will appear elsewhere. We need a way to counter the infection.'

'I've been both angry and disgusted before,' Kiriyama said slowly. 'But not to this degree.'

'I can't say if this peculiarity of theirs is unique to Earth,' Kitamura went on. 'Which is to say, whether there's something about human XX chromosomes that makes them especially good as a growth medium, or whether it holds for all gendered lifeforms.'

'Which kind is our visitor?' Kiriyama asked. 'Male, female, other, or all of the above?'

'None of the above,' said Kitamura. 'Don't ask me how they reproduce. There may be a separate form that gestates offspring or lays eggs. Or maybe they grow their young the same way they grow their food. In any case, I'm certain it isn't here alone.'

'What makes you say that?' Dan asked, honestly curious.

'Infecting—or cultivating—two women would produce a surfeit of food. More than it needs to stay alive.'

'Maybe it has a way to preserve the surplus,' Kiriyama said thoughtfully.

'And who do you suppose it would be saving all that food for?' Kitamura said. 'Whether or not it's alone now, I'm sure there are more on the way.'

'Or already here,' Dan said darkly. The other two men looked at him uneasily. 'Animals were stolen from different places around the world, and no one's found a trace save for weird prints in the sand or dirt. But now one's gotten into HQ undetected. Whoever these aliens are and whatever they want—besides food—they have extraordinary camouflage/macro-encryption capabilities.'

Dan leaned forward, resting his elbows on his knees. 'But they can breathe our air, they can live under our gravity, and they can make food out of people—excuse me, *some* people. Maybe they wouldn't understand Earth customs and laws any more than we would understand theirs, but the one thing common to all species, whether they breathe air or chlorine or nothing, is: the drive for survival. *Nobody* wants to die.'

'I've got three of the Ultra Guard out in the Hawk-1,' Kiriyama said. 'And I've had the TDF send out underwater drones, but we should have manned subs searching as well.'

'Have the drones use ground-penetrating sensors,' Kitamura suggested. 'In case they're hiding *under* the ocean floor. The water just off Iritahama is relatively shallow for ten kilometers out. Then it drops off sharply.'

'And in the meantime, what about Anne and her friend?' Kiriyama said. 'What can we do to try to help them, if anything?' The captain's desire to find some way to save the women was so intense, Dan could practically feel it vibrating the air around him.

'Working on that,' Kitamura said. 'Initial analysis of the alien's remains indicates it's been traveling for a long time and its last port of call before Earth was Saturn. Or more precisely, one of its moons.'

'Was it Titan?' asked Kiriyama tensely. 'I thought we had a treaty with those aliens.'

'No, this moon is located in the A ring,' Kitamura replied. 'There's a gap in it—the Enke Gap—where a small moonlet called Pan orbits. The alien's inorganic material contains evidence of certain isotopes of transfermium elements, which are extremely rare here—in fact, none of them occur naturally in the Earth's crust but they're fairly abundant on Pan.'

'What a coincidence,' Kiriyama said.

'I'd call it serendipity myself,' said Kitamura. 'Transfermium isotopes are extremely radioactive and they decay very quickly. I don't know what would account for their presence on Pan. It could be natural—Mother Nature is full of surprises and many of them are highly improbable. As a young scientist, I was told when you hear hoofbeats, think horses, not zebras. But sometimes, they *are* zebras—*alien* zebras.'

'Maybe that's why our instruments missed them,' Dan said. 'They don't have a setting for alien zebras.'

Kitamura turned to look at him with a surprised chuckle. 'Young man, you may be more right than anyone knows.'

Dan pressed his lips together so he wouldn't burst into hearty laughter. He was roughly seventeen thousand years older than the avuncular professor, but at the moment, he felt as young as Dan Moroboshi was supposed to be, and he found that he liked feeling that way. And why wouldn't he? After all, he *was* Dan Moroboshi.

But only temporarily, he reminded himself. Only temporarily.

'What do you suppose alien zebras are like?' Kiriyama was saying. 'Besides radioactive.'

Now Dan did laugh. 'They've got no stripes, they walk upright on two legs, and they shield their radioactivity so we can't find them with Geiger counters.' He looked from the captain to Kitamura. 'What do you think, professor? Am I close?'

'Damned if I know,' Kitamura said. 'It's the transfermium isotopes that really puzzle me. They've been added to the aliens' biochemical profile but I don't see anything like a natural explanation as to why.'

'Condiments?' Kiriyama blew out a short breath. 'Maybe transfermium isotopes make their food taste better.'

Kitamura turned to look at him. 'That might not be the joke you think it is, Captain. The long-range spice trade began on Earth around 1,000 BCE and continued for the better part of a millennium, with the Arabs as the sole middlemen. Making food taste better has actually played a major role in the development of human civilization.'

'These aliens aren't just seasoning stews,' Kiriyama said.

'No, they've also discovered that half the Earth's population is an optimum growth medium. The fact that these—' Kitamura paused, looking thoughtful, '—"human farms" are conscious, intelligent lifeforms seems to be beside the point to the aliens. Or perhaps *that's* what makes their food taste better.'

'Which brings us to the question: what can we do about it?' Kiriyama said.

'Well, there *is* one thing we've discovered, and purely by

accident,' Kitamura said. 'When the women are exposed to negative beta particle decay, it slowed the growths very slightly.'

Kiriyama looked heavenward for a moment. 'Pardon me for saying so, Professor, but you should have led with that.'

'I said *very slightly*,' Kitamura replied. 'We can't just expose Dr. Yuri and her friend to negative beta particle radiation and wait for them to get better—the women would die of radiation poisoning first. And we aren't yet at a point where death is our best option.'

'And never will be, I'd hope,' Kiriyama said firmly.

Kitamura looked apologetic. 'Of course not. But if we had a way of focusing a highly concentrated beam of beta-minus radiation directly into the growths, we could probably kill them off without killing the women.' He stood up and stretched. 'And now I need to get back to work. I'm growing a few cultures I need to check on, and I prefer to be within arm's reach of Dr. Yuri and her friend.'

As Kitamura turned to leave, Dan caught a splash of everything on the surface of his mind—his fears for the women, his dread that the spores could become an airborne contagion, and the waking nightmare of a planet inhabited by sad, defeated humans that had become food animals, all of them female, with a small number of men tending to them.

Kiriyama nudged him. 'Hey—not going to be sick, are you?'

Dan shook his head. 'Sorry, Captain. For a second there, I felt overwhelmed.'

'And that's why we never swallow a crisis whole,' Kiriyama said. 'We break it into chunks—' His wristcomm chimed with an incoming call from the Hawk-1.

'Soga here, Captain. Have any underwater drones reported activity anywhere?'

Dan handed Kiriyama his tablet so he could check. 'Not that I can see,' Kiriyama said. 'Why?'

'Then either their sensors are broken or they're in the wrong ocean,' came Furuhashi's voice. 'Because right now, we're watching a whole lot of alien vessels coming up out of the water and assembling at an altitude of two thousand feet.'

'What's "a whole lot?"' Kiriyama asked.

'I lost count after thirty,' Soga said.

'You know what to do.' Kiriyama's voice had a slight edge to it.

'And we'd love to do it,' Furuhashi replied. 'But the lead vessel shot us with something that disabled our splitters. We can't divide into three separate aircraft, not even manually.'

'I'd better get out there in the Hawk-3,' Dan said.

Kiriyama nodded. 'I'll send a squadron of TDF fighters with you.'

'Uh, I think you should hold off on that,' Dan said. 'Keep them back, out of range, while I try some maneuvers, see what the aliens are capable of. They don't need to know what kind of fire power we've got.'

'I'll keep the pilots on standby.' Kiriyama looked at Dan thoughtfully. 'Unless you come up with a way to take all the aliens out at once.'

'Not me,' Dan said, with a slight emphasis on the last word.

'Dammit,' said Furuhashi, 'there seem to be more of them every time I look. Amagi, what are you getting from the scanners?'

'Not much,' Amagi said glumly. 'The readings flicker in and out. I can't get a fix on any of the ships long enough to find out if they're carrying live passengers or what kind of weapons they have.'

'Then assume we're outgunned,' Furuhashi snapped.

'I always do,' Amagi replied patiently. 'But I'd rather know what we're outgunned by—laser, plasma, or old-school cannonballs.'

'Uh-oh,' Soga said, a heartbeat before one of the alien vessels exploded. All the others scattered in every direction as two more blew apart. 'That wasn't me!'

'Sure wasn't.' Amagi was grinning from ear to ear. 'Dan's here in the Hawk-3 and not a moment too soon, I'd say.' He activated the cockpit communicator. 'Hawk-1 to Hawk-3, Amagi here. How ya doin', Dan?'

'I'm okay, but damn, these aliens are tricky,' came the answer.

'Copy *that*,' Amagi said with a grim laugh. 'I was calling to tell you the same. Don't depend on instruments, seeing is believing— you gotta aim by eye.'

'Then I'm glad I've got a good aim.' Dan's determination came through clearly.

'Just be careful,' Amagi said, more concerned now.

'I don't think anybody ever got the best of these guys by being careful,' Dan replied. 'Let's see how they react when I do this.'

The three men in the Hawk-1 watched as the Hawk-3 climbed another two thousand feet.

'Oh, man,' said Furuhashi. 'I really hope he's not gonna do what I think he's gonna—' He cut off as the Hawk-3 went into a dive, its nose aimed squarely at the largest of the alien vessels. 'Aw, dammit, he is. Hawk-1 to Hawk-3—Dan, stop! Never play chicken with aliens!'

Lightning suddenly flickered around the largest alien craft and quickly spread to all of the others.

'Dan, don't! They're ready for you!' Furuhashi fired into the alien formation. Two ships exploded; a plasma bolt bounced off the largest vessel and blew up a smaller one close to it.

'Hawk-3! Pull up! *Pull up!*' Soga shouted. 'Are you crazy?'

At the very last moment, Dan did pull up, the belly of the Hawk-3 almost skimming the top of the lead spacecraft. Furuhashi expected it to break formation to pursue Dan, and prepared to give chase as well. But the largest vessel only changed position in the formation, with several of the smaller ships firing on the Hawk-3, one of them scoring a glancing hit near its tail.

'What's he trying to do?' Soga wondered, watching Dan execute a wide turn before climbing again. Four smaller spacecraft broke from the group and followed him.

'He knows they're on his tail,' said Soga as the Hawk-3 pulled ahead of the aliens, still climbing to an even higher altitude than before.

'He wants to see what they can do,' Amagi said.

'Just hold it steady, Dan,' Furuhashi prayed, watching the Hawk-3 slow its ascent. As soon as the aliens reached the same altitude, Dan rolled the Hawk-3 over and let it drop belly-up. The smaller vessels dived after it and Dan picked them off one by one.

'Now that's some fancy flying,' Furuhashi said, impressed. 'I gotta get him to teach me that move.'

The Hawk-3 continued to drop but it was no longer returning fire from the aliens. 'I think something went wrong,' Amagi said.

'He must have passed out!' Soga said. 'Dan, wake up! Dammit, *wake up!*'

The Hawk-3 rolled right side up but then it kept rolling, tumbling down toward the ocean below, its wings in flames now. Seconds later, they saw a bright flash and then clouds of black smoke rising up from where the Hawk-3 had hit the water.

'Guess he didn't wake up,' Soga said in a small, bleak voice.

'Or maybe he was rescued at the last second,' Amagi said in a ridiculously cheerful voice that made the other two men stare at him. 'But don't take *my* word for it,' he added, pointing at the right-side window, where a familiar red and silver figure was soaring high over the black smoke from the crash. The alien ships scattered in every direction again.

'He always knows!' Soga crowed, pumping his fist in the air (and denting the ceiling). 'How does he always know when we need him?'

'He's Ultraseven,' Amagi and Furuhashi said together.

* * *

And now he owed the Ultra Guard one very expensive, state-of-the-art airship, Ultraseven thought as he flew a tight circle around the Hawk-1.

The last thing he'd wanted to do was crash the Hawk-3, but it couldn't be helped. He had run several thousand scenarios in his head and the most successful ones—i.e., those in which the Hawk-1 *wasn't* destroyed with no survivors—involved crashing the Hawk-3. Later, he could show up at the base and tell them he'd hit the eject button, but he must have banged his head because the next thing he knew, he was waking up on the beach; apparently Ultraseven had saved his butt again.

But that was a concern for later. Right now, the alien vessels were reassembling. Had there always been this many or had more come out of hiding?

He stretched forth his awareness, then withdrew it quickly. What these aliens called 'hunger' was an irresistible drive to consume, with no bounds, no end, and for the people of Earth, no future. They were going to swarm the planet, overwhelming it, cultivating and consuming as much food as possible before the population was played out and they had to move on.

Hoping the aliens would follow him, he flew away from the Hawk-1 and they did, surrounding him. That was all right, he thought, raising his hand to the lamp in his forehead. The Emerium Beam took out half a dozen at once, forcing them to rearrange the formation around him, with the largest one close to him. He raised his hand to the lamp again but the Emerium Beam crackled and suddenly went dark.

Which was impossible—these aliens could not be advanced enough to neutralize the Emerium Beam.

Abruptly, he realized: the aliens had formed an energy sink around him. The more he struggled to get out of it, the stronger its hold on him would become. What he had to do was keep his own energy level below a certain threshold, where he could still think clearly without triggering an attack.

The energy sink wasn't something the aliens had developed; a species of ever-hungry marauders wouldn't have the patience. They'd have taken it from one of the worlds they'd eaten, or perhaps some unfortunate civilization had offered it to them in the hope they'd take it and go away rather than turning it back on them. Or maybe—

The energy sink dragged the idea away.

'We've got to get them away from him before they suck the life out of him,' Amagi was saying to Furuhashi.

'How?' Soga snapped. 'I can't get a stable fix on any of them.'

'We don't need precision for what I've got in mind.' Furuhashi glanced at the other two men with a wicked grin. 'Strap in, I want to try something.'

For a second, he wasn't sure if he was having a spectacular dream of watching the Hawk-1 execute a move called the Corkscrew.

The trick was a big hit with flying show audiences (and a major cause of airsickness among flight crews). He caught a quick sense of Furuhashi's unflinching calm, Soga's terrified excitement, and Amagi's complete faith holding them all steady as the Hawk-1 spiraled through the air between himself and the alien vessels, breaking their connections and forcing them to scatter.

He followed the Hawk-1, ready to act if Furuhashi couldn't bring it out of its continuous roll, but Furuhashi managed just fine, maintaining control as he extended the wingspan to stabilize the aircraft and level off right side up. Now he saw Furuhashi's smiling face through the aircraft window and gave him a snappy salute. Furuhashi's grin broadened as he returned it.

In the distance, he heard the TDF fighters approaching. The aliens were regrouping again but there definitely weren't as many as before. He could leave the mopping up to them and his teammates while he obtained the substance that would save Anne and Ruriko.

Only a few hours ago, the two women had been at a party, but it seemed so far removed from the present it might have been a lifetime ago. No one had imagined the evening would end with them slowly turning into alien food. He couldn't let the process finish.

Achieving escape velocity took more effort than he'd expected, but once he had, the light from the local star hit him with full, unfiltered force, instantly restoring him to full strength. Even his mind was clearer. He could stretch forth his awareness easily now to orient himself within the planetary system.

Locating the ringed planet with respect to Earth was just as easy. But if he was going to save Anne and Ruriko, he couldn't travel in the usual way. He had to make the journey as a Being of Light, something he'd done only a few times previously and, until now, never without permission.

The Ultras would know. They always knew when a conscious, intelligent lifeform traveled at light speed. What would they do about it? Take him into custody for a tribunal? Or simply summon him home to answer not only for zipping through space at maximum natural velocity but also for abandoning his assignment to map the galaxy?

He couldn't worry about that—couldn't even care, really—until Anne and Ruriko were safe, and that was so much easier said than done. Even at the speed of light, the round trip would be a little over two hours on the human clock, and that didn't include how long it would take him to find the cure for alien zebras, or rather, alien zebra food.

* * *

If he hadn't known better, he'd have mistaken Saturn's innermost moon for a saucer-shaped alien vessel. Granted, it would have been a phenomenally *big* vessel, with a thick center seam. But it was only an orbiting lump without even single-cell life, which made it easier to extract the right transfermium isotopes in just the right quantities.

The process of extraction went more slowly than he'd have liked, and he had to force himself not to rush so the isotopes would remain discrete and intact. The measures had to be precise and he had to hold them in stasis by force of will so they wouldn't decay before he got them back to Earth.

Leaving Saturn's orbit, he stretched forth his awareness over the entire solar system. There were scant few signs of life except for the colony on Titan, still small and well-hidden, and the very busy, very noisy Earth. This part of the galaxy was so empty and dark.

For an astral moment, he turned toward the ever-bright center of the Milky Way, where countless worlds had never known darkness. If he resumed his mapping assignment, he would never have to be alone in the dark again. He felt the pull as much as ever, but now it wasn't as strong as what he felt when he pictured his teammates... especially Anne.

In one way, that was irrational. How could he feel so profoundly drawn to humans, or even just one of them? He had been born a Being of Light, had grown, learned, matured among others like himself for thousands of years, and yet he had bonded to humans in the space of a heartbeat.

It was because he'd taken human form, he realized. The brevity of the human lifespan made living an extraordinarily intense experience, as illustrated by the fact that although he wasn't in human form now, he could hardly wait to get back to Earth and resume Dan Moroboshi's life. And when he looked for reasons why, he saw Anne's face among them.

'Ultraseven left a message confirming that my treatment plan is exactly right,' Professor Kitamura told Kiriyama as they set up the shielded box containing the transfermium isotopes next to Ruriko's bed. The professor was all business, but Kiriyama could detect a hint of pride in his voice. 'We radiate the growths on the women's skin, not the women themselves. We should start with Ruriko, since her condition is more advanced.'

Kiriyama looked down at Ruriko through the plastic faceguard in his hazmat suit. Her left arm was completely covered and new growths had appeared on her neck and under her chin. By comparison, they had appeared more erratically on Anne—there were a few on her arms, but a new growth had appeared below her left eye and she now had rings of them around both wrists.

The professor would have liked to study the growths, Kiriyama knew, but Ultraseven had been very clear: they were to use the transfermium to eradicate every last bit of alien tissue, nothing was to be saved for research. Until they had better technology to contain it, the threat to humanity was too great.

He had half-expected Kitamura to protest in the name of scientific curiosity or something. But the professor had acceded to Ultraseven's terms with a resigned nod. Apparently research scientists knew they had to pick their battles.

'Ready?' Kitamura asked, bringing him back to the moment. Kiriyama nodded and the professor activated the machine.

There was no visible beam, but within a few seconds the green began fading from Ruriko's skin. Once she was back to her normal coloration, the growths turned gray and crumbled to dust.

'I'd say that bodes well for Dr. Yuri,' Kitamura said, deactivating the machine so he could move it around to Anne's bedside.

'Hey, there's no penicillin in transfermium, is there?' Kiriyama asked suddenly.

Kitamura stared at him, bewildered. 'Of course not. Why do you ask?'

'Just wanted to make sure,' the captain said. 'Anne's allergic.'

'Ah.' Kitamura nodded. 'No, I'm confident Dr. Yuri will tolerate the treatment as well as her friend did.' He checked the readouts on the top of the machine. 'Quickly now, before there's any further decay.'

Kiriyama hadn't realized he was holding his breath until it came out of him in a relieved rush at the sight of the alien growths disintegrating on Anne's skin. He was about to call the rest of the Ultra Guard to tell them the news when they buzzed the door for entry. Kitamura let them in.

'How are they?' Amagi asked as he, Soga, and Furuhashi hurried to Anne's bedside.

'No longer green,' Kitamura said as he stuffed his used suit into a hazmat barrel in the corner.

'Definitely an improvement,' Soga said. 'When do you think they'll wake up?'

As if on cue, both women opened their eyes, startling Soga so that he jumped.

'Anne?' he said, looking anxiously into her face.

'That's my name,' Anne said with a drowsy smile. 'Don't wear it out.' She turned to Ruriko, who was looking around at everyone in a daze.

'What happened?' Ruriko said. 'And is there any birthday cake left? Answer the second question first.' She and Anne laughed together.

'Where's Dan?' Anne asked Kiriyama, her expression turning serious.

'I'm right here.'

Dan was standing in the doorway, looking more than a bit rumpled but otherwise alive and well. Kiriyama felt his jaw drop, and he wasn't the only one.

'Where on Earth did you come from?' Furuhashi demanded, incredulous and happy.

'Well, that's quite the complicated question.' Dan chuckled in his good-natured way that could make his friends forget there had been anything wrong. 'But the short answer is, someone was kind enough to give me a lift from Iritahama, even though I was dripping wet at the time.'

'You should get some rest,' Kiriyama told him.

Dan looked mystified. 'Me? Why?'

'You dumped the Hawk-3 in the Pacific,' Kiriyama replied. 'You're gonna need all your strength for the paperwork.'

'Stop trying to scare him,' Anne said, her eyes twinkling. 'There isn't any actual paper.'

'We're just glad you're alive,' Kiriyama told him. 'But what took you so long?'

'Oh, the person who picked me up had to run an errand and it took a couple of hours,' Dan said as he moved to Anne's side and took her hand. 'But better late than never, right?'

'*Always* much better than never,' Anne said.

The image of all of them gathered around Anne and her friend lodged in Kiriyama's mind with the staying power of a snapshot. It came back to him again and again in the following days, a happy memory, but for some reason, something about it also seemed like a warning.

CHAPTER

SEVEN

'Attention, carbon-based vertebrates, with or without feathers! We are now leaving the troposphere and entering the stratosphere!' Amagi announced from the navigator's position in the cockpit of the Ultra Hawk 1. 'The stratosphere is most famous for being home to the ozone layer, which protects us all from the sun's harmful ultraviolet radiation!'

In the pilot's seat, Furuhashi sighed heavily. 'You're going to keep doing that, aren't you?'

'I'm trying to get comfortable with presenting,' Amagi said. 'Otherwise those elementary school kids in Chuo City are gonna eat me alive.'

Furuhashi looked at Dan on his right; they burst out laughing.

'I'm glad you two find my imminent and untimely demise so hilarious,' Amagi said stiffly.

'You're making it sound like you're going to be locked in a room with fifty rabid wolverines, all off the leash,' Furuhashi said. 'They're just kids.'

'Yes, but I'm not a performer or a presenter,' said Amagi.

'So that wasn't you explaining the alien camera back at HQ?' Dan asked.

'That was different,' Amagi said. 'I didn't have to convince you it was interesting and exciting.'

Dan and Furuhashi laughed again. 'I guess that's one way to describe an alien device that steals souls,' Furuhashi said after he wound down. 'What do you think, Dan? You're the one with firsthand experience. Was it interesting and exciting to have your soul stolen?'

'I'll have to get back to you on that,' Dan said, chuckling. 'Right now, I'm busy keeping an eye out for strolling asteroids. Or asteroid-shaped UFOs, or something.'

They were into the seventeenth hour of a twenty-four-hour patrol; Dan thought, all things considered, they were doing pretty well. Both Amagi and Furuhashi were sure that Global Watch at the Ultra Guard Headquarters in Paris had been faked out by a phantom phenomenon that had somehow come to be known as 'the strolling asteroid.' According to Furuhashi, it would be two or three days before GW officially declared it to be a false alarm and issued a general stand-down.

'Hey, Amagi,' Dan said cheerfully, 'what comes after the stratosphere?'

'Glad you asked,' Amagi said in a hearty voice. 'Next we'll be entering the mesosphere.'

'That's it?' Dan twisted around in his seat to look at him. 'Your audience'll want to know more than that. What kind of fun stuff do we find in the mesosphere?'

Amagi was staring past him. 'Uh… a flying island?'

Dan glanced at Furuhashi, who was also gaping at something straight ahead of them, and turned to look.

The thing in the sky really did look like a flying island, Dan thought. It could have been one of the many Pacific islands that appeared, disappeared, and reappeared at the whims and vagaries of weather and ocean, except those were a few hundred miles south of their current location. On his left, Furuhashi hit the comm button without looking away from the thing.

'Furuhashi to HQ, please respond,' he said, adding a very emphatic, 'Please.'

'HQ here, Furuhashi,' said Anne's voice from the speaker in the ceiling. 'What's your status? Any strolling asteroids in your vicinity?'

'Currently have eyes on a very large airborne object that could be an asteroid,' Furuhashi replied, his voice tight and tense. 'Except it's more like a flying island. An island in the sky.'

There was a half second of hesitation. Then Kiriyama's voice said, 'Say again, Hawk 1.'

'We've found a flying island up here,' Furuhashi said, carefully enunciating each word. 'If you want to call that strolling.'

'You can save the jokes for Happy Hour,' Kiriyama said. This was followed by a burst of static.

'No joke, Captain, there's an island in flight up here,' Furuhashi said earnestly. 'And it's coming right at us.'

Kiriyama's answer was lost in another burst of static.

'Amagi, send HQ the feed from our forward cams,' Furuhashi said.

'Already done,' said Amagi. 'But I'm resending, just to make sure.'

More static from the speaker; this time, it was continuous.

'I thought I heard the captain's voice in there,' Amagi said. 'But I can't make out the words. Sorry.'

Furuhashi turned the volume down on the comm without turning it off. 'Dan, can you tell how far away that thing is? The instruments can't get a fix on it.'

'Two kilometers, maybe,' Dan told him. He didn't add that he wasn't sure they were looking at a solid object. The asteroid registered on his Ultra senses as a patch of free-range noise. Maybe it was a phantom, he thought as they drew closer to it; a little something cooked up by uninvited visitors wanting to have a little fun by scaring the locals. Except there was no sign of any other presence.

Abruptly, the island accelerated toward them.

'Evasive action!' Furuhashi shouted over a new burst of static coming in via a different channel. 'Everybody, hang on to your—'

A beam of harsh white light shot out from the island and hit the Hawk-1. The impact shook the whole aircraft.

'What was that?' shouted Amagi.

'Nothing good,' Furuhashi said grimly. Or maybe he'd said it himself, Dan thought, since the exact same words had been on the tip of his tongue.

He opened his mouth to tell Furuhashi they should split the Hawk-1 into three aircraft, but something pulled his voice out of him, the same pull that had taken hold of his arms and legs and everything else in the cockpit, even the air. That was one very sophisticated tractor beam. All they could do was watch the island/asteroid grow larger and larger.

Now he could see the island had a deep stone foundation, and for a few fraught seconds he thought they were going to end up as a gory smear all over the front. But the tractor beam lifted the Hawk-1 at the last moment. Dan caught a glimpse of terrain covered in thick, low-lying fog and, in the distance, something that could have been a silo.

It was his last thought for some time.

As soon as they'd lost contact with the Hawk-1, HQ had gone on full alert. TDF jets were scrambled, satellite coverage was diverted and refocused, and through it all, Anne sat at the communications console in the Strategy Room reconfiguring the protocols in hopes of re-establishing contact.

After a couple of hours, Kiriyama had tried to get her to rest, but she refused to budge for another ninety minutes. Even then, she insisted on going out with Kiriyama and Soga in the new Ultra Hawk 3 to look for their missing teammates.

The search continued through the night and into the next morning, albeit with fewer personnel. No help for it—even with half the Ultra Guard missing, life with all its attendant responsibilities, obligations, and problems went on.

'I hope those guys had a better night than we did,' Anne said to Soga after the captain ordered them both to get some rest. 'Because when they finally do show up, I'm going to make them clean the whole clinic as punishment for making me worry. While I watch old movies and eat bonbons.'

'Have you ever had a bonbon?' Soga asked as they walked back to the Ultra Guard living quarters together.

'No, but I'm sending away for a case,' she replied.

'What if you don't like them?'

Anne shrugged. 'Then I'll make those three bad boys eat them for me.'

Consciousness returned slowly, in ragged bits and pieces.

Eventually, Dan became aware that he still had his helmet on. As he started to remove it, his gaze fell on Furuhashi, slumped in his seat as if he'd dozed off in midflight. Unbuckling himself, he knelt on his seat cushion to look around and discovered Amagi hanging half out of his chair like a lanky rag doll.

Furuhashi groaned then and pulled off his helmet. 'Okay,' he said, yawning. 'I'll buy breakfast for the first person who can tell me where the hell we are.'

'Remember the flying island?' Dan asked, yawning himself.

'Are you sure?' Amagi untangled himself from his harness and looked out the windscreen at the fog-covered landscape. Removing his helmet, he ran one hand through his hair, making it stand wildly on end. 'Who forgot to turn off the disco fog machine?' He got up and made his way over to a side window to get a better look at the sky. 'And if this island was flying before, it isn't now.'

'And neither are we,' Furuhashi grumbled, flipping switches and pushing buttons on the dashboard in front of him. Nothing happened. 'Dammit, I can't even get a diagnostic to run.' He sat back heavily in his seat, which gave an ominous creak. 'But you know the really awful part?' he added, turning to Dan with a glum expression. 'When you crash the Hawk-1, they bill you for *three* aircraft.'

'We'll all chip in,' Dan said. 'Three of us, three aircraft.'

'It's still the mother of all bills to pay off,' Amagi said, leaning on anything available to make his unsteady way back to his seat. 'Especially for you, Dan, since you're already on the hook for the Hawk-3. You're not gonna be able to retire before you're a hundred and seventy-five, at least.'

'I hadn't planned to,' Dan said matter-of-factly.

Amagi stretched, lost his balance, and sat down heavily in his seat. 'And no one's going to point out how absurd this conversation is?'

'Not in my job description,' Furuhashi, speaking through another yawn.

'And I'm not awake enough yet,' Dan lied. In truth, he wasn't sensing his teammates quite as sharply as he usually did. Something seemed to be blocking him and it wasn't anything natural. This asteroid or island or flying chunk of alien whatever was still putting out a storm of interference.

No, he realized, feeling foolish; not interference but encryption.

Or maybe camouflage would be a more accurate term, since the asteroid had slipped past the TDF's keenest and most advanced sensors. For all he knew, it could confound human senses so thoroughly that a person could look directly at it and see nothing.

Dan tried to remember which civilizations in the Milky Way had this kind of technology. Those near the center were capable and most would be conscientious enough to deploy it on the galactic outskirts to avoid unauthorized contact with less sophisticated lifeforms. But why would any of them come all the way out here at all?

'Don't see anything that looks familiar,' Furuhashi was saying. 'And I can't see what's under all the disco fog. But the sky's blue, which means there's Rayleigh scattering and air we can breathe.'

Amagi gave a short laugh. 'So far, so good, I guess?'

'Just because we can breathe, doesn't mean we're safe,' Furuhashi added. He got up and went to a cabinet at the rear of the cockpit to pull out three courier bags with shoulder straps. Slinging one across his back, he gave the other two to Amagi and Dan.

'What about weapons?' Amagi said.

Furuhashi looked annoyed. 'What about them?'

'They might not work right with all the interference.'

'Bring 'em anyway, of course,' said Furuhashi. 'If they work, great. If they don't, they're clubs with fancy handles. Dan, you've got our six. Amagi, behind me.'

Disembarking took some effort—the door had to be cranked open by hand. Furuhashi did it himself, and had Dan and Amagi keep their weapons trained on the doorway, just in case something was lying in wait to surprise them. But other than a few wisps of fog, nothing rose up out of the thick, snow-white mist blanketing the terrain.

'We keep to the high ground,' Furuhashi told them as he moved from the open door up onto a slightly higher stone ridge. 'And whatever you do, don't step into anything if you can't see the bottom.'

'Copy that,' Amagi said, following him.

Dan hesitated, looking around.

'What's the matter?' Amagi asked him. 'Fog got you spooked?'

'Not exactly,' Dan replied, kicking at the tendrils of mist at the edge of the doorway. 'I'm just wondering how the fog is connected to the interference.'

'We don't know that it is,' Furuhashi said. 'So many questions, so little time.' He tapped his helmet. 'Headgear on, Dan.'

'Right,' Dan said, feeling foolish again. The crash-landing had rattled him. Or maybe his memory lapse was down to the interference. But if that were the case, he thought as he stepped onto the ridge with his teammates, the situation was even more dangerous than any of them knew.

'I feel like I'm on a sci-fi movie set,' Amagi said with a nervous laugh, waving one hand to disperse the shreds of fog rising up around them. 'Anyone tried calling HQ again?'

'I'll try,' Dan said, 'but I'm not optimistic.' He activated his wristcomm, then winced at the hard-edged electronic whine in his headphones and shut it off again.

'We can get up higher,' Furuhashi said, moving up the ridge to a rough wall of striated rock. The ridge took them another twenty feet, where it ended in a sudden sharp drop into an abyss filled with fog.

'At least the air's a little clearer,' Amagi said, holstering his sidearm.

'Yeah,' said Furuhashi. 'Now if only we had something interesting to look at.'

'Just before we hit, I thought I saw something,' Dan said. 'A building of some kind.'

'Anything like those?' Amagi asked thoughtfully, staring into the distance.

Dan turned to follow his gaze. In the distance, the three structures protruding from the fog looked like nothing so much as giant coiled springs, each one capped by a bowl. To catch samples? Dan took out his binoculars and focused on them; it didn't make them any less puzzling.

'Theories anybody?' Amagi said, using his own binoculars. 'Another alien power station? Or alien condos? Or the disco fog distributor for the inner planets?'

'Were they here when we crashed?' said Furuhashi. 'I mean, who knows how much farther this place flew after we were forced down. We could be anywhere on Earth—or off it.'

In spite of everything, Dan couldn't help chuckling. 'Could be,' he said. 'But we're not only still on Earth, we're still in Japan.' Dan had moved several yards farther down the path; he beckoned for the others to join him and pointed at two jagged escarpments. The mist had cleared enough to let them see a rather spectacular view of Mt. Fuji in the early morning light.

Furuhashi's long, relieved sigh had a laugh in it. 'We're not too far from our own stomping grounds—the Terrestrial Defense Force training grounds and armory should be nearby.' He paused, frowning. 'Unless we landed *on* them.'

Amagi's complexion turned ashy but Dan shook his head. 'Listen,' he said, pressing a finger to his lips. 'Hear that?'

'No,' Amagi said, eyeing him warily.

'Exactly,' Dan said. 'If we'd landed *on* them, all hell would have broken loose. HQ would have called out the armed forces.'

'I guess,' Furuhashi said. 'I'm just wondering what kind of civilization or society would travel by asteroid instead of building a spacecraft.'

'Good question,' Amagi said. 'Maybe too good. It's going to bother me all day.'

They moved on toward the structures. The fog didn't clear so much as it shifted to lay close to the ground. It seemed to disperse as they walked through it, but when Dan looked back, it was thicker than ever. Eventually they came to a broad flat expanse of reddish stone, where they paused for a break and tried calling HQ, to no avail.

'Maybe the aliens are glampers,' Amagi said suddenly.

Furuhashi laughed. 'Alien glamour campers—that's a good one. I wonder what they have instead of air-conditioned tents and TVs.'

'Whole buildings, of course.' Amagi nodded in the direction of the structures. 'I don't know why glampers don't just stay home. That's what I do.'

Under normal conditions, Amagi's feelings would have come through to Dan much more vividly. The flashes of memory—insect bites, rocks under his sleeping bag, the distant sound of animals running through the woods—were muted, like a muffled voice in another room. Normally, humans didn't even get that much, Dan knew, but it was little consolation. He was feeling impaired, deprived, and alone.

They moved on and came to a narrow channel cutting through solid stone for almost a whole kilometer, letting out only yards from one of the coiled-spring structures.

Furuhashi drew his sidearm and flicked the safety off. Dan and Amagi did the same. Moving as quietly as they could, they found something that looked like a door, except it had no markings, no signs, and nothing like a handle, a knob, or a lock to pick.

'Is this the main entrance or just for deliveries?' Furuhashi wondered aloud.

'Hey, guys!' Amagi had moved around to the left of the putative door. 'I found a window!'

Dan and Furuhashi rushed to his side. The window was oddly shaped, four-sided but a trapezoid rather than a square, and heavily tinted. They had to press their faces against it and cup their hands around their heads for a glimpse of colored lights blinking on and off.

'I don't see anything moving around in there,' Furuhashi said. 'Not even a maintenance bot on wheels.' He pressed one gloved hand to the center of the glass for a few seconds, then stepped back. 'Must be real quiet in there—I didn't feel even the slightest vibration.'

'I think this "glass" is a lot thicker than it looks,' Amagi said. 'A lot more compressed than our glass. I don't think we could break it with anything short of a grenade.'

Furuhashi was back at the door, running his hands along a nearly invisible seam in a search for some kind of access, finding nothing, and stood back. 'Maybe it's a giant fog machine and interference is a by-product.'

'Or vice versa,' said Amagi. 'Or it's all automated, like that underground power station we took out.'

'That would explain why we haven't seen any signs of life,' Furuhashi said. 'I mean, if someone crash-landed in my front yard, I'd come out to see if I could help.'

Amagi laughed a little. 'It's still pretty early. Maybe they're not up yet.'

'We could try knocking,' Dan suggested, and rapped his knuckles on the door. There was no sound.

'Damn, that's thick,' Amagi said. 'Maybe if we pounded with our fists—'

There was a sudden mechanical noise like large metal gears engaging. Furuhashi pushed them all back as the door shuddered and slowly began to swing outward.

Amagi had been right—Dan estimated the door was at least eighteen inches thick, more like something that belonged to a bank vault, except there were no visible mechanisms on the door or the frame. It opened about halfway and then stopped.

'That says, "Come on in," to me,' Amagi said. 'But maybe only one of us should go in. Or stay out here—'

Furuhashi shook his head emphatically. 'We *don't* split up. And we go in *fast*—I don't want anyone caught in that door if it slams.'

'I don't think this door slams,' Amagi said.

'Me either, but we don't know, so I'm not taking any chances,' Furuhashi said. 'Amagi, behind me.'

As soon as they were inside, Dan sensed a change in the air, as if the energy level in the room had increased, and perhaps it had; some of the lights on the consoles seemed to be flashing more quickly. Amagi paused, looking uncertain, and touched a hand to his temple.

'I feel—I don't know, a little funny. Like I'm in an electromagnetic radiation hotspot.'

'Maybe you're allergic to alien EMR,' Furuhashi said. 'Should we leave?'

'No, I want to investigate this... stuff.' Amagi's attention was focused on three square frameworks on pedestals. They were lined up side-by-side, each with an orange light that waxed and waned in a slow, steady rhythm.

'What do you make of that?' Furuhashi asked him finally.

Amagi shook his head as he turned to a hexagonal frame containing several small boxlike objects, each about the size of a deck of cards, slotted into a flat, square board. Dan could tell the placement was specific but that was all; interference hid anything else.

He and Furuhashi followed Amagi over to a large, free-standing console. These lights, Dan saw, were arranged in squares of seven by seven, but they blinked on and off in no discernible rhythm or order.

'Hey...' Furuhashi sniffed. 'You guys smell that?' He looked at Dan, then at Amagi, who paused in his inspection of the console then shook his head.

'I think it's more like the *absence* of a smell,' Amagi said. 'Like in a computer clean room. Those always smell funny to me before I get acclimated.'

Furuhashi frowned, then shrugged and ambled over to another framework on a pedestal. This one was hexagonal and contained a square box covered with translucent panels slightly larger than postage stamps; some of them lit up, others stayed dark, under a small yellow light that waxed and waned on a slow cycle.

Amagi joined him, although he was more interested in the yellow light than anything else. 'What do you suppose that's for?' he said after half a minute.

'Maybe it's like a heartbeat,' Furuhashi said.

Amagi straightened up and stared at Furuhashi with a thoughtful, mildly surprised smile Anne referred to as his *Aha!* look. 'That didn't even occur to me. But it could be.'

'I wasn't really serious,' Furuhashi said, glancing at Dan uneasily. 'I don't think it's alive or anything.'

'But it *is* activated—it's *on*. As opposed to *off*.' Amagi spotted something else and started toward it, putting a hand on the framework he and Furuhashi had just been looking at. There was a sudden, loud noise like gigantic cymbals crashing together and they all jumped.

'What the hell was *that*?' Furuhashi whispered, raising his weapon.

They all held very still, waiting for something else, but nothing happened.

'Maybe it's an alien MP3 player?' Furuhashi said, lowering his weapon but not holstering it. 'No, wait—I know, it's an alien car alarm. You know—"Step away from the… uh, thing?"'

Amagi gave him another thoughtful *Aha!* look. Careful not to touch anything, he went over to a console in the middle of the room. This one was slightly larger than the communications console in the strategy room, only with many more lights, all of them blinking. In the center of the console was a clear, flat space that might have been a desk or some other kind of worksurface, featureless except for a number of very thin black lines. Dan had the impression that these weren't decoration.

'Oh, look—a map of their subway system,' Furuhashi said. 'It's even more indecipherable than anything we've got.' Amagi burst into hearty laughter and Dan joined in to cover his own *Aha!* The lines *were* a sort of map or schematic, but the interference hid any other details.

This was starting to get annoying, Dan thought. He waited for Amagi to spot something else but he stayed where he was, staring at the lines as if he was waiting for them to reveal something. Then he suddenly touched the center of the flat area with his index finger.

Instantly, every light on the console flashed and began blinking rapidly in different patterns; Dan could sense a very strong yet subtle vibration emanating from it.

'This is a transmitter,' Amagi said confidently.

'I'll take your word for it,' Furuhashi said, moving around to the other side so he was facing Amagi. 'But what's it transmitting, and who's on the receiving end?'

'We are,' Dan said before he could think better of it.

The other two men stared at him. 'But why?' Furuhashi said. 'We're right here with it.'

Amagi started to say something when they all heard what sounded like a loud, hydraulic hiss.

'The door!' Furuhashi ran for the entrance and reached it a fraction of a second after it snapped shut. 'Okay, everybody stand clear.' He backed up, preparing to take a run at it.

Dan stepped in front of him. 'Don't. You know how thick it is, you'll break *yourself* before you get it to budge.'

Furuhashi made a face. 'Maybe it's not locked.'

'Or there's a release switch or control on this side,' said Amagi, and began searching for something on the door frame. Furuhashi did the same on the other side while Dan felt for something along the bottom.

After some unmeasured time, Furuhashi made a disgusted noise and went to look out the window. He found a small protrusion at the bottom of the frame and tried pulling on it; it telescoped into a small table.

'Good work!' Amagi enthused, and rushed over to examine it. On finding nothing, he pressed down on it to see if it would hold his weight, then sat on it. 'Now what do we do?'

As if on cue, the whole place began to rumble and shake so much, he fell to the floor and Dan and Furuhashi nearly fell on top of him. The tremor lasted almost fifteen seconds, then stopped just as suddenly as it had begun.

'Earthquake?' Furuhashi said, looking around. 'Or maybe the escape room doesn't like it when you play with the furniture?'

Amagi started to reply but Dan shushed him. 'Do you feel that?' he said.

Nobody said anything; they didn't have to. The island was moving again.

Communications in the Yamanashi and Shizuoka Prefectures went from intermittently glitchy to hit-and-miss before finally going down altogether, along with the power grid. The problem spread quickly, traveling in a northeasterly direction into the Kanegawa Prefecture. Boats along the coast of Sugami Bay bobbed in their moorings; any with instruments were fried. Train passengers were stranded and all aircraft had to be grounded; not that any could take off. Authorities banned all nonessential road travel in the affected areas, although any vehicle more sophisticated than a bicycle was unusable anyway.

At TDF HQ, operations were in disaster mode. The base itself was well shielded—the lights stayed on, climate control and basic utilities continued to function, but Kiriyama and Manabe scaled back on any nonessential activity. Research labs shut and nonemergency medical services were limited to ibuprofen and butterfly bandages, leaving Anne free to accompany Kiriyama and Soga on an unofficial search mission.

'I know the Pointer is armored from most kinds of interference,' Soga said as they headed southwest on an eerily empty road. 'But it could be a real long walk home if we break down and can't call for a tow.'

'There's a flare gun in the glove box,' Kiriyama said, keeping his tone serene and confident. 'There are a few energy bars in there, too, in case we miss lunch.' He chuckled inwardly as Soga opened the compartment to see what flavors they had. 'If we do end up stranded in the middle of nowhere, I'll make it up to you when this is all over.' *If we're all still here when it's all over.*

'I trust you, Captain,' Anne said from the back seat. She was smiling but there was a hint of tension in her voice.

'I do, too,' said Soga. 'I worked on the shielding install with Amagi and I know the Pointer can pretty much stand up to anything short of a catastrophic solar flare.' He gave a small laugh. 'To be honest, the empty roads are getting to me.'

'You prefer being stuck in traffic?' Anne teased.

'No, it's just that it looks like one of those end-of-the-world-as-we-know-it movies and we're the last three people left.'

'Thanks for that—very cheerful,' Anne said. 'Are we going to Mt. Fuji, captain? Is that where you think the Hawk-1 is?'

'Their last known position was in that vicinity,' Kiriyama said.

'If they cr—ahem, were forced to land there,' Soga said, 'wouldn't they have sent up a flare?'

Kiriyama nodded. 'I'd like to know why they didn't.'

The silence that followed was filled with deafening anxiety and Kiriyama was almost sorry he'd said anything. Soga and Anne were the two youngest members of the Ultra Guard; they were well trained but their experience was limited. Neither of them had ever had to deal with losing a teammate.

'You know, I heard about a TDF crew that had to make an emergency landing on one of those islands that's barely a bump in the ocean,' Anne said chattily, as if she was just making conversation on a long drive. 'All the doors of their VTOL got jammed, and of course their comms were out, too. Even their emergency beacon was dark. They were stuck for three days before a search drone located them.' She laughed a little. 'They all ended up in therapy for claustrophobia.'

'Did you treat them?' Soga asked.

Anne shook her head. 'It happened at one of the other bases. I don't remember which one. But it wasn't Paris.'

'Of course not, because nothing ever goes wrong in Paris,' Soga said with more than a little envy. 'They get all the hottest tech before the rest of us even know it exists.'

'I know,' Anne sighed, just as envious. 'They recently upgraded their urgent care clinic and you wouldn't believe half the stuff they've got now.'

Soga and Anne were still discussing the wonders of the Paris branch thirty minutes later, when Kiriyama turned off the highway onto a road less well maintained. Satnav was out of the question, but he knew the area well enough to find the shortcut to the Fuji-Hakone-Izu National Park without help.

The road went from badly paved to packed dirt. As they passed the Dainichido Shrine, however, Kiriyama considered turning back. They'd seen nothing out of the ordinary—no sign of a strolling asteroid, an alien spacecraft, or even just an alien footprint. Comms were still out—he'd been spot-checking—and he was starting to think he'd set the three of them on a fool's errand, just because he felt the need to *do* something.

He was about to tell Anne and Soga they were turning around to head home when Anne suddenly lowered the left-side window and stuck her head out.

'Captain, stop! Nine o'clock!'

Kiriyama stood on the brakes and stared out the driver's-side window. 'Anne, pull your head back in,' he ordered as he grabbed his tablet off the seat beside him and began taking a flurry of photos. Even if there was no way to send them back to HQ, he wanted as many pictures as possible because he wasn't sure how to describe what he was seeing.

It might have been an asteroid but it looked more like an island, and it was floating on a thick layer of fog barely twenty feet above the ground, if that. He could see more fog spilling over the edges of the island from somewhere on its surface, or perhaps from within. Was the fog keeping the island aloft? If so, that was some powerful fog. Alien fog; who knew?

'I guess we found the strolling asteroid,' Soga said. He was sitting in the open passenger-door window, using the camera function on his wristcomm. 'Or it found us.' Paused. 'I'm surprised more of it didn't burn off on its way down.'

'That's because it didn't *fall* through the atmosphere,' Anne said, peering at it through binoculars. 'It *strolled*.'

Kiriyama stared at the undulating clouds of fog under the island or asteroid or whatever it was and had a sudden wild hope that it was a holographic projection, a publicity stunt for a new movie or TV show. But it was a fleeting notion that blew through his mind like a scrap of paper in a windstorm and was gone.

'Captain?' Anne's voice roused Kiriyama from his trance. 'It's getting lower. That thing—it's *descending*.'

She was right, he realized; the island was sinking down, its attendant cloud of mist flattening out under the stony base.

'Windows up,' Kiriyama ordered. He put the Pointer in gear

and turned it around so they were facing the island, which seemed to be sitting right on the ground now. 'I'm going to try getting a little closer. Get low, you two.'

'I'm good, Captain,' Soga said. He'd drawn his sidearm; so had Anne.

Kiriyama inched the Pointer forward a few feet, then stopped. When nothing happened, he pressed the accelerator gently, but this time the Pointer didn't move.

He tried again, pressing until he heard the back wheels spinning. Great; he must have found the only mud hole for fifty miles. Annoyed, he checked the side mirror, using the interior control to angle it so it showed him the rear left tire. It was on dry, level ground. He did the same with the other mirror; no mud hole on the right, either.

'You know, the last time this happened,' Soga said, 'Dan Moroboshi was sitting on the roof.'

Kiriyama shifted into reverse and was relieved when the Pointer backed up with no problem. He put it in drive and tried again; the Pointer rolled forward and stopped in the same place, its wheels spinning.

'Maybe we should check the roof?' Soga laughed nervously. 'Dan's a real character.'

'I've got a better idea,' said Kiriyama and activated the Pointer's flight function.

The car rose up five or so feet. But when Kiriyama tried to go forward, the Pointer's nose lifted, as if he were trying to drive *up* an invisible wall.

'The force-field lab ought to see this,' Soga said.

Kiriyama set the Pointer down on the ground. 'Okay, we can't drive and we can't fly,' he said. 'I guess we'll have to walk.' He opened his door. 'Unless you want to wait in the car?'

Nobody did. The three of them gathered in front of the Pointer. There was no damage to the car that any of them could see; also, no sign of anything like a wall or a barrier. Kiriyama took a few steps forward, stepping carefully although the ground felt normal,

Soga moved up on his right, waving both arms in front of him. 'I don't feel anything yet.'

Kiriyama stopped and bent to pick up a rock, hefted it, tossed it up and down a few times, then hurled it at the asteroid. It flew a couple of yards and bounced off nothing at all. All three of them moved back.

'Let's see how it does with a laser beam.' Kiriyama nodded at Soga. 'Medium strength.' He and Anne moved a little farther back as Soga reached through the passenger-side window for the laser control on the dashboard.

The invisible barrier deflected the laser beam at a point Kiriyama estimated to be yard closer than where the rock had rebounded. Kiriyama told Soga to increase the strength thirty percent and fire again; the same thing happened.

Anne climbed up on the Pointer's roof with her binoculars. 'Captain?'

'See anything?' Kiriyama asked.

'The Ultra Hawk 1.'

Kiriyama hurried to climb up beside her; she handed him the binoculars. It was indeed the Hawk-1, he saw, slightly worse for wear after scraping its belly on the stony surface to fetch up against a ridge, but it was still intact. There were no scorch or burn marks but he couldn't tell if any of the crew were still inside. He watched for a full count of sixty while Soga tried to raise Furuhashi, Amagi, or Dan without success. When he gave up, Anne tried, but to no avail.

'I was hoping we were close enough to get through,' Soga said, disappointment large on his young face.

Kiriyama handed the binoculars back to Anne and slid down from the roof. 'There's no catastrophic damage visible,' he said. 'We should assume they survived.'

'Do you think they're trapped inside?' Anne's forehead puckered with worry.

'It's possible, but—' Kiriyama cut off as he realized the strolling island was moving toward them. 'Everyone back in the Pointer *now*!'

Without waiting for them to buckle in, he accelerated in reverse. The car shot back several yards; then Kiriyama yanked the steering wheel hard to the left while pulling up on the handbrake. Both Anne and Soga gasped as the back end of the Pointer slid around in a half-circle so they were facing away from the asteroid. Releasing the handbrake, Kiriyama stomped on the accelerator. The Pointer lurched forward, zooming back along the dirt road.

'Captain, it's *following* us!' Anne said, looking out the back window.

'You think it knows where we're going?' Soga said, fumbling with his safety belt.

'I don't know.' Kiriyama upshifted and stamped on the accelerator again. 'But we'd better get there first.'

'Are you getting anywhere yet?' Furuhashi asked, sounding so pitiful that Dan had to press his lips together to keep from laughing out loud. He and Furuhashi were bent double so Amagi could stand on their backs to get at the machinery above the front door. Amagi had been absolutely certain he could find some way to force the door open, but after ten minutes they seemed no closer to getting out than before.

'Hey, that's my *kidney* you're digging your heel into,' Furuhashi complained.

'Sorry,' Amagi said and shifted, momentarily putting all his weight on Dan's back. 'Is that better?'

'Well, it's *almost* not worse,' Furuhashi grumbled.

'Just try and stay as still as possible,' Amagi said as they all swayed with the asteroid's movement.

'Take your time, we're fine,' Dan said. 'Aren't we?' He looked at Furuhashi.

'Yeah, we're *great*. Never better,' said Furuhashi. 'But next time you ask for *backup*, I'll know better.'

Dan let out a surprised laugh. 'Good one!'

'Thanks.' Furuhashi winced. 'Dammit—after this, I'm going to need *months* of physio.'

Dan tried to see how Amagi was doing, but in his current position it wasn't easy. Amagi's head was enveloped in a cloud of red and blue wires. How he was making sense out of anything was beyond him. But then, neither Amagi nor Furuhashi was as sensitive as he was to the interference. So far, he'd covered pretty well, but if they had to stay much longer, his teammates were bound to notice he wasn't at full capacity.

The asteroid suddenly swerved to the right while simultaneously moving upward. Both Dan and Furuhashi went sprawling, leaving Amagi hanging from the open panel, kicking his legs and yelling for help.

'Sorry, Amagi,' Dan said as he and Furuhashi hurried to get back into position. 'There's nothing we can hang onto.'

'Tell me about it,' Amagi said, steadying his feet on their backs again. 'Whatever this place is, it wasn't made to accommodate an operations crew.'

'A spacecraft can go farther and faster when you don't have to worry about providing air, sustenance, or lifeboats,' Dan said. 'I mean, that's what I think. Plus, it can self-destruct anytime.'

Furuhashi turned his head sharply to look at him. 'You think this might be like a time bomb?'

'Hold still, will ya?' said Amagi.

'We *are* holding still,' Furuhashi said as he and Dan swayed from one side and then to the other.

'Well, hold still-er,' Amagi said. 'I've almost got—ouch!'

'Are you all right?' Dan asked.

'Yeah, just caught my finger.' Amagi sounded annoyed. 'Dammit, everything is wired into everything else. Dan, I think you're right—this thing can self-destruct, and I think it's going to do exactly that. The way it's wired, it's...' He floundered for a second. 'It's hard to explain but it's not set up to last.'

'You still think we're headed toward HQ?' Furuhashi asked.

'It hasn't made any major changes in direction,' said Amagi. 'So, yes—hey, I think I've got it!'

A moment later they were all tumbling backward as the door swung open, a little wider than before.

'Great work!' Furuhashi scrambled to his feet and offered hands to Amagi and Dan. 'Now let's see if we can get off this thing before we're in range of our better weapons.'

They ran for the Hawk-1.

'If its current rate of speed remains constant,' Anne said, showing Kiriyama and Manabe the graphic on her tablet, 'the strolling asteroid should amble into the parking lot in about fifty-three minutes.'

Kiriyama looked at Manabe, who took a breath and let it out. 'And you saw no sign of any survivors?' Manabe asked.

'No, but the Hawk-1 was intact,' Kiriyama said firmly. 'All three men are almost certainly still alive, possibly injured but not critically.'

Manabe's troubled expression deepened. 'We'll give it another thirty minutes.' He tapped a spot on the tablet screen. 'I'd rather it didn't get any closer to Tokyo than that point. Otherwise the whole city'll go dark.'

'You're thinking of using the Killer,' Kiriyama said.

Manabe heard the hint of accusation in Kiriyama's voice. 'With half the Ultra Guard trapped, possibly injured on that thing, it's not what I *want* to do. But something on that asteroid's made hash of our communications and disrupted normal operations. The Killer is self-contained, air-gapped, and unhackable.'

'Not to mention powerful,' Kiriyama said, seemingly more to himself. The TDF had tested the Killer on an uninhabited island; when the smoke cleared, the island no longer existed and effects of the blast had gone halfway through the Earth's crust. The Killer in their armory was somewhat smaller, but Kiriyama still considered it a last resort.

'Captain?' Manabe said.

Kiriyama nodded reluctantly. 'Get it prepped and into position. But we fire only on *my* command.'

'It's your operation, and your people,' Manabe assured him. 'I'd do the same.' He left to oversee the Killer prep.

Furuhashi sat back in the pilot's seat and watched ragged sheets of mist blowing across the Hawk-1's nose. 'If Anne were here, I bet she'd have found a way to get through the interference by now,' he said unhappily. 'Maybe if we went back—'

A deep, powerful rumble came up from somewhere far below the aircraft. For a moment, everyone was frozen in place, waiting for it to happen again.

'I don't know what that was,' Amagi said finally, 'but something tells me our interference problem just got worse.'

'The TDF isn't going to just let this thing stroll in and take up all the spaces in the parking lot,' Furuhashi said. 'If I were in command, I'd have any weapon still working prepped and on the ready line, no matter who was still in harm's way.'

'Like the Killer?' Amagi said.

'It's what I'd do,' Furuhashi said, although Dan didn't think he was completely convinced. 'And I'd do it before Tokyo went dark.'

'I believe you,' Dan lied. He pulled open the armaments cabinet next to the door. 'Since we can't get out of the line of fire, maybe we can let HQ know we're still kicking, trying to shut down the interference before they have to use the Killer.' He held up a chem charge. It was deceptively small, about the size of a wallet, containing two chemical mixtures in separate compartments. Both were stable on their own, but when combined, the explosive force left craters.

'What are you doing?' Furuhashi watched him tuck three charges into the front of his jacket.

'What I should have done in the first place.' Dan looked at the charges nestled around his Ultra Eye, then added two more before sealing the pocket. 'I don't know if these can take down an entire strolling asteroid, but I'm betting if they're in the right place, they can give it a black eye and a bloody nose.' He turned to leave.

'Wait, I'll come with you,' Amagi said. 'Or we'll all go—'

'No,' Dan said, giving Furuhashi an apologetic look. 'I know you don't want us splitting up, but I can do this faster alone. If—no, when the interference goes down, get ready to bug out fast. Copy?'

'Just get back here asap,' Furuhashi said. 'Make us leave without you and I'll write you up for insubordination.'

Amagi nodded solemnly. 'He will. He's kind of a jerk that way.'

'Copy that,' said Dan, laughing a little. 'Back before you know it.'

He slipped through the partially open door and ran back the way they had come. Once he was out of sight of the aircraft, he veered off on a ridge overlooking the three alien structures, pulled out the Ultra Eye, and pressed it to his face.

Nothing happened.

He was about to try again when he heard a loud, vicious animal roar.

'Oh, come on—seriously?' he said aloud, looking skyward.

The roar came again, louder, closer, and he saw a monstrous, reptilian creature emerging from a pool of mist.

Dan felt his mouth drop open. Not because of the creature's huge, glowing purple eyes or the alligator-type jaws filled with rows of pointed fangs, or even because at this point, the sudden appearance of a kaiju was so absurd that it seemed like an alien practical joke, but because he recognized it.

Among certain civilizations, the beast was known as a Rigger, and, left to its own devices, it tended to gravitate to areas of high radiation. Some less savory aliens had found ways to pair them to asteroids or moons as a way of staking a claim—or, as seemed likely here, as a way of clearing out any inconvenient indigenous lifeforms.

Dan tried pressing the Ultra Eye to his face again; still nothing. In his thousands of years of existence, he had never heard of anything that could block a Being of Light from their Ultra nature.

Another roar, even closer than before. If the Rigger saw the Hawk-1—

No, too late, Dan realized; it already had.

'Oh, for—where the *hell* did *that* come from?' Amagi said, gaping at the monster as it lashed its long tail from side to side and bellowed loudly.

'From deep in the heart of the Ultra Guard dharma,' replied Furuhashi, sounding bone-weary. Amagi turned to look at him, his expression a mix of alarm and bewilderment. 'But I'm just guessing. If you mean literally, that rumble we heard earlier was probably its cage opening somewhere underground.'

Amagi shook his head slightly as if to clear it. 'That thing could bite Dan in half and gulp down the pieces before he even knew he was dead.' Pause. 'If it hasn't already.'

'Not on our watch.' Furuhashi went to a larger cabinet. Inside were three heavy-shot plasma bolt rifles. These were the new, upgraded model, programmable on the fly, with twin barrels that could be discharged together, separately, or alternately, as well as selective targeting to avoid collateral damage when possible, and enough memory to preserve modes and settings. He tossed one to Amagi and grabbed another for himself. 'I've been dying to try this out on something other than targets on the range.'

Amagi hefted it with one hand. 'Wow, it's a lot lighter than the previous model.'

'I just hope its shielding holds against the interference,' Furuhashi said. 'At least long enough for us to bag a purple-eyed kaiju.'

Amagi followed him out of the Hawk-1, around the rear of the aircraft and up a steep stone incline with a crumbly coating on the surface; the two of them had to close their visors to avoid getting a face-full of rock shards and powder.

Furuhashi found a place that seemed made for sharpshooters— plenty of cover and a clear line of sight to where the creature was growling, bellowing, and kicking up bursts of soil and rock along with the ever-present fog.

'I'm sorry Soga's not here,' Amagi said, settling in beside Furuhashi. 'He's just what we need right now.'

'I saw your last range scores,' Furuhashi said, 'and I'm glad to have you on my side. Now let's waste this lousy lizard so we can fix the Hawk-1, find Dan, and get off this strolling rock before, one way or another, it blows.'

'Ready when you are,' Amagi said, taking aim.

'On my mark, five seconds continuous fire, then stop. Copy? Good.' Furuhashi adjusted his sights. 'Three... two... one... *mark!*'

The creature disappeared in a cloud of smoke and fog. Amagi saw flashes from direct hits and heard the monster's bellows rise in pitch. It seemed like much longer than five seconds before Furuhashi called, '*Cease fire!*' and even longer than that before the smoke and fog cleared enough for them to see the result.

The monster was roaring and flailing but it was still upright, obviously enraged, and not nearly as injured as they'd hoped.

'I thought for sure that would knock it down,' Amagi said, and was disconcerted to see its reptilian head swing around to look at them.

Furuhashi pulled him down behind the stone wall. 'I think it saw us.'

'Then it's got better vision than I do.' Amagi rose up and peeked over the rock.

The creature was laboriously clambering out of one pool of mist and into another, whipping its thick tail around as it moved in their general direction. Its rear limbs were flattened, he saw, and its feet were webbed.

'I don't think that thing really belongs in this place,' Amagi said to Furuhashi. 'It's more like a duck.'

'A *what*?' Furuhashi lifted himself up to take a look.

'See? Its rear limbs show it's a swimmer.'

'No wonder it's in such a lousy mood,' Furuhashi growled. 'Aw, *dammit*.'

The monster had made a small detour, Amagi saw. It brought one clawed forelimb squarely down on the Hawk-1, which crumpled like tinfoil. Roaring furiously, it kicked the wreckage out of its way. The Hawk-1 disappeared over a ridge; in the next moment, an enormous fireball blew upward from where it had landed.

'There goes our ride outta here,' Furuhashi said grimly.

'And here comes our latest crisis,' Amagi said as the kaiju scrambled over the edge of another fog pool. It seemed to be heading straight for them, its purple eyes glowing even more brightly and its jaws open in a classic predator's grin.

Furuhashi beckoned for Amagi to follow him down the ridge to a stone overhang, and then to the junction of at least half a dozen ridges so close together they were like stone pleats. Amagi headed for the ridge directly in front of them, but Furuhashi gave him a hard push to the left toward another overhang, then up a short but very steep incline to a promontory behind a pile of boulders.

The two of them crouched there, catching their breath and watching the beast stick its long snout into the place where they had been when they'd fired on it.

'I'm open to suggestions,' Furuhashi said.

'Give me a minute,' said Amagi. 'I'm thinking.'

Watching the monster crush the Hawk-1 and kick it away, Dan could get no sense of where Furuhashi and Soga were. The fireball marking the aircraft's destruction felt mercilessly final but he couldn't detect even a hint of anything organic in it. He could only hope that meant his friends were still alive, and it wasn't just interference blocking him from sensing what had happened to them.

No, it wasn't—they *were* still alive, he told himself; the loss of two humans he'd become so close to would be too great for interference to screen out. Besides, the creature was obviously hunting for something, the way it was nosing along the ridges and into crevices too small even for its snout.

All right, that was the good news. The bad news was everything else. And the worst news was, his Ultra Eye still didn't work. If anyone had told him there was a kind of interference strong enough to block his Ultra nature from himself, he'd never have believed it.

What would his teachers have said? Would they have put it down to his inexperience? Or would they just say something about how all lifeforms were subject to the laws of nature and he had to find a workaround?

Abruptly, he realized he already had a workaround and it was right there in his pocket, waiting for him to remember it. He pulled one of the capsules out of his trouser pocket.

'All right, Agira,' he whispered to it. 'Keep that monster too busy to eat us for lunch, okay?'

Standing up, he hurled the capsule toward the monster as hard as he could.

'Look!' Amagi clutched Furuhashi's arm hard enough to make him wince.

Near the purple-eyed creature, white bands of energy were spiraling up from the ground—and then there was a second creature. To Furuhashi, it looked like a triceratops that had evolved to walk on its hind legs.

'Where did *that* come from?' he said. 'Now we've got *two* monsters after us?'

'No,' Amagi said, catching hold of his arm as he turned to get away. 'I don't think that one's here for us. I think a friend sent it to help us out till he can get here himself.'

Furuhashi was about to argue, then shut up as the second monster threw itself on the kaiju's back and wrapped its massive arms around its neck, forcing it to the ground.

'Ultraseven!' Furuhashi looked around wildly. 'Where is he? Why doesn't he just fly in and kick that thing's ass?'

'I think he's got a problem with the interference,' Amagi said.

Now Furuhashi looked utterly baffled. 'You really think the asteroid's interference could be too much even for him?'

'It's *alien* interference,' Amagi reminded him. 'And I can't think of any other reason why Ultraseven isn't here already.'

Furuhashi blew out a long breath. 'I really hope Dan gets those charges planted.'

'And I hope he took enough of them,' Amagi said. 'Because if he didn't—'

The two men looked at each other.

'Yeah,' Furuhashi said. 'I hate when that happens.'

The door was still open when Dan reached the structure. He ran inside and set the charges, putting three of them on the console Amagi had said was a transmitter and the other two at the base of an interior, load-bearing wall. The shortest delay was fifteen seconds, which didn't give him much time to get clear. But if they worked the way he hoped, it wouldn't matter.

After activating each of them, he sprinted out the door and flung himself over a mound of earth and rock into a ditch. In the distance, he heard Agira roaring and bellowing as it battled the monster.

In the next moment, it was as if a giant fist slammed down on the ground beside him. He felt himself thrown back against something hard and lumpy as dirt and rock rained down on him. Then everything went away.

Crunch time. That had been what one of Kiriyama's training officers had called that magic moment when you had to decide to do something or give up on everything. The problem was, using the Killer felt more like giving up. Either way, it was now or never—they couldn't use the Killer on the asteroid if it got any closer or the radius of devastation would bite well into the Tokyo suburbs and beyond.

Kiriyama's gaze fell on Manabe standing nearby, waiting for his command. Sometimes there were only bad choices and worse choices, he thought. He opened his mouth to give the order to fire the Killer when fate or destiny or plain dumb luck smiled down on him and communications suddenly returned, startling a roomful of TDF personnel so much they all jumped.

'Captain, the interference is gone!' Soga shouted. A screen to Kiriyama's left lit up with the feed from Furuhashi's body camera, which seemed to be showing a movie about giant monsters fighting each other. One looked like a biped triceratops; the other seemed to be a cross between an alligator and a dragon, with glowing purple eyes.

Anne was already at the main comm board. 'HQ calling the Ultra Guard! Please respond!'

'Furuhashi here,' came the reply.

'We copy,' Kiriyama said, leaning over Anne's shoulder. 'Return to base immediately.'

'Sorry, captain, unable to comply,' Furuhashi said cheerfully. 'Due to an unforeseen kaiju attack, our ride home got trashed. But now that the interference is gone, maybe you can swing by and pick us up before you blow this asteroid to smithereens?'

'On our way.' Kiriyama looked from Anne to Soga. 'You heard the man—let's go!'

Dan regained consciousness to the sound of roaring and bellowing somewhere in the distance. Two very large beasts were going at each other full-on, without mercy. One of them definitely had the upper hand, or paw, or claw, and it wasn't the one whose bellows he recognized.

Memory fell on him like a flood of cold water and he jumped to his feet, looking around until he spotted Agira. The kaiju had wrapped its thick tail around the capsule monster from neck to midsection. In the next moment, it snapped its tail like a whip, sending Agira into a pile of rocks. The pile blew apart as Agira rebounded into an uneven stone wall and tumbled over it. The purple-eyed monster roared in furious triumph and reared back, preparing to deliver a killing blow.

'Agira!' Dan hollered, holding up his hand. 'Come back to me now!'

The white bands of power reappeared around Agira and he was gone. Dan felt the monster rematerialize in his palm, reassuringly weighty, and stuffed it back into his trouser pocket.

Then he realized the interference was gone.

Did he dare to believe that? Without giving himself time to answer that question, he clapped the Ultra Eye to his face.

This time, the transformation was like having his senses restored after an eternity of deprivation. The interference had blocked his Ultra nature so completely, he'd lost all sense of what it was to be a Being of Light.

Now he looked up at the bright blue sky, feeling the sun's energy surge through him, feeling the light suffuse his mind and spirit as well as his body. He drank it in, then turned to the kaiju, roaring and flailing in a pool of mist; so close to him, he was on it in a leap.

'Captain, the drones we sent out earlier are back online,' Manabe said.

'So I see.' Kiriyama grinned broadly at the sight of Ultraseven straddling a monstrous beast with long alligator jaws full of mean pointed teeth and an even meaner disposition.

There'd been nothing to indicate the presence of such a creature—but then, there'd been nothing to suggest there wasn't. All that mattered was the Killer could go back to the armory, unused.

'Soga!'

'Right here, Captain!' Soga was at his side.

'Prep the Hawk-3 for immediate departure.' Kiriyama nodded at Anne. 'We can't leave *everything* to Ultraseven. Let's go!'

* * *

Furuhashi was sure there had never been a noisier fight than the one between the purple-eyed monster and their unofficial seventh teammate. Every blow seemed to reverberate and the creature blustered, wailed, and roared in fury, its jaws snapping at Ultraseven's arms and legs as the red and silver figure darted forward to strike, then danced out of the monster's reach. The din was so loud, Furuhashi didn't think he'd have known the Ultra Hawk 3 had arrived if he hadn't seen it land.

He and Amagi ran to meet Kiriyama, Anne, and Soga as they ran across the stone terrain, weapons in hand. The five of them met up just as something underground detonated with enough force to make the whole asteroid wobble.

'Where's Dan?' Anne said by way of hello.

'He went to plant chem charges, hoping to knock out the interference,' Furuhashi said. 'I guess it worked. Amagi must have been right about the transmitter.'

Amagi wasn't listening; he was using his wristcomm's scanner function on the monster. 'Captain, I'm getting a new signal from something in that creature's head. It's a homing beacon.'

Reflexively, they all looked up at the sky. 'How close do you think the invading force might be?' Soga asked, his face puckered with worry.

'I suspect they'll send in a few more asteroids before they get here with the moving vans.' Kiriyama used his own wristcomm to call Manabe with an update. 'Raise readiness to DEFCON 1 and keep the Killer on standby, just in case.' As he disconnected, his gaze fell on the plasma bolt rifle slung over Furuhashi's shoulder.

'I'm afraid this was all we managed to save from the Hawk-1,' Furuhashi said, his face apologetic. 'The burning wreckage is...' He looked around. 'Well, it's around here somewhere...'

Kiriyama shook his head, unperturbed. 'We can replace an aircraft a lot more easily than any of the Ultra Guard.' He was about to say something else when another violent tremor shook the ground under them, then kept shaking it harder than anything Kiriyama had experienced, even in the prefectures along the Sea of Japan.

'Captain, this, uh, strolling asteroid has become unstable,' Amagi said. 'We should get airborne before it comes apart altogether.'

'But *where's Dan*?' Anne demanded.

'I've been trying to raise him since we got comms back,' Furuhashi told her. 'But it's like he disappeared—like he's not on the asteroid anymore.'

Kiriyama frowned as sheets of mist blew over the group. Visibility was getting worse; fog was coming up out of more crevices and cracks in the rocky landscape. 'We'll search for Dan from the air,' Kiriyama said. 'Once we find him, we'll lower a lifeline and reel him in.'

'What if he's unconscious?' Anne asked.

'Then we'll lower *Furuhashi* on a lifeline to pick him up,' Amagi said.

Everyone looked at Furuhashi. 'Works for me,' he said. 'Now let's go!'

While the rest of the Ultra Guard sprinted for the Hawk-3 and the asteroid shuddered and shook, the battle between the Ultra Being and the Rigger raged on. This particular Rigger had never encountered an actual Ultra before, although there was information about Beings of Light from the asteroid's data vaults. Or there had been, before the control center had blown up.

The asteroid's interference had served to shield the vaults, allowing the data to remain holographic. The first chem charge Dan had set had knocked out the interference completely; the next had scrambled both the data and the process that allowed the asteroid's artificial brain to create a workspace. The fourth and fifth had cracked the maintenance chamber, destroying the asteroid's ability to repair itself.

The civilization that had developed this method of conquest and acquisition had persisted with it for millennia despite repeated warnings from other, more advanced lifeforms, including the Ultras. As a species, they hadn't been inherently aggressive, or at least no more so than any other beings still on their way to enlightenment. Somewhere in their distant, unrecorded history, something had tweaked their vision and made them see the universe in terms of conquerors and those conquered. Now they took planets from their original inhabitants simply because they always had.

Sending unmanned vessels—asteroids—to clear populated worlds ahead of their arrival was efficient and effective. Of course, one asteroid wasn't enough to clear an entire planet, even one as small as Earth. It usually took four or five at least, which was no problem: asteroids were ubiquitous. They were space flotsam, often accumulating at what Earth people called the Lagrange points of any body orbiting a star. The planetary system Earth belonged to had an orbital path occupied by nothing *but* asteroids, which would be very convenient for future conquests.

Agent 340 hadn't mapped any world conquered in such a fashion; otherwise, he would have reported them to his superiors as a crime against life in need of immediate correction. Now as he grappled with the Rigger, he couldn't help imagining his Ultra teachers shining their approval on him, even with his assignment unfinished. Surely preventing invaders from exterminating humanity was far more important, he thought. In the final reckoning, whenever that would come, an incomplete mapping assignment would be a peccadillo compared to preventing a conscious, intelligent species from being wiped out for their real estate.

Wouldn't it?

He dodged the Rigger's long, sinuous tail to grab the creature around the neck, twisted hard, and forced it down on the stony ground. The Rigger flexed, undulated, and suddenly it was on top of him while he strained to keep its snapping jaws away from his neck.

Abruptly, he felt something deep underground cracking and coming apart. The charges he had set off had scrambled the asteroid's programming so that it had flipped into self-destruct mode. If it blew now, it would trigger the next wave of invaders—more asteroids would arrive to begin wiping out the population. After that, the invaders themselves would arrive to pick through the ruins and decide what they could use to remake the world for themselves. And before they'd even finished sweeping up the debris, another asteroid would be launched, to go in search of the next world to conquer after this one was used up.

Deep inside, his human aspect asserted itself: *Not on* my *watch.*

He broke out of the Rigger's grasp, rolled away and, in one smooth motion, jumped to his feet, swept the Eye Slugger from atop his head, and slung it at the monster. It sliced through the creature's neck and flew back to him before the thing knew it was dead.

Several meters away from the clumsy, still-twitching body, the head kept snapping at the air with its jaws, its purple eyes glowing. Apparently, it still didn't know it was dead; the beacon in its skull was transmitting more strongly now, drowning out all the other signals from its nervous system.

Grabbing up the severed head, he launched himself into the sky just as the Hawk-3 took off with all five of his teammates aboard, safe and well. They'd done their part; now it was up to him to get rid of the asteroid.

As he flew higher and higher, he sensed the asteroid chasing him; its damaged artificial brain had locked onto the beacon in the Rigger's head as the only signal it could understand. All he had to do was get it out of the atmosphere and off the plane of the ecliptic, which would send it into the intergalactic void, away from living beings.

He had just reached the edge of space when the asteroid blew.

A surge of horror went through him for all of a second before he saw the asteroid had shattered into countless infinitesimal pieces; they disappeared in tiny bursts of light as they fell through the atmosphere.

For a long moment, he hung there on the threshold between Earth and space, looking out at the stars. Seen from here, starlight was steady, constant, unblinking. It hadn't been that long since he'd last been here, thinking again of how easily he could go back to his life as Agent 340. Instead, he had chosen to remain even after traveling all the way to the ringed planet and back.

For Anne. For all of them, really, but most of all for Anne. Who right now would be asking where Dan Moroboshi was.

Twinkling stars had a beauty he had come to appreciate. Besides, letting Anne and the others believe he'd been blown up with the asteroid was no way to treat people who had willingly accepted him into their lives.

CHAPTER

EIGHT

Dan woke with a start, sure he'd heard someone call him, not as Agent 340 or Dan Moroboshi but by the wordless name that meant himself. For a few seconds, he was lost in the dark. Then his gaze fell on the silly owl clock on the wall, its eyes looking left to right, moving counter to its pendulum.

The silly owl clock had been a gift from Anne. *If you wake from a crazy dream in the middle of the night and you don't know where you are, you can look at the owl and know you're right where you're supposed to be,* she'd said. *The silly owl clock will tell you you're home.*

Furuhashi, Soga, and even Amagi had teased him about it unmercifully, until Anne had threatened to use only rectal thermometers in the clinic. That had shut them right up, much to Dan's amusement.

There was nothing to be amused about now, not even the silly owl clock, which had always made him smile. He was covered in sweat again, for the seventh night in a row. Or was it the eighth? The tenth? He wasn't sure. Whatever crazy dream he'd awakened from was gone except for a few barely remembered fragments. It was a quarter to three—if he didn't get a move on, he'd be late for his shift.

He pushed the damp sheet away, swung his legs over the side of the bed, and got up to shuffle off to the shower, hoping that would wake him up. It did, but not as much as he'd hoped. He felt like he'd barely slept at all, he thought as he pulled on his uniform and headed for the hangar to sign in.

Finding Soga there filling out his end-of-shift report was a pleasant surprise. Since he'd joined the Ultra Guard, he'd developed a genuine affection for Soga, who was always good company—seldom grouchy, quick to laugh, and easy to talk to.

When Soga saw him, however, his smooth young face took on a worried expression. 'Jeez, Dan, did you get any sleep at all? You look like the living undead.'

Dan forced a laugh. 'I asked myself the same question. I know I got some sleep but it sure doesn't feel like it.'

Soga's concerned expression intensified. 'You want to go back to bed and try again? I can take your shift for you.'

'Nah, I'm fine,' Dan assured him. 'I've just got to wake up some more.'

But Soga wasn't satisfied. 'You've been tired a lot lately. Being tired all the time can be a symptom, you know. Maybe Anne should give you one of her super-thorough workups. It's not fun but you might need it.'

'I'm not gonna wake her up now.' Dan chuckled. 'She'll whip out the rectal thermometer.'

'Maybe she should,' Soga said.

'Not before my shift in the cockpit,' said Dan. 'I'm fine, Soga, really. If I wasn't, I wouldn't be here. Honest.'

Soga hesitated, looking uncertain. Then: 'All right, I guess you know how you feel better than I do. Meet up later for a game of *Outrun*?'

Dan grinned. The vintage racing game was Soga's latest off-duty obsession. 'Count on it. Leaving you in the dust always puts pep in my gitalong.'

'Step,' Soga corrected him. 'It's "pep in your step" but "a hitch in your gitalong."'

'Whatever.' Dan laughed. 'I don't know where you get that stuff.' He started toward the elevator.

'Oh, hey, I almost forgot,' Soga said, making him stop. 'Kurata's back on Space Station 3. He's in Overwatch for your shift.'

Dan sagged a little. 'Thanks for the warning.'

'Yeah, I guess everyone down here got sick of him, so they put him back in orbit.'

'Kurata's good at what he does,' Dan said, more to remind himself. 'He's just...' He thought for a couple of seconds. 'Unhappy.'

'And he doesn't mind sharing it,' Soga said, nodding. 'Race you later.' He trotted off to the stairs quickly enough, though not before Dan sensed he was thinking about talking to Anne about him.

If he'd felt slightly more energetic, he might have gone after Soga and tried harder to jolly him out of his concern. But he knew his friend probably wouldn't say anything to Anne. That would have been an official, on-the-record action akin to what humans called *snitching*, which was unacceptable except in extreme circumstances. Soga wouldn't do that to any of his teammates, and neither would he.

Although he'd been tempted to leave an anonymous note for Psychiatric Services about Kurata's perpetual hostility. The guy hadn't been reticent about expressing his displeasure at Manabe recruiting Dan into the Ultra Guard. It was no mystery why—he'd applied twice and been told both times he needed more experience in the TDF. From Kurata's point of view, Dan had walked in off the street and leapfrogged over him into a position that should have been his.

Being assigned to a space station was hardly scutwork—it was the kind of plum job that would have given anyone else a sunnier disposition. But Kurata wouldn't be satisfied with anything other than the elite squad.

Well, with any luck, Dan thought, he'd have no reason to communicate with him.

The Ultra Hawk 2 had just crossed the threshold from the exosphere into outer space when Dan heard Kurata's voice in his headphones.

'Hawk-2, this is V3. If you're out there, please respond.'

If you're out there. Apparently, Kurata knew it was his shift; he was already locked and loaded.

'Hawk-2 responding to V3,' Dan said, keeping his voice neutral. 'What's going on where you are?'

'What's "going on" here? Well, let's see,' Kurata said in a flat voice. 'We've got a full schedule here. Unidentified spacecraft detected. Sending you coordinates.'

Dan checked the message screen on the dashboard. 'Coordinates received. Have you tried sending out a drone?'

Kurata gave an offended sniff. 'Exploratory drone deployed earlier, has since vanished. Debris detected. Unknown vessel hasn't responded to any calls. Pursue, scan, and take any defensive action necessary.'

'Copy that, V3.' Dan hesitated. 'Suggest you deploy another drone.'

Kurata gave a single harsh laugh. 'What for, Hawk-2—so the unknown vessel can get in some more target practice? *We* can't afford to lose expensive hardware, we don't have the Ultra Guard's budget. Procedure is: pursue, investigate, and defend, Hawk-2. Unless you have something more important to do?'

'Will investigate and report, V3,' Dan said briskly. 'Hawk-2 out.'

He cut the connection and set the display on his larger dashboard screen to real-time recording. The unknown spacecraft appeared as a large point of white light against a starry backdrop. Magnification showed him it was actually a rectangular box with wings, but no other marks or features.

Dan scanned it for the presence of lifeforms and wasn't really surprised when the result came up as undetermined. Vibrations in the spacecraft's hull were confounding his instruments. He'd have to keep trying to find its resonance, and that would take some time.

If Kurata didn't like that, Dan thought, he could complain to the aliens who had sent it out.

'Hawk-2, respond now! V3 calling Hawk-2, dammit, are you out there?'

Dan came to with a start. 'This is Hawk-2,' he said automatically, hoping he didn't sound as foggy and disoriented as he felt.

'Hawk-2, I've been calling you for the last *two minutes!*' Kurata's angry voice was loud enough to rattle the speakers. 'What the hell's wrong with you?'

'Nothing's wrong,' Dan replied. 'What's *your* problem?'

'*My* problem? *I* don't have a problem except I'm waiting on a visual from *you*. What happened, did you doze off?'

'Wide awake, thanks for asking.' Dan found the alien vessel had slipped past him and was now entering the atmosphere. He was changing course when the fire alarm went off.

'Hey, Hawk-2, don't look now but your tail's on fire.' Kurata sounded positively gleeful.

'No kidding? Thanks for the heads-up,' Dan replied, activating the fire suppression system. 'Any other obvious things you'd like to point out?'

'Hawk-2, identify yourself,' Kurata snapped.

As if he really didn't know, Dan thought, answering with his ID.

'Yeah, I thought so,' Kurata sneered. 'Who else would it be? Good luck with your emergency. Try not to sleep through it.'

'Yeah, you have a nice day too,' Dan said, checking to make sure the fire was out before he followed the spacecraft's trajectory—

—and came to again just as the alien vessel fired on him.

Alarms were blaring but his eyes kept trying to roll up in his head. It was a struggle to stay conscious as he fired back.

Something was scraping the underside of the Hawk-2— treetops, he discovered with some alarm. Ahead of him, the alien ship was in flames. He was steering away from it when his eyes were suddenly so heavy he couldn't keep them open.

This time Dan jerked awake to find himself in sick bay. Immediately, Anne was beside him, pushing him back down on the bed as he tried to sit up.

'What happened?' he asked, too drained to push her hands away.

'You were chasing that uninvited guest and the both of you crashed about two kilometers from the base,' she told him. 'So for the next forty-eight hours, you belong to me.'

Dan blinked at her. 'I—wait, what?'

'You heard me.' Anne was smiling but her eyes were serious. 'Dan Moroboshi, you are *not* well. You're presenting like someone who hasn't slept in three days and probably hasn't eaten for even longer. I'm prescribing a course of rest and good nutrition, to be carried out *here*, so I can keep you under observation. If you haven't improved to my satisfaction within that time, I'll need to run a full battery of tests.' Her smile faded a bit. 'You know, you're not the first member of the Ultra Guard or the TDF I've treated for exhaustion. I want to make sure it's *only* exhaustion and not something more serious.'

'I can't just lie around here for two days,' Dan protested.

'You can if Captain Kiriyama says you can,' Anne said evenly. 'And he does.'

Dan sighed. 'I can sleep in my quarters just as easily.'

'But then you wouldn't be hooked up to monitoring equipment that'll tell me how well you're sleeping,' said Anne. 'If you're not getting proper sleep, you need treatment. Fortunately, we've got a sleep specialist on staff.'

'I don't need a specialist,' Dan said. 'I'm fine. I just need some rest.'

Anne was unmoved. 'If that's true, we'll all be relieved.' She paused. 'Look, Dan, I wouldn't insist except Kurata's sent an incident report to Kiriyama saying you blacked out on duty. And then you went and crashed. We had to take action.'

Hearing this made Dan feel even more exhausted. 'Should've known,' he said, sighing. 'Just because I took a few extra seconds to answer him on comms, he thought I'd dropped into a coma.'

'Kurata can be a major pain in the ass,' Anne said. 'And he'll never win any popularity contests. But he'd never do this to someone just because he didn't like them—no, not even you. If he made a report, it's because he had good reason to believe you were in some kind of trouble. He might be petty and spiteful, but if he'd really wanted to hurt you, he'd have kept quiet when you crashed.'

Dan made a face. 'Still…'

'Cheer up,' Anne ordered him. 'I won't keep you locked up here. Tomorrow you can get some gentle exercise in the gym if you're feeling up to it.'

'I feel up to it now,' Dan lied.

'Too bad—tomorrow is soon enough. Obey your doctor,' she added as he opened his mouth to protest. 'Don't make me take your temperature.'

He slumped back against the pillows.

'Here.' Anne pushed a tablet into his hands. 'Read a book or watch a video. Or both. Learn how to relax—you'll live longer.'

A day later, Anne couldn't help feeling a little guilty as she watched Dan on the video feed from the basketball court.

She told herself she was simply being a conscientious doctor assessing a patient's overall fitness. Everybody knew there were cameras all over the gym, including the basketball court; it wasn't like she was spying on him, not really. Only it sure felt like it.

If he'd been anyone else, she'd have sat in some inconspicuous corner to observe and make notes, and the patient in question would never have known she was there. But she could never do that with Dan; somehow he always knew when she was around, and he'd distract her by suggesting they go for a walk or take a tea break in the cafeteria. Then, after a while, he'd suddenly remember he'd left some paperwork unfinished or he had a report to write and that would be the last she saw of him for hours.

His reluctance to submit to medical treatment wasn't unusual. Everyone—Ultra Guard or TDF, officers or rank-and-file, men or women—they were all terrible patients. Anne was baffled. These were educated people and they understood how important it was for all of them to be fit for duty. But getting them to hold still even for a quick routine check was next to impossible.

And Dan was the worst of all. That instinct or whatever it was he had for knowing when she was nearby meant she could never catch him off-guard. It made her wonder if he was what her grandmother referred to as *gifted*.

Soga was sure Dan was a genius like Amagi. Amagi himself had remarked that he never had to simplify an explanation for Dan, while Furuhashi claimed Dan could have been a professional athlete. If he'd been watching Dan now, he might have changed his mind, Anne thought. When he dribbled, he kept losing control of the ball, and he'd missed every single shot he'd taken at the basket.

Well, it hadn't been that long since the crash. Nobody would be ready to be in the starting lineup for a game of catch after something like that. At least he hadn't had any more blackouts. Those really worried her.

She sighed as Dan took another shot at the basket and missed. He let the ball bounce away and sat down on the court, his elbows on his knees and his head in his hands. Whatever was eating him was taking big bites.

'Why are you suffering alone?' she whispered. 'Why won't you talk to me?'

As if he'd heard her, he raised his head and looked directly at the surveillance camera. Startled, she turned the screen off, then immediately felt like an idiot. For all his keen awareness, Dan could not possibly have sensed her watching him on a screen. He'd probably just remembered the gym surveillance and felt self-conscious about his poor performance; the timing was nothing more than coincidence. After all, Dan was only human.

Wasn't he?

She turned the screen back on. The basketball court was empty.

'Our space stations have sighted more unknown objects in the past month than we've seen in the past year,' Kiriyama said to the Ultra Guard assembled in his office. 'Dellinger effects have been recorded every day and they're the kind of sudden ionospheric disturbances we'd normally see with solar flares. Except there haven't been any solar flares.'

'It's all been playing merry hell with communications everywhere,' Amagi put in. 'Not to mention the migration patterns of certain birds.'

'So carrier pigeons *aren't* a viable alternative when comms go down?' Furuhashi asked. Everyone laughed except Kiriyama, who managed only a perfunctory smile.

'Mixed in with all these disturbances are a lot of phantom signals,' Kiriyama went on. 'We've been able to determine most of them don't come from actual alien vessels, but the general public doesn't have our sophisticated tech. Which means every amateur UFO spotter is calling in to report suspect phenomena. Even invisible invaders.'

'"Invisible invaders,"' Furuhashi marveled, then looked wary. 'Wow, I really hope not.'

'Civilians are also getting into accidents chasing what they think are alien spaceships in remote areas. This is starting to spread to the suburbs.'

Dan sat up a bit straighter in his chair. 'Do you think the false alarms could be deliberate?' he asked, knowing Kiriyama was considering the possibility.

'I'm not sure what to think,' Kiriyama said. It wasn't really a lie; the captain had always tried not to jump to conclusions.

And Anne was sneaking another glance at him. Lately, whenever she looked at him, he sensed it as distinctly as if she'd tapped him on the shoulder. Her attachment to him was growing stronger, and it wasn't just human nature. A connection between Ultras was more than an abstract kind of thing. Granted, Anne wasn't an Ultra, but he'd been here long enough that she was becoming attached. They all were in their individual ways but Anne most of all. She had no idea how substantial the connection was between them, only that she had come to care for him, which made it imperative that she determine the cause of his exhaustion.

It came to him suddenly that the cause might be Anne herself. Not *just* her, but everyone on the Ultra Guard as well as the TDF, and any—every?—other human he came into contact with. He sensed so much about them but it wasn't mutual. He expended far more energy on them than they could on him.

Kiriyama ended the meeting by advising them to be ready for anything on short notice, then dismissed them. Dan was the first one out of the room, projecting the air of a busy person with no time to talk, but Anne caught up with him.

'I was observing you just now,' she said.

'I thought my forty-eight hours were up,' he said lightly, not slowing down.

'Dan, you look like you're carrying the weight of the world on your shoulders,' she said, trotting to keep up.

'That could be a stray Dellinger effect,' he said, hoping she'd laugh; she didn't. 'You cleared me for duty. I hope you haven't changed your mind?'

'No, but—' She practically had to run now to keep pace. 'I think you should have a complete workup. Blood tests, X-rays, CT scans, the whole package.'

'Maybe after things quiet down,' he said.

'I'd rather not wait. I've got time today for a few tests.'

Now Dan did stop. 'Absolutely not. You heard the captain—if something happens, I don't want to be caught in an X-ray machine in my underwear.'

'But—'

'I said *no*, dammit!'

Anne stared at him, her face full of surprised hurt.

The right thing to do now was apologize. But if he did, she would keep after him.

'Is that clear?' Dan added, then walked off without waiting for an answer.

As he'd hoped, she didn't chase him. But her hurt feelings stuck to him like glue.

* * *

'Agent 340.'

Dan's eyes flew open. He could hear the silly owl clock ticking steadily in the darkness but that was all. It must be nearly time for him to get up, he thought, and he must have had another dream. No one had called him Agent 340 in such a long time, although it really wasn't, not for an Ultra. Even on Earth's highly shortened scale of duration, it wasn't all that long. But so much had happened since he'd come here that his life as Agent 340 seemed more distant than it really was.

He waited and still heard only the silly owl clock. His eyelids became heavy and he let them fall closed.

'No, I should call you by the name you're known by here on Earth—Ultraseven.'

Instantly he was wide awake again, blinking up at the tall red and silver figure standing over him. The pattern of his colors was different from his own but there was no doubt that this was an Ultra. Joy surged in him at the sight of another like himself, joy and a feeling of having something restored to him that he hadn't realized was missing.

'Your time here has taken quite a toll on you,' the other Ultra went on. 'You remain here on Earth at your peril. It's time—past time, really—for you to return home to the Land of Light.'

'I would,' Dan said. 'I want to. But this beautiful world has been a target for hostile forces. I can't leave it unprotected.'

'Even Ultras reach a point where they have to think of their own wellbeing,' the other said. 'Staying here will mean your death.'

'But I *can't* leave now,' Dan insisted. 'I've seen the signs. Something terrible is imminent. I can't just turn my back on Earth.'

'Listen to me!' said the Ultra and Dan sensed him bristling with urgency and impatience. 'Understand this if nothing else—

each battle you've fought has used up part of your life-force and now you have precious little left. If you expend any more energy fighting for these humans, you'll never be able to return to your own world. You must not—you *cannot* transform!'

The Ultra made a sweeping gesture at his uniform jacket hanging on the back of a chair and Dan saw his Ultra Eye fly out of the front pocket to land on the silly owl clock.

'If you transform again, *you will die.*'

In the next moment, his eyes opened and he jumped, startled. Sitting up, he reached for the lamp on his nightstand, turned it on. There was no one else in the room; another crazy dream. But just in case, he hooked his foot around the chair with his jacket, dragged it over, and looked in the front pocket for the Ultra Eye.

It was gone.

The pit in his stomach was an abyss as big as a planet as he searched the other pockets and felt the lining. Then he checked the floor and under the bed. Finally, he turned to the silly owl clock.

The silly owl's eyes slid from side to side in the bright red frames. The Ultra silly owl clock; Dan went over to it. Was he still dreaming? He reached for the Ultra Eye, bracing himself to find that as soon as he touched it, he'd be back in bed, waking up again, for real this time (he hoped). But nothing happened. The clock went on ticking; the eyes slid left as the pendulum swung right, and vice versa, just like always. Nobody here but him, no other Ultras, no humans, no aliens, not even us chickens; just good old Dan Moroboshi, Ultra Six, and from time to time, Ultraseven, when needed.

A chill ran through him, intense enough that he could feel all the little hairs on the back of his neck and arms stand up. Anne had told him this was a phenomenon called *horripilation* and it was often a physical manifestation of fear, although it could also happen in response to something extraordinarily beautiful.

Tonight, he could definitely rule out beauty.

The Ultra had spoken the truth: he was damaged, and what sunlight came through the filter of Earth's atmosphere wasn't enough to restore him completely. If he'd been at full strength, he'd have already known what sort of menace Earth was facing. In his present damaged, impaired state, he could only feel it was something pernicious, and as merciless as it was malign. And yet, as impaired as he was, Earth had no chance without him.

Mapping the galaxy had been an assignment but Earth was where his life was, and if his life ended here, then it ended. As Furuhashi would have said, he knew what he'd signed up for.

'Hawk-3 to Hawk-1, are you seeing what we're seeing?' Soga's voice was even and steady but half an octave higher than normal.

In the Hawk-1 with Kiriyama, Furuhashi, and Anne, Dan was briefly overwhelmed by their reactions: Furuhashi's frustration at wanting to be more capable mixed with Kiriyama's anxiety that he may have overlooked something, and Anne's worry for everyone, Dan Moroboshi most of all.

'Not yet, Hawk-3,' Kiriyama replied. 'We have your position but—'

The alien vessel they'd been chasing for the last half hour suddenly emerged from a puffy cumulous cloud, and everybody in the Hawk-1, including Dan, gasped at the size.

'Hawk-3, you weren't kidding when you said it was *big*,' said Furuhashi. He glanced at Kiriyama sitting beside him in the pilot's seat. 'Captain, should we divide into three?'

'Not yet,' Kiriyama said tensely, his eyes fixed on the alien spacecraft. 'Hawk-3, have you been able to make contact?'

'Amagi here, Captain. So far, the alien ship hasn't responded to our presence at all. We scanned for lifeforms but results were inconclusive.'

'Either it's carrying live passengers or it isn't.' There was a testy note in Kiriyama's voice.

'I'm getting the same readings, Captain,' Anne said apologetically. 'See for yourself.'

Kiriyama checked the dashboard screen to the left of the yoke. 'And it isn't a problem with the scanners?'

'If it is, our scanner is broken exactly like the Hawk-3's, and that just doesn't happen.'

'Hawk-1, I have a theory.' Amagi sounded slightly more confident than apprehensive. 'The ship may be full of modular bots with organic enhancements on standby. Once that thing lands, they'll activate fully.'

'Should we shoot it down?' Furuhashi asked.

'*No*,' Kiriyama said emphatically. 'I don't want to spread whatever's inside all over Japan.'

Dan sensed Kiriyama looking at him but didn't take his eyes off the alien spacecraft. It was another rectangular box with wings, made for a one-way journey. And whatever was inside was only the beginning.

'Furuhashi, give them a warning shot across their bow,' Kiriyama said. 'See if that gets their attention.'

'Hawk-1 to Hawk-3, firing warning shots,' Furuhashi said.

'Copy that, Hawk-1,' replied Amagi. 'We're ready to back you up.'

Furuhashi sent a short series of plasma bolts past the alien vessel's nose. It didn't change course or fire back.

'You think it could be unmanned?' Furuhashi asked Kiriyama.

'That would make it one helluva big drone,' Kiriyama said.

'Maybe *they're* big—the aliens,' Anne said. 'Bigger than we are, anyway.'

'Or they want us to think so,' Furuhashi said with a grim chuckle.

Abruptly, the alien ship did change course, made a wide turn, then began slowly spiraling downward. Dan watched as it passed over the western edge of the Tokyo suburbs to set down in the middle of several hundred acres of undeveloped land.

The Hawk-1 and Hawk-3 circled above it, waiting to see what would happen next. Three minutes passed; no activity.

'Hawk-3 to Hawk-1, scanner readings have changed,' Amagi said, his voice a bit strained. 'Now they indicate the presence of one large organic entity.'

'We're getting the same thing, Hawk-3,' Anne said. 'Maybe the modules have assembled into one unit?'

'Let's take it to ground level and find out,' said Kiriyama, and changed course, heading for a level area just beyond a line of trees.

As soon as they disembarked, a pit in Dan's stomach opened up again, deeper and more uncomfortable than ever. But when the six of them came together, the feeling lessened, almost as if they weren't just the Ultra Guard but Ultras.

Except they *weren't* Ultras, Dan reminded himself. There was only one Ultra and he wasn't at full strength. Nonetheless, he could sense all of his teammates' feelings, jumbled together and yet distinct, with the captain's dominant as he divided them into three teams: Soga and Amagi would approach the alien ship from the southwest while Dan and Anne went at from the northeast, and Kiriyama and Furuhashi would introduce themselves up front.

Kiriyama was carrying the Heavy-Shot, recently upgraded to fire grenade-level charges; the rest had their sidearms, also upgraded so they were more powerful. Dan sensed Kiriyama's mild surprise at how good it felt to carry a big weapon, how right it felt in his hands, and how glad he was to be in the field with his team rather than giving orders from afar. The warrior-barbarian aspect of human nature had been eclipsed by civilization but not erased. Still, in the back of Kiriyama's mind, he was admonishing himself not to enjoy the big weapon *too* much.

Furuhashi slipped easily into warrior mode; he always had. He would slip out of it again almost as easily, although a small part of the warrior within was always awake and vigilant, just in case.

It was Soga and Amagi that Dan felt less certain about, but it wasn't like he could try to persuade Kiriyama to have them hang back in Overwatch—well, not unless he revealed his Ultra nature to the whole team. Perhaps he should have done that already, right after they'd rescued Jiro Satsuma. That would have put a whole new spin on their underground adventure, not to mention the team—they'd never have been the same after that.

Well, he'd never know, and he certainly couldn't hit them with the revelation now, when they were about to face an alien attack. And there was Anne to consider. She was trying not to worry about his physical condition because she wanted to trust him to be as well as he claimed, and yet she couldn't quite believe it. Finding out he was Ultraseven wouldn't ease her mind, it would give her a whole new set of worries—

A small but very hard fist punched his arm. '*Dan!* What are you, asleep?'

He turned to look at Anne blankly.

'I *said*, there's a trench ready-made for us!' She pointed ahead of them. 'Probably left over from the last monsoon. It's deep enough to hide in but we'll still have a good view of the alien ship.'

'Good thinking.' He hopped into it, turned to help her but she managed on her own. Which for some reason made him feel slightly rejected.

'All right, so what do we do now?' Anne said in a low voice.

'We wait to see whatever we're going to see.' He drew his sidearm and she did the same, bristling with impatience.

'I *hate* waiting,' she fumed.

'I do, too.' It came to him then that part of her frustration was left over from his refusal to submit to medical tests. In spite of everything, it made him smile—but inwardly, where she couldn't see it.

'Did you see that?!' Amagi grabbed Soga's arm as they crouched together in a gully.

'Ow! See what? *Ow!*' Soga pried Amagi's hand off his bicep, wincing.

'I don't know what it was, but I just saw it. Right there!' Amagi pointed at a mound of rock and dirt several yards away. 'I'm pretty sure it was an alien.'

He and Soga drew their sidearms and waited. A minute passed.

'I'm gonna move closer.' Amagi got to his feet, staying low.

'I don't think there's anything there,' Soga said.

'Then it won't hurt me.' Amagi made a move toward the mound and Soga caught his arm.

'Maybe it was never there and you're being lured into a trap.'

'Then I'm glad I've got the best shot in the Ultra Guard backing me up,' Amagi said with a grim little smile, and, bent double, moved toward the mound.

Soga stared after him with a pained expression. Amagi was supposed to be such a tactical genius but this couldn't possibly be good strategy, he thought. What was Amagi trying to prove— that he wasn't scared? Furuhashi was the fighter on the team, and he'd said more than once that anybody who *wasn't* afraid was too dumb to join the Ultra Guard.

Amagi was maybe fifteen feet from the mound when Soga saw something pop up from behind it. It was about as tall as he was, with long dark hair and a silvery face, featureless except for the two black holes of its eyes. There was a glow around it that made Soga wonder if it was really there; perhaps it was a holographic projection, he thought.

The alien suddenly threw something at Amagi.

'*No!*' Soga cried out, thinking it was a grenade. Amagi threw up one arm defensively but there was no explosion. Instead, a huge transparent sphere popped into existence like a giant soap bubble, with Amagi inside. Soga had one last glimpse of Amagi beating his fists against it before it zoomed off into the sky.

Soga caught the glow in his peripheral vision just in time to dodge a second object. It hit the dirt where he'd been a second before, and then an empty sphere was zipping up into the sky. The alien tried again; Soga leaped out of the gully, sure he had felt the curved surface of the bubble brush the sole of his boot as it soared away.

Crouching on all fours, Soga stared at the alien, waiting for it to raise its arm for another throw. The alien's face wasn't really featureless, he saw now; there was some kind of pattern or design embossed on it. Maybe it was a mask; maybe the glow was a protective shield.

A second later, the alien simply melted away like magic. Soga let out a loud cry of terror and then Furuhashi and Kiriyama were on either side of him, as if they had just melted *into* existence.

'They got him! They got Amagi!' Soga babbled. 'He flew up into the sky in a great big bubble! They took him away in a bubble—' He cut off, hearing himself. 'But it's true. I saw.'

Furuhashi took the Heavy Shot from Kiriyama and pointed it toward the alien ship, steadying the thick barrel on the edge of the gully. 'Then let's knock on the door and see what they've got to say about that.' He fired all barrels at once, and kept firing.

Soga crouched behind him with Kiriyama, and then remembered he was still holding his own weapon. He moved up beside Furuhashi, took aim, and fired a few shots before Furuhashi ceased firing and made him do the same. All three men waited, watching the smoke clear.

'See anything?' Kiriyama asked after a bit.

'A lot of smoke, but other than that…' Furuhashi made a face. 'Doesn't look like I even scratched the finish.'

'So what's *that*?' Soga pointed at the top of the vessel, where a panel had opened. No, not a panel—the whole roof was flipping back. The walls collapsed outward and something big rose up. As the smoke dissipated, they saw it wasn't just big, it was immense, gigantic, and bright red, with a thick body, muscular arms, and a strangely long neck topped by two sharp beaks on either side.

'What. The actual. *Hell*.' Furuhashi stood up. 'Is *that* what put Amagi in a flying bubble?'

'Not even close,' Soga said solemnly.

The creature lumbered forward on its massive legs, its long neck twisting to brandish one beak, then the other. Kiriyama took the Heavy Shot back from Furuhashi and aimed it. 'I think we'd better knock this thing down. Resume fire!'

The creature staggered under the barrage from their weapons but didn't go down. It turned the beak on the left toward them and gave a loud, hard squall that made all of them cringe. Still squalling, it turned the other beak toward them and let out a long stream of fire; the ground behind them became an inferno.

Horrified, Soga looked from Furuhashi to Kiriyama.

'Well, *of course* it breathes fire!' Kiriyama snapped. 'Unless you want to see all its other talents, *keep firing*!'

'I don't know *what* that is,' Dan said to Anne in response to a question she hadn't asked. 'But the Hawk-3 has the most fire suppression foam.'

'On it.' Anne turned to leave, then stopped. 'Are you—'

'I'm fine,' he said. 'Hurry now—you're a better flyer than I am.' He bent and interlaced his fingers to give her a boost up out of the trench. As soon as she was gone, he reached into his jacket for the Ultra Eye.

If you transform again, you will *die.*

The image of the Ultra was so vivid that for a moment he thought he was back in his quarters, even with the crackle of flames and the smell of burning wood, leaves, soil, and rock. The monster let out a louder squall, then laid down another stream of flame in front of the three men in the gully, trapping them there. Bellowing again, it picked up an enormous chunk of broken stone, and Dan knew it was going to slam it down on his teammates before Anne could even get airborne.

The Ultra Eye lay in the dirt where it had dropped from his fingers. If he didn't transform, his teammates would die, and they'd only be the first. The rest of the country would follow. And after that—

He couldn't let that happen. He *wouldn't.*

Anne had just made her first pass over the flames to drop fire suppressant when she caught sight of the titanic red and silver figure bounding toward the monster. Smiling to herself, she made a tight turn to fly back the other way. Kiriyama, Furuhashi, and Soga became visible briefly through the smoke, waving at her and cheering. Had they seen Ultraseven yet, coming to help them the way he always did?

She brought the Hawk-3 around in a wide turn, passing over the trench where she and Dan had been hiding. He wasn't there anymore. Well, wherever he was, she'd find him; she could see everything. Ultraseven could take care of the monster, she'd take care of the Ultra Guard.

'You'd better be okay, Dan Moroboshi,' she muttered. 'You'd just *better* be.'

* * *

Pandon.

He remembered now, this monster was called Pandon; it came to him as he shoved it away from the gully where his teammates had been trapped by the flames. The creature had been enslaved by the Alien Ghose, a species that followed what Earth people referred to as a scorched-earth policy—literally. They liked to keep their conquests simple by offering a choice to the inhabitants of any world they conquered: surrender, or burn.

Now he reached for the monster, intending to slam it down on the ground it had torched so thoroughly, but only succeeded in knocking it over. Thick smoke swirled into his face as he turned to make sure his teammates were safe, and all at once he felt the world tipping sideways. Staggering, he tried to shake off the dizziness: then two giant paws grabbed him around the neck from behind and started to squeeze.

Dan struggled to free himself but the power he needed was beyond him. His muscles felt drained of strength as he yanked on the monstrous paws, unable to free himself. He tried to slide out from under them, but the thing tightened its hold on him. Dark patches appeared in his vision. Or was that the smoke, still thick in the air?

Abruptly, he felt a jolt—something had struck the creature's bizarre head. It lost its balance along with its grip on him. Dan shoved it away, lunged forward, then saw the Hawk-3's belly as it passed only a few yards over his head, gone before the creature could make a swipe at it.

Good one, Anne, he thought at her as she took the Hawk-3 higher, then banked to come back the other way. He couldn't see her in the cockpit but her image was so clear in his mind, he could sense her position in the pilot's seat, her hands, her arms, her face turned toward him, sensed her belief in him to protect them because he always did.

Going down on one knee, he raised his hands to the lamp in his head, two fingers on either side of the gem that would blast the creature with the Emerium Beam. The energy gathered within him; now the beast would fall.

Except nothing happened.

Concentrating harder, he tried again, visualizing the beam streaming out of him in a continuous, unbroken ray of power that the brute could neither comprehend nor withstand.

Nothing. No ray, no power.

He fell forward on his hands, barely able to raise his head. The monster gave a raw-throated shriek of triumph, grabbed hold of him and flung him to one side so that he flopped like a ragdoll.

Dan pushed himself to his knees and the monster kicked him over with one thick hind leg and pounded on him as he tried to get away. The beast hauled him to his feet and threw him down on his back. He rolled with the movement and kept rolling, letting momentum carry him away from the monster. If he could just clear his head, he thought, reaching up for the Eye Slugger.

The next thing he knew, the Eye Slugger was lying in the dirt and an immense red paw slammed him between the eyes. He tumbled backward, disoriented again, unsure which way was up.

A long harsh bellow told him the creature was behind him. He turned, spotted the curve of the Eye Slugger on the ground just as the monster's outsized clawed foot came down on it. Dan reached for it and the monster kicked him back.

And then Pandon was screaming in outrage and pain, lurching away from him under a barrage of plasma bolts from the Hawk-3. The aircraft zipped past the creature's twin beaks, still firing. Anne wasn't showing off; she was doing her best to keep the thing's attention away from him.

He could sense her more strongly than he ever had, her energy so high she glowed like the sun in his mind, filled with a power possessed by those special, unselfish souls who reach out not to take but to give.

Because she was in love with Dan Moroboshi.

Oh, Anne, he called to her silently, knowing she wouldn't hear. Reaching deep within himself, he found the last of his strength; it was enough to get him up on his feet with the Eye Slugger in his hand, and he ran at the monster, making two well-placed swipes at it.

Pandon wavered, then screamed as its left arm fell to the ground. It gave another raw wail and took a step toward him; its right leg dropped off. Screeching and shrieking, it collapsed heavily on its side and lay still.

Dan replaced the Eye Slugger and waited to see if the beast would try anything else, but it didn't move. Which was the first lucky break of the day, Dan thought, sinking to his knees, because he could barely move now except to return to his human form.

The small relief he'd expected to feel once he no longer had to carry the full weight of his existence as an Ultra on Earth didn't come. Resuming human form had failed to lighten his load the way it always had before.

Was this what dying felt like?

Perhaps, but he wasn't dead yet.

Did the Ultra who had come to him know he hadn't died?

Would he return with the same warning—*If you transform, you will die?*

But he hadn't died, Dan was sure of it. A dead man wouldn't have felt all the aches and pains that were part and parcel of human existence.

How long had he been unconscious, alone in dark silence? His limited human senses were further blunted from fatigue and the beating he'd taken. Not just that beating, but all the beatings he'd been through in defense of this beautiful little world.

Impaired as he was, he knew Amagi was still missing, taken by the Alien Ghose. They would be poring over the knowledge in his mind and Amagi would be unable to block them from learning everything, starting with the location of the base.

He had to wake up all the way now, he had to gather himself for one last big effort to protect Earth, or it would be raided, looted, and picked clean, and human life eradicated. Full awareness... he had to find his way to full awareness...

Some unmeasured time later, he sensed Anne sitting at his bedside in sick bay. She was waiting for him to wake up so she could tell him about the battery of tests she wanted to run. Most were the same tests she ran on everyone, and the results would be unremarkable—his human form was authentic enough that any anomalies would be within the normal range of variation.

But she also wanted to do an MRI of his brain. Magnetic resonance imaging was high tech on Earth, but rather primitive compared to what most civilizations were capable of. Nonetheless, it was sophisticated enough to reveal he wasn't what he appeared to be, that he was an alien who'd been walking among them in disguise.

They wouldn't assume he meant them no harm. If he had really come in peace, why hadn't he told Kiriyama who and what he really was? Or Manabe, who had been so quick to bring him into the Ultra Guard?

Dan could imagine Soga and Furuhashi and Amagi looking at him differently, wondering why he hadn't trusted them with his secret. And Anne...

Anne knew he was hiding something, he realized. The doctor was good at reading people, even people who weren't exactly people. She'd been biding her time, waiting for him to open up to her. Now she thought his secret must have something to do with his health, that he had some kind of physical problem that would end his career with the Ultra Guard.

What would she think if she knew the truth?

At the same time, she was certain she *did* know the truth about him. Or all the truth that mattered, anyway, to wit: he was good at heart if not terribly forthcoming, and everything he did came from a place of goodness. If only he would let her all the way into his life, she could help him.

He couldn't lie there indefinitely. Taking a deep breath, he opened his eyes.

'Dan!' Anne grabbed his hand, her face filled with relieved joy. 'We've all been so worried! I couldn't find you anywhere after Ultraseven killed the monster, and we still haven't found Amagi or those weird aliens that took him.'

As she went on, he let the images from her memory flow over him so he was seeing everything again from her point of view. And then there were things he hadn't seen at the time—how Furuhashi and Soga had carried him unconscious to the Hawk-3 and she had rushed him back to HQ.

'Professor Kitamura wanted to give you an MRI the moment we arrived,' she was saying. 'But every time we tried to get you ready for it, you fought us off.'

Dan blinked at her. 'Fought you off? How?'

'I don't think you were really fighting *us*,' she said with a small rueful laugh. 'You just wouldn't let anyone touch you. The professor tried to take your pulse and you did this tricky little twist to get out of his grasp. Then you slapped him. He wanted to strap you down, but I said no.'

'Thank you,' Dan said, meaning it. Then something else occurred to him. 'I didn't hurt *you*, did I?'

Anne shook her head. 'I was afraid you'd hurt yourself, so I told the professor the MRI would have to wait till you regained consciousness.'

'Anne, I...' He floundered for a couple of seconds. 'I can't have an MRI. I just can't."

'Why not—is it the dye?' she asked. 'Are you allergic to it?'

'Yes, that's it,' he said quickly. 'I'm badly allergic.'

'Is that really true?' She gazed steadily into his face. 'Or are you afraid of what we'll find?'

The emergency klaxon went off, saving him from having to answer.

'Oh, for crying out loud, what *now*?' Anne got up. 'Let me find out what's going on. I'll be right back.' She paused at the door, one foot on either side of the threshold, and looked back at him. 'Wait here,' she ordered; the door whispered closed behind her.

But he couldn't do that, either.

As the Hawk-3 approached the spot where Ultraseven had fought the enormous red kaiju, Furuhashi switched on the spotlights in the aircraft's belly. 'Okay,' he said to Soga, 'what do you see?'

'One monster arm, one monster leg, no monster body,' Soga replied. 'Don't ask me what happened to it. You think the aliens recovered the body?'

Furuhashi frowned. 'By extra-large bubble, maybe. Or they're hiding out somewhere nearby. My money's on the Kumagatake crater. Lots of reports of strange lights over it and some people claim they've heard rumbling, like the old volcano's waking up.'

'I hope not!' Soga said feelingly. 'That last thing we need in the middle of an alien attack is a volcano erupting!'

'Oh, I don't know,' Furuhashi replied, banking the Hawk-3 for another pass over the place where the monster's severed limbs lay. 'Maybe a volcanic eruption is just the thing to make those aliens think twice about invading.'

'HQ to Hawk-3!' said Kiriyama's voice in the cockpit speaker. 'Return to base immediately! We're under fire!'

Soga and Furuhashi looked at each other. 'Hawk-3 to HQ, we're on our way,' Soga said. 'How many attackers?'

'Unknown, dammit, just get back here!'

In the distance, they could hear the sound of anti-aircraft weapons.

The strategy room shook so violently, Kiriyama looked up, expecting to see the metal ceiling buckling, but it was still holding. The base had been constructed to withstand anything short of the planet breaking apart, or so Kiriyama had been told. Up until now, the worst they'd experienced were normal earth tremors, none of them exceptionally strong.

There was another blast and Kiriyama staggered sideways, almost falling on one of the TDF officers at the tracking console.

'Dammit, how many of these things are hitting us?' he asked the officer who'd steadied him.

'Still not clear,' the woman said calmly, as if he'd asked about the weather. Kotani was a veteran of several natural disasters, Kiriyama remembered; someone not easily rattled by tremors or loud noises. But there was nothing natural about this.

'If you had to guess,' Kiriyama prodded. 'Just off the top of your head.'

'Half a dozen?' She shrugged. 'I managed to tag two of them but tracking is glitchy. The two I tagged are actually quite small—I think they're looking for a way to physically enter the base.'

'Then we'd better make sure they stay out.' Kiriyama stepped back and bumped into someone behind him. 'What are you doing here, Kurata?' he said, annoyed. 'You're supposed to be back on V3, aren't you?'

'I extended my leave because I thought you'd need the extra help,' Kurata said in a stiff, formal tone. 'And I see I was right to do that. Moroboshi's unfit for duty. I can pilot the Hawk-1—'

'Dr. Yuri's an excellent pilot,' Kiriyama said shortly.

'But she's busy nursing Dan Moroboshi, isn't she?' Kurata's voice had an insolent edge that didn't quite rise to open insubordination but made Kiriyama want to punch him.

And then, as if on cue, Anne ran in, obviously upset. 'Is Dan here?'

Kiriyama shook his head. 'I thought you and the professor were giving him an MRI.'

'We can't,' she said. 'And now I can't find Dan anywhere!'

Kurata gave a single hard laugh. 'Isn't *that* perfect! Aliens attack and the great Ultra Guard prodigy bugs out!'

'And you're not at *your* post, either.' Kiriyama stepped to him so their faces were inches apart. 'Find some way to be useful or I'll throw you in the brig.'

Alone in the darkness, Amagi tried to make his wristcomm work while he waited for the Alien Ghose to come and kill him. Which they were definitely going to do, he was sure of it. They would have to, because he had no intention of cooperating, no matter what they did to him.

So far, however, they hadn't done much other than give him a wild ride in a bubble. He'd thought it was headed for a spacecraft in low orbit. Instead, it had looped around and dived into the Kumagatake caldera, where the aliens had been making themselves at home.

The subterranean base was actually not too dissimilar to HQ. Obviously, this hadn't been a rush job—they must have been working on it for months, more likely years. He tried to remember when the rumors of the volcano waking up had begun—quite a while ago. Now he knew it had been the Alien Ghose, establishing themselves right under the TDF's nose.

That almost certainly meant he wouldn't be the first human they'd grabbed, Amagi thought, shifting uneasily in his dark, cramped prison. They must have learned a lot while they'd been in hiding but they weren't getting anything out of him.

Until the aliens figured that out, Amagi had decided to pass the time trying to get a message to HQ, to tell them where they aliens were based. He wasn't optimistic—the aliens' shielding-cloaking tech had kept them practically invisible while they prepared to attack. But since they weren't in hiding anymore, there might be gaps in their shield.

And then again, maybe not; he actually had no idea. Even for aliens, the Ghose were baffling. While they were about the same size as adult humans, there was something about them that reminded him of adolescents. Part of it was the way they moved, like youthful beings full of energy. But an even bigger part of it was how openly emotional they were. Their default mode seemed to be somewhere between high alert and anger, although the anger didn't always appear to be directed at anyone—not at each other, not even at him. He'd decided to maintain a dispassionate manner and keep his eyes open.

So of course, they'd confined him alone in some dark place, where his open eyes had nothing to see. No doubt they were observing him and they knew what he was trying to do with his wristcomm. If he could get even just a one-second blip through, the TDF comms people could trace it.

And if he couldn't manage even that much, fiddling with the wristcomm took his mind off the one thing he really wanted to do: straighten his legs. This chamber they'd thrown him into was more like a box than a cell.

Amagi felt for the tiny jeweler's kit in his jacket, and was relieved the aliens hadn't taken it when they'd grabbed his sidearm. If he could get the back off the wristcomm, and not lose any tiny pieces in the dark—

Abruptly, the top of his cramped prison slid back and bright light flooded in, blinding him.

'Hello?' he asked politely.

Many hands reached in and hauled him out.

'What are you doing?' he asked, trying to sound dignified.

No answer; they didn't even look at him. Two of them grabbed his arms and dragged him forward. He stumbled, almost fell, and got a hard push from behind.

'Stop it, I can barely see!' Amagi said, but they kept forcing him to move forward. 'Can't you wait until my eyes adjust—'

Cold mist blew into his unadjusted eyes, as well as his mouth, nose, and ears. He tried to protest but the mist was coating his throat, blocking his voice.

A wave of fear rolled through him. Then the cold mist was gone, and the two aliens were marching him into the room the bubble had delivered him to before disintegrating. An alien was sitting on a large chair on a dais surrounded by several others standing guard, all of them watching him closely. The one in the chair waved at something overhead. Amagi looked up to see something like a booth descending on him.

The structure had six sides, with a window in each one. Maybe they were going to exhibit him; see the funny Earthling in the box. It came down and clicked into place, and then there was no sound at all.

Let me out! he yelled, or tried to; he couldn't speak, couldn't make a sound. He twisted around to look at the alien in the chair— or was that a throne? The alien gestured for him to turn around, and though he had no intention of obeying, he did exactly that.

The cold mist was back in his throat. He tried to turn around and look at the alien again, but something had happened to his motor functions.

* * *

The largest monitor in the strategy room suddenly went dark. Kiriyama was reaching for the controls when it lit up again and he found himself staring at Amagi. The room around him went silent.

'Captain—' Manabe started, then cut off when Amagi began to speak.

'Attention, Terrestrial Defense Force,' Amagi said in the stilted tone of someone unaccustomed to making announcements. 'We are the Alien Ghose and we demand your immediate surrender.'

Kurata opened his mouth to say something and both Kiriyama and Manabe glared him into silence.

'Surrendering will ensure your survival as a species,' Amagi continued. 'We will transfer your entire population to an underground habitat on Mars, where you can live out your lives in peace, while we make use of this world. In time, you will die out painlessly, without violence.

'Your new home is ready for you now. But if you don't surrender, we are prepared to attack all of your major cities simultaneously and destroy them. There will be no escape for you and no mercy. We can exterminate every last human, and we will.

'The choice for you is clear: surrender or die.'

The screen went dark.

Dan woke with a start, which seemed to be the only way he woke up now that his body was failing him. Finding himself slumped over sideways in the Pointer-1's front seat, however, was definitely something new.

Sighing, he pulled himself up by the steering wheel while he tried to remember what he'd intended to do. He rubbed his forehead, waiting for his mind to settle.

Right—he'd been in sick bay, with Anne watching over him. So what was he doing here?

If you transform, you will die.

Yes, yes, he knew that, but there was something else.

Professor Kitamura wanted to give you an MRI…

Then someone opened the driver's-side door and he toppled out sideways.

Two pairs of hands caught him, one pair gentle but strong like Anne's, the others small, like a child's.

'Good heavens, what's a member of the Ultra Guard doing here?' a woman asked. 'I think we'd better get you to a hospital.'

'No!' he said sharply and saw the woman draw back from him, pushing a young boy behind her as she did.

'I'm sorry, I'm so sorry,' Dan said, holding the steering wheel to keep himself upright. 'I didn't mean to snap at you, I was just startled. I'm really all right, I just need to rest.' He reached over to pull the door closed.

'We're *not* going to leave you here by the side of the road,' the woman told him, still keeping the boy behind her.

'It's okay, I'll be all right,' Dan assured her, wishing she would just hurry up and leave.

'You can come home with us,' the woman said in the brisk, no-nonsense tone Anne used on uncooperative patients. 'I'm *not* going to be the woman who left a member of the Ultra Guard to spend the night in the breakdown lane!'

'Yeah,' said the boy, peering at him from behind her. 'If you're all right here, then you'll be all right with us. Right, Mom?'

'Right, Akio,' she said. 'Now, can you walk a little?' She was already helping him out of the Pointer.

'Yeah, no problem,' Dan said, understanding that either he went with her and the boy or she'd call an ambulance, whether he liked it or not.

* * *

When the largest monitor in the strategy room lit up again, Kiriyama braced himself for the sight of Amagi under alien control. Instead, it displayed the Arc de Triomphe in Paris. He was about to say something when the monument disappeared in a fiery explosion.

There were horrified gasps and shocked cries before the whole room fell silent.

'I want to know if this is real,' Kiriyama snapped, hoping his tone masked his own sick horror. 'Someone get me Paris HQ—'

'They're offline,' said one of the TDF officers on comms. 'We'll keep trying.'

The fiery destruction on the screen abruptly changed to Amagi's blank face and empty eyes.

'We have spent decades placing explosives in critical locations under your largest, proudest cities, and you, in your arrogance, never suspected. Now your "City of Lights" is all lit up in a way you never intended, and you know we're not making empty threats. We'll give you thirty minutes to surrender, or another of your so-called "great cities" will be destroyed. You don't have to answer promptly to find out which city—unless you want to save millions from the fate of the Parisians. Perhaps you don't. But if you do, you'll respond on this frequency.'

The screen went dark again.

'Captain Kiriyama?' said one of the comms officers in a small unhappy voice. 'Paris HQ is really gone.'

'Thank you for the status update,' Kiriyama said stiffly. 'Keep Tokyo on the line, and contact London, Edinburgh, Kyiv, Madrid, Rome, and New York.'

'Done,' said the officer. 'Ekaterinburg, Beijing, Cairo, and Johannesburg are requesting conference. Should I transfer them to your office?'

'No, transfer them to mine,' said Manabe, 'and patch Captain Kiriyama in from here.' Manabe hurried out.

* * *

Dan blinked at the Ultra Guard, all six of them, himself included. They smiled down on him with the confident air of people who always knew what to do. Eventually he understood he was looking at a photo stuck to the underside of a bunkbed.

'Cool picture, huh?'

He rolled his head around to his left. The kid—Akio, he remembered—was sitting cross-legged on the floor beside the bed, grinning.

'I'm gonna join the Ultra Guard when I grow up,' Akio told him. He was holding a model of the Ultra Hawk 1; it was a scale model, Dan saw, carefully built and detailed with precision.

'Good for you,' Dan said. Where was the kid's mother, he wondered. He concentrated and finally sensed her presence on the floor below. She was calling a doctor. That was his cue, for sure. It took a lot of effort, but he sat up.

'What are you doing?' the boy asked, looking alarmed.

'I have to leave,' Dan said.

'You can't,' the boy protested. 'You're not well. My mom says she thinks you might have a head injury.'

'What I have is a mission and a duty.' Dan hung on to the bunkbed to pull himself to a standing position, looking around. The room was filled with all kinds of things human children loved—toy planes, rocket ships, and action figures, most of them wearing the insignia of the TDF or the Ultra Guard. 'I have to finish my mission or some very bad things will come to pass. Some very, *very* bad things have already happened. I've got to stop them. Do you understand?'

The boy's head tilted to one side quizzically. Dan sensed the boy did understand; he just thought Dan talked funny.

'I've got an idea,' the kid said. 'A place where you can go. Let me show you.'

* * *

The boy sneaked him out of the house by way of the patio door in the living room while his mother was in the kitchen, putting together a late supper. Dan felt more than a bit guilty as they slipped through the sliding door. He couldn't say he was a very good influence on Akio, he thought, as they hurried away from the town house toward what looked like a gardener's shed on the edge of a parking lot some three hundred yards away.

Akio pushed him inside ahead of him and turned on the light. It was indeed a gardener's shed, but all the gardening equipment was neatly confined to one corner. The walls were festooned with posters and pennants, some from universities or sports teams but most from the TDF and the Ultra Guard.

'This is *my* mission HQ,' Akio told him proudly. 'Mr. Ikeda says it's okay as long as I don't touch his tools or mess with the fertilizer.' The kid made a face. 'Not that I would. Fertilizer—*ew!*' He led Dan over to a small workbench that looked like a sawed-off picnic table.

Dan sat down, leaned his elbow on the table, and rested his chin in his cupped hand. 'I just need to rest,' he said, then wondered how many times he'd said that in the last few hours. And how many more times would he say it before he actually rested?

He activated his wrist comm, set it to access online news. Then he sat staring dumbly at the burning ruins that had once been Paris, feeling sick.

How could he not have sensed all those deaths? How could such a thing happen and the terrible pit in his stomach had not opened till now? He knew the Alien Ghose wouldn't stop at just one city. If Earth surrendered in the next ten seconds, they would still destroy two more—at least two—by way of showing humans how powerful they were. The ensuing panic would result in even more deaths, leaving fewer people for the Alien Ghose to get rid of.

His gaze fell on the Ultra Eye in his jacket. He'd told the boy he had a mission and a duty, and that meant one more transformation, one more at the very least. Because he had to; Ultraseven had to. Dan got up and headed for the door.

'Hey! Wait!' The boy ran to him and grabbed his arm.

'I *have* to go,' Dan told him firmly. 'I can't do what I need to do here. It would mess up Mr. Ikeda's bags of fertilizer.' He pulled out of the kid's grasp and went out into the dark, acutely aware of the boy's eyes on him. There was enough open space around him so his transformation wouldn't damage anything except maybe a few tree branches that the gardener was probably planning to prune anyway.

As soon as he took the Ultra Eye out of his pocket, the image of the Ultra filled his vision.

Stop now. *If you transform again, it will be the last time. You can never return to human form and you will survive only if you go back to M78 and heal.*

The boy was still watching him. If this really was the last time, it didn't matter what the kid saw. He started to raise the Ultra Eye to his face when two big, bright headlights suddenly blinded him.

And now he was hallucinating for sure, he thought, because he'd left the Pointer by the roadside. So it couldn't possibly be here. Then the driver's-side door opened and Anne stepped out of the Pointer-2. She ran to him.

'What are you doing here?' she demanded. 'Why did you bug out like that? Do you know what's happened? After HQ was attacked, Paris—'

'Is gone, I know,' he said gently.

Anne folded her arms. 'Do you also know the aliens took Amagi and brainwashed him? They're going to keep burning cities, you have to come back with me before they decide it's Tokyo's turn...' She tried to pull him toward the Pointer-2 but he didn't move.

'I can't, Anne,' he said. 'I have to stop them. *I* have to. And I can't do it from HQ.'

'I don't understand!' Anne clutched his arms, tried to shake him. 'What's going on? What's *wrong* with you?'

Dan hesitated. If this was his last time, he had to tell her, but there was no easy way to do it. 'I couldn't let you and Kitamura give me an MRI or a CT scan because it would have showed you I'm not... human.'

'What are you *talking* about?' She looked him up and down, her eyes wild and frightened. 'You're Dan Moroboshi!'

'And Dan Moroboshi is Ultraseven,' he said.

'You... you...' Anne stared up at him and he sensed the tears she was holding back.

'That's who Dan Moroboshi is, Anne,' he said. 'No one knew until now. I'm sorry, this wasn't how I wanted to tell you.'

Anne's grip on him loosened but she didn't let go. 'You know, I think part of me always knew there was more to you than any of us imagined. And I mean *you*, Dan Moroboshi. Because no matter what, that's *still* who you are!'

'I'm sorry to tell you that Dan Moroboshi's time on Earth has come to an end,' he said sadly. 'I must return to my home in M78 or I won't survive. But there's one last thing I can do before I go to save this beautiful world.'

'Will we see you before you leave?' Anne asked. Then, in a smaller voice: 'Will I?'

'When the morning star shines in the western sky, look for a single light flying upward. That'll be me.' Dan touched her face gently, thinking that now he understood the human phenomenon of heartbreak. 'Tell the team for me. Goodbye, Anne.'

His transformation didn't damage the trees or the landscaping or anything else as he soared into the starry sky. He could sense Anne and the boy below, gazing after him.

* * *

Deep beneath the earth, the Magma Riser traveled unmanned, by remote control, through a maze of tunnels, some natural, some manmade. Even from a thousand feet up, Dan could track it simply by Kiriyama's regret and sorrow. No, not just Kiriyama—Furuhashi and Soga felt the same. And Anne, too, because the Magma Riser was carrying the Killer, and the aliens that were its target still had Amagi.

But he couldn't think about that now. He had reached the volcano caldera well ahead of the Magma Riser and dived straight into it. There was no solid barrier—he passed through the bottom of the caldera and into an area that reminded him in some ways of the place he'd been calling home for the past few months.

It must have taken the Alien Ghose a decade or more of slow, patient work, he thought as he flew through the huge subterranean chambers filled with structures that lined the walls, jutting out to make platforms with yet more equipment.

But even with all that hardware, he noticed the air here was filled with particulates, many more than on the surface. Perhaps that was what the Alien Ghose called breathable. He marveled that Amagi had been able to speak without coughing.

This was why the aliens were going to destroy all the cities, he realized—to make sure there was plenty of particulate pollution in the atmosphere. A small planet like Earth wouldn't last long under those conditions. When the Ghose moved on, the world they left behind would be as barren as the moon.

Amagi's presence shone like a beacon even in the prison of a mind-control booth. It drew him to a compartment barely larger than the box the aliens were keeping Amagi in. Dan broke through the wall and pulled him out, chamber and all, only a minute or two before the Magma Riser drilled up from below, to breach the aliens' hideout and detonate.

* * *

When Anne felt the road tremble under the Pointer's wheels as she headed back toward HQ, she thought the volcano had actually awakened angry after all, just like the old stories had predicted. In the next moment, she stood on the Pointer-2's brake pedal with both feet and just managed not to hit the structure in the middle of the road. It looked like a gazebo, although why anyone would leave a *gazebo* (of all things!) in the middle of a—

Then she saw the man inside and left the Pointer-2 parked crosswise on the road as she got out and ran to it. Amagi's uniform was rumpled but not ripped or stained. His eyes were closed and his face was peaceful, as if all was right and normal in this little corner of the world.

Anne activated her wristcomm and called Kiriyama directly.

The TDF vehicle wasn't as fancy as an Ultra Guard Pointer, but it delivered the three remaining Ultra Guard teammates to Anne's location in record time.

'How did you manage this?' Soga asked Anne as he and the others circled Amagi's booth, examining it as closely as they could without touching it. Inside, Amagi remained completely still, with no sign of waking.

'I didn't manage anything,' Anne said. 'But we need to get him out of there. He needs medical attention.' And then she immediately jumped in front of Furuhashi as he drew his sidearm. 'No, you can't! You might hurt him!'

Kiriyama pulled her out of the way as Furuhashi set his weapon on low incendiary and aimed it at a panel seam behind Amagi, moving slowly along the length of the panel, then the width. When he was finished, Soga handed him a crowbar he'd fetched from the TDF vehicle. As strong as Furuhashi was, it took some time and no little effort for him to pry open a gap large enough for them to pull Amagi through.

As soon as he was out of the booth, Amagi came to, looked around frantically, and found Kiriyama. 'We've got to attack the volcano, Captain,' he said urgently, taking hold of Kiriyama's arm. 'They're going to blow up all the major cities and they're going to keep blowing everything up, even if we surrender—'

The ground began to tremble again. This time, however, there was a bright burst of light on the horizon and a thunderous explosion that made them all drop to the ground, covering their heads. But no burning chunks of rock rained down on them, although the ground continued to shake in short bursts and spasms.

'There's no lava flow,' Soga said, looking toward the volcano.

'Because the volcano isn't erupting,' Kiriyama said. He was almost giddy with relief until the ground began trembling even more violently. Cracks appeared, running swiftly along the road. The five of them retreated eastward into darkness. Kiriyama looked back and saw the TDF car tilt nose-first into a widening fissure before it slid into the gap and disappeared.

Dammit, Kiriyama thought; he was never going to hear the end of this from Manabe.

Part of the road suddenly exploded upward. They heard a raw-throated bellow of rage, followed by the last giant monster any of them expected to see.

But he'd *killed* Pandon, Dan thought, sprinting toward the monster, intending to tackle it. In the fraction of a second before he slammed into it, he registered the metal arm and leg. Apparently, the normally wasteful and profligate Alien Ghose had brought only one giant monster, thinking it would be enough to cower all the humans on this tiny planet.

Maybe that had been true on some other world, he thought, almost amused. But even if he hadn't been there to defend them, he knew humans would never have made conquest that easy for the aliens.

Dan grappled with the beast, refusing to give in to the familiar drag of fatigue trying to overwhelm him. The creature's movements were clumsy, as if it wasn't used to its replacement limbs. Because it wasn't, he realized; it was still in pain from the grafting procedure. He struggled to get it off balance and the thing forced him back, then threw him to one side.

Letting the momentum carry him in a controlled tumble, Dan sprang to his feet and took a step toward Pandon. Abruptly, he was struck by a *very* strong sense of his five teammates. They were nearby—too close for his liking and their own safety, which was probably why Anne's voice came to him so clearly and distinctly, as if she was sitting on his shoulder.

'Ultraseven is actually our own Dan Moroboshi.'

Reflexively, he put himself between them and the monster, hoping the fatigue wouldn't pick that moment to redouble its effects. Pandon got both arms around him and slammed him to the ground, but his strength held. Sensing his teammates, protecting them had not taken energy from him—if anything, they seemed to be radiating strength *to* him. Because now, they knew.

He sensed all of them more powerfully than ever, as if they were fighting Pandon with him. Because they would have; because they were willing.

The creature took hold of him again, squeezed the breath out of him, and flung him down on the ground. Dan rolled away, felt more of his strength return, and stood up. Pandon charged toward him and he grabbed its metal arm, twisting as hard as he could. If he could twist it off—

But Pandon twisted him instead, much harder. His feet left the ground, and suddenly he was rolling over and over in midair before hitting the ground so hard that it trembled.

He rolled to his feet, checked for his teammates' collective presence.

They were gone.

Displeasure flashed white-hot in Kiriyama at the sight of Kurata in the cockpit of the Hawk-3. But there was no time for dislikes, and he could only hope Kurata was professional enough to know that.

And perhaps he did—his expression as he ceded the pilot's seat to Kiriyama was wide-eyed and tense. Although it was also clear to Kiriyama that the man had counted five of them, not six.

'If you're wondering where Dan Moroboshi is now,' Kiriyama said to him, 'look out the window. He's the one fighting the monster for us.'

'But he did rescue me first,' Amagi said matter-of-factly, taking the copilot's seat.

Kiriyama could practically see Kurata's mind at work. Wisely, he moved to a seat at the rear, without comment or argument. 'What about the other TDF aircraft I called for?' Kiriyama asked him.

'Holding back, just waiting for your signal, captain,' Kurata replied.

Kiriyama consulted the readout on the dashboard, found the aircraft, and sent them a message to assume attack formation.

'First, we make a pass right over the monster's head,' he told the TDF pilots on cockpit comms. 'Then we bank, come around, and go back the other way, unloading on that monster every second, without let-up. I don't know if we can put it down, but we can hurt it. At the very least, we're gonna kick its ass enough to give Ultraseven an edge. Copy?'

The aircraft gathered, then headed off toward the two giants locked together in a dance to the death.

Five individual presences burst in on Dan's awareness again as Pandon swiped at him with its metal arm and knocked him over. He rolled away but the monster followed, kicking him with its metal leg when he tried to stand.

Dan looked up and saw the Hawk-3 leading a tight diamond-shaped formation with several other TDF aircraft as they all passed dangerously close to the monster's head. Now he caught a sense of the pilots, but the Ultra Guard were emitting so much power, they eclipsed everything else.

He took a breath, felt new energy come alive in him, enough to keep him from weakening any further—but only for a short while, he knew. As much as his teammates wanted to back him up, they weren't Ultras; they only had intention, and weapons.

As the Hawk-3 came back toward him and Pandon, it opened fire on the monster again and the TDF aircraft did the same. Dan staggered back, out of the line of fire, watching the monster waving its arms and roaring. Soga was on the weapons; no surprise, he was the marksman who always hit what he aimed at.

But who was the sixth person in the Hawk-3? The presence was so overshadowed, Dan had almost missed him completely. But he recognized it now: that was Kurata, sitting alone and wishing that it was he, not Soga, who was trying to shoot off the monster's metal arm.

Dan tackled Pandon, brought him down without losing his hold. They rolled over on the ground while he sensed Kiriyama leading his attack force around in a tight turn; they had just enough firepower for one more run.

Pandon broke away, twin beaks screeching. Dan let it go,

grabbed the Eye Slugger from the top of his head, and hurled it at the creature.

The monster raised its metal arm and caught it.

The shock of seeing his Eye Slugger in Pandon's metal paw was like a physical blow. The beast waved it around like a trophy, squalling loudly. Its dim brute brain remembered what had happened the last time Dan had thrown the Eye Slugger, and it intended to return the favor.

The TDF ruined its celebration with a barrage of plasma bolts, explosive projectiles, and laser beams. Pandon screeched furiously as the aircraft passed over just out of its reach, and then slung the Eye Slugger at Dan as hard as it could.

But it was Dan's Eye Slugger. He dug deep into his remaining strength and willed the Eye Slugger to change course in midflight. It sailed back toward Pandon, sliced effortlessly through the base of its neck, and returned to him.

The monster's neck and body parted company, the former dropping away while the latter stayed upright, not yet aware it was dead. The carcass actually took a couple of steps forward before it crumpled lifeless to the ground.

Dan rose to his feet and spotted the morning star in the deep, end-of-night sky. In the east, the sky was beginning to lighten. He could still feel the presence of his friends and the pull of their wish that he could stay. But in the new day, the pull toward home was stronger.

It was now or never.

'There he is!' Soga shouted, pointing at the sky ahead of them.

The Ultra Guard plus one watched the fast-moving point of light rise, and then recede until it disappeared.

'Will he survive?' Soga said. 'Or was this last fight too much for him? All those times he fought for us, rescued us, saved our lives…'

'He'll live,' Furuhashi said stoutly. 'He will. He'll heal and grow strong again, and he won't forget us. And someday…' He stopped and looked around at the team, his gaze finally coming to rest on Anne.

'Yes,' she said. 'Someday, we'll see Dan Moroboshi again. I'm sure of it.'

THE FREAKIN' END

ACKNOWLEDGEMENTS

A mountain of thanks to Fenton Coulthurst, brave editor, and George Sandison at Titan Books.

Also to Jeff Gomez at Starlight Runner for having the answers.

And the wonderful people at Tsuburaya Studios who keep the spirit of the Ultras shining bright.

ABOUT THE AUTHOR

PAT CADIGAN is a science fiction, fantasy and horror writer, three-time winner of the Locus Award, twice winner of the Arthur C. Clarke Award, and one-time winner of the Hugo Award. She wrote the novelization of *Alita: Battle Angel*, and a prequel novel to the highly anticipated film, *Iron City*. She also wrote *Lost in Space: Promised Land*, novelizations of two episodes of *The Twilight Zone*, the *Cellular* novelization, and the novelization and sequel to *Jason X*.

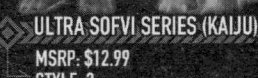